Advance P

"*Meadowlark* is a stirring debut a
to the choices adults make and th   r
heart of this book is the refreshingly fierce Rebecca Archer pushing
back against the isolation of grief and neglect, the betrayal of forgetting. In pitch-perfect prose, Wendi Stewart delivers a nuanced,
visceral portrait of small towns and family farms, memory and identity, and most achingly, the liberating beauty of friendship."

— Krista Foss, author of *Smoke River*

"In this evocative coming-of-age novel, Stewart's characters find a
way to challenge the confines of the world they inhabit. Powerfully
rendering life in small town northwestern Ontario, Meadowlark
grips a reader from first page to last."

— Anne Simpson, author of *Falling* and *Loop*

"*Meadowlark* is an impressive debut novel that encapsulates the heartache and immediacy of young lives upended. In Stewart's evocative depiction of Rebecca Archer, we meet a girl who is willing to
be different, to be brave, to beat back against unspeakable tragedy
without losing tenderness."

— Fran Kimmel, author of *The Shore Girl*

Wendi Stewart's *Meadowlark* is at once a manifesto of grief and a
testament to all that can be gained when there's nothing left to lose.
This novel drew me in gently and never let go—not even after I
had read its final passages. Stewart writes with beautiful, painful
honesty about the divide that can exist between parents and children, the resilience that must be cultivated once innocence is lost,
and the redemption that can be found through friendship and love.
Her observations about childhood are clever and graceful. It's a rare
book that makes me cry and laugh the way this one did.

— Marissa Stapley, bestselling author of *Mating for Life*

Other books in the Nunatak First Fiction Series

Meadowlark

Meadow

A Novel

lark

Wendi Ste

Library and Archives Canada Cataloguing in Publication
Stewart, Wendi, 1955– author
      Meadowlark / Wendi Stewart.
(Nunatak first fiction series ; no. 41) Issued in print and electronic formats.
ISBN 978-1-926455-38-9 (pbk.).—ISBN 978-1-926455-39-6 (epub).—
ISBN 978-1-926455-40-2 (mobi)
      I. Title. II. Series: Nunatak first fiction ; no. 41
PS8637.T499M43 2015   C813'.6   C2015-901793-9
                                            C2015-901794-7

Board Editor: Leslie Vermeer
Cover and interior design: Michel Vrana
Cover illustration: Plate 136 of *Birds of America* by John James Audubon depicting Meadow Lark.
Author photo: Chelsea Yeaton Photography

Excerpt(s) from *The Myth of Sisyphus* by Albert Camus, translated by Justin O'Brien, translation copyright © 1955, copyright renewed 1983 by Alfred A. Knopf, a division of Penguin Random House LLC. Used by permission of Alfred A. Knopf, an imprint of the Knopf Doubleday Publishing Group, a division of Penguin Random House LLC. All rights reserved.

NeWest Press acknowledges the support of the Canada Council for the Arts, the Alberta Foundation for the Arts, and the Edmonton Arts Council for support of our publishing program. We acknowledge the financial support of the Government of Canada.

NeWest Press and the author acknowledge the support of Arts Nova Scotia and the Ontario Arts Council.

NeWest Press
#201, 8540-109 Street
Edmonton, Alberta T6G 1E6
www.newestpress.com

No bison were harmed in the making of this book.

Printed and bound in Canada

To Lor—you were right
and
To Aimee, Samantha, Laurie, and Thea—for believing

In the midst of winter, I found there was,
within me, an invincible summer.
— Albert Camus

Prologue

MY MOTHER LEANS OVER ME WHEN I SLEEP, HER VOICE A WHISPER, her lips tickling my neck. Her heavy braid falls down and wallops me on the side of the face, and we giggle. There is frost on my bedroom window. I can hear the snowplow in the lane straining to move the snow, lights flickering on the walls. My mother puts her hands out and wiggles her fingers at me to come and peek out the circular space in the frost's lace-patterned surface. She holds her palm against the glass, enlarging the circle. *Come, Rebecca,* she says. I try to resist; I bury my face in my pillow. *Rebecca,* she whispers. My baby brother howls from behind her. I reach out my arms. *Mommy,* I cry. Her fingertips graze her lips. *Good night,* she says and vanishes.

Rebecca

One

MY MOTHER PULLS HER KNEES UP IN THE BIG CHAIR BY THE morning window. That's what she calls it, the morning window, where she sits to forget she lives in a place where winter comes and stays too long. Godforsaken, she says at times, when she thinks she can't possibly bear one more minute of a northern Ontario winter.

It was here, she said, pointing to the ground beneath her with an angry jab of her finger, that the glaciers stopped and burped, leaving a tract of farmland in between the rocks and lakes, along the Rainy River, before they, the glaciers, continued on with their gouging and tearing up the soil and scraping down to the bare rock, carving out the Canadian Shield. She shivers and pulls her shoulders up and closes her eyes, probably trying to imagine that winter has gone, that the sky is blue and warm and calm.

"As if England's any better," my father says, an accusing tone in his voice as he flings insult for insult. My mother never lets on, shakes her head and closes her eyes.

The rising sun shines in through the window's glass and drenches my mother in light, the many shades of yellow woven in and out of her hair pulled back in a braid. Her hair is almost always tied back, gathered with her magic fingers, fingers that work on their own without her eyes, without a mirror. I can't remember her hair ever hanging loose. She holds a white porcelain mug up to her face, the steam from the coffee rising up around her. She breathes in as though the smell itself might warm every cell in her body. She looks like she is dreaming.

I want to stand in front of her and memorize the details of her, the colour of her cheeks, flushed slightly on either side, her eyebrows thick but perfectly shaped, her lashes long and sweeping, her eyes a deep blue, somewhere between blue and green, a single dimple, the mirror image of mine, on the left side, a deep fissure where I am tempted to place my finger, wiggle it to see where the hole goes. I want to memorize the way she runs the backs of her fingers along her jaw and drops her eyes when she is tired, as if her mother might have done the same when my mother was little, a genetic motion. I want to memorize how she stands up tall, her back arched with her hand on her forehead, her teeth together, a look that says *I've had enough*, a warning to everyone but me.

Jake is my baby brother. He is eleven months old, not even real enough to be measured in years, as if he is still a test model, waiting to become a real boy. He pounds his fists into the tray of his high chair and squirms, trying to get free. He shouts merely for the sake of shouting. I look at him with disgust, at the bits of toast stuck to his hair. The toast has been cut precisely the size for his mouth but instead he jams several pieces in at once.

"Yuck," I say, closing my eyes so I don't have to see the mess. He does a lot of food flinging and dragging his sticky hands through his hair, leaving his appearance a bit startling. He wears a bib that is soggy with his drool, wet and sloppy.

"He's teething," my mother says. He's always teething, has been teething since he took his first breath. His cheeks are red and enflamed as if the skin might crack. My mother hands him an ice cube to bite on through a tiny face cloth. He winces and then sucks on it with a fury like he's suddenly gone mad for ice, his eyebrows jumping up to his forehead and his eyes looking crazed. He is usually jolly, but annoying and demanding. I try to remember my life before he came along and upset the balance, when my parents lifted me off the ground and I hung between them from their hands, my feet walking on air. It was magic. But now their arms are taken up by Jake, his fists closing around their thumbs, his heavy head falling asleep on their shoulders, his thumb stuck in his mouth like a plug. The rest of the time he is loud and laughs and everyone laughs with him. Except me. I don't find him funny, not one bit.

My father is tip-toeing through the kitchen like a cartoon character, a big grin stretched across his face as if he has a secret and can't hold it for one more second. Jake squeals at him. My father knocks his flat open hand on the kitchen table and the silverware jumps.

"It's today," he shouts, as if he has become an evangelist, shouting about being saved. We had one of those at our church, an evangelist, but our congregation preferred not to be shouted at, my mother said. My father fidgeted and said good grief, as if he knew he didn't want to come to church and wanted to remind my mother again.

"We've packed a lunch and we're driving up the lake today to clean out the cabin for its new owners."

My father throws his arms over his head and turns his back to my mother. "We're selling the cabin and with the money we're going to build this farm into something Jake can take over. Isn't that right, Jake," my father says, bending over with his face close to Jake's.

Jake clobbers my father's nose with his spoon and laughs with his crazy noise-making voice. He can't even talk, says only *mom-mom-mom*, pressing his lips together, his dimples like deep holes on either side of his mouth. He has two dimples, as if he is more balanced than I am. *I am like Mommy*, I want to say, to shout into his face. That makes me better.

"I want to be a farmer," I say, my throat feeling dry and sore all of a sudden, as if I swallowed something too big.

My mother opens her arms and I run and bury my face in her apron. Her fingers instantly begin weaving my hair, like a reflex, as if she can't help herself. I would have left my face there forever, her fingers calming all the worries a six-year-old might have.

"Robert," her voice stern with a warning sound to it. I look up at her face. Her teeth are pushed together and her lips pulled straight across, as if something stung her, but my father doesn't seem to notice, keeps his face turned the other way.

"Right, right," he says. "We're all farmers."

We aren't really farmers, though. Not yet. We don't have huge hogs in our front field like the Mennonites down the road, hogs that look like bulldozers digging in the soil. The hogs get down on their front knees, pushing their wide snouts into the dirt, pulling up roots and twigs, their small curled tails wiggling with what looks like pure joy.

"Happy as a pig in shit," Mr. Katz from next door says. He is a bachelor and doesn't know not to talk like that around children, but I say his words in my head and they make me laugh. *Happy as a pig in shit. Happy as a pig in shit,* I sing while I jump with my skipping rope on the hard-packed mud in the driveway.

We don't have lovely black-and-white cows like Mr. Krueger, cows that know when to come down from the pasture field to be milked, coming all on their own with the help of two border collies, Nip and Nancy. They are very smart cows, cows that stand quietly under a tree when they are full of grass and chew their cud and make milk, cows that don't run and jump around while they refill their large udders. They look dazed, burdened with the huge sacks of milk they carry around, and I wonder if they'd like to unhook those udders and leave them at the edge of the field while they run and play and chase each other.

The calves are in a separate field, not allowed to run with their mothers. They drink instead from large glass bottles or pails when they learn how, but they want to suck, want to suck so bad that they suck on each other's ears, not caring that no milk comes, desperate to be sucking, wanting their mothers, bawling at the fence that separates them, protesting this separation that they can't quite figure out. Their mothers have forgotten them, more interested now in making milk, eating grass and making milk.

"Why can't they be with their mothers?" I ask Mr. Krueger and he looks at me with impatient tolerance.

"That milk is not for them," he says.

The calves would suck the fingers right off my hand if I let them. They leave my fingers slimy and wet, their rough tongues tickling my hand.

"All babies need to suck," my mother says. "It's only natural."

We stopped in a couple of times to buy milk for one of our orphaned calves and I wanted to play with the dogs, but Mr. Krueger snarled at me.

"They're working dogs," he said, waving me off like a mosquito.

"Why do they have friendly names, then?" I asked my mother.

"Good question," she said, her fingers in my hair.

We aren't really farmers like a lot of farmers on our road, like Corkums who have a field full of small black cows whose calves look like cuddly teddy bears. The Black Angus frolic and play, wrestle and disagree with their heads pushed together, cows that run with their tails up over their backs like they are alarmed and running from imaginary danger just for fun.

"Can't keep those Angus buggers in," Mr. Corkum says. I like that word, *bugger,* and practise saying it in my head, knowing I won't be allowed to use it in a regular sentence. I tried it once.

"That Jake is a noisy bugger," I said, and my mother pulled her apron up over her mouth and shook her head rather seriously, her eyebrows trying to be angry.

Mr. Corkum is always fixing his fences and chasing calves down the road. Corkums have eight children to do the chasing, eight children who run around like ants, laughing and pulling at one another, and they never notice me standing and watching, wondering if I might join in. I lean forward and back from my heels to my toes as if I am trying to jump into a skipping rope that is turning too fast for me. I suppose Mr. Corkum never notices how much time it takes to keep his cows inside their farm.

We aren't even farmers like Harold Prescott, who milks cows, some Jerseys and Brown Swiss and Holsteins, in his tumbling-down barn, selling cream to the neighbours. Prescotts have pigs and chickens, too, and Mr. Prescott works hard, but not smart hard, my father says. We buy their cream. Mr. Prescott always seems angry. My mother doesn't like him, says she doesn't think she has ever seen him being kind to his children. Farming can do that to a man, my father says, but my mother shakes her head. It's not right, she says.

My mother is the real farmer, or more a farmer than the rest of us. She has a huge garden that she tends as if the seedlings, the little bits of green life pushing through the soil, were her own flesh and blood. She gets on her knees and pulls the weeds, the invaders that try to crowd out her vegetables. She plants a thick band of marigolds along the edges of her garden and places crushed eggshells around her tomato plants, the plants tied up to wooden stakes with her old nylon stockings. The carrots she thins with tweezers so they don't crowd one another, and all the while she explains what she is doing, and hums, a white bandana tied around her hair. She looks earthy and exotic, both at the same time.

She keeps a stack of old bed linens on the back porch, and every night that threatens frost she covers her garden plants, tucks them under the sheets, placing bricks along the sheets' edges so the wind can't tear the sheets away. In this part of Ontario the frost seems to threaten twelve months of the year. Farmers have to be smarter, my father says. The window of opportunity is smaller, fewer days to get things to grow, less heat to let things ripen. Farming in the north isn't for sissies, he says. It's the world's biggest gamble.

I have no idea what gambling has to do with farming, but I picture my father at a card table with other farmers, all of them chewing on cigars.

"I'll raise you a second cut of hay," one farmer says.

"I'll see your second cut and raise you some corn silage," says another, but before they can throw their cards down, Mother Nature tips the table over and the cards go flying.

My mother's garden shifts and changes, and what starts out as tiny seeds in the palm of her hand becomes something magical. In the fall, when the last potato has been dug and the last carrot pulled and all the tops are stacked in a pile to rot and decay, to be put back on the garden, my mother cries, weeps quietly at the edge of her garden. It's over, she says, as if she might never have the chance to garden again.

The summer after Jake was born, my mother's precious garden was forgotten, overrun by weeds, the rabbits and deer eating off the blossoms until my father took the lawnmower to the whole garden, levelling it flat.

We aren't really farmers at all. My father works in town three or four days a week, picks up shifts at the sawmill pushing and lifting logs. We have four Hereford cows and my mother's eight hens with rich copper feathers. Gwen, the biggest hen, lets me carry her around like a doll, and when I stand and stomp my feet on the wooden platform at the back door, she comes running right to me. My father says chickens are stupid, but I think Gwen is *brilliant*, a word I borrow from my mother. She uses that word only when something is very good. Gwen is just such a very good something.

* * *

"Let's have a picnic at the cabin," I say, clapping my hands together and jumping up on my tiptoes to make myself taller.

"It's too cold," my father says, a matter-of-fact sound to his voice as if everyone, including me, should know such things.

"We'll have a picnic right inside the cabin, Rebecca, right on the floor on a blanket, and we'll pretend it's summer," my mother says.

The idea sounds lovely. My father clicks his tongue on the back of his teeth. "We'll have to get in and get out. The days are still too short for such nonsense."

"Robert," my mother says, and it makes him wince and suck his breath in a little, but he doesn't turn to look at her. She says his name as though that might guide him to turn left or right or pause, as if she can put all that instruction into just his name and the sound she gives it. Mr. Lowe can do that with his voice to his team of big black horses. They know to turn right or left or get going just by the sound of Mr. Lowe saying their names. He adds a whistle at the end, after he calls out their names, but they've already started to move.

"We can leave Jake behind with Mrs. Klein, so it won't be so hard to carry everything," I whisper to my mother, trying to make it sound like a good idea. My mother shakes her head but smiles at me, a knowing kind of smile as though she understands the burden of loving Jake.

I think I love Jake. He is still more a baby than he is a boy, so he doesn't have a lot of practical use and spends his days taking up all my mother's time. He drags the pots and pans out of the cupboards and bangs on them like a maniac. He pulls anything he can reach off the cupboard or the coffee table and makes a terrible mess. My mother spends a lot of time leaping at him, shouting *Oh Jake*, as he pulls the lamp off the end table and flings ashtrays across the room and tries to electrocute himself by pushing anything he can find into the electric outlets.

My mother bathes him in the kitchen sink and ladles soapy water over his head, and they both laugh while I watch from the chair. She massages shampoo into his head, but he doesn't have much hair so I wonder why she bothers. His head has more of a yellow glow than real hair, although his curls are beginning to grow. She has the electric heater on the kitchen cupboard aimed at Jake, the coils brilliant red with heat. My mother puts her arm out in front of me. "Be mindful," she says to me. She lifts Jake from the sink to a big fluffy towel, letting the water drip from him. He pulls up his legs and I look at the small sac hanging between his legs.

"I wish I had a penis," I say.

My mother smiles and wraps Jake up tight in the towel like a parcel. He howls. He hates being confined and throws his arms and legs around, making too much noise, and I clamp my hands over my ears. My mother wraps her arms around him and muffles the sound.

"Shhh," she says. "Shhh," and he eventually quiets down. I'd like to put him out in the barn when he cries so he is far enough away not to be heard. But when I suggest that, my mother eases into the rocker by the fire and slowly moves back and forth and I forget that he is bothersome. She lifts her shirt and pulls Jake's face into her breast, his head in the crook of her arm. He wiggles his head slightly to get himself lined up properly. I used to try to see what he was up to, all the slurping and sucking, but now I know. I'm not included in this private moment between my mother and Jake, even if I already had my own private moments, moments I can't remember. So I lift my shirt and pull my doll Rachel into my chest, crossing my legs and leaning back. Jake's hand reaches up to my mother's face, his chubby fingers caressing her. I close my eyes.

* * *

"Jake, eat your breakfast," my father urges.

"At least he's occupied," my mother says. She leans against the kitchen cupboard and holds her stomach like it is trying to get away. She is more silent than usual. She catches my look and her face softens into the kindest smile I will ever see. I want to be as lovely as my mother.

The washing machine hums in the corner of the kitchen. The letters WESTINGHOUSE are spaced in chrome around the circular lid on the front. The clothes bump and slosh from right to left while the soap bubbles cling to the glass, pleading with me for help to escape. Slosh, slop, slush.

"I'll get these sheets on the line before we go," my mother says, and my father immediately glances at his watch but says nothing. "Rebecca, get your snowsuit on and you can help me," my mother says. As she pulls the sheets from the washer I climb into my snow-suit, red corduroy with soft white rabbit fur worn through in several spots around the hood. She hurries through the deep snow in her boots with only a sweater on, me at her heels. Her nose turns red and her fingers move quickly to snap the sheets and hook them to the line. I hand her the pins. The sheets are stiff before we are done, but I know they come in from the clothesline with a smell more wonderful than anything else. My mother makes my bed with me in it, the fragrant sheets floating down to cover me, feeling much like I imagine butterflies fluttering close to my skin.

"Can I hear a meadowlark?" I ask, looking in the empty plum trees and pointing to the little birds flitting in and out of the branches, listening for a melody that has more notes than most songbirds', and I mimic the sound, the call that floats in my summer window.

"Not in the winter," my mother says. "You won't hear them sing until this nasty winter is done for good. Not until everything wakens and starts again."

"I wish I could hear them now," I say.

"I hate the cold," she says and shivers before turning to run to the house.

There is more scurrying around, keeping Jake awake so he will sleep in the car and not bother everyone with his howling. We all understand he hates his bunting bag. I want to shout into his face, *We get it!*

My father backs the station wagon up to the back door so we can set in our picnic lunch and the toboggan we will use to carry things from the cabin to the car. We have our heavy winter clothes on and I feel like a block of wood with all the layers of my clothing and I can turn my head only slightly with a scarf wrapped around my head several times.

Winter is harsh; rivers and lakes are supposed to freeze over like iron. Lots of people drive on the ice in the wintertime to get supplies to their cabins. It's much easier than loading supplies onto the small boats they use in the summer. I like summer best when we climb into the boat and push away from the dock and leave the world behind. I can see my mother untie the rope from the dock, my father sitting at the back with his hand on the motor. My mother pushes off from the dock, gracefully, one leg dragging over the surface of the water, her toes barely touching, as if she were a ballerina.

* * *

We drive up to Five Mile Dock. Mr. Challis is standing at the landing looking out over the ice with his arms folded across his chest. My father rolls down the window.

"Heading up the lake today?" my father asks.

"I don't think so," Mr. Challis says, rubbing his short well-groomed beard. "I think it's too late in the season."

"It's been bloody cold," my father says.

Mr. Challis shakes his head. "I don't trust the ice. I wouldn't be going if I were you."

My mother braces herself and reaches across my knees to touch my father's arm. He brushes her hand off. Mr. Challis talks about the new causeway going in that will make getting up the lake much easier and no one will have to go on the lake.

"That will be quite the thing," Mr. Challis says.

My father says he likes the wide-open space of driving on the lake, like driving on the prairies. Mr. Challis shrugs his shoulders and my father rolls up the window as he steers the station wagon toward the ramp that leads down to the lake. My mother sucks in her breath and pulls up her shoulders. My father doesn't say a word until we are a long way out from the shore.

"Look, it's a perfect day for a drive on the lake," he says. "There's hardly any snow." He begins to hum.

Jake murmurs in his sleep, his lips making a sucking sound as though he's dreaming about having a bottle. I can't see him. His car bed is on the back seat and I can't turn my head on account of the scarf that is strangling me. So I pull my feet under me and rest my hands on the dashboard.

The shore is blanketed with snow, rocks jutting through the surface. In some places the ice is pushed up against the rock like broken glass. The lake is speckled with ice-fishing huts like tiny hotels from the Monopoly game. I see smoke coming from a couple of the huts, and I wonder how they can have a fire on the ice and not fall through.

Two

RAINY LAKE'S WATER TEEMS WITH PICKEREL AND BASS AND northern pike hiding in spots the best fishermen know about, the fishermen who guard their secrets well. My father says no one tells the truth about where they catch the best fish, but lying is allowed, expected even. That's where a fish tale comes from, he says. There are lake trout, too, my father says, but they like the water cold and deep. He showed the difference between the fish, laid their dying, flapping bodies out on the dock. The northern pike with its long toothy snout. The bass with its oval shape and friendly red eyes. The yellow pickerel with its lovely olive-and-gold sides. Walleye, my dad said. Like Jake and Jackson, Jake's proper name. Or Becca and Rebecca, I offered, but he merely shrugged his shoulders with an indifferent nod. He never called me Becca. After a bit, the fish looked the same, all sad and struggling to breathe and dreaming of the lake.

Rainy Lake is large with all its bays and inlets and islands, like tentacles on an octopus going in every direction. A fisherman could be on the lake all day and never see another boat. That seemed very large to me. We never went fishing; there wasn't time. We'll go, we'll go for sure. Later, when Jake can hold his own rod. That's when we'll go, my father said. I can hold a rod. I can even cast from the dock, but I never catch anything except a twig loaded down with green slime.

The cabin used to belong to my mother's family. The Claydons. My mother's family didn't fit together particularly well, she told me, because their edges were different shapes. She took two of the mismatching pieces from Jake's easy picture puzzle and tried pushing them together, but they wouldn't fit. "See," she said. "They just don't fit."

Then she used the puzzle to explain why she thought I needed a baby brother, a baby brother who cries in the night like a locomotive blasting its warning whistle. "Look," she said, with two matching pieces. "A perfect fit." She said it would be too lonely to be an only child.

My mother fell in love with the magic of Rainy Lake. I pictured the lake with a big top hat and a rabbit inside, or a lady swimming in the lake with a sparkling suit like at the circus, her arm over her head and her hips pushed to the side. My mother's parents said lake property was always money well spent. People want to be by the water. A good investment. My mother was lucky to spend her summers learning to swim and picking blueberries and paddling her canoe back and forth across the bay and driving the motorboat all by herself.

"Oh, Becca," she said, her voice breathy and far away. "It was brilliant to come here. Deliciously fun. To escape lessons and going to the dentist and cars and all that madness," and she hugged me. I hoped the magic was flowing from her body to mine.

I couldn't quite get the part about her parents leaving her at the cabin and not coming back for her, and I wondered if they got tired of being parents and just didn't bother to take her back to England with them on their last trip, as if they arrived at the train station and checked they had their bags and their tickets and their snacks and raincoat and a bottle of pop, but forgot my mother. Maybe that was when my mother found my father; maybe he offered her a lift when he saw her standing alone on the side of the road with her suitcase. In all my six years, the ones I remember, my mother's family didn't visit or call on the phone. Maybe they are so old they have become senile and completely forgot about having two daughters, not just one. Maybe my mother really was an afterthought, an afterthought that became a forgotten thought.

My mother and I spent the summers at the cabin, and then after Jake came along, it became the three of us. My father stayed home to make hay while the sun shines. He said that often, too often, and mostly on Sundays when others thought God would punish him for working on a church day. My father's crops were never that good so perhaps God did do my father a bad turn. My mother said God didn't get involved in such things, because He was busy trying to prevent wars and famine and left the small stuff up to us.

The cabin now belongs to my mother, not the Claydons. My mother isn't a Claydon any longer. She became an Archer, left her name at the back door of the church when she and my father got married. I have never met these Claydon people, other than a single photograph on the top of the piano, a photo of the four of them at the train in Roddick arriving for the summer. My mother is right; the Claydons are very old, even my mother's sister, the one in the middle of the photo looking bored and annoyed.

The cabin is tucked in among the birches and poplars, and in the summer when the trees are full of leaves, I can't see the cabin from the boat, the cabin's russet-red coat blending in with the forest. The long bank of windows on the front of the cabin open, lift to the ceiling to be hooked in place, to let all the smells and sounds drift up from the lake, the smell of earth and plants, all rich and real and thick and musty at times. I can hear the laughter of water, the canoe bumping against the dock, the sound hollow and simple, feel the canoe as it swayed and bumped against the dock and I fell asleep. I gave my mother quite a start, and when she found me asleep in the canoe I couldn't decide if she was angry or sad. Maybe both. I didn't mean to fall asleep, but I couldn't help it.

The cabin floor has smooth wide planks and the doorways are covered in heavy dark fabric, a deep cranberry with black swirls, swirls that look like part of a coat of arms. The curtain ties back during the day and lets down in the evening for privacy. A large pine harvest table stretches along one wall, and I sit at the table and practise printing my name and writing the numbers from one to twenty, staying between the lines on the page, a big primary pencil in my fist. I hold it tight as if at any moment someone might try to take it away before I have finished.

The summer ride is rough on the open lake, the aluminum boat pounding down on each wave. I hit my chin on the edge of the boat once and split the skin open. My father said I bled like a stuck pig, but my mother pushed on the cut with a cold wet cloth and eventually the bleeding stopped. She put two pieces of narrow tape over the split, holding the skin together.

"There," she said, rubbing her palms together. "You won't need stitches."

I was relieved. I imagined my head at an uncomfortable angle with my chin feeding through my mother's sewing machine. The image made my stomach hurt.

"We won't have a rerun of the lip incident," my father said, sounding annoyed, remembering the fuss he said I made when I split my lip after I was bucked off my rocking horse. I don't recall the details. I can see my new scar when I place a mirror below my chin. I like my scars. My mother says they are evidence of having had a childhood and then she smiles.

"You're a lucky girl," she said.

A lucky girl.

Going to the cabin is an adventure like no other we do as a family. It is stepping out of our regular, ordinary life and into another, and we become a different set of people with new names and a different history or maybe no history at all, just starting here in this moment in this place. I wanted to be called Susie or Penny or Gabriela or Felicity. When I asked my mother what she would like to be called, she said, Guinevere would be nice. When I wrinkled my nose she said, But not Gwen. Gwen is just for chickens, not a pretend name.

The trees are full of birds and it takes a lot to scare the birds out of the trees, so they sing their whole songs, complete with verse and chorus. The sounds at the lake are not cluttered with car doors banging and tires on pavement and shouting and horns honking. The quiet is filled with different sounds, sounds that hypnotize me. The air is different at the cabin; the sun is gentler and the sounds are deeper and richer. At the farm I can hear the meadowlark through my bedroom window in the morning, with her distinctive sound, her long melody so different from the robin or the blue jay. The meadowlark's song changes from eighth notes to quarter notes, with more to say. At the cabin the meadowlark sings a different song, uses her summer voice, her birch-tree voice when she perches there. She tells the whole story without having to hurry.

The wind rustles the birch and poplar leaves and they are clapping about our holiday, as if they too are glad we came. The water laps at the shore, slaps it playfully, tumbles over and over on the sand. The slapping sounds like laughing, inviting me to jump through the waves, a Styrofoam duck tied around my waist, always with my mother's warning.

"Don't go too far," she says. She is watching and I feel completely safe to leap farther and jump higher because my mother is there; I know she will kick off her shoes and run into the water to save me, not worrying about her pedal-pushers getting wet. She will dump Jake down on the sand and run to me. I know it. So when the waves knock me down and wash over top of me, pushing my face under the water, I am not afraid.

The frogs are different at the cabin, in the little pond behind the beach where the sand rises up and sinks low again. The frogs are less worried about me catching them. They don't hop away in fear, so they grow larger and their skin is older and darker and they tolerate me with their patient eyes and heavy tummies, the white of their throats moving in rhythm to their beating hearts. They are warm and slippery in my hands, and I put them up to my face hoping they have something to say.

Rocks peek out between the trees and in between the rocks the blueberries flourish. We can fill an ice cream pail in a half hour if we try hard and resist the urge to eat the blueberries. Sometimes my mother and I give up and sit down on the rock and fill our mouths and then stick out our purple tongues.

"Don't tell anyone," she says, laughing.

The sound of the waves on the beach comforts me, and I close my eyes and hear the sound any time I want to.

We go to the cabin in the winter, when the lake isn't a lake, when the lake becomes a road and my father lets me ride on a toboggan behind the car when we drive right on top of the lake. Jake isn't old enough and I alone am going to zoom over the ice on the toboggan. My mother hooks my thick mittens through the sisal rope on the long toboggan that could hold six of me.

"Hold on tight. Not too fast now, Robert," my mother says, and her voice has that warning sound to it again. Just before she climbs into the car, with her hand on the door handle, she turns and runs back to me. "I'm riding with you," she says with breathless excitement and climbs on behind. She waves her arm over her head at my father and he drives slowly. My mother drags her heels on the ice so the toboggan won't slide under the back of the car. "There," she says. "We're safe."

Where the ice is swept clean I expect to see through the ice like a window, see the fish swimming back and forth at their slow winter speed, maybe with scarves and mittens and warm hats, see the turtles sitting on the bottom of the lake waiting for spring so they can climb out and lay their eggs. But the ice is cloudy and grey and cracked. I can't see anything beneath it at all, not one single thing.

* * *

We pull into the cabin's bay. The snow has drifted heavily near the dock so we leave the station wagon a long way out from the shore and begin the hike in. We put Jake and his car bed on the toboggan along with the lunch basket. My father starts up the path that is only a slight imprint in the deep snow. His snowshoes keep him on top of the snow most of the time. Every now and then he breaks through the crust of snow and I hear him struggle to dig himself out. The going is difficult and my legs begin to throb. I turn and wince at my mother, wanting to cry, wanting to complain, but knowing I shouldn't.

"Lie down and make a snow angel and let your muscles stretch," my mother says. "I'll do it, too."

We fall straight back into the snow with a soft thud, the thick snow a soft mattress, and begin moving our arms and legs in and out. The snow gets in around my wrists and bites at the skin.

"Hey, you two," my father shouts. "Have you given up? Lazy lugs. Letting the men do all the work."

I hear Jake screaming, wanting out of his bunting bag that he barely fits into now.

"We're coming," my mother groans, trying to get her feet under her.

Something tells me to clip this moment from my memory and put it somewhere safe, the two of us in the snow, our perfect angels beneath us, the snow on my mother's cheeks turning the skin pink and her eyes more intensely blue. She drags her bright-yellow wool mitten under her nose as she sniffs gently, nostrils flared, her winter coat worn at the elbows and the collar flat, the zipper torn from its seam part way up. Her eyes are perfect blue, her lashes long and sweeping, and her lips red and full. She is beautiful, my mother. She is lovely. We trudge the rest of the way through the snow to the cabin.

My father shovels off the back deck that runs the width of the cabin.

"Look," he says, pointing at the kitchen window's screen, the mesh hanging shredded. "A bear tried to get in. I should have brought my gun."

"No, no," my mother says. "The bears were here first and besides, they're asleep."

"That's bloody nonsense," my father says and keeps shovelling, his head wiggling back and forth like he's trying to dump my mother's thoughts out of his head and into the snow. "Women," he mutters, with something about having no idea.

My mother tears up bits of newspaper and gathers bark and wood chips from the bottom of the wood box. She builds a loose nest inside the woodstove while Jake squats beside her and peers inside, his fists tucked in below his tummy.

"A fire needs air to give it life," she says to me over Jake's head, and I smile, glad he isn't old enough to learn about fires.

She strikes a wooden match and the kindling leaps into flames. "We'll be warm in no time," she says, rubbing her hands together and scooping Jake away from the woodstove. She puts her hand out toward the stove. "Hot," she says with a frown and a very firm voice. Jake just kicks his legs and squeals. He's not very smart. I suppose he will be; I suppose he will grow into smart. I try to give him credit for being a baby and not plain stupid, but it's hard. He gets away with just about everything because of his dimples and his sparkly eyes and his blond curls and cuddly body. He doesn't have to be smart; he's adorable instead.

My mother empties cupboards and fills boxes with candlesticks and photographs and some dishes wrapped carefully in towels and rags. She folds quilts and piles games while the fire snaps and cracks and Jake toddles between chairs, feeling quite free in this large open space. My father gathers tools out of the shed and drags them down the hill to the lake and into the back of the car. Something special is ending. I can feel it on my skin and it makes my mother quiet while Jake squeals non-stop. My mother piles books on the table.

"Choose only your favourites," my mother says. "We'll leave the rest."

They are all my favourites, all the ones I learned to read while my mother watched over my shoulder, encouraging me to try, when I could crawl up on her knee and open a book while her lips rested on my head. My finger ran along the words like the letters were Braille. When I stopped at a word, my mother waited and then made the first sound: *st, st, st.* And then she waited some more. *Stumble,* I said, and she whispered *yes* at the edge of my ear and the whisper tickled my ear and tickled right inside my head, into my brain, tickled all the way through to the other ear.

My mother looks at all the belongings in front of her and wipes at her forehead. She smiles, but there is a knot between her eyebrows.

"I've been coming here since I was a little girl," she says, turning slowly in a circle. "Just a little girl." She collapses in a chair, dropping the stack of books on the floor, and leaves her hands at her feet, her face resting on her knees. "I planned for it to be yours," she says.

Tears roll down her cheeks, just three or four trickling down into the crease around her nose. I don't know how to comfort her, so I put my face against hers and say nothing. Jake squeals and my mother gets up, the moment gone.

Eventually, everything is sorted and packed, and the station wagon is loaded to the roof. Tucked in the middle of all the belongings is Jake's car bed and Jake sleeping inside, swaddled tight inside his bunting bag. My mother had to wait until he was asleep to zip him up. He fell asleep quickly and I think he may have been snoring.

My mother puts me in the front seat and climbs in the back, in the small space left on the seat. Her fingers can just barely reach the edge of Jake's car bed in the very back. My father throws himself into the car, exhaling loudly, and loosens his jacket.

"All set?" he asks, looking over his right shoulder to my mother.

"Yes."

I can't see her, can't turn my head at all.

"Oh, wait. I forgot my old teddy bear. I promised it to Becca," she says. She starts to open the door.

"Leave it," my father says. "We can't fit one more thing in this car."

"I can't. I promised," she says. "I'll go."

"No, I'll go," my father says. "Then I can grumble about it all the way home. We have to get going. It'll soon be dark."

"The bear is tucked in on the middle bed. Thanks, dear," she says, a grateful sound in her voice.

"I'm grumbling," he says before slamming the car door.

I watch him trudge up the hill, the crust of snow not supporting him. He throws his arms over his head every now and then, like he's making a fuss. A loud bang echoes across the bay and before the front of the car rises up and blocks my view, I see my father freeze in his tracks. Then I feel the world fall out from under me.

Jake starts screaming after I hear the stack of books tumble over on him. My mother is crying.

"Oh dear, oh dear," she says.

And I'm not sure who is making what sound. My mother tells me to roll down the window while she strains her arms through all the boxes in the back trying to grab at the car bed. My father is suddenly in the water that surrounds the car. He is trying to swim in the broken ice with his heavy parka on. He grabs the side of the car, moving his way along to the window, hand over hand, his face as grey as the ice, his lips already blue.

"Rebecca," my mother urges, pushing me, her voice afraid. I want to hold on to her and bury my face in her, but she is pushing and my father is pulling.

"Get Jake. Get Jake," my father is shouting through the open window in a voice I have never heard before. He is pulling at the door handle but the door won't open. The darkness is smothering me while my father tries to pull my bulky frame through the window. The cold makes it hard to breathe. Then I can't see, and I am fading far, far away.

Three

I SEE MY CHEST MOVING UP AND DOWN LIKE I'M BREATHING, BUT I'm not sure I am. My chest rises up, then waits a bit before lowering, deliberate and mechanical like a robot. My chest hurts so I take a little air in, a sip, and then let it out slowly. I'm afraid to breathe in again so I don't, until I can't help it, and I try not to gasp. My whole body is aching like it is being squeezed in a vice, like the one in my father's workshop that he cranks tighter and tighter while he grits his teeth. I wonder if my eyes are bulging. My fingers feel thick and numb except for a million needles being pressed through the skin, right up to my elbows, my feet, too, with no feeling and every feeling all the way to my knees.

The ceiling in the room is high, too high, with brown stains leaking out from the corners on the tiles, as if someone forgot to clean there, forgot to look up. I wonder how tall I'd have to be to reach them, to wipe at them, because they are ugly. I'm in an ugly room and I don't know where this room is. I keep taking little sips of air. I close my eyes because the room is too hideous, but my eyes won't stay closed.

"You're awake," a too-loud voice says as she peers into my face with a wave of perfume and the smell of stale coffee that makes me slap my hand over my nose. I pull in my chin and sink deeper into the pillow.

"I'm Mrs. Middleton. You're in the hospital," she is saying.

I am counting the tiles on the ceiling. One, two, three, four.

"I'm taking care of you," she says, not quite so loud, but with the sound of pretend kindness in her voice.

Mrs. Middleton tucks my hair behind my ears, her cold fingers nipping at my neck, and it stings. I want to call out, to cry for my mother, but I clamp my lips together and tears run down the sides of my face into my ears and make my ears itchy and the tears are bubbling in my ears, making a gurgling sound. I keep counting inside my head. One, two, three.

Everything is noisy. Trays banging and clanging, a shrill metallic sound, and drawers and cupboard doors are slamming and all the sounds echo on top of each other and make my head hurt. The nurses talk in their too-loud voices as if I'm not really here. They talk about the accident. *Poor Robert hasn't been the same since the accident.* One nurse puts her hand on her chest when she says *the accident* as if saying the words might give her a heart attack. That little girl in Room 207 was in the accident. It was a terrible accident.

The nurse says the cold water stopped my heart in its tracks a couple of times after my father rescued me. Good thing they got you to the landing or it would have been a different story.

A different story. I want a different story.

* * *

"She's not talking," Mrs. Middleton says to the doctor as they both peer into my face. The doctor is wearing a white shirt that buttons up on the side, like the shirt my father's barber wears. Maybe the doctor does both jobs; maybe he is a part-time doctor and a part-time barber. He has a stethoscope around his neck like a necklace, and I wonder if he stops people in the hall and listens to their hearts. "Let me listen," he would say and he would know all about the person when he listened to her heart and what was going on inside of her. "Oh my, you're not feeling good," because he could hear it. He could hear that her kitten got run over or that he fell off the teeter-totter and scraped his back. He could even hear what she is hoping for her birthday. "Hmmm," trying to decipher the sounds.

The doctor breathes in through his nose, loudly, his nostrils flaring open. He puts the cold metal on my back and tells me to breathe, but I'm already breathing so I count the tiles some more. One, two, three.

"In and out through your mouth. A big breath now," he says, and his voice is all business without a sound of kindness in it, the business of breathing.

It hurts. I wince and hold my breath.

"That won't hurt in a little while," he says and then pulls my fingers and looks at each one, then my toes. He looks in my ears, stares at the tears bubbling inside my head, and then pulls the sheet back up to my chin. "You can get up and play with the toys when you're ready," he says. "You're going to be just fine."

Just fine. I don't know what *just fine* means. Does it mean I will grow and my feet will need longer shoes and the sleeves on my jacket will be too short? Or does *just fine* mean everything will be as it was? Does *just fine* mean it won't matter what happened up the lake? Does *just fine* mean I'm going to be okay?

Toys are spread out on the floor beside the bed, but they aren't mine. A wire contraption holds orange and yellow and green beads that can be moved back and forth on the wire. I think of pulling the beads off and letting them loose on the floor. There is a big walking doll standing in the corner, her arms and legs stiff, and she doesn't have a friendly face at all, as if walking takes all her concentration. One of her eyes is stuck halfway open, giving her a frightening look. There is an eight-pack of Crayola crayons on top of a stack of three or four colouring books; Casper the Friendly Ghost is the colouring book on top. I have an urge to colour Casper orange, but not enough of an urge to move me out of bed. There is a game of Chutes and Ladders, the box crushed in the corners, the lid threatening to slide off, and a Barbie with one leg severely chewed. There is a small canister of Play-Doh, all the colours rolled together and the lid left off so the clay will be hard and useless. There is a Pull-a-Tune, a xylophone on wheels, and a box of Little Red Schoolhouse building bricks.

A sock monkey sits on the shelf laughing at me with his big red mouth, his long thin arms folded in front of him. I am tempted to take him down to hug, but he doesn't belong to me. What if the other child comes in and wants the monkey back? I'll leave it on the shelf. My chest hurts. I'm cold. One, two, three.

There's another bed in the room. The sheets are smooth and tucked in tight. Only someone very skinny could fit under that sheet. I get out of bed slowly and look down the hall, and then I pull the sheets up, pull their edges from under the mattress and heap them all up in the middle of the bed as though someone is already using the bed so there won't have to be another accident, no one else will fall through the ice and be brought here to warm up and play with toys that aren't hers.

"Jell-O," a nurse sings out, carrying a tray with a bowl of green jelly in it, only the jelly doesn't even wiggle. It has tiny bits of fruit in it, not sinking or bobbing to the top, just trapped inside the green.

"Everyone loves green Jell-O," she says, looking over at the messy bed and frowning.

That's not true. She doesn't know. Green is all wrong. I roll over and bury my face into the pillow and count until I can no longer hear the nurse or see her dreadful green Jell-O. One, two, three. I want orange Jell-O with a plop of whipping cream on top, at the very last minute, like a surprise, orange Jell-O that tries to wiggle off my spoon like it is alive.

I try hard not to think of my mother but I can't help it. She is smoothing the hair off my face, putting her face against my cheek, her skin smooth and clear, not a single mark on it as if life hasn't hurt her at all. She presses the sheets against me and rubs the bottoms of my feet through the blanket. I keep breathing deeply to smell her apples and lavender. One, two, three. My breathing gets faster and faster like I'm running down a hill and can't stop, my arms flailing like windmill parts. I want my mother, I want my mother, until I feel dizzy and my chest hurts again and the room begins to move so I close my eyes. I can't see and I can't think.

When I open my eyes, the room is cold and empty, and a large sob bursts out of my mouth and startles me and I hold my breath to make it all stop. But it won't stop, won't even slow down.

I want my mother. I want my mother. Please, please, I want my mother. I consider crying out, but I am afraid. Afraid I might wake up and know I'll never see her again. There is no one in the room but me, and the empty space is pressing hard on my chest. My mother is gone, my mother is gone, over and over in my head as I continue to stare at the ceiling. One, two, three.

I want to feel her hands in my hair twisting and braiding. I want to hear her voice saying *there, there*. I want to lay my cheek against hers, her arms all the way around me. Mommy. Mommy.

The hospital room is a pale colour. The nurses discuss the colour as if they are trying to describe the room to a blind person.

"Susan, would you say these walls are green?"

"No, not green. More beige."

"What colour do you think the walls are, Rebecca?"

I don't answer. I don't care what colour the walls are. Then they talk about chicken casseroles and Cynthia's dreadful haircut.

"Why she thought she needed a new look is beyond me," one of them says.

Gossip, my mother calls it.

A picture of Jesus hangs on the wall next to the window. He looks forlorn and hopeless, as if there is nothing he can do to help me. His eyes are heavy. He too knows. I half expect his face to start moving slowly back and forth. No, Rebecca, his face says. She is gone.

Accidents happen, my mother said when I spilled my milk or fell and hurt my knees while skipping. What if this was no accident? One, two, three. What if, what if.

Nuns rustle through the hall in their penguin suits that flow behind them like sails. I don't hear any shoes clomping down the hall, just a whooshing sound that gets loud and then fades away. Maybe their feet never have to touch the ground at all. Did Jesus walk on water or was that Moses? I stare at the ceiling trying to remember Mrs. McDermid's Bible lessons, but I decide if Moses could make a sea move apart from itself with his magic stick, then walking on water would be easy.

The nuns all look the same, one after another sailing down the hall as if they're all headed to the same place but can't quite figure it out. *Make haste,* I think of saying, sitting up in bed and using my minister voice.

One of the nuns told me my mother went to be with Jesus, that He called her home. She tucked the sheets in around me tight.

"We don't want you falling out of bed, now do we," she says

Jesus must be close by if his picture is on the wall in the room I am in. This must be his home because people put pictures of themselves on their walls. I sit up and can feel my heart bumping around in my chest, getting louder and louder, as I start breathing in and out, faster, not worrying about it hurting. I want to call out to my mother. Mommy, mommy, come home. I check under the bed and in the closet. I think about running through the halls calling her name. It takes me a while to figure out the hospital doesn't belong to Jesus; it's not his home. The nuns just borrowed his pictures.

No mention is made of Jake being called home, but the nun read me the words under the picture of Jesus: *Let the little children come unto me.* Maybe the nun thought I knew that Jake would have been called right away, like the door at the Shop-Easy that opens on its own when I get close to it and swings shut after I walk through. Maybe the door to heaven works the same way for little children. Maybe if you've not had much chance to be very good, you get in on a pass, with a wild card, like landing on free parking in Monopoly and getting all the money. I wasn't sure of all the rules of believing in Jesus. The whole idea of being called home confuses me, so I take Jesus off the wall and put him face down in the closet.

The minister from our church comes to see me. He brings me a new book. I can read when my mother helps me, but the thought of trying to sound out a word without my mother is too much so I shove the book under my pillow. Reverend Jacobs frowns and shakes his head slightly as if he is expecting something else. He puts his hand on my forehead, pushing on it slightly, and looks into my face.

"This wasn't your fault, Rebecca," he says.

I begin to scream. I throw my head back and scream as loud as I can, never taking my eyes off him. I pull my eyebrows together and lean my head back and scream even louder. The nurses rush in and brush the startled reverend back. His eyes open wide and he holds on to his neck, saying, "Oh my, oh my," as though he's never heard a child scream before. I scream at his face until the nurses roll me over and jab something in my hip. I slap the nurse, not on purpose. My hand jumps up off my blanket and slaps her. She has the needle and syringe in her hand, and my finger catches the end of the needle and begins to bleed. I stare at it.

I think for a minute I must be dead, but if I'm bleeding I can't be dead. I stare at the blood again, until the nurse wipes the blood off with a tissue. The nurse herds Reverend Jacobs out the door like he's infected with a disease. She may have even said *shoo*, like he is a pesky fly. She looks back at me, but my eyelids are collapsing and I can feel my eyes rolling back into my head and the water is pouring in around my ears. *Help,* I cry, but then I don't care if the water devours me.

Reverend Jacobs comes again and I think of screaming when he walks back into the room, for that second when his foot comes down in the doorway, but I don't even whimper. I heard the nurses say that screaming is a good sign. When I made a fuss my mother said, Rebecca, there's no need for noise like that, so the nurses are wrong. I decide not to scream ever again.

"The nurses say I can take you to see your father," Reverend Jacobs says, bent over with his hands on his knees, with a too-big smile, standing back from me a bit as if I might be contagious with some screaming disease.

His face looks like a sock puppet, the mouth huge and not real. He wears his collar, the flat white band, around his throat instead of a tie. My mother called it a uniform. A costume is more like it, my father said. I wondered if it was hard to figure out a uniform for everyone, so none of us would look the same, so a police officer wouldn't be confused with a doctor or a doctor wouldn't be confused with a bus driver. How do we keep it all straight? Wouldn't it be easier not to know what everyone was before we met? I could put Reverend Jacobs's collar on, but I don't think anyone would confuse me with a reverend. Reverend Rebecca. If I were a reverend I wouldn't talk so loud and I would always use mouthwash before I go visiting.

"Would you like to see your father?" Reverend Jacobs asks, like the carrot I hold out for Daisy to come to me when I want to ride her. Here, Daisy, I say, holding out the carrot in front of me, like a promise I won't ride her, but then I break the promise. Every single time.

I nod.

We walk to the end of the hall. I pad beside him in hospital slippers that are too big for my feet, but I manage to keep my feet in them by scrunching my toes into the soft but worn fabric. He tries to hold my hand, but I don't want him touching me. I want to remember what my hand felt like holding my mother's hand. Holding his hand will spoil it so I keep my hands in my sleeves. As we pass the nurses' station I hear one nurse say, "Children adjust so quickly."

My father is in his bed, looking small and almost invisible with his shrunken and shriveled body, his arms empty balloons, flat and wrinkled. He is staring at the ceiling just like I had been doing. He doesn't seem to be counting; his lips aren't moving. My father doesn't seem to hear a word the reverend is saying. He eventually turns to look at me, as if I just arrived, and his eyes are watery and puffy, his face a terrible white, his hair pressed tightly to his head as if melted into his skin. He begins to sob but doesn't raise his arms, doesn't reach for anyone, just lifts his pointer finger of his right hand in my direction, the hand that is not bandaged. He lets the tears and snot leak out and run down into his ears, a steady stream. I grab a tissue off the little table that stretches across his bed. I was going to dab at the wet spots but instead I just crumple the tissue in my hand. I am not sure daughters are supposed to do nose-wiping. The rules are all muddled now.

There was a time when I would crawl into bed with him, lift his heavy arm and let it drape over me like a shield to keep the scary things away. I placed my head on his chest, listening to his heart swoosh and purr like a double pendulum: beat-beat, beat-beat, my mother's hand on my back, patting me back to sleep.

I want to put my face against his chest the way I used to then, listening to the hum of his voice. I want him to gather me up in his arms and make the pictures in my head go away. I want him to throw me over his shoulder the way he did with Jake and drag his Saturday whiskers across my belly until I beg him to stop, only I wouldn't beg him to stop; I just want this morning to be Saturday, exactly how it used to be, every day for the rest of my life.

I look at Reverend Jacobs for help, but he is stuck in the door-way, his head down and his lips moving. I crawl up on the end of my father's bed and rest my head on top of his lower legs. I feel the warmth through the blanket. My head bumps up against his fingers, but just for a second until his fingers retract into his right sleeve. I watch his face for some clue that he is still my father.

"Is there something I can do for you, Robert?" the reverend asks.

"No," my father says. "There's nothing. I've got nothing."

Instead of a family, my father is stuck with me; the teams are chosen and I am the only one left standing. If we were in the yard, he would lift his head, tip his chin as if to say *come on,* but he has already given up, certain he will never win. He would drop the ball at his feet, leave it there in the mud as he trudged home, ignoring my calls for him to stay.

Four

A BLACK CAR, SLIPPERY AND SHINY AND SINISTER LOOKING, comes to the hospital to take my father and me to the church. There's no dust on the car, no fingerprints; it shines as if perfectly new, the edges straight and sharp, with great wings off the back of it as if it might be able to fly. I stare at my reflection in the car, and I am wide and short and my face is strange and bloated. Everyone is quiet and the driver smiles at me in the rear-view mirror with a strange kind of smile, as if he didn't really mean to smile at all, as if the smile slipped out with a mind of its own and he is trying to pull the smile back in, as if this were the wrong time to smile.

Somehow my father's suit appeared and a dress that is too big for me. It isn't my dress and it feels wrong. I already know it's not right when I pull the dress over my head, getting lost inside its prickly fabric, a whole lot of stiff fabric sewn inside the dress to make it puff and flounce. I don't want puff or flounce; I want straight and smooth, nothing that will draw attention. I don't want to be noticed, don't want to be seen. One of the nuns buttons the dress at the back and ties a big pink bow, snugging it tight around my waist.

"This is a lovely dress," she says, patting me on the shoulder, the sound of her voice saying I should agree.

The dress has a large white collar and the skirt fluffs out, but it feels too long or too wide or too thick. I don't like dresses, with my bare legs and underpants all there to be seen if someone lifts my dress, if the wind catches the hem, if I decide to climb a tree. A girl can't play in a dress, not real play. A dress makes a girl stand at the edge and just watch.

The nun pulls a brush through my hair, pulling my head back when she hits a tangle. She must not have had much practice with a little girl's hair because my mother never yanked on my head, she never hurried, and when she got to a tough spot she whispered in my ear, her lips tickling me, and I forgot about the tangles.

Tears start to drip off my chin, but the nun keeps dragging the brush through my hair, pulling my hair into a ponytail at the base of my neck. Everyone knows that ponytails are meant to be high, high enough so the bottom of my hair will tickle my neck. Everyone knows that. Everyone but nuns. She leaves some white ankle socks and shiny patent shoes by the bed. I don't want to go to a party. I've not been invited to any party. Not once. Not one single birthday party, in all my six years, not even my own.

"You're going to the funeral," the nun says. She turns me around and stares in my face. "Do you know what that means?"

I nod. I don't want her to tell me. I have no idea what a funeral is. *Funeral.* The word sounds like *final.* The end of everything.

The black car, with my father and me sitting in the back seat, parks at the front of the church. Two markers keep anyone else from parking where we need to. *Funeral Today,* the two signs say, as if something wonderful is about to happen and everyone is invited, like the circus is in town today, but you can't park here; park somewhere else.

Reverend Jacobs opens the car door and helps my father out. My father's friend Barry is on the sidewalk looking worried.

"Robert," he says, the name coming out on his breath and saying all manner of things besides my father's name. Barry smiles at me, the same strange smile the driver had. His arms wrap around my father in an awkward way, and my father's head drops, his lips moving like they're sharing a secret, making plans to rob a bank or knock off the post office.

My father limps around the side of the car and steps up on the sidewalk. Barry lowers him into a wheelchair, and then we head for the side door of the church. Two women stop on the sidewalk and watch, their hands over their mouths as if the sight of us is too shocking and they need to catch their breath, their purses swinging from their wrists. They put their heads together and wait until we move past.

"He could only save the one," one woman says.

Reverend Jacobs tries to hold my hand, but I fold my arms in front of me. No, no, no, I want to say and I want to stomp my feet and scream and I'm sorry now that I've made the promise about never screaming again. I slip my hands into my armpits.

"You can let me hold your hand," Reverend Jacobs says. "I won't hurt you."

I stop in my tracks and put my stiff arms at my sides, and I shake my head and use my angriest eyes. Reverend Jacobs has no idea how memory works or he wouldn't say that. He wouldn't even ask to put his fingers on mine, where my mother's fingers had been. Ministers should know such things. That's why they get to be at the front of the church, because they are supposed to have a better understanding of how things work, what the rules are. They're meant to be wise, wiser than the rest of us. So I give him my angry look, my I'm-going-to-scream-in-a-minute look even though I won't. I tried the look on Jake once or twice, but it didn't do any good. It works on Reverend Jacobs.

Barry pushes the wheelchair into the crying room. That's what our Sunday school teacher calls it. It is just off to the side of the altar at the front of the church, set in behind sheer curtains that have a hint of green to them, faded and worn, the dust woven right in. Some of the older boys hide their Sunday school books behind the curtains on their way by after the children have been excused from church.

"That room's for crying," one of them said. "You can't go in there unless you're making a fuss."

Barry wheels my father in beside one of the chairs. I stand at the edge of the curtain. I can't see much of the sanctuary from where I am standing, but I can see people begin to take their seats. It's terribly quiet and no one is smiling or talking. Two boxes sit side by side at the front of the church, shiny dark brown boxes with big handles on each side. I wonder at first if there is going to be a magic trick like I saw at the circus where someone got sawed in half or disappeared from one box and sat up with her arms over her head when the magic person opened the other box. *Ta-da*, I imagine my mother saying. *Fooled you.* But the two boxes sit perfectly still, a big one and a small one like a toy. Jake had a little tractor just like my father's big tractor. My father flopped Jake's chubby baby body down on the toy tractor on Jake's first birthday. "You're a farmer just like Daddy," my father said.

At first, I don't know what is in the boxes. The reverend asked my father a few days ago if the caskets should be open.

"No," my father moaned. "No," shaking his head back and forth and back and forth until I felt dizzy and had to sit down.

"Jake and Grace look very peaceful," Reverend Jacobs is saying to my father now, his hand on my father's shoulder. "Do you want the caskets open?"

It is now, this very moment, that I know my mother and Jake aren't stuck at the bottom of the lake trying to get out of the car; they are right here in the sanctuary in those boxes. I want to throw up the lids and let some fresh air in, but all I can do is sit and be a good girl.

I think of Todd the Turtle in the little blue necklace box with a bit of ribbon tied around to hold the box shut when we planted him in the garden next to the raspberry canes after he died. My mother asked if I wanted to say a few words, so I said *umbrella* and *pendulum*, because they were big words and I had just learned them and Todd might like to hear big words, but then I got wondering if turtles even had ears. I added *sunshine* and *giggle* at the last minute because they seemed like happy words.

I hear the chimes, just a second before my father does. My head jerks up and lifts my body right out of my chair and, before I can stop it, *Mommy* flies right out of my mouth. Reverend Jacobs puts his hand on my shoulder and gently pushes me back into my seat.

"No music, no music," my father says, and his voice is strange and frightening.

"It's for Grace," Reverend Jacobs says. "For Grace and Jake. A call to worship."

My father sobs as the chimes continue. I close my eyes and let myself perch beside my mother on the organ bench when she turned sideways from the organ's keyboard to press the few keys in the tiny oak box that worked the chimes, such a small keyboard for a sound that can be heard all over town. My mother played the organ; the church music was because of her, the Sunday music and the everyday music. She played for everything, all the parties that go on at church.

"For Grace," I whisper. I don't say *Jake*. I don't think of Jake.

"Everyone is seated, Robert. I'll take you and Rebecca in," Reverend Jacobs says.

"I'll take them," Barry says. He lifts my father by the elbow out of his wheelchair. "You can do this, Robert. You can do this," he says though my father doesn't seem to be listening. I follow behind.

We come out from behind the curtained room just as Reverend Jacobs speaks from the front of the church.

"We gather here today," Reverend Jacobs says with his Sunday voice that is loud and sharp, "to mark the life of Grace Archer and to say our farewells to her and to Jake."

A terrible silence falls over the room, and all I can hear are my father's slippers dragging along the tiles. I stare at his slippers, wondering why he forgot his shoes, forgot he was going to be in church. For just a second I consider running home for his shoes. I was going to tug on his sleeve and point to his feet, but something about him said *don't touch*.

The church is fuller than I have ever seen it, even at Christmas when all the *part-time Christians* come. Mrs. Zaback, our children's choir director, called them that. "You must sing your best this Sunday," she says. "There'll be lots of part-timers in the pews."

Mrs. Zaback could play the organ and use her head to tell the junior choir when to sing and when not to sing. My mother said Mrs. Zaback was the most musical person she knew.

I stop for a moment, as if my shoes are stuck to the floor, looking at the faces searching for someone I might recognize, but they all blend in together in a smear of sadness. There are no children laughing and squirming, being hushed by their mothers. There is nothing that reminds me of anything, not the Fall Fair when bodies push up against the rail to see the horse races or the Santa Claus Parade where faces line the sidewalk straining to see what is coming, to see if Santa is on the next float. All these faces knew the terrible truth: my mother is dead and she is never coming back.

Barry reaches up and touches my shoulder, and I sit quietly beside my father. There is no organ music. My father said no one was going to play my mother's organ, especially on this day. The minister didn't say anything about the organ not being my mother's, didn't say about it belonging to the church. Mrs. Zaback is ready to play, Reverend Jacobs said in the crying room, but my father said his *no—no—no* again, only louder.

With no organ, the church feels broken, as if all the pieces are just bumping around inside but nothing works. People begin coughing and clearing their throats. I stare at my shoes. The strap moves across the shoe or slips down behind the heel. I couldn't decide which was best so the left shoe has the strap over my foot and the right shoe has the strap behind. I stare at my shoes really hard when Reverend Jacobs begins to talk.

"Heaven is better for having Grace and Jake," he says, so loud that I jump. "Let us pray," he says.

Everyone in the church shifts in their seats, as if bowing their heads requires them to straighten their backs. I think of Jesus in the closet at the hospital and wonder if someone put him back on the wall.

They stand behind us to sing the hymns, but my father stays in his seat as if he's stuck. I pull on his sleeve, but he doesn't move. The singing is awkward, as if no one knows when to start and when to stop. The ladies in the choir are warbling like their mouths are full of marbles, and Mr. Drazinski, the only man in the back row of the choir, sings too loud and it hurts my ears. My mother asked him at practice to sing *a little quieter*, her fingertips waving him down. *A little less, Mr. Drazinski, a little less.* I watched Mr. Drazinski from the organ bench while I sat beside my mother, and he looked annoyed, like she didn't really know anything at all about leading the choir.

I don't want to sing now. I know all the hymns, like the ABCs, but I keep staring at the straps on my shoes, one forward, one back.

My mother sang with me while she played the piano. Her voice was clear but never loud. It reminded me of water running over the rocks, a gentle sound, soft and comforting.

"Grace was our neighbour, our friend," Reverend Jacobs says. "She was a wife and a mother. Before she was that, she was a daughter," and he extends his arm in the direction of my father. My father's head flops forward and I hear someone breathe in quickly behind me, like he's been punched. I turn in my seat. A strange man and woman are looking to the front of the church and sitting very straight. They are old, with skin like an accordion. The woman looks at me so I whisper.

"Are you my grandma?"

She nods and puts her finger to her lips when I start to tell her about the picture on our piano. The man moans. The woman wipes at her nose with a rolled-up hankie, the other hand fidgeting with the string of faded pearls around her neck. On one of the fingers is a huge ring with jewels on top and the sides. A bracelet hangs from her wrist. My mother wore only a narrow gold band on her finger, thin like a gold thread.

"I'm so sorry," my father says, turning slightly in his seat toward the man, but Barry turns him back. There are no more sniffing sounds from the noses behind me.

Reverend Jacobs talks about the happy circumstance of my mother calling Roddick home and how she shared her smile and talent with her community. "She became one of us," he says, and the man behind me whimpers just slightly.

I don't hear the old people fidgeting the way other people seem to be. I concentrate on the pain inside my stomach that feels like I am being squeezed to death very slowly. While I sit there, I think about Jake having all my mother's attention now in heaven and wonder if I miss him at all.

People stand and sing and sit and someone says something, but I've quit listening. I feel numb and airy like I might just crumble into dust. They file past my father and me when the service is over. Reverend Jacobs invites guests to stay for refreshments in the church hall, where the church ladies have everything ready for us. He uses his happy church-is-over voice. We said goodbye to my mother and Jake, and now Reverend Jacobs thinks tea will make it all better.

The man and woman wait in their seats until everyone has said what they came to say to my father. People glance at them quickly on the way by. A few people extend their hands and nod and make a sort of smile.

"Sorry for your loss, Mr. Claydon," the bank manager says and nods at the woman.

Tears roll down my father's cheeks but he doesn't make much sound while his shoulders move back and forth. "You've been through so much," people say. Most of them say they are sorry, as though it is their fault. And then everyone has passed by, no *Sorrys* left.

"Robert," the old man says as my father struggles to get to his feet. Barry helps him. Barry looks over my father's head and mouths the word *please*. The man nods and closes his eyes.

"I tried," my father says, and then he shakes his head back and forth, as if he's forgotten what he was going to say.

The woman fidgets with the ends of her sleeves, and I think the fabric must be itching her wrists or the blouse is the wrong size. She looks at me, but her eyes dart away.

I stick out my hand. "I'm Rebecca."

"Hilda," she says.

It sounds funny, an old person with a first name, and I almost giggle out loud. Almost. I want to stare at her hair, white and fluffed up high like thick cotton candy. My mother said I should never stare, but some things require staring just to figure them out.

"We can take you to see the beavers," I say. I imagine leading them back to the beaver pond on my own, showing them the way, telling them to be careful of the mud on their English shoes. I would explain how the beavers built their dams and why they chose this spot, why it was our farm the beavers wanted to call home.

"Rebecca," my father squeaks.

The man clears his throat again, and I look at him.

"I'm sorry we won't have time." He looks at me long and hard as if he recognizes me from somewhere.

"This is Rebecca," the old woman says while the man nods. "She is so like her mother." The man looks away.

She is so like her mother. I start repeating that sound in my head, over and over, making the words sound just like when the woman said them.

"I wish," my father starts to say.

"We're past wishing, Robert." Then the old man sticks out his hand and my father takes it with his right hand, putting his bandaged left hand on top. "Goodbye, Robert," the old man says. No smile. He nods at me, and the woman puts her cheek against mine. She smells exactly like my mother. I start to slip my arms around her neck, but I hesitate and she stands up.

"Goodbye," she says, and they turn and leave, the opposite way everyone else has gone. The woman leans on a polished stick she is carrying, but keeps her body straight, rod-like. I want to shout something after them that will make them stay, something that will make them see I am their family, too. I can't think of a single thing.

We go to the church auditorium for tiny sandwiches and sweets, but none of them look inviting to me. There is a hum of voices speaking quietly. Mrs. Fairweather says their furnace needs repair and Mr. Corkum says his calves are coming early and someone has a new car. No one does much but pat me on the head or jiggle my shoulder. I hear the tinkling and clinking music of the tiny china teacups and see the little sandwiches and a cookie tucked in on the saucer like we're all playing house.

My father lets go of my hand, and I wiggle my fingers to get the feeling back. He tries grinning at me once but he seems to have trouble looking into my face, and when he does he looks as if he can't remember who I am. The look on his face is the same as when he was holding his breath under water trying to pull me out the window. Maybe he is still holding his breath.

Five

THE HOUSE SOUNDS EMPTY, AS IF NO ONE HAS EVER LIVED HERE. It smells strange, too, that locked-up smell that lets loose the bad things that happened inside the house: the burned toast, the potatoes that boiled over on the stove, Jake's diapers, the rotten cabbage that someone forgot to throw away, and all the bad smells that come from an old house: rotting wood and stale air, the whole lot in that first smack in the face when we opened the door, as if all the bad smells came out to play while we were away, while the doors and windows were closed up and no one was in the house to chase them away.

I'm not sure which is louder, the smells or the silence, as if we are disturbing this tomb, this emptiness that not even air has been allowed to move about in. The house has been frozen, holding its breath, petrified in the pose it was in when we all left, when we left for a drive to the cabin, left this life, left the house alone.

We may have been away a week or a month or years, I don't know, but we have been away long enough for the house to forget our voices and our way of walking, to forget we even live here, and now we're strangers. I don't remember where my hand fit into the groove by the back door that I used to swing from and not lose my balance. I can't find the light switch at the bottom of the stairs in the dark. I'm not sure if the bathroom door latch will catch every time.

I take my shoes off because they echo on the wooden floor and the sound bumps into me and hurts my head. "Keep your shoes on," my mother said. "You'll get slivers." I have to risk it, the slivers, so I wear my thickest socks, my silent thick socks. They were hand knit by a lady of the Hospital Auxiliary. That is a really hard word to say. My mother broke the word into pieces so I could practise. She wasn't a member of the Auxiliary. You have to be invited; someone has to want you to join, to become one of them. You can't just go along to one of the meetings and say here I am, I'd like to join. My mother didn't want to join. "A little more gossip than I like," she said to my father. So instead she bought their mittens and socks and played the piano for their meetings sometimes.

"Don't be ridiculous," my father said.

"Telling someone's story when you have no business thinking you know," she said. "That's gossip."

I wonder if those stories were about her, her story, the parts she didn't want told, the parts that someone would take away, and she wouldn't be able to get the parts back, such as a bad dream she'd had and woke up crying and calling for her mother or when someone might have knocked her down at school and taken her sandwich and she decided to fight back and got in trouble or maybe she stole some penny candy from the store on her street and the proprietor caught her and threatened to call the police but she tried to explain that it had been a dare. Or maybe how she came to stay in Roddick and was left behind by her parents, maybe that's the part she wanted to keep for herself, her own story.

* * *

There are a lot of dishes in the refrigerator, some with notes attached to them. Bake for this long and have the oven this hot and stir halfway through. The mail is piled up neatly, the larger envelopes on the bottom. The newspapers are off to the side. Front page on top says *Rainy Lake Ice*, but that's all I can read, the only words I can recognize before my father turns the paper over after staring at it without moving, as if he suddenly forgot how to read.

Mrs. Klein from next door comes over with her apron on. She taps on the door and opens it slowly. Her hair is piled up on her head, all grey and dark, and some of it stands straight up as if there were no way to tuck it in. *You can't get me*, the hair seems to say, and I can't stop staring at it. Mrs. Klein waves at her hair like it is full of flies.

"I've been watching for you," Mrs. Klein says, whispering too loudly, like she just broke a paper-bag balloon, her words jumping out and scaring us. I expect her teeth to shoot across the room with the whistle that comes between each word.

My father told my mother that Mrs. Klein was a windbag. He didn't look happy that she was a windbag. She has a great laugh, my mother said. My father exhaled with a big humph. She sounds like a big fat chicken, he said. That's harsh, Robert, my mother replied and shook her head, but her eyes were laughing a little bit, too, as my father mimicked Mrs. Klein.

"Never you mind me," Mrs. Klein says. "Pretend I'm not here. I'm going to fix your dinner and get these dishes put away. Those sheets need to come off the line," she says. "I think they've been hanging there long enough. Surprised they didn't blow away. We've had some big winds this past week."

I look at my father as if he should say *uh-huh* or nod or something, but he doesn't react, just stares at his knees. Mrs. Klein keeps talking, not even bothering to notice whether anyone is listening. She says all the neighbours are going to take turns making meals until my father is on his feet.

"When do those bandages come off?" she asks. Then she steams ahead with, "Mr. Katz will feed your cows. He's got nothing better to do this time of year, no family to bother with." My father jumps like he's been pinched, and she keeps on going. We hear about the Corkum kids and chicken pox and how they are dropping like flies. And how Mrs. Sutherland's mother is so forgetful she can't live alone and why would she want to in that great big giant house of hers, really, at her age. The Fisk girl is getting married and a little too quickly, if you know what I mean. And Mrs. Klein fans her face like she's suddenly too hot.

Mrs. Klein bangs around in the kitchen, her arms going in every direction, and not once does she stop talking. My father sits in a chair near the kitchen table with the newspaper on his lap that he's not bothering with, his feet and left hand still bandaged. He closes his eyes and rocks back and forth slowly, ever so slightly. I sit at the table with my knees under me, watching Mrs. Klein.

"I hope you don't lose your fingers and toes," she says. "What does the doctor say?" She doesn't wait for my father to say anything back. She drops a mug of coffee down on the table in front of him.

"No sense in giving up now," she says, putting both her hands on the table in front of my father and looking right into his face. "You have a daughter to raise, and take my word for it, daughters come with all sorts of issues. You can take that to the bank," and she cackles, throwing the tea towel over her shoulder. My father was right: she does sound like a chicken.

People come and go. The casseroles disappear and the cakes and buns stop coming. I saw my father dragging a laundry basket to the ravine and emptying food from the dishes over the edge. The sheets are off the line. I didn't help.

The bandages came off my father's feet and hand. Barry came to the farm to drive my father to the doctor's office. The bandages were brown at the edges and frayed and dirty though I hardly recall my father leaving his chair.

"You've got to shake out of this," Barry said, helping my father into the passenger side of the car and looking right into his face, but my father never looked up. He only has a thumb and pinky on his left hand, so he keeps his hand stuffed in his pocket. He has no toes. I saw him staring at his feet when he was putting his socks on. I wanted to ask, but instead I just stared, too. The skin is tight and pulls over the end of his foot all raw and red.

Mrs. Klein no longer comes to the house. "No, thanks," my father said when she called. "I'm okay. I can take it from here," and he sounded glad, if only slightly. He used words like *much appreciated* and *you went above and beyond* and ended with *thank you, Mrs. Klein.* They had been neighbours since before my father was born, and she was still Mrs. Klein to him, not Bernice or Phyllis or Flo, but Mrs. Klein.

My father shuffles around the house and makes me toast for breakfast and toast for lunch and sometimes toast for supper. He piles peanut butter on thick and says it has protein in it. He buys fruit sometimes but leaves the fruit sitting in the bag, and pretty soon little flies have found it and form a fog around the fruit and I don't want to eat it. "Have some fruit," he says if I'm looking hungry.

He tries to do all his jobs without taking his left hand out of his pocket. Sometimes he gets mad and kicks things, turning around and using his heel. I try to figure out when he needs me to help. He doesn't ask, but I can tell when I should open the drawer or hold the other side of the garbage pail.

"You're a good girl," he says.

A good girl.

I've started making his bed and making the toast and opening the cans of beans and soup. I watched Mrs. Klein put the dirty clothes in the washer so now I do it on my own. I take the garbage out to the burn barrel before it smells, and I sweep up the mud that wanders in from the back porch.

The silence in the house is growing, like the ivy climbing the telephone pole at the edge of the driveway, trying to get to the very top. My father takes me everywhere he goes, but leaves me sitting in the truck. He goes into the hardware for nails. He goes into the pharmacy for toilet paper. He goes into the bank for money. He goes into all these places while I stay in the truck. Sometimes I stay in the truck so long I pee my pants but I don't tell him. When we get home I change my clothes and stuff the wet ones in the bottom of the laundry pile. I pretend he takes me everywhere so he can keep me safe. He doesn't try to hold my hand.

The only place my father lets me out of the truck is the grocery store: Mr. Lyons' Food Basket with its creaky wooden floor and large walk-in freezer at the back of the store where the cold air comes out like a fog when Mr. Lyons opens it. I catch a glimpse of large slabs of meat hanging in the frosty air. Mr. Lyons' apron is crisp and white except where his tummy pushes up against the counter; there it is soiled with blood. Mr. Lyons always hands me a sucker when we come to the store, orange, like he knows it is my favourite. My father leans on the grocery cart and shuffles his feet along under him. He doesn't lift his feet anymore, and I wonder if a person can't lift his feet if he doesn't have any toes. I scrunch my toes up in my shoes and it is hard to lift my feet. I wonder if I should walk like my father, if he'd feel better if my toes were gone, too.

"Good morning, Robert and Rebecca," Mr. Lyons says, and he sounds like he is singing. He seems to be sharpening his knife all the time, like he's conducting an orchestra, his arms waving in big circles. "How are you two on this glorious day?" he says, even when it's raining. Mr. Lyons makes me smile on the inside, where it is safe to do such things. I worry about smiling in case my smile means I've forgotten my mother. My father only nods at Mr. Lyons.

My father has a grocery list that he follows carefully. He goes up and down every aisle like he's lost, checking every shelf. The kid who carries the grocery bags out to the cars asks if he can help.

"Mr. Archer, can I find something for you?" the boy says.

"No," my father says and keeps looking. If it isn't on the list we don't buy it. I could whisper to my mother about a candy necklace or a can of fruit cocktail with the cherries. "Great idea," she said. I don't whisper in my dad's ear.

"There is no honey left," I say, an announcement sound to my voice, stopping to stand beside the bear-shaped squeeze bottles and wide-mouth jars from Meyers honey, a happy bee on its label. He glances at his list, turning the paper over a couple of times, and then continues down the aisle. I hold my ground. He turns to stare at me like I am someone else's child that he's been stuck with and the humour of it has worn off.

"It's not on the list," my father says. He turns to go, but I don't move. He turns his whole body to face me and holds up the list. "Not here," he says, and his eyebrows jab at each other.

"We need honey."

"No, you want honey. Big difference," and his lips are pulled back in a snarl. He rubs the skin under his nose with the side of his finger and shrugs inside his too-big coat. "Come along," he says, like he does when he is urging a cow through the barn gate. I cross my arms in front of me.

"Rebecca," he says, and the sound of his voice should have been a warning, but I don't move. I point to the honey.

"You are not in charge of what we buy," he says. His teeth are clenched.

"Neither are you. Mommy does the groceries," I say.

His right hand squeezes into a fist at his side. Then he swipes at the shelf with his right arm like he has suddenly become a Frankenstein monster. Cans and boxes crash to the floor. Everyone in the store stands perfectly still. I grab a squeeze bottle of honey and bolt for the door.

"What's all this?" Mr. Lyons asks, wiping his hands on his apron as I push past him into the street.

I run until I come to the river, puffing and gasping to catch my breath. I stare down at the grey-and-brown water. I look at the smiling bee on the label of the honey bottle, the bee's perfectly happy face, and I fling the bottle overhand into the river. The bottle bobs along on the water, turning end for end in the current, and then disappears.

I sit in the grass by the river and wait, wait for someone to find me. I feel a little more than sure that I'm going to be in trouble, that someone will tell me that I'm not a good girl at all, but a bad girl, a very bad girl.

Eventually, Barry's car pulls up, and he slowly climbs out. He is so tall that I wonder if his arms and legs fold up like the small table in our hall closet so he can fit inside his car.

Barry walks toward me as if he is thinking about each step before he puts his foot down, and then squats down beside me.

"What are you doing here?" he asks, like he really doesn't want an answer, like he's making conversation.

"Throwing honey in the river," I say matter-of-factly, avoiding the saucy tone that my mother told me not to use.

"I'll take you home," he says. "Your father's having a tough time. You're both having a tough time. It's going to get easier. In a while."

I climb up off the grass and crawl into the front seat of his car, and without another word, Barry drives me home.

Things start disappearing after that. Photos of Jake in the frames on top of the piano are the first to go. They were there and now they aren't. His little baby shoes collecting dust inside the china cabinet are gone. The wedding photo of my parents standing in a garden, my mother holding a single flower, a fat peony, disappears next. She had on her best dress that day, my mother told me, saying my father looked more like a boy than a man. "We were just foolish kids," my mother said. "Foolish kids in a hurry." The photo is gone.

My favourite is a photo of my mother sitting at a grand piano when she was sixteen, on a big stage at a concert hall in England. She looks proud and happy and is smiling off to the right to someone she must have recognized, someone important. She looks like she is about to exhale, to let out a big blow of air that she has been holding for a long time. Her shoulders are high and tight against her neck like she has a secret she is dying to tell. I take the photo and hide it between my mattress and box spring, a long way in where not even my father's arms could reach if he tried. I know he wants to ask me where it is. I practise shrugging my shoulders to look innocent. I stare in the bathroom mirror at my face, but no matter how I open my eyes or move my mouth I still look guilty.

Mr. Lyons from the grocery store says *guilty as charged*. Saw you at the movies Saturday night. Guilty as charged. You've got the best pork chops in town. Guilty as charged. Stole the photo of my mother. Guilty as charged.

Four of the Mennonite boys show up at the back door. They're tall and broad, and I can't tell who is older. Their cheeks have a slight pink to them, with no sign of whiskers like the ones that grow out of my father's chin.

"Come in, come in," my father waves in front of them, throwing the back door open, his eyes to the floor. "I won't be able to help much," he says.

Help what? I can feel panic start to bubble up in my insides.

"Never mind, Mr. Archer," they all mumble, like a choir of shyness.

"Right on in here," and he leads the way to the room off the kitchen, the room with the floral paper that's dull and pale, peeling in spots, and the grey flat rug stained with rust where something must have stood a hundred years ago. I want to throw my body in front of the door. I want to shout and run around screaming to distract them. Don't take her piano, I want to plead. Please. My father doesn't look at me, so I stand frozen in the kitchen, watching them hoist the piano out the back door and into the shed to sit up on cedar boards, covered with a heavy tarp, watching them remove the last evidence my mother lived in this house.

I don't go to the grocery store anymore. No more waiting in the truck. My father leaves me at home if he has an errand to do.

"I'll be back in a while," he says. "Don't turn on the stove," as if I'll suddenly have the urge to cook a meal as soon as he goes out the door. I'm tempted to drag a chair over to the stove and put the big pot on the front burner with some oil in the bottom and a cup of popcorn in it, but I don't know how much oil or how much popcorn, and I imagine the kitchen full to the ceiling with popcorn when my father comes back. He would open the door and look at me with a shocked face. *What on earth is going on?* he would say. So I don't risk it. But I do lie on my father's bed, curled up in the blankets. I dig in the back of the closet and find my mother's special-occasion dress and pull it over my head. I hike up the stiff taffeta skirt and spin round and round with a regal rustling sound until I'm dizzy and collapse on the bed in a heap. I put my feet into her going-out shoes and feel princess-like. And I start sneaking out to the shed and lifting the tarp off the front of my mother's piano.

Chuck

Six

THE BUS IS COMING, TURNING THE CORNER DOWN THE ROAD, THE road following the bend in the river. Chuck is waiting at the end of his lane, beside the rusty mailbox caved in on top as though some- one drove a sledgehammer into it, the mailbox atop a post with a suggestive lean to it. His left arm is up over his face like a shield. Harold, Chuck's father, paces back and forth behind Chuck, his hands in and out of his pockets, his teeth jammed together.

Chuck wishes he had his cape on, the red one, the one that flows out behind him like wings when he runs, the one with the shiny fabric that's slippery and smooth to touch, always cool when he rubs it against his upper lip. If he had his cape he could hold the bus back with one hand, his left hand, even though his mother says the world is built for right hands and to stop using his left one, an instruction that comes with a slap to the back of the head. He could jump in front of the bus and hold his hand out in front of him like a traffic cop.

"Not today," Chuck would say, leaning into his raised hand. "No one's going to make me get on a school bus. Superheroes don't go to school."

Instead Chuck cries when the bus pulls up, clunking to a stop with a big cloud of diesel smoke behind it, like a big fart, and he would have laughed but he is busy crying.

Farts almost always make him laugh, involuntarily; even thinking about farts, especially in church, makes him laugh right out loud and then he has to hold his hand hard over his mouth so no sound can get out, but he's still laughing, on the inside.

This morning Chuck can't help crying. His stomach aches and it is squeezing him. He wants to shout about not wanting to go to school, not today, not ever. He wants to grab on to the broken-down mailbox post and refuse to let go. He considers digging his fingernails into the splintering wood and screaming at the top of his lungs if someone tries to pull him off, but he knows that wouldn't be a battle he'd win, not today, not any day.

"Stop that," Harold says, slapping at Chuck's arm. "Christ almighty, you'd think you were a girl."

Mr. Basaraba opens the bus door. "Come on up, son," he says. "Morning, Harold," he adds with a disinterested drawl.

Harold nods. "His grandmother babies him," he says, laughing his it's-really-not-funny laugh.

The first step of the bus is a doozy. Chuck grabs the rail and hoists himself in, holding on to his lunch box with a death grip.

"Find a seat," Mr. Basaraba says, his hand ready to pull the door closed behind Chuck, his face saying *Let's get the show on the road.*

A girl named Rebecca is in the second seat on the right. She moves over as soon as she sees Chuck. They're Sunday school friends, but Chuck goes to Sunday school only when his Gran feels like it. Gran comes down from her room some Sunday mornings, not many, with her black church dress on and her hat pushed down on her head hiding her messy hair, and that means get upstairs and get your cleanest pants on and be down here in ten minutes because we're going to church. Gran smoothes Chuck's hair down with her spit and tells him not to worry about the hole in his pants or the broken shoelace in his right shoe.

Chuck slides quickly into the bus seat with Rebecca and wipes his sleeve across his nose and tries hard not to cry anymore. Rebecca has a brown paper bag on her lap. She printed her name on the bag with blue crayon.

"Your mother died," Chuck says between leftover crying gulps and looking at Rebecca.

"Yah, I know," Rebecca says.

"What's in the bag?"

"My lunch."

"Why don't you have a real lunch box?"

Rebecca shrugs.

"What've you got for lunch?" Chuck asks.

Rebecca pulls open the bag and shows Chuck a bruised apple and a sandwich wrapped in wax paper. The sandwich is squished almost flat.

"It's honey. Peanut butter too," she says, lifting the edge of the bread as proof. "I cut the crusts off."

"Did you make it?" Chuck asks, the sound of shocked surprise in his voice. "I didn't know kids were allowed to make sandwiches."

They're quiet again for two stops. Rebecca looks across the aisle at the tin lunch boxes. The Lone Ranger on one kid's knee and Woody Woodpecker on another. She puts the paper bag down beside her and shoves it a little bit behind.

"I like Mighty Mouse," she says, pointing to Chuck's lunch box. "I wish I could fly."

"I'm going to fly," Chuck says. "I'm going to be a superhero. I already have my cape." And with that he jumps out of his seat and throws his arms up over his head. "Here I come to save the day," he sings out with his best impersonation of the Mighty Mouse theme song.

"Sit down, kid," Mr. Basaraba says, looking at Chuck in the big mirror on the front windshield.

Rebecca smiles. Their friendship is sealed.

They sit together on the bus every day and beside each other at school. There are six grade ones in their two-room school: twins with blonde hair who look exactly alike except one is shy and doesn't say much; another kid who is chubby; another who is Chuck; another who never brings a lunch; and one with a dead mother. Mr. Pedorski teaches the senior class, grades five to eight, the older kids. The very tall Mrs. Bell, with dark red lipstick and spiked high heels that clomp and echo in the hall, teaches the juniors.

Mrs. Bell is very everything. When she sings "God Save the Queen," she throws her head back and her mouth hangs open in a long oval and her teeth are stained red from her lips moving up and down as she sings. Some of the kids snicker and others clamp their hands over their ears. Mrs. Bell doesn't seem to notice. She keeps singing.

Rebecca joins in, quietly at first, only slightly more than mouthing *Long live our noble Queen.* By the end, Rebecca is challenging Mrs. Bell's volume with *Long to reign over us.*

"Well done, Rebecca," Mrs. Bell says, running her hands down the front of her dress to smooth out the bumps and gather herself after her morning-exercises performance, as if she imagines she's just been on stage at Massey Hall. Chuck claps, his hands out in front and slightly above his head. Nancy, one of the blondes, starts to cry, pointing at Mrs. Bell's teeth as though Mrs. Bell has become a zombie during the opening exercises.

Mrs. Bell towers over her students and walks with a yardstick in her hand, swinging it back and forth like she might whack them, Chuck thinks, if they get out of line. Back and forth, back and forth, and all the kids watch the yardstick except Rebecca; she is reading. Mrs. Bell's hair is puffed up like a thick spider web, and when she walks through the door she leans her head to the side slightly just in case her hair rubs on the doorframe; she's that tall. Chuck thinks little kids at school should have a small teacher, a short one, one who blends in and makes the students feel at home and comfortable. Mrs. Bell is frightening.

"Should you be reading?" Chuck asks, leaning over to Rebecca's desk and whispering.

She nods without looking up. "My mother teaches me," she says, a matter-of-fact tone to her voice, her finger running along the words.

"Come up on the carpet, children," Mrs. Bell says. Everyone clambers out of the desks, and the boys collapse on the floor with tremendous fanfare, their legs flopping over their heads. Mrs. Bell clucks at them and speaks sharply. "Boys, boys, boys," she says, each *boys* louder than the one before. Chuck pulls at Rebecca's arm.

"Rebecca, will you be joining us?" Mrs. Bell asks.

"No," Rebecca says. "I know how to read."

"Well, then, there's no point in you coming to school, is there?" Mrs. Bell says, turning her attention to the others. Rebecca looks annoyed but slides her book into her desk and joins the other children sitting on the carpet. Chuck holds her hand, lacing his fingers through hers. Mrs. Bell holds up a book and asks who can tell her the name of it.

Brenda's hand shoots up. When Mrs. Bell points to her, Brenda suddenly comes down with a case of amnesia.

"Don't put your hand up unless you know the answer," Mrs. Bell says, pointing at Brenda with the yardstick to make an example of her. No one else volunteers to answer.

Someone from the senior class stands in the hall waving a hand bell up and down like she is warning ships off the rocks, the bell clanging its announcement that recess has begun. The big kids explode from their classroom, the doors banging against the wall, the students grabbing baseball bats and basketballs. The little kids wait to be dismissed. Some of them walk to the playground door pressing their bodies against the hallway wall, not sure yet where they're supposed to be, not sure they even have permission to be alive. Chuck is one of them until Rebecca finds him, takes his hand firmly, and heads for the door.

"Come on," she says, a no-nonsense sound to her voice.

There are no swings or slides on their playground. It is a small country school with an even smaller budget for play than for classroom supplies. Rebecca grabs a small ball from the wire cage full of oddly sized balls, most of them flat on one side.

"Let's kick the ball between us," she says. They find a patch of grass at the bottom of the playground, near the ditch, and stand about twenty feet apart and kick the yellow ball back and forth, back and forth, until one of the nine-year-olds wanders over. He doesn't ask to play, just stands closer to Chuck than Rebecca, moving closer each time the ball is kicked, standing forward on his toes.

Rebecca kicks the ball, and the kid jumps in front of Chuck and grabs the ball off the grass. He is just turning to run away when Rebecca slams into him with full force and knocks him off his feet. He didn't see her coming, and the surprise and impact knock the wind out of him.

"Our ball," Rebecca says as he writhes on the grass, his mouth open, trying to get air into his lungs. Rebecca stands over him, almost daring him to try to take the ball from her. She raises her eyebrows, which seem to ask a question all on their own—*What's it going to be?*—but Rebecca doesn't say anything at all. The nine-year-old climbs to his feet and rejoins the game of dodge ball going on beside the school, looking back at Rebecca every few seconds to be certain she isn't going to take him down again.

Chuck stares at Rebecca, a little bewildered by her and a whole lot impressed. She kicks the ball back to him and carries on as if nothing has happened. Chuck doesn't say a word about it, kicks the ball a little harder now, a little more on target. The bell is clanging again, only this time Mrs. Bell is hanging out the school door, one hand on the doorframe and the other waving the bell.

"Recess is over," she shouts.

* * *

"School was great," Chuck says, bounding through the door and dropping his lunch box and jacket on the floor before kicking off his shoes, one hitting the wall and leaving a dark scuff mark. His Mighty Mouse lunch box flops over on its side, and Chuck sets it back upright.

Gran is there to welcome him, to say she's glad he's back, to say there are cookies on the counter and come and tell her all about his day, putting down her book and opening her arms.

"I have a new best friend and she knows how to read and she's not afraid of anything," Chuck says, and then he sticks his tongue out as if has run out of air. "Her name is Rebecca."

"That must be Rebecca Archer, from down the road. You know her from church," Gran says while Chuck nods vigorously.

"You've got chores," Harold says, sticking his head in from the kitchen. "Farmer chores. Change your clothes and come on," he says, before slamming the door.

Chuck looks at Gran, a pleading don't-make-me-go-to-the-barn look. Gran nods. "Go on now," she says.

Chuck throws himself on the floor, spread-eagled. His eyes close. "But Gran," Chuck says. "It'll be the death of me."

"Just fly up the stairs," Gran says. "Use your superhero powers."

Chuck groans and climbs up off the floor. "I don't want to do chores. I want to fly." And he spreads his arms and runs around the room, jumping over the footstool and around Gran's rocker before sailing up the stairs.

"What the hell is going on?" Harold says, coming in from the kitchen looking ready to punch something, but Chuck's door has already slammed and his bed bounces above the ceiling in the living room, while he jumps, up and down, pulling off his going-to-school pants in between bounces. Up and down, touching his head and hands on the sloping ceiling. One leg out, two legs out, the pants sailing through the air, landing on the chair next to his small desk where a model of the Norseman sits, the best plane every built.

Chuck flops on to his back and pours off the bed like he is made of liquid, able to flow into cracks or under the door or just about anywhere if need be. He pulls on his barn jeans that are already a bit short, which is good news. "I'm growing," he says right out loud. "Finally."

"You're slower than molasses. Slow, slow," Harold says, meeting Chuck at the bottom of the stairs, giving him a shove. "We've got to bed the cows down and move some of that pig shit out of the pens. Get your rubber boots on."

Harold grumbles about daughters and too-small boys and any number of other complaints while he marches to the barn three or four strides ahead of Chuck. Living with older sisters, much older sisters, had been an adventure into mystery for Chuck. They are like aliens, creatures that have little or no genetic connection to him. They are always embroiled in a struggle, it seems to Chuck, one trying to outdo the other. Gran says having those two break trail for you is just a bit of bad luck.

Geraldine was born first, but only by eleven months. Gerri, everyone called her, mostly everyone. Harold didn't call her anything. Frances must have been in the starting blocks when Geraldine was born, because Frances spent every second trying to overtake her sister.

There is always some ruckus going on in the room the girls share. A line has been drawn down the middle of the room with sticky black electrical tape. The understanding is that neither girl is to take one step over or on the line. The neutral area is the space both need to get in and out the bedroom door. But that line of tape doesn't stop them from throwing things on each other's beds or arguing about closet space. There is an occasional wrestling match, complete with hair pulling and biting over a dress or sweater.

No amount of yelling from Chuck's mother discourages their warfare tactics, nor does it reduce the amount of bad language flung between them. Gran even covers Chuck's ears sometimes, trying to protect him from a display of unacceptable behaviour. The girls compare test results but aren't inclined to boast of a better mark over the other, because neither is a particularly good student.

"If you'd just apply yourselves," Chuck's mother says, staring at their report cards as if the reports have been written in Latin, the results making her wilt.

"Those girls would turn any mother off mothering," Gran explains. But then after a moment or two of thoughtful consideration, Gran shakes her head and mutters about which comes first, the chicken or the egg.

Geraldine and Frances peck at each other, going for the same worm, so to speak, says Gran, and with loud emotional wrestling until one gives in, but giving in isn't a notion either embraces with any vigour.

The girls move to town as soon as they finish high school, both in the same grade having been born in the same year. They bolt from the farm as though they are on fire, and they live in a small apartment above the drugstore.

Before they change their address they regularly seize Chuck and hold him captive in their room, dressing him up for play. They tease his blond curls, making his hair appear like a mad scientist's. They cover his eyelids with brilliant blue shadow that extends to his eyebrows in an alarming way. His pouty lips are made even more so with a dramatic red that borders on clown-like. They hang bobbles and clusters from his ears, shrieking with delight when they stand back to survey their efforts.

All this is brought to an abrupt halt when Harold throws open the girls' bedroom door, the doorknob cracking through the plaster.

"What are you two up to?" he shouts, grabbing Chuck's decorated body from the bed by one arm. "You'll turn him into a faggot."

Instead of being fearful of their father's wrath, the girls squeal and cackle, running from the room, leaving their father pulling Chuck's shirt over his head and furiously rubbing the makeup off, nearly taking Chuck's skin with it. It is the only co-operative play Geraldine and Frances ever engage in.

* * *

Chuck's mother turns in the lane just as Chuck is climbing the barnyard fence, his chores finally done. He waves, a feeble sort of wave, not wanting to be distracted from walking along the top rail, his arms stretched out to balance him.

"Don't you dare fall, Charles Prescott," his mother shouts, climbing out of the car looking tired beyond tired. Her thin hair is pulled back into a thick rubber band. She always looks thinner when she arrives home from work, as though all the air has been let out of her on the drive home. She gets out of the car and grinds a cigarette into the dirt with the toe of her shoe. She has to crawl out the passenger side, as the driver's door no longer opens. The colour of the car is anyone's guess; it has a green back door on the driver's side and a red hood and a black fender on the back passenger side. Gran calls it the Christmas car, a real gift.

Chuck's mother is thinner than thin. Everything about her is thin: her hair, her skin, her wrists, her eyes. She needs inflating, Gran says. Her hair is a washed-out brown, limp and feather-like. Her eyes are an almost translucent blue, watery and pale. Her lips are firmly pinched together to keep anything from escaping. Everything is locked up tight.

Penelope works at the hospital in the laundry room. People at work call her Penny. Chuck likes that name better than Penelope, which seems too much of a mouthful. He calls her Mom, but they seldom have a conversation that requires him to call her anything. She sits at the kitchen table when she isn't at work, her legs crossed and a cigarette in her fingers. The ashtray is always full, and it seems she stares: stares and smokes with a magazine open in front of her.

Chuck asked her once what she wanted to be when she was his age. She looked at him, shook her head, and didn't say a word.

"Your mother's tired of mothering," Gran says when he is shooed away from his mother's knee like lint. "Come on over here, my boy. Gran's knee happens to have a vacancy." When Chuck climbs up on Gran's knee, she lays her lips against his cheek and he rolls himself into a ball under her chin, snuggling against her marshmallow breasts.

"Don't let Harold see you babying that boy, Mother," Chuck's mother says, not looking up from her magazine.

"You let me worry about that, my dear. I think I've earned my own free will."

Seven

CHUCK'S PONY IS WILD AND WILY, EVEN WITH THE REGAL NAME of Prince. Prince is handsome with a steel-grey body and a full silver mane and a tail that flows like silk in the wind. Prince can run like stink—Chuck's expression, not Rebecca's. When Prince is feeling fresh, he tucks his nose into his chest and raises his front feet slightly off the ground, suspended in air, steadying by touching down one foot every few seconds, poised, waiting for Chuck's urging, and then he bolts as if he might run right out from under Chuck.

There was a time when Chuck was afraid of Prince, not willing to ride him outside the corral. He had to stand on an overturned pail to get Prince's bridle on, to be tall enough to reach Prince's ears. Prince knocked him off the pail from time to time, leaving Chuck clinging to Prince's neck, dangling, Chuck's feet off the ground.

"Keep trying," Rebecca says, no sound of impatience in her voice. "You'll get it."

Prince is inclined to nip when he grows weary of Chuck's inability to get the job done, and the nip usually makes Chuck cry.

"You're okay, aren't you?" Rebecca says, staring into Chuck's face. "You're very brave."

Then Chuck discovers the magic of Prince's speed and it is as if he is airborne. They become a precision team, galloping everywhere at full speed. Chuck throws the reins over Prince's head, then grabs a bit of mane, his shoulder pressed to Prince's; then his leg swings up over Prince's back and they are off in one simple fluid movement.

Rebecca's pony is sensible and calm, never in too much of a hurry. Daisy is safe, Rebecca's mother said, the only thing that really matters. Grace bought Daisy for Rebecca's fourth birthday, running a yellow ribbon all the way from the end of Rebecca's bed to the pen in the barn. Rebecca could scarcely believe it, her hands up over her mouth while she squealed and danced.

"I didn't even know I wanted a pony," Rebecca said to her mother, her eyes shiny and wet.

Daisy is snowy white with a large patch of black hair encircling her left eye. She looks like she is winking. The patch gives the impression Daisy's head is slightly tilted. Rebecca's mother placed Rebecca on Daisy's bare back and squeezed Rebecca's hands around the pony's long white mane.

"Sit up straight, keep your chin down, and squeeze with your lower legs," Rebecca's mother said, her hand on Rebecca's leg, pushing it in on Daisy's side. "That's it, that's it," she said, walking Daisy around the yard. "Keep your heels down."

She kept Daisy and Rebecca in the yard that first year, not willing to trust Daisy completely. Rebecca tumbled off once or twice, slipped off the side of Daisy and into the grass. Rebecca's mother chuckled and bent down to console Rebecca. "There's a brave girl," she said.

Daisy dropped her head and waited while Rebecca climbed to her feet, Daisy's eyes closed as though she was taking the time to grab a nap. Daisy never hurried. Rebecca practised sitting perfectly balanced, her arms stretched out to the sides, imagining she was part of a band of circus performers. "Steady as she goes," Rebecca's mother encouraged from the fence once she let Rebecca go on her own.

* * *

Rebecca can put Daisy's halter on by herself now, has been able to since she was five. She untangles the thick forelock so the halter's crown band sits flat behind Daisy's ears; Daisy drops her head in co-operation. Rebecca trims the hair behind Daisy's ears, at the top of her mane, for the halter. She ties some sisal bale twine to each side of Daisy's halter to use as reins to steer. Daisy doesn't need a bit in her mouth to control her speed. There are no outbursts in her repertoire of paces.

Rebecca catches Daisy out in the pasture and then climbs up on the fence. Daisy pushes up against the fence so Rebecca can slide her leg over Daisy's broad back. Sometimes, Rebecca jumps on her pony's back in the pasture and while she grazes, Rebecca lies on Daisy's back and gazes at the clouds. Rebecca sees dogs and dragons and castles in the swirls and puffs of the cumulus clouds. For moments at a time she forgets where she is and who she is. She forgets about loss and loneliness and doesn't think about how life changes without any warning. She forgets about belonging to the secret club of the grieving.

Rebecca imagines her life is different, that her father isn't her father but a strange man she has to care for, imagines next Tuesday she is going on holiday and what she will pack and where she will go. She might go on a large boat across the ocean to England to find her mother's family, a boat so large it could stretch from one wave to another and the boat will never have to go up or down. She might go on a large balloon with orange and green and red stripes on it, a huge balloon, bigger than the *Wizard of Oz* balloon. Or on a train, a speeding locomotive, and she will see the whole countryside from her seat. But imagining gets harder and harder, so she stops and looks at the clouds instead and empties her head when she can.

* * *

Chuck and Rebecca are on the same party line. On Sunday mornings they both pick up the telephone at precisely eight o'clock to make their daily plan.

"Are you there?" Chuck says.

"Yah," Rebecca says.

"Meet you halfway," Chuck says, always breathless, like he is ready to run out the door to win some unspoken race. They never meet halfway, though. Chuck and Prince almost always meet Rebecca at the end of her laneway. Prince is dripping with sweat, his nostrils flared and glowing brilliant red like a fire is burning inside him. He tosses his head, and his long mane makes waves in the air. He pushes his nose toward Daisy, who puts her ears back against her head and swings her hind end around like she might kick Prince, but it's all for show. Daisy can't be bothered to expend that much energy, and Prince would be gone before she lifted a foot. The whole routine makes Rebecca shake her head, the absurdity of Chuck racing against himself and Daisy thinking she might kick something. Neither of them know much about the truth.

Chuck and Rebecca ride without saddles, their bare legs bouncing against their ponies' sleek summer coats. They gallop and imagine they are cattle rustlers and bank robbers if Chuck is choosing, pony express riders and Indian braves if Rebecca chooses.

Rebecca rides all the way on those days when Chuck is under yard arrest for not locking the gate properly and letting a fox in with the chickens, or if Chuck is sick, or any number of things that get Harold riled. This means Rebecca can curl up next to Gran on the swing under the birch trees and hold Gran's ball of knitting wool while Gran's fingers fly, the needles clacking against each other making a friendly sound.

"I'm a terrible knitter," Gran says, laughing. "I only pretend I can knit when I'm feeling old, like I should act my age." Gran examines her knitting. "Look at this sock," she says, holding up her work, the stitches uneven and holes the size of dimes here and there.

"You're funny, Gran," Rebecca says.

"I like it when you laugh," Gran says, putting her knitting down and pressing her forehead against Rebecca's. "You should laugh more often."

Gran is a storyteller, a person of the remembering kind. She needs an audience so she can channel back in time, when life had choices, forks in the road where she had to decide to veer right or left, when she wondered about things like what kind of person she might choose to be, when there were still sentences to complete, words whose meanings to figure out.

"Did I ever tell you your grandfather had a team of horses?" Gran says.

Rebecca nods, but Gran keeps going anyway.

"We think all early farmers had horses, but that was a very rare thing. Your grandfather was lucky, got those two old horses from a neighbour, some sort of gambling story," Gran says, picking up her knitting again. "Those horses listened to your grandfather like they knew exactly what he was saying to them. They pulled logs out of the bush in the winter. Your grandfather whistled once sharply for them to step ahead. Old Edward bent his right ear back and then swung his head around to your grandfather as if he maybe wasn't sure. Sort of like he was asking was that one whistle or two. George was the bigger of the two, but he did whatever Edward told him to."

Gran lets her hands flop down on her lap. She hasn't knit a single stitch while she is talking.

"When Edward got too old for the heavy work, George went on his own, but it wasn't the same. What a pair those horses were."

Gran nods, letting all the details flow in like a dam letting loose. She closes her eyes as though she has stored the texture and taste of each word attached to any particular memory.

"Your grandfather was coming down the hill toward Old Edward one Sunday afternoon. You grandfather never farmed on a Sunday. No sir. You don't mess with God. That old horse lifted his head and looked at your grandfather, nickered at him, and then dropped dead, right there in the field. Your grandfather said there was no finer way for him to go."

Rebecca drops the wool and grabs her stomach like she's been punched. She looks at Gran, Rebecca's face white and empty, and then jumps off the swing, on to Daisy's back, and gallops out the lane.

Gran gives Rebecca time to get home and then drives over to the Archer farm, not even bothering to knock on the door.

"Pay no attention to me, Robert. I have some business with Rebecca," she says, heading for the stairs. She stops and looks around the room and up the stairs and frowns and shakes her head. "You need a damn railing on these stairs. Someone could fall to her death," she says, stopping to talk to the back of Robert's head. "Good god, clean this place up, make it look like someone lives here."

Gran climbs the stairs, leaning into each step, holding the wall, and muttering complaints as she goes. She knocks on the only closed door. "Can I come in?"

Rebecca is sitting on the edge of her bed, her hands folded in her lap, staring straight ahead. The room is sparse, the wall around the dormer window sagging, leaving bits of insulation on the end of Rebecca's bed. No toys or clothes are scattered around. Her single bed fits into a corner of the room, under the window with a tattered green blind behind white ruffled curtains. The walls are a soft butter yellow; the wide wooden floorboards have been painted white. Rebecca's bed has a bright yellow quilt on it, and on one wall hangs a child's large painting of a single dandelion. A wooden apple box, painted white, is turned on its end beside Rebecca's bed and on top of the box are three neatly stacked library books with a flashlight beside.

Gran touches Rebecca's shoulder before sitting down on the bed.

"I won't tell any more dying stories. I promise. When you get to be as old as me, sometimes dying stories are the only ones you remember."

Rebecca doesn't move while Gran massages the fingers on Rebecca's left hand. The two of them sit in silence for several minutes. Gran plants a little kiss on Rebecca's cheek.

"You don't have to be old to remember dying stories," Rebecca says.

"You're right about that," Gran says, exhaling and giving Rebecca a squeeze.

The two of them sit on Rebecca's bed, Gran's finger tracing the line of the quilting threads. No talking. Gran would like to scoop Rebecca up in her arms and take her to a place where grief doesn't live, but where might that be?

"We'll pick you up in the morning. About ten. We'll make it a library day," Gran says, getting to her feet and placing her hand on Rebecca's head before she closes the door quietly behind her.

* * *

Rebecca and Chuck sit in the back seat on the way to the library, fingers entwined while Gran drives. Rebecca sits quietly while Chuck fidgets and chatters like a chipmunk. Sometimes he lies in the back window. Gran watches them in the rear-view mirror, wishing Rebecca would sometimes misbehave, break the rules, but Rebecca sits perfectly still, the expression on her face never changing, as if every emotion is zipped up tight.

Gran turns the radio up, puts the window down a little, and sings along, a cigarette perched between her fingers on the steering wheel or stuck to the corner of her mouth. Rebecca thinks Gran must have had a job as a ventriloquist at one time. Her lips stay firm on the cigarette while she talks, the thin trail of smoke finding its way to the open window. From time to time, Gran lets her fingers lean against the glass and pivots the end of the cigarette, and the air rushing by grabs hold of the ash and tears it off. Gran doesn't actually draw any smoke into her lungs, the cigarette more of an accessory, and she never smokes anywhere but in the car.

Chuck and Rebecca are dropped off at the corner where Law's Hardware and the post office stand across the street from each other, forming the landmarks, the bearings to find any other building in town—turn right at the post office; three doors down from the Hardware; watch for the traffic lights at the post office—as though the town's entire range of activities pivoted from this point.

Chuck scrambles to the window of the Hardware, pressing his face against the glass, his hands on either side of his face blocking out the sunlight.

"There it is," Chuck sighs, almost drooling over the red Schwinn with white-striped fenders and upright handlebars standing proudly on display in the window, tormenting Chuck, making his stomach ache, the red catching the light. Chuck uses his fingers to count out the bike's amazing qualities, finishing with a coaster brake and chain guard. "I want it more than anything else on earth," Chuck says for the third time this month.

"You said that about Prince," Rebecca says.

"It'll never be mine," Chuck says, ignoring Rebecca and collapsing against the side of the hardware store, pouring down the wall.

Rebecca doesn't have the heart to tell Chuck that a brand-new CCM Super Cycle, brilliant blue with white streamers hanging from the handlebars along with its very own bell that sounds more like a tinkle than a bell, is in her back shed leaning up against the wall behind the tractor.

The bicycle showed up five days before her tenth birthday in April. She found it standing beside the house next to the back door. She stood in the grass beside the bike, letting the streamers flow through her fingers, imagining what she might carry in the white woven basket that hooked on to the handlebars. She wanted to ask her father if it was hers, imagined him saying, *Surprise. Happy Birthday.* But he didn't say a word about it until the morning of her birthday, as if he hadn't noticed it at all until then.

"Claydons sent some money to the hardware and they delivered that bike for you, for your birthday. I told them it wasn't your birthday yet and to leave it by the house," he said, not looking up from his oatmeal.

"Today's your birthday," he added before taking a long swallow of coffee.

Rebecca stood in the kitchen door, her arms hanging limply at her sides. She waited, waited for a sign that her father still existed in some recognizable form, waited for a hint that he knew she turned ten today, that he might celebrate one second of joy, that he might pull a cake from the cupboard, a bit lopsided and undercooked, but iced with maple butter frosting with bits of cake showing through, the candles lit and flickering feebly, and they'd laugh at this pitiful excuse for a cake and he'd look at her with a face that said, *I tried. I'm still trying.* Instead she wheeled the new blue bicycle into the shed so she could think about it. She marched back into the house and leaning over her father, her mouth right next to his ear, she whispered clearly, pausing between each word, her lips pulled tight across her teeth.

"I. Know. It. Is. My. Birthday."

* * *

"Big deal," Rebecca says to Chuck, the same matter-of-fact tone she always employs. "You have a pony. You don't need a bike."

"But I want one," Chuck whines, looking at Rebecca for support. "If I rode it down Murphy's Hill I bet I could almost fly." He climbs back up to his feet with a newfound enthusiasm. "I could get a job."

"Who's going to hire a ten-year-old and for what?"

"I could help your dad with fencing," Chuck says, sounding breathless.

Rebecca considers the front pasture fence being propped up where the posts have rotted through. The fence is barely enough to keep their six cows in. Luckily, there's enough pasture so the cows don't bother pushing their heads through the fence, their long rough tongues reaching for the grass in the ditch.

"He doesn't have any money," Rebecca says. "Besides, you hate farming."

"No, I hate milking cows and forking manure and stacking hay. I don't hate fencing. I could cut Mrs. Klein's grass and weed her garden."

"She'd pay you with a cake or a box of cookies. You can't buy a bike with cookies."

"I could sell the cookies to Gran or my mother."

"And when exactly are you going to cut the grass? Before or after your chores?"

"You're a spoilsport," Chuck says.

"I'm realistic."

"I don't even know what that means."

"It means accepting life the way it is," Rebecca says.

"We're ten, Rebecca. We're supposed to dream."

"Come on, we have to meet Gran at the library in a half hour and I haven't had a chance to choose my books yet," Rebecca says, striding off so Chuck has to run to catch up.

"I still want that bike," Chuck says, with one last longing look over his shoulder. "Maybe Mr. Law would let me buy it over time."

"That's no way to buy anything," Rebecca says, forming a plan in her mind.

* * *

The library is a stately stone building with columns on either side of the doorway, the words *Let There Be Light* etched in the stone above the door. One corner block has the numbers 1915 carved into it. It was an Andrew Carnegie library, Rebecca's mother had explained, using words like *philanthropy* and *caring for the common man*. This Mr. Carnegie built one hundred twenty-five libraries in Canada, and Roddick was one of the lucky communities. He asked for nothing in return, her mother said.

"Rebecca," Mrs. Mason says with exaggerated friendliness each time Rebecca appears in the library, no matter how frequent. "My favourite patron." It has become Mrs. Mason's signature greeting.

"What's a patron?" Chuck whispers at Rebecca, but she merely shoves him aside.

Mrs. Mason fusses over Rebecca when she comes to the library, can't help herself, always encouraged when a child wants to read. Rebecca was shy at first. Came in with her mother every week when Rebecca was little. A lovely woman—a little distant, though, set back, a little unsure—but the way she looked at that child of hers. You could almost see the swelling of pride in her chest, the utter amazement that said *I made this, this perfectly beautiful child.*

Rebecca came in on her own two years ago. She walked up and down the aisles, letting her fingers run along the books, her steps deliberate and slow, one foot ahead of the other like she was walking through a minefield. She didn't remove any books from the shelves, but she admired them, leaning over to read the words on the books' spines.

"What do you like to read?" Mrs. Mason asked. Rebecca looked at her, ready to run away. Mrs. Mason kept asking questions, changing the words around to find a way to get at Rebecca's thoughts. What do you want to be, who do you want to be, what do you think you'd like to grow up to be, what do you imagine you'll do when you're all done growing up? Will you be a veterinarian? Lots of girls want to be a veterinarian, and on and on. One Saturday morning Rebecca was the only child in the children's section of the library.

"I want to build bridges," Rebecca said, standing beside Mrs. Mason's desk and not really looking like she was talking to anyone in particular. "I'm going to be an engineer."

"Let's see what we can find on that," Mrs. Mason said, opening the little drawer filled with tiny cards under the heading of subject. "When we've read all these we'll go upstairs and get more from the adult section."

* * *

Chuck pounds down the library stairs ahead of Rebecca to the children's department and shuts the door behind him, holding it so Rebecca has to knock. Mrs. Mason looks straight at Chuck over the top of her glasses, her hands on her hips.

"No running in the library, Mr. Prescott."

"I don't run. I fly," Chuck says, releasing the door for Rebecca and leaning in toward Mrs. Mason like he's confiding a great secret. "Did you know February this year had no full moon? First time in history."

"Run along, Charles."

"Good morning, Mrs. Mason," Rebecca says, squaring her shoulders.

"Rebecca, my favourite patron," Mrs. Mason says. Chuck pokes Rebecca in the ribs with his elbow. "I've set some new books out on the corner of my desk. They've just come in and there's one on beavers and another on bridges. Have a look."

Chuck opens his arms and pretends to fly up and down the rows of books.

"Charles," Mrs. Mason almost shouts with her friendly shout. "No flying in the library."

Eight

GRAN PULLS OVER TO THE CURB NEXT TO THE POST OFFICE. SHE bumps into the concrete that edges the sidewalk, uses it as a guide before she turns the wheel, and then slams the gearshift into park, slams it so quickly that the car rocks forward and back as though the car itself is uncertain which way to go.

"Like bumper cars," Gran says with a laugh.

Rebecca doesn't move from her seat.

"Do you want me to come in with you?" Gran asks.

"No, thank you," Rebecca says, but she doesn't move. She seems to be counting in her head, her lips moving slightly and her hands clasped tightly together.

"You're very mysterious today. Are you on a secret mission?"

Gran smiles her you-can-do-it smile, a smile that says *You're an equal, not some stupid kid.*

Rebecca opens the car door and gives Gran one last look. No smile.

Rebecca hardly laughs, doesn't play pranks. No outbursts of fun. It's like she is concentrating on every tiny detail of living so that not even breathing is a reflex.

"I'll wait right here," Gran says. "And if you run out of the hardware with guns blazing, the get-away car will be ready to go." She puts her hands on the steering wheel and pats it a few times. "And if it's a heist you're planning, get enough for the both of us." Gran laughs and slaps her knee. "I'm so damn funny."

The corner of Rebecca's mouth tips up, and she pushes the car door shut with a firm shove. She looks both ways and then marches across the street with a don't-mess-with-me stride. Gran watches Rebecca lean back from the heavy glass door of the hardware store, letting her body weight help her open the door.

Gran lights a cigarette, telling herself it will be her last, then coughs. Rebecca has disappeared into the hardware store. She's quite the kid, Gran thinks, shaking her head. Rebecca is all business. Chuck's lucky to have her for a friend. A safe spot. Lord knows he needs it. Gran runs interference as much as she can, but it's not easy.

She sighs and picks at a hangnail on her thumb, the smoke from her cigarette rising into her eyes and making her squint. She can't even remember when she started smoking or why. Everyone smoked. Not the greatest reason, but there it is. She fiddles with the radio trying to clear out the static, glances at the hardware store wondering if Rebecca is okay.

Gran's chin falls down on her chest, her eyelids heavy. She flicks the cigarette out the window before she lights herself on fire. She thinks about Chuck and Rebecca and parenting. Had she been a good mother to Penelope? Not really. She could blame Thomas, put the responsibility on him or the memory of him, his leaving her the way he did, getting up from the supper table, leaving the room, leaving the house, leaving their life, without looking back, without a sound or an explanation. Gran used to tell Penelope and anyone else who asked that Thomas would be home by Thanksgiving or harvest or Christmas or whatever damn-fool holiday stretched out in front of her. Everyone quit asking, eventually, even Penelope. Thank you, Thomas, Gran used to say to the sky, to his empty chair, to his favourite coffee mug that she ended up flinging across the room and watching smash against the wall. She didn't have to bother with a divorce and there were no funeral costs.

Gran knew Penelope didn't have it in her to do much mothering, left it up to Gran to care for Chuck. He was premature, a weak little fish, pale and limp. Harold and Penelope seemed repulsed by the baby, but Gran didn't mind. Probably kept him on her knee too long. Chuck was a different sort of kid, not rough and tumble like most boys, a bit anxious most of the time and nervous, with some habits that she tried to ignore. He chewed his fingernails. He had a hard time sitting still. Enough calls had come from the school saying that very thing. *Charles can't sit still. Charles doesn't pay attention. Charles is a daydreamer.* Every now and then Chuck surprised everyone with a demonstration of confidence, but not often enough.

Gran stretches, tries to wake her slumbering brain that is doing too much wandering back through the past. That never does anyone any good. She sees Mr. and Mrs. Kovalchuk walking toward her, Mr. Kovalchuk slightly ahead, the missus hurrying to keep up with her husband, her rotund belly making hurrying awkward. An empty look in the man's face reminds her of Thomas. She thinks she might busy herself in the glove box so she doesn't have to acknowledge Mr. Kovalchuk, but she can't be bothered. She wants to roll down the window and shout at both of them, *Take me as I am.*

Men are a strange bunch, Gran thinks. Men in general, the whole lot of them. Who can really understand how a man's thinking works? Robert had seemed a fine young man, seemed in awe of this lady, his wife, maybe couldn't imagine the great fortune of landing this exotic bird, this bird he caged when she lighted with no real plans to stay. He snared her, laid his trap, getting her pregnant and barring all the escape exits. Seemed like he was always apologizing to her when Gran saw them out, like Robert needed Grace's permission simply to be.

Gran lights another cigarette. The Kovalchuks move past Gran's car, and she lifts her hand to Mr. Kovalchuk's nod and his wife's faint smile.

Men almost ran off to war, thinking it an adventure, willing to put their lives in harm's way, a reflex, a bloody need. Gran got the honour of that, standing up against an enemy, but it was about adventure, fighting the odds. When men have to fight their own battles, their own grief, they often forget they have little ones who need a hand up, who need to be lifted to safety. Their brawn seems to be only about hoisting weapons, never the clean-up. Forget it and move on, or don't forget and be consumed by it. Nothing in the middle.

Gran twists her wedding ring around on her finger, fiddling with it, the thin silver band that says maybe at one time she had it all, had hope and plans, the whole shooting match. Mental illness was the invisible adversary that held Thomas in its grasp after the war. Thomas never spoke of the war. He'd been a sharpshooter, using the skill he developed as a boy picking off raccoons and gophers and squirrels, while he trained his eye and his finger. *How many men did you kill?* Gran asked. *None,* Thomas said. After a long silence, he added, *They were the enemy, not men.*

Thomas used to sink into spells of silence, hardly ate, lay awake in bed at night, staring at the ceiling. Gran had tried affection, a comforting voice and a warm hand on his forehead, but in the end, mental illness repels assistance if left untreated and leaving was his only recourse. He may have started over, tried with another family to get it right, but he would always end up back in the same place.

Women don't suffer the same fatigue. They're hard wired to accept what's in their path and make the best of it. As a rule. Penelope didn't exactly make the best of her misfortune. She turned off, a bit like her father. Maybe it had nothing to do with the war but rather with genetics. Maybe Penelope had no more choice than Thomas.

Gran stretches to see inside the hardware store. Rebecca has been in there quite some time now, Gran thinks. What is that girl up to?

* * *

"I want to exchange my bicycle," Rebecca says to Mr. Law, her eyes fixed on the row of batteries behind the counter.

There were several customers in the store; one was looking for a refrigerator light bulb, another for some kind of glue to fix a china horse that the grandchild broke the leg off of. The broken china required a story, the details of where the china horse came from in the first place and how the granddaughter couldn't leave it alone. I warned her over and over, the man said. Another customer needed the right latch to keep the dog in the backyard, one that might shut on its own. You know how kids are, always leaving the gate open and that darn dog gets into the neighbours' garbage. Kids today. They talked about the weather and how it might change or not change, that robotic conversation that doesn't require listening or thinking, that is more like white noise that calms the discomfort of being exposed in public, of having left the safety of the house. The customers finally finished their business and left the store.

Rebecca continues her rehearsed monologue.

"I haven't ridden it, the tires aren't even dirty, and there's some cobwebs on it from being in the shed. I can ride it to town if you want me to, but I don't know how to ride a bike and I don't think I want to bother learning now that I am giving it back, but I could if I had to, but then the bike would get dirty." She sounds like she is reciting a poem that she has rehearsed carefully to get each word right. She nods now, relieved she got all the words out and in the right order.

"Is your father with you?" Mr. Law asks, looking somewhat puzzled and leaning to look out the window on to the street in case Robert is there.

That bike was delivered months ago, Mr. Law thinks, trying to remember the exact details of the transaction, fidgeting with the list of charge receipts impaled on the single metal spike on the front counter beside the cash register. Business is tough, sales down. Customers have choices now, don't always have to rely on Law's Hardware store like when his father owned it and sold everything from nails to sugar. Mr. Law really wanted to be a veterinarian, not a store owner relying on the whim of shoppers who decide to fix the lock on their back door or not, whether or not they need rat poison for their sheds or a new washing machine for the wife.

Rebecca looks around to her left and right and then directly at Mr. Law, placing her hands above her on the counter. She conjures up her best no-nonsense face.

"It's my bike, and I don't want it. It came from this store. I don't know how to ride it and I want to exchange it for the red boy's Schwinn that was in the window. The red Schwinn is for Chuck Prescott and you're not to tell anyone and when you deliver it to his house on the River Road three driveways past our farm, you can pick up my bike and then we will be even." Rebecca exhales like she couldn't have held her breath for one more second.

Mr. Law looks at her as if he's just met her, his face serious, and when he opens his mouth to speak, Rebecca jumps in.

"The tags are still on the bike."

"You've got it all figured out," Mr. Law says, crossing his arms in front of him and leaning back slightly.

Mr. Law looks hard at Rebecca. He doesn't know her, not really, not the way you know someone without having to think about it, that automatic recognition when someone walks through the door and you recognize by his walk whether he's having a good day or fretting about his bank account. He knew Rebecca's story; everyone in town knew Rebecca's story, but they've all quit talking about it long ago. There have been plenty of fresh tragedies to take up people's time and conversation. Garfield Lowe fell off his garage roof and broke his back a few months ago. He won't walk again and his wife is already closer to death than not, fighting a losing battle with some kind of cancer in her woman parts, parts that no one really wants to say out loud. The fact that Rebecca lost her mother and baby brother hasn't been forgotten. There's just been too much real life in between, too many accidents that take her particular catastrophe off the hot-topics list. People ran out of ideas of how to get Robert Archer out of his house and back with the living. They've quit extending their neighbourly hand not because they don't care, but because it is too darn hard to keep fighting the fight. Everyone in town had their way with the wrong and right of it, the chewing over driving on the ice in March, the wondering how he pays his bills and was it bad sense to marry above him. Only a few dared go in that direction, or were foolish and stupid enough to go in that direction. It takes only about a year and a half, sometimes less, to gnaw through any particular subject, before people move on for good, even the stragglers, the ones who really want to help this child.

"I'll have to go and see if we still have that bike. In the basement. I'm pretty sure I didn't see it ride on out of here, but I'll check and you wait here," Mr. Law says.

* * *

Rebecca stands alone at the counter. She imagines for a second getting up on a chair behind the counter with an apron on, because all store clerks should have an apron that says they're in charge, a uniform that says they work here. But kids can't be in charge. There are rules about that sort of thing. Rebecca thinks it would be fun to push the buttons on the cash register and feel the cash drawer pop open with the sound of a bell and collide with her belly, imagines counting out the dollars and quarters and dimes for change, a bit like playing store, except the pretending part is real. Oh, our hammers are in aisle two next to the handsaws and screwdrivers, except she would say *my* hammers as though the store belonged to her.

A man comes in. Rebecca recognizes him from somewhere, probably from passing on the street, but she doesn't have a name to put to his face. Makes no difference; he's an adult. That puts him in charge. If he looks at her she'll have to move aside. That's what kids have to do. All adults are parents, someone's parents, even if they don't have children. Adults get to call the shots, get to run the world, and kids don't have any power, are a nuisance, are invisible, until they grow up and move on.

* * *

Mr. Law comes back in from the doorway to the basement.

"I'll be right with you, Jim," he says. "I'm busy with Miss Archer here."

"No, I'll wait," Rebecca says, giving Mr. Law an it's-private look.

The man called Jim has a wad of cash in his fist and asks Mr. Law to put it on his account. Rebecca knows what that means; she does that at the feed store for her father. He gives her money to put on his account, which simply means he hasn't got it all. That's why he doesn't go in himself, why he sends Rebecca, because he can't pay it all. Rebecca knows what these words mean. *On account:* a promise that he'll come back with more money when he can.

Mr. Law licks his pointer finger and counts out the cash; it was quite a stack of one- and two-dollar bills.

"Eighty-four dollars," he says, and the man nods. Mr. Law writes a note that says Jim put eighty-four dollars on his account.

Mr. Law looks at Rebecca and his eyebrows rise as the man leaves the store, the signal to her that she's next.

"That bike of yours cost more than the Schwinn. You'll have to take some money back, or my books won't balance."

"That will be fine," Rebecca says. "When can you come and get my bike and what will you say to Mr. Prescott so he won't take the bike away from Chuck?"

Mr. Law scratches the skin along his jaw on the left side of his face.

"That's a tough one," he says. He drums a pencil on the counter and Rebecca waits. "Harold Prescott can be an unfriendly guy all right." He keeps drumming his pencil. "Now let me see," Mr. Law says after another long pause.

"We could say he won it in a contest and it's for Chuck because those are the rules of the contest. Simple as that," Mr. Law says, lifting his hands above his shoulders. His mouth falls open, astonished by his own brilliance.

"You'd have to practise saying it or Mr. Prescott would know it wasn't true," Rebecca says, a look of hope creeping into her face.

"You leave that to me. I can handle Harold Prescott," Mr. Law says.

"You'd have to give the bike to Chuck in front of Mr. Prescott so he'd know that you know the bike belongs to Chuck, and you might check on it some day to see how Chuck is making out learning to ride it and stuff, because Mr. Prescott will want to take it away and throw it in the ravine beside his pasture field. He'll want to," Rebecca says, a fearful look on her face like the hope balloon sprang a leak.

"Absolutely," Mr. Law says, understanding all too well the nasty side of Harold Prescott, the only side of Harold Prescott. Mad, always mad, like a rabid dog, ready to fight for everything; not a hint of a kind word ever came out of that man.

"I won't take the bike off the truck unless both Chuck and Harold are there. Don't you worry. I know how to play the game." He starts scribbling on the paper taped to the counter beside the cash register.

"I can come tomorrow and I owe you eighteen dollars and fifty-three cents."

Rebecca opens her hand in front of her and Mr. Law carefully counts out the money.

"A pleasure doing business with you, Miss Archer," he says.

Rebecca smiles up at Mr. Law and for a minute, she feels care-free and happy, someone without a worry in the world.

* * *

Rebecca climbs into the front seat of Gran's car, her fist still holding the eighteen dollars and fifty-three cents. A penny slips out, and she shoves the money in her pocket, digs into the carpet on the floor of the car for the penny.

"All done your business?" Gran asks.

"Yes, thanks," Rebecca says. Nothing more, her lips closed tightly. Gran knows not to ask any more questions.

Rebecca leans her head back against the seat and closes her eyes and they don't say another word the whole drive home. Gran drops Rebecca off at the end of her lane.

"No need to turn in," Rebecca says. "I can walk from here." She slams the car door firmly and almost struts across the road and into her driveway, confidence in her stride.

Nine

REBECCA SLIPS THE MONEY FROM MR. LAW INTO ONE OF HER OLD socks, one that is almost worn through. She pushes the sock between her mattress and box spring until she can feel the edge of the picture frame against the tips of her fingers. She hears her father's shuffle in the hall and leaps to her feet as he opens the door.

"I'm going to town," he says. Not one to ask many questions, but his face looks suspicious as he surveys Rebecca's room, as if he wonders what Rebecca is up to, but she doesn't take any chances. She nods at him and then carries on tidying up as if she had been doing that the whole time.

He thumps down the stairs, one at a time, like a toddler learning to manage the stairs on his own. Rebecca can hear his right hand sliding down the wall, adding to the stain already on the paint, a dark smear that forms a well-worn path where his right hand automatically goes each time he descends the stairs. There is no handrail to grab hold of should someone decide to fall, no banister to steady, just walls on either side like a tunnel. Rebecca considered nailing a two-by-four to the wall in the stairwell for her father to hang on to when he descends the stairs and to pull himself up with when he climbs the stairs, but she can't quite figure out how she will hold the board and nail it at the same time. She thought of having Chuck help her, but he's never been inside the house and she isn't sure it's worth the risk. Maybe her father prefers that there is no rail so the option is always available to hurl down the stairs without a chance to reconsider and grab on to something, an all or nothing with no alternatives. There were times she wondered about pushing him down the stairs and watching his body tumble to the bottom, but those were fleeting thoughts, thoughts that left her with the pain of guilt. She had enough guilt crawling around inside her, feeding on her like a parasite, pinching and stinging and keeping her from standing upright. Why look for more?

Rebecca used to help her father into his coat, ran ahead of him and got it down and helped button or zip it up, depending on which he was wearing. He told her to stop, grabbed the zipper right out of her hand. He said he needed her help, but didn't want it, didn't want her feeling sorry for him like some pathetic pet, pretending she was playing house and he was a toy she put in a chair and pretended to offer drinks to or force fed. He had finished off that particular rant with a *Get away from me* that came with a big swing of his right arm.

Then it felt as if she was floating around the house, like a balloon losing its air but slowly, getting caught on the little currents of air that moved from room to room, and she bumped into the walls and furniture and couldn't hang on to anything, barely lighter than air with no string tied to the back of a chair or to a door handle to keep from drifting toward an open window where she might float right out and keep on going, never ever landing anywhere. She hoped all her air would be let out so that she wouldn't get sucked out the window, so she wouldn't have to fight with weightlessness forever, up in the sky where no one would notice her, trying to dig her fingernails into clouds or snowflakes or the very droplets of rain, anything at all that she might feel against her skin.

She listens for the rumble of the old truck as it burps to life with a little effort, usually a couple of pumps on the gas pedal. She knows by heart the routine that her father follows: check that the gearshift is in first gear and push the clutch all the way to the floor with his left foot, put his fingers on the key and let them sit there for three or four seconds like he's listening for something, some cue that says, *Go ahead and turn the key*, a couple of kicks at the gas pedal while he turns the key and then starts over when the engine doesn't fire. Check the gearshift, fingers on the key, and so on. The same pattern no matter how many times it takes before the engine concedes and ignites. Then her father drops his head as though he has defeated something and is humbly acknowledging his success, as if it nearly drained him, this starting of the truck. He then takes a deep breath and moves the gearshift into reverse and slowly begins to back up, an inch at a time at first, and Rebecca thinks he might win some world record for how slowly an individual can move a motorized vehicle. Maybe she should call Guinness World Records and have someone come and verify this feat, this wonder.

She stands beside the bedroom window and watches, watches him steer the truck down the lane, driving slower than slow. One time she couldn't stand it and ran down the lane behind the truck and then passed it. She kept running until she couldn't run any further and collapsed in the ditch. He drove right on by her lying in the grass and never gave her so much as a sideways glance, kept his eyes focused straight ahead and his right hand on the steering wheel. She thought it was funny and had a laugh bubble right out of her while she stood in the middle of the lane, watching the back of the truck as it lumbered away from her, and she stood in the driveway screaming obscenities at him.

"Shit. Damn. Fuck. I'm right here." She laughed and kicked dirt at him and walked home.

Rebecca can still see the truck from her bedroom window. Her father turns the truck onto the main road and speeds up, but only slightly. She can see the Corkums come up behind him in the green Rambler they stuff all their children into. The Rambler passes her father as if he is standing still, as if he is stuck in a slow-motion replay.

Rebecca exhales a little more dramatically and completely when her father leaves the house, as if being alone is easier when he's not here to remind her there might be something different, could have been something different. She doesn't let herself linger on those thoughts. *What is,* that's all she can work with.

She vaguely remembers a conversation between her parents. The details are dim but she sensed an argument, though they never argued, not the way Chuck describes the arguments that go on in his house: the throwing of things, the hurling of ugly words, the slapping and pushing and slamming. She remembers her mother talking to the back of her father, him gripping the edge of the sink, his knuckles white. He looked hollowed out.

It is what it is, her mother said, and then she'd gone to the piano and played for what seemed like a long time, her eyes closed, her head and upper body swaying with the music, she and the piano all part of one instrument, no start or finish. Her fingers moved over the keys knowing where to go all on their own. The sound lifted up from the piano as if each note was carried inside a tiny fragment of glass, so light that it could float on the air, the sound crystal clear.

Her father had come and closed the door to the room off the dining room where the piano sat against one wall. The latch clicked into place with an almost indiscernible sound, but it broke the spell, her mother's hands falling to her knees while Rebecca watched from under the small table that sat next to the wingback chair where her mother did her reading, the light over her right shoulder, *as it should be.*

* * *

Rebecca sighs and digs under her mattress for the picture frame and once her fingers find its edge, she pulls it carefully toward her. The frame is made from a thin but heavy wood, dark and polished, and inside, under its glass, her mother is imprisoned, safe from all that was, not yet knowing the disappointment of all that could have been.

The photo is a black-and-white image with a name in the bottom right corner, a professional photographer's name. Rebecca takes the photo into the bathroom where the light is good, shines right on the mirror. She holds the photo of her mother next to her own face, up close to the mirror. First she looks at her mother's face, her eyes wide, the smile filled with excitement, the teeth straight and even, the lips thick and full, her long thick hair pulled over her right shoulder, tied together with a dark ribbon. Then Rebecca looks at her own face, her eyebrows thick and a bit woolly, her lips not nearly so plump, a bit flat when she pulls them into a smile. It's not a real smile, not the kind that makes the eyes twinkle like they're catching a reflection. Rebecca's eyes are dark and heavy, but the line of her face and her chin and her nose, they look similar. She can pull her hair to the same spot as her mother's, just below her shoulder, on the meaty part of her chest. She leans closer to the mirror, her heart beating a little quicker now. It's coming, she thinks. Her face is a little bit more like her mother's every time she stares and wishes. She has to try harder, will it to happen. What had Hilda said? *So like her mother.* Yes, there it is. So like her mother.

She pulls the photo into her chest, wrapping it tight in her arms, and the ache swells up, the hunger and the wanting and the remembering her mother's touch, her mother's whisper, her lips against her hair. Rebecca bends double at the waist and lets out a deep groan from the emptiness in the pit of her stomach, the sound of loneliness. Before she can help herself, she collapses on the bathroom floor, sobbing for her mother, sobbing for every child's right to be loved.

* * *

She hears the truck burp and bounce when it makes the last turn into the yard, creaking when the wheels roll in and out of the puddles, hollowed-out circles in the gravel that get deeper after every rain fall. Rebecca climbs up off the bathroom floor, wiping her hair back. She slips the photo back under her mattress, floats down the stairs barely touching each step, and with her shoes in her hand eases the front door open and pulls it shut behind her without making a sound, jumping off the doorframe into the grass.

The front door has no steps beneath it, a door that leads to nowhere, on the side of the house like an idea, a sentence that was never said, started to get someone's attention and then quit before the thought was complete. Rebecca creeps around the side of the house waiting for the sound of the back door closing so she can make a dash for the plum trees, into which she can vanish.

The plum trees are old and gnarled, producing less fruit each year. They are short, squatty trees with rough, peeling bark that likes to jam its bits under Rebecca's fingernails when she climbs them, so she doesn't climb them, not anymore. Thick and unruly, the trees are a great place to hide, like some medieval forest that might come to life at night.

Rebecca slips through the orchard and down to a creek that runs through a stand of spruce and balsam fir at the edge of the lawn, where the creek spills into a little pond. Three logs stretch across the pond where frogs of various sizes swim and float with their legs stretched out behind them. Rebecca runs across the logs, drops down to the pond's edge, and stretches out against the embankment, listening to the frogs plop into the water. She can see only the roof of the house and likewise only the roof can see her.

She imagines sometimes that her father will return home from town and call out to her. *I'm home*, he might say. *I've brought you a surprise*, and he'll pull out a candy bar or a book or a new pair of socks, anything that says he was thinking about her while he was away. That never happens. In fact, he comes home in a more brooding mood, probably from having been out among the living, having to hear *Hello* and *How are you* that he never seems to care for. Rebecca is fairly certain her father responds with a shrug and a more hurried step.

Would it be so terrible, when someone asks how he is, that he might answer with the truth? *My life is terrible. I'm living in a nightmare. I don't like my daughter. I wish I'd never saved her. Wish we'd all gone to the bottom of the lake so no one would have been left to carry on, to pretend we're living when we're not, obligated to play these roles that we have no idea how to play.*

If he said the truth out loud, someone might nod and listen, her finger on her chin like she's contemplating a solution, and then she would have some words of wisdom that would make Rebecca's father change, so he could shed the grief he wears like a heavy coat, the grief that has curled his spine and ruined his eyesight so that all he can see is misery and emptiness, all he can hear is silence, and he can't feel a single solitary thing.

She doesn't really know what goes on inside her father, but she's given up trying to figure it out, given up imagining anything positive or hopeful. She lets him be. It is what it is. He is what he is.

Rebecca wishes she could sit by the pond until the day is over, until darkness rolls in like a blanket and covers her, until she sleeps and her body floats up to bed without her ever having to get her feet under her.

"It is what it is," she says out loud, nodding her chin toward the house and pushing on her hands to stand up.

She creeps around behind the plum trees, watching the back window for any sign of her father watching her, which she realizes is ridiculous. He will be in his chair in the living room, the newspaper on his lap that more often than not he never opens. She lifts up the back window of the shed and wiggles through on her stomach to a workbench that she has cleared off so she can pull herself on to it without knocking anything off or hurting herself. The front door of the shed has a big lock on it and the key, Rebecca suspects, is on her father's keychain with the truck key and everything else he locks. He has a cupboard that holds a twelve-gauge shotgun, the gun for the common man, the every-farmer-needs-a-gun kind of gun, and the cupboard is locked. A liquor cabinet with strange-looking bottles that she has never seen him take a drink of is locked. A grey cash box in the drawer under the radio with only coins in it, as far as Rebecca knows, is locked. Everything locked up tight, yet he never locks the house when he leaves, never shuts the windows even if it looks like rain; locks on the shed and locks on boxes and trunks and drawers in the shed, but no locking the house. Nothing in the house worth protecting.

She lifts up the heavy tarp that covers her mother's piano and quietly raises the keyboard cover and lets the backs of her fingers drag along the ivory keys, cold to touch, pressing them down softly so the note barely makes a sound. She places her ear next to the key and presses middle C and then hums the same sound.

Do-re-mi-fa-so-la-ti-do, she sings, more of a whisper than anything as she presses each key in order up the C major scale. She loves the cool touch of the keys, so smooth and white.

She hears the key in the lock and immediately drops the tarp down, covering both herself and the piano, crawling under the keyboard and pressing her body into the bottom panel of the piano. Her father shuffles in, standing inside the door like he is listening. She can't remember if she shut the window behind her after she crawled through. She winces with worry.

She imagines him letting his eyes adjust to the dusty darkness and then she hears the scuffle of his feet and sees the shadow at the bottom of the tarp. He stops, and Rebecca tries her best to breathe shallow silent sips of air, her mouth puckered slightly, her eyes squeezed shut, her fingers pressed into a fist. The shuffling continues and then he drags a trunk out from under one of the tables, making a loud scraping sound on the concrete floor. The keys jingle and the lock gives way. She hears him sigh and probably drop to his knees.

"Grace," he whispers, an empty, broken sound.

Rebecca hears papers shuffling and a tin of some kind opening. What could he possibly be keeping out here, she wonders. The desk in the hallway is buried in a mountain of bills and letters and junk mail, not a single personal letter or card. He sometimes takes a pile out to the burn barrel but tells her not to touch anything on the desk, it's none of her business. She has seen a few papers with *Past Due Notice* and *Pay Immediately* stamped in red, but they too eventually disappear.

He shoves the trunk back under the table, pulling firmly on the lock, and then stands, like he is listening again. Rebecca's legs are beginning to cramp so she wiggles her toes. She sees the shadow move past the bottom of the tarp again and holds her breath. Then the door closes and the lock is clicked into place. She hears her father's dragging feet on the gravel, but she stays hidden, stretches her legs out in front of her, waits, patiently, giving him enough time to return to his chair and fall asleep like he does several times a day.

Too bad his sleepless nights can't be spent unplugging the kitchen sink or fixing the drywall at the edge of the bathtub that is crumbling or fixing the hinge on the back door that has loosened, letting the door drop a bit. To shut it tight, Rebecca has to use all her strength to pull the door snug in the frame. All these jobs require daylight, a good pair of hands, and a willingness to keep things in repair, none of which Rebecca's father has.

While she waits, Rebecca thinks of her mother's piano and the three songs that Rebecca has mastered in her short life. How is she going to become more like her mother if she can't play the piano the way her mother did? She closes her eyes and hums softly.

* * *

Rebecca can hear pounding on the back door of the house, and her name echoes out across the yard.

"Rebecca, Rebecca," she hears Chuck shouting, his voice loud and urgent.

Rebecca crawls out the window and runs around the side of the shed. Chuck is on the back step pounding his fist on the door. He is out of breath and can hardly get a word out between his gasps for air. He waves in the direction of the driveway, bent over, his face red.

"I won it," he says. "I won the bike. I wanted it so bad that it made me lucky and I won it. Come on."

Chuck bounds down the steps, having regained enough oxygen in his lungs. He throws his leg over the bicycle seat and plants his hands on the handlebars and starts reciting all the facts he had memorized for months about this bike, the bike he absolutely had to have.

"I can't believe it. I can't believe it. A contest. I'm a winner," and he rides around the yard with his hands stretched up over his head, grabbing the handlebars every few seconds to steady the bike. "I didn't even know I entered the contest," and he whoops again.

Rebecca stands on the back landing, her hands pressed into her thighs, watching Chuck fly round and round the yard as fast as he can go, squealing the whole time.

"What's going on?" Rebecca's father asks through the crack in the back door.

"Chuck won a new bike, and he's happy. People make noise when they're happy. That's how people behave when they're alive," Rebecca says, almost shouting, and then runs down the steps and chases after Chuck.

Ten

CHUCK TAKES THE TELEPHONE RECEIVER OFF ITS CRADLE THAT hangs on the wall in the back door hallway. He feels a bit like a spy or a secret agent. He doesn't have to dial Rebecca's number, lifts the telephone quietly so no one else in the house knows, and listens for the sound of her breathing.

It's ten past six in the morning. He's been hiding at the top of the stairs for ten minutes waiting for Harold to get his boots on and leave for the barn. Harold decided to be slow this morning, to take time for a cup of instant coffee. Harold opens the refrigerator and stares inside while Chuck watches from the shadows. Harold is beyond lean; he is skinny. Though he is strong, lifting with ease things Chuck can't even budge, he has no bulging biceps, no sculpted chest. Chuck thinks Harold is a lean, mean dog, a scrapper who can fight dirty and whip any opponent, not with strength or skill but with outright meanness.

Harold slams the fridge door like he's annoyed that nothing leapt out ready-made for him to eat. The dishes in the cupboard clink against each other. Harold never worries about being quiet in the mornings. If Harold has to be up early to milk cows, then the whole house should know, especially Gran, whose bedroom is behind the kitchen.

"I don't hear a thing," Gran says, probably for Harold's benefit. Chuck wants to warn Gran that saying such things will only encourage Harold to try harder to disturb her. But Gran would only laugh and shrug it off.

"You there, Rebecca?" Chuck whispers into the telephone.

"Yah," Rebecca says. "You're late."

"I had to wait until Harold went to the barn," Chuck says, his hand covering his mouth and the telephone. "He's going to be mad if I skip out on chores," Chuck continues, sounding unsure.

"He's always mad. He'll just be madder."

There's dead air on the phone while Chuck digs in his right ear with his pointer finger, to pry out his decision to go to the beaver pond with Rebecca or not. Rebecca isn't afraid of Harold. She holds her ground and stares Harold right in the eye when he rants at Chuck and sometimes she takes a step closer, almost daring Harold to turn his rage on her. That's usually when Gran steps in with a distraction of some sort, usually something to eat. But Rebecca is never the first to look away where Harold is concerned. Chuck doesn't know where she gets her courage and fierceness; it impresses him and also makes him feel shame.

"You don't have to come," Rebecca finally says, without any hint of impatience.

Chuck is relieved about the patience part. Rebecca pushes him but never demands him to stand up to Harold, though he'd like to. He'd like to stand on a chair and tell Harold a thing or two about kindness and tolerance and patience, none of which Harold understands.

"I'll go on my own," Rebecca says.

"No, wait for me. I'll hurry through my chores and then we can go," forgetting his courage from yesterday when they planned to check out the beaver pond early in the morning when the world is quiet, to see if they can see the new little beavers that should be swimming on their own now.

"It's not worth getting him riled. I'll pay for it for days," Chuck says, with a defeated kind of sound. "Give me an hour."

"Don't tell him where you're going or that you're going with me," Rebecca says.

Chuck hangs up the phone and scrambles into his boots while pulling on his jacket and crashes into the doorframe of the back door, nearly falling down the back steps.

"You're goddamned late," Harold says, halfway up the walkway from the barn.

Chuck would like to say, *not goddamned late, Harold, just late*. Chuck has imaginary retorts in his head and thinks if he rehearses them enough, one day one will fly right out of his mouth and things will change, Harold will stop treating Chuck like an annoyance, like a sliver in his thumb, something that constantly irritates.

"Sorry," Chuck says, running past Harold, leaving enough space that Harold can't take a swipe at him. Chuck plows through the barn door, grabs a small steel pail, and begins feeding calves before Harold is through the door himself.

"What are you up to?" Harold asks, removing his cap and roughing up his hair.

"Making up for lost time," Chuck says without looking up.

"I suppose you and your little girlfriend have plans. Well, think again," Harold says.

Harold doesn't like when Rebecca hangs around. She isn't allowed in the barn. I don't need any goddamned girls in my barn, Harold says to Chuck, using his fist to drive home his point. Harold is pretty sure that Rebecca does most of the barn work for her father. Harold feels uneasy with Rebecca, not really certain if there were a battle of wits that Rebecca wouldn't win. He feels exposed when she is around, like she can see through his mean exterior and discover he is cold to the very core, and afraid, always afraid. He admires her, though, a little, wonders where she gets such fierce determination considering she is damn near an orphan. Her father is practically a cripple, hardly gets out of his chair most days, or so the stories go. But this kid of his, this girl. The guys at the feed mill tell stories about Rebecca and how she manages that pitiful farm. Where does she get that? Harold's children are useless: the two girls hardly have a brain between them and Chuck is plain weak, coddled by his meddlesome grandmother who thinks she has all the cards, she owns the land, but by god he does all the work and owns everything else—he and the bank.

Harold has little tolerance for his mother-in-law, so little in fact that he doesn't even pretend to like her, doesn't make small talk, usually tries to pretend she isn't in the room. He doesn't call her by name, doesn't call her anything. Sometimes he has to think for a minute what her name actually is, it's been so long since he used her first name. Calls her *the mother-in-law* when he's out and anyone asks. Not many do.

Esther Randall. What kind of a name is Esther? Some kind of Bible name. Truth be told, he has only a hint more tolerance for his wife. Penelope. Another ridiculous name. He and Penelope went to school together and he had trouble pronouncing her name properly a couple of times and she went on about it with all manner of ridiculing. Their teacher didn't allow for any shortened names. Richard was never Dick. James, not Jim. Harold, not Harry, though no one he could think of had ever tried to call him Harry. Maybe his mother, but she's been dead so long he can hardly remember a single detail about her other than her sitting in a chair by the window and shrinking and disappearing a little bit more each day until all that was left was a bag of bones. She'd quit speaking or opening her eyes, and his father sometimes left her in the chair overnight and she smelled awful. Then his mother was gone and he can't remember the sound of her voice or the colour of her eyes or even how old he was when she was gone.

He should have called Penelope some other name like Dimwit because she was a terrible student, barely passed any mathematics class, and he wasn't sure she could even read when they were in school. Though, of course, everyone can read, but she wasn't a good reader. He could have called her Puny, Puny Penelope, to shut her up, but instead he married her. She got herself pregnant and they were only seventeen. Being pregnant shut her up, that and the bloody scandal that hung over her head, dragging him into it. So her interfering mother invited them to live with her. She said Harold could farm her land and wouldn't that be a great idea, and he fell for it lock, stock, and barrel. Then after Geraldine was born, Penelope announces there's another kid coming, setting Harold's nose against the grindstone with no let up in sight. And then there was Frances alongside of Geraldine, the two of them wailing into the night, and he wondered if he'd ever get a good night's sleep again.

Everything makes him angry, and the fact that he works with little notice or thanks from anyone, well, that drives him crazy, and then that he should feel some kind of gratitude to Penelope and her mother, some kind of respect neither of them has earned, turns his blood cold. This son of his, the runt of the litter that came long ten years after Frances like a reminder that life could keep knocking him down. This weakling who spent the first six years of his life crying and complaining, afraid of everything, and the kid looks at Harold like he expects something more, as if Harold owes him anything more than a roof over his head and food on his plate. He can work for his dinner like Harold did; only Harold worked at any job he could get and gave every cent to his father. Shouldn't Harold expect the same from his kid? But no, he asks Chuck only to do chores, to learn the ropes so he can take over and Harold can finally have a rest. Harold has earned at least *that*.

Harold hasn't had a vacation since his family went to see Lake Superior when he was five or six. His mother was well then, almost well. She told him to pretend the huge lake was the ocean, but without the salt water. The waves were huge and he couldn't imagine the ocean's waves being any bigger and the water was terribly cold, too cold to swim in. There was a Sleeping Giant in the harbour and his mother told him about the legend, but he's long forgotten the details now. That was his first and only holiday. Even when he and Penelope got married, they spent only one night at the Rainy Lake Hotel and ordered room service for breakfast. He felt ridiculous eating breakfast in his underwear and sitting on the bed. It felt awkward and uncomfortable, and Penelope was sick, throwing up every five minutes and blaming him.

Harold wonders what on earth God is punishing him for, what on earth he has done so wrong to deserve this pitiful life. No one understands him; no one even tries. There hasn't been a single soul who hasn't disappointed him, not one who hasn't come up short. None of the friends he had in school even bother with him now. They nod when they see him in town and judge him because he doesn't bother to take his barn boots off before going into the bank or the Hardware. Makes him want to put a fist through the wall. Now he laughs when he leaves the bank, knowing they won't be getting that cow-shit smell out of their precious carpet anytime soon. He even drags his feet a little to make sure they know Harold Prescott has been to the bank.

A cow fusses while he tries to milk her and lifts her inside back leg as if she might kick him, so Harold stands from his tiny stool and drives his fist into her ribs. She groans and drops to her knees. She stands quietly after, but her eyes are bulging.

"Chuck!" Harold hollers. He opens the barn door to turn the cows out. "Where has that kid got to?" Harold mutters. The calves are fed; he sees that the pigs have been slopped and the chickens are busy scratching for corn, running off in a hurry when Harold approaches. The old dog is tied to the tree and the pony's gate is swinging wide open.

Harold shakes his head with fury. "Can't take my eyes off that lazy kid, thinks he can spend all his time daydreaming with some notion of flying airplanes."

"Chuck!" Harold hollers again, but his voice bounces off the barn roof and then dies. *It's Sunday, I'll give him that*, Harold thinks, trudging to the house.

* * *

Chuck creeps up behind Rebecca. She and Daisy are waiting inside the forest where the trail to the beaver pond narrows. Rebecca is sitting on one of the stumps that remain from the land being cleared. Daisy's head is hanging like she's asleep though she's not even tied, could run off if she felt like it. Rebecca has a blade of grass between her palms, trying to make it whistle while she sits in her thinking pose. Rebecca is always thinking.

"What are you scheming?" Chuck asks. Daisy's head jerks up, startled awake.

"Nothing," Rebecca says, gathering up Daisy's reins. "You were quick." She clucks to Daisy and Daisy moves over beside the stump so Rebecca can slide on.

"Some cowboy you are," Chuck says.

"You're jealous."

They ride the rest of the way to the beaver pond in silence, Daisy leading the way, Prince snorting and prancing behind her. They tie the ponies to separate trees so they can't fuss with each other, and then Rebecca and Chuck climb up into their beaver watch house. They built the fort a couple of years ago. The two of them dragged lumber and tin and even an old window that Rebecca expropriated from the shed where it had been leaning against one wall, ignored and decaying. She confiscated nails from the workshop in one side of the large granary and unearthed a couple of hammers. They pounded their body weights in nails to be sure the fort was solid. They had hammering contests. *One-two-three go*, and Rebecca almost always won, except when she noticed Chuck wilting; then she hammered with less gusto. It was a great fort, high up in an old elm tree that stood on a small incline above the pond.

"I love this tree," Chuck says as he does every time they come to see the beavers.

"She's the lady of the forest," Rebecca says with her usual calm self-assurance, running her fingers over the jagged edge of an elm leaf.

Rebecca raises her father's binoculars to her face and gazes out over the water.

"Look how graceful she is," Rebecca says, pointing to a beaver swimming in the pond and handing the binoculars to Chuck.

"They're so different in the water from how clumsy they are on land. I guess that's why they live in the water," Chuck says.

"You think?" Rebecca says, a laugh sneaking out with her words.

Chuck gives her a shove. "You know what I mean," he says, handing the binoculars back to her.

"I see a little one," Rebecca says, leaning out of the tree. "And another."

"I see them. There are three babies," Chuck says, pointing and almost falling out of the tree.

"They're called kits," she says.

"I know. It's a stupid word," Chuck says with a groan.

Rebecca stares through the binoculars and watches the beavers display their aquatic skill. There was a time when everyone wanted to come back to the beaver pond, when Robert and Grace Archer had friends. Robert hoisted Rebecca to his shoulders and Jake was swaddled in Grace's arms to protect him from the razor-sharp edges of the bulrushes. Robert spouted beaver facts like a tour guide. Largest rodent in North America. Its tail is a foot long and is used as a rudder in the water and slaps on the water's surface sounding like a gunshot when danger is near. Rebecca soaked all the facts in like a sponge. Now she doles them out sparingly to Chuck.

Rebecca admires the beavers, admires that they stay together as a family, the female in charge, having mated for life. The young beavers stay with the family unit until they are two or three years old and then wander off in search of their own pond. Rebecca imagines them tucked under the ice safe and warm in their dens, all together to keep warm like a big mound of beavers, unable to see where one beaver starts and another stops, all of them safe.

"The beavers build dams only to keep the pond deep enough so it won't freeze to the bottom, so they can get in and out of their dens from under water," Rebecca says.

"I know," Chuck says, rolling his eyes. "I know all about it."

Prince sneezes to clear his nostrils, and Daisy lays her ears back on her head and lifts her hind leg in warning.

"Daisy's cranky," Chuck says, starting to climb down the ladder.

"She's in heat," Rebecca says plainly.

"She's always in heat."

"Every twenty-one days. It only seems like all the time."

Prince throws his head around and snorts, pulling to the end of his lead rope to stay out of Daisy's reach.

"Wanna race home?" Chuck asks.

"No. I want to enjoy the scenery. Race with yourself."

Chuck tries to keep Prince at a steady walking pace, but once Prince is turned toward home he runs as if on rocket fuel. His feet prance and his head tucks and his ears flip forward and back, listening for a signal from Chuck to go. Rebecca moves Daisy in front when the trail narrows to single file, and then she digs her heels into Daisy's sides. Daisy jumps forward into a full gallop, like she knows. *Game on.*

Chuck holds Prince back until Daisy is about a hundred yards ahead, and then he lets loose the reins and whispers a *go* in Prince's ears. Prince's front feet come off the ground and he bolts, gobbling the distance between them in seconds. As they round a corner, a fallen tree consumes most of the trail as Prince comes up beside Daisy. Daisy's ears go back, and Prince redirects his speed and in one fluid movement tucks his feet under him and sails over the fallen tree. Just as fluidly, Chuck soars through the air end over end until his back hits the fallen tree with an ugly cracking sound. Prince continues toward home, racing with the shadow of the reins flopping from side to side.

Rebecca pulls Daisy up and leaps from her back, pulling the reins over Daisy's head. Daisy will stand without moving when her reins hang in front of her, while Prince has no such manners. Chuck's mouth is hanging open, trying to find enough air to re-inflate his flattened lungs. Tears are leaking out the corner of his eyes.

"Are you hurt?" Rebecca asks, leaning across him and wiping Chuck's hair back off his face. Chuck nods and points to his left shoulder, his face an alarming white underneath the skid mark of mud along his jaw.

"Probably a broken collarbone," Rebecca says. "I'll go for help."

"No," Chuck manages to burp out and tries turning his head, but winces more.

Rebecca kneels beside him and spits on her fingers and wipes the mud from his chin and dries it with the edge of her sweatshirt.

"Harold will kill me," Chuck says, barely able to talk.

"Get your breath and you can ride Daisy home. I'll walk her. Can you move your fingers and toes?"

Chuck wiggles them and smiles, a relieved sort of smile. He closes his eyes and starts to breathe normally, his right hand in Rebecca's as she massages and worries his fingers. Chuck cries for a few minutes, quiet, contained sobs, not caring what Rebecca thinks of his crying. Rebecca lets him lie still, waits for him to regain his composure, to come back to himself.

"Okay, let's get you up," Rebecca says, and Chuck opens his eyes and raises his right arm toward her.

Rebecca braces her feet against Chuck and pulls slow and steady, and he rises up, his left arm hanging useless at his side.

"It hurts," he says, trying hard not to cry again.

"I know, I know," Rebecca whispers. "Stand up here on this stump and I'll help you ease on to Daisy's back."

Rebecca holds her hands under Chuck's right elbow and practically lifts him onto the stump. She pushes Daisy's side and the pony moves in tight to Chuck. All he has to do is lift his leg over her back and slide on.

"I wish Prince were this well behaved," Chuck whimpers.

"No, you don't."

Chuck doesn't argue and they begin the long walk home.

Eleven

IT TAKES ALMOST AN HOUR TO GET CHUCK SAFELY HOME, STOP-
ping every ten minutes or so to give him a rest from the jiggling.
Daisy's pace isn't exactly smooth, but she plods without darting left
and right, always willing to stop. Rebecca sees real terror in Chuck's
face when he worries over Harold's reaction, something beyond
anxiety. She wants to wrap him up and keep him safe from Harold.
She wants to be a shield. She grits her teeth and her fingers tighten.

"He was already mad I was late this morning and then I snuck
away after chores and now this." Chuck wants to cry, wants to let
it all out right there on Daisy's back, the grief of not being loved.

"It'll be okay," Rebecca says, only imagining the limits of
Harold's rage, if there were any limits at all. She tries to distract
Chuck with beaver facts, but he doesn't respond. She talks about
plans for school, but he doesn't offer anything. She holds on to his
ankle while Daisy strolls toward home, as if that one hold will keep
him safe, and she stops talking.

They turn in the driveway and Prince raises his head from the
front lawn, the reins now barely hanging on behind his ears, his
mouth full of grass, the grass tangled around the bit that lies across

his tongue. He gives a snort and trots off toward the barnyard looking proud for having got loose.

"What the hell?" Harold says from the top step of the front veranda. "Why is that goddamned pony loose?"

Chuck opens his mouth to speak, but no sound comes out. Rebecca drops Daisy's reins in front of the garden fence and takes hold of Chuck's right arm to help him down off Daisy's back. Rebecca takes a deep breath.

"Chuck had a fall," Rebecca says. "His collar bone is broken." She hollers for Gran.

"What's happened?" Gran says, coming out the front door. Her eyebrows shoot up when she sees the worry on Chuck's face. She heads for the steps, but Harold moves in her way.

"Oh, no, you don't," Harold says. "There'll be no sucking-up baby crap. He wants to get out of chores. You're fine," he says, pointing at Chuck, Harold's arm raised like a menacing weapon. "Now get that pony caught and put away before he gets hit by a car and I have to pay the damage. I'll shoot him. I damn well will, right through his goddamned head."

"Oh, Chuck," Gran says and tries to get by Harold.

Harold gives Gran a shove and she falls backwards on the veranda, hitting the side of a small wooden chair, the chair breaking apart from the impact. Chuck's head collapses onto his chest and he cries out like he's been punched. Rebecca runs up the three steps to the veranda, past Harold, and takes Gran's hand to help her up. Gran shakes her head, catching her breath.

"What a bunch of pansy-asses you are," Harold says, his hands clenched. He slashes the air with his fist. "You are not getting out of chores. I'm so goddamned tired of you lazy good-for-nothings."

Rebecca helps Gran to her feet and checks Gran's scuffed elbow.

"I'm okay," Gran says, brushing herself off and moving her head slowly back and forth, like her jaw is stuck.

Rebecca turns to face Harold and takes a step closer.

"We are taking Chuck to the hospital," she says, with a sound that is filled with every ounce of courage she can muster.

"The hell you are," Harold shouts at her, but he takes a step back.

"That's right, we are," Rebecca says and moves to stand right in front of him. Her teeth are clenched, her lips pulled apart. "He's hurt. Your son is hurt. And when a person is hurt you help him." Rebecca turns to Gran. "Are you okay to drive, Gran?"

"I most certainly am, and Harold, if you know what's good for you—" Gran says, but doesn't bother finishing her sentence.

Harold kicks one of the chairs across the veranda and into an empty flowerpot that tumbles off its stand and shatters.

Chuck hasn't moved. Tears are dripping off his chin and his nose is running, but he doesn't bother to wipe it, not even with his sleeve. His head is dangling like he's paralyzed, unable to hold any part of him upright.

"Chuck, come and sit here and I'll put Prince away. I'll ride Daisy home, and you and Gran can pick me up there. I'll hurry," she says.

She turns to walk down the steps. Harold hasn't moved.

"Mr. Prescott, get out of my way." She pushes by him and takes Chuck's arm and whispers to comfort him.

"Aren't you a sight? Crying like a little baby. You disgust me," Harold says.

"You disgust me," Rebecca says, turning to face Harold and barely restraining her voice from shouting. "Why are you always so angry? Why can't you ever be kind?"

"Get off my property," Harold says in a low growl. "And don't step one foot on this farm again."

"Ah-hah, my good man," Gran says, twisting her neck to get it realigned. "This is my land. Let's not forget that."

Harold turns to go back into the house and kicks the screen door hard. The door bounces back, slamming Harold in the rear end.

Gran smiles at Rebecca. "I'll get my purse."

Rebecca runs for Prince, but he's having none of it, evading her right and left like they're playing a game of tag. She reaches down and picks some of the same grass he's been eating and then squats in place. Curiosity gets the better of him and he reaches out his nose to her without moving his feet, his lips wiggling at her, his neck stretching closer and closer.

"Gotcha, you cheeky bugger," she says, lunging at him and grabbing the reins before he can dart away. She trots him over to the barnyard and opens the gate and pulls his bridle off in one fluid movement. She runs into the barn and hangs the bridle on a nail inside the door next to the light switch. Then she makes a dash for Daisy.

She can see Harold watching her from the kitchen window but doesn't let on. She feels an ugly twist in her stomach, like she would like to punch Harold right in the face. She'd like to give him a taste of his own rage. She grits her teeth thinking about it. She picks up Daisy's reins, grabs hold of a handful of mane, and throws her leg over Daisy's back. Driving her heels in and urging Daisy on with a *get up*, she gallops for home. Daisy's ears move forward and back, waiting for a cue from Rebecca to slow down, but Rebecca keeps urging Daisy on, leaning down over her neck.

"Go, Daisy," she says when the pony hesitates and begins to slow and Rebecca tries very hard not to cry.

She turns Daisy loose in the paddock and runs for the house. She throws open the kitchen door and lets the door slam into the wall. She screams one loud scream that sounds more like a shout and sees her father's legs jump where he sits in his chair. She marches over to him and without hesitation says, "That's right, I'm screaming. Chuck is hurt and I'm screaming. I'm screaming." She leans closer to her father's face and screams again. Robert squeezes his eyes shut and says nothing.

* * *

Rebecca helps Chuck out of the back seat when Gran pulls up by the Emergency entrance at the hospital.

"I'll park and meet you inside," Gran says. "You're okay, my boy."

Chuck is pale and sweating and feels sick to his stomach. He stops halfway up the sidewalk and vomits into the pail Gran gave him for the ride in. Rebecca wipes his mouth with the facecloth she's been holding. He can't help but cry out when he heaves.

"Just about there," she says. "Steady now."

A nurse sees the two of them standing at the door and comes toward them.

"What have we here?" the nurse asks.

"A fall from a pony. Something is broken," Rebecca says.

"Okay, let's get you in," the nurse says, taking Chuck's right arm from Rebecca while Chuck continues to whimper. "Are you right-handed?"

Chuck moves his head slightly back and forth, his head still dangling and tears dripping from his chin.

"That's too bad," she says. "You give his name to Iris there behind the desk," the nurse directs Rebecca. "Is there a parent with you?"

Rebecca nods.

The nurse squeezes Rebecca's arm. "We'll get him fixed up," and she walks Chuck through the door. "Iris, page Dr. Hutchinson for me. Thanks." She turns her attention to Chuck. "You've had quite a day," she says as the door closes behind her.

Rebecca gives all the information to Iris. Chuck had his tonsils out when he was little so his name is on file. Gran comes through the door breathing hard. A dark-blue stain is beginning to grow on her cheek.

"Gran, your face," Rebecca says.

"Never mind," says Gran. "It'll be fine." But she has a weary look about her, as if it's all too much. "Penelope is working down in Laundry. I should go and get her," Gran says, collapsing into a chair. "But I can't be bothered. We've got things well in hand."

Rebecca sits down beside Gran, feeling tired, too.

"We do," Rebecca says.

Rebecca can't help staring at Gran's face. The blue stretches down over Gran's chin with one dark blue line almost like it had been drawn there with a ruler, the edges mottled in varying degrees of red and blue.

"Try not to look at it," Gran says, closing her eyes and exhaling deliberately.

Two women come in the door, and one goes over to Iris. Rebecca recognizes Mrs. Martyn, who sits down to wait. Mrs. Martyn comes to the school to play for concerts and when some of the children sing in the festival. She pulls a magazine out of her purse and begins to flip through it. She looks up at Rebecca and then at Gran.

"Is that you, Esther?" Mrs. Martyn asks, leaning forward.

Gran opens her eyes, startled. "Yes, it's me. Hello, Sandra. How are you?" Gran says, barely able to hide her fatigue.

"Better than you, I think. What happened?"

"My face. Oh, it's nothing. I had a run-in with a screen door," Gran says, putting her hand on Rebecca's knee when Rebecca straightens up in her seat. "I'm here with my grandson. Fell off his pony. Kids. He's in there getting put back together," Gran says, resting her forehead in her hand, a motion that seems to say *Leave me alone.*

Rebecca keeps looking at Gran's face, a bad taste filling her mouth. Gran lied, and though Rebecca knows Gran wouldn't tell the truth or couldn't tell the truth, it seemed so easy for her to lie, almost automatic, like she's done it many times before. Rebecca thinks about the time Gran was on crutches and said her arthritis had flared up. Or the time she had her wrist bandaged and said she wrenched it, but Rebecca saw bruise marks stretching out beyond the bandage. Chuck has his own bruises and scratches, and she wonders now if he too is a liar.

Rebecca never told a lie to anyone before, not even to her father. She doesn't always tell the truth, but that's not the same as lying. She refuses to answer when she can't tell the truth and after her father repeats the question a few times, he quits asking where she's been. He never asks her any questions about much else, except did she feed the chickens, has she crushed barley for the calves. He doesn't ask if she brushed her teeth or did her homework. He doesn't ask if her shoes are too tight or if she needs longer pants. She tells him when her toes hurt or when she can't do up her pants.

She doesn't answer Mrs. Bell's questions about homework or where her gym shoes are. Rebecca doesn't bother with any made-up excuses such as her pages got too close to the woodstove and burst into flames or some stray dog chewed up her running shoes. She says nothing.

Mrs. Bell kept asking, leaning over and looking in her face. "Well, then, you can stay in with your head down on your desk at recess if you have nothing to say."

Rebecca has taught herself not to react, to keep staring straight ahead like she is in a trance.

"Maybe I'll have a chat with your father," Mr. Pedorski said when she started grade five.

Go ahead, Rebecca wanted to say. *Good luck getting anything out of him.* She knew Mr. Pedorski wouldn't call her father. He was bluffing. No one called her father. In the years she's been going to school, no one has ever called to ask why Rebecca isn't singing in the festival or whether she is allowed to go on the grade five trip through the paper mill. No questions. So she gives Mr. Pedorski her I-dare-you look.

She sometimes wishes she would stop growing, that her feet would stay a size four and she would never have to be embarrassed about her pants being too short, though she has quit worrying about that. No one dares to tease her at school, not since she flattened Marty McKelvie in grade three when he called Chuck a crybaby. She made Marty cry, pushed him down on the playground and held her knee in his back. "Don't call people names," she said in his ear, and her voice frightened even Chuck.

"I'm telling," Marty said between whimpers, climbing to his feet.

"Go ahead," Rebecca said, taking a step toward him before he ran off shouting about revenge.

"Holy cow," Chuck said, looking dazed.

Rebecca called it a pre-emptive strike. She'd heard that term on the news and looked it up in the dictionary. *A surprise attack to keep the enemy from doing it to you.*

Chuck says the kids at school are afraid of her, even the big kids, even big fat Gerard in grade eight. They all give her a wide berth in the hallway. She doesn't care. Pre-emptive. She wishes she could plan a pre-emptive strike against Harold. She is too late, though; he's already got a taste for being mean, was maybe born with that particular taste in his mouth. All he knows is anger and shouting.

* * *

Mrs. Martyn's sister comes out, and they both get ready to leave after a brief visit with Gran about the weather and hoping Gran doesn't have to wait too long and how sometimes you have to wonder about the medical care in this town. Rebecca can hardly sit still.

"Gran, how much do you think piano lessons cost?" Rebecca says after the two ladies have made their way out of the Emergency waiting room, leaving Rebecca and Gran alone.

"I don't have any idea," Gran says. "Did your mother use to teach piano lessons? Or was that before you were born? Or I guess when you were little because you came along right quickly after your mother moved in down the road." Gran continues her conversation with herself.

"I don't remember her teaching piano lessons," Rebecca says. "I should know that."

"Oh no, that was before Jake was born, I think, so you would have been too little to remember."

Rebecca shakes her head, like she's trying to wiggle loose a memory but can't. It is unthinkable that she has forgotten something about her mother, and the thought makes her clammy and cold.

"Gran, why did you lie to Mrs. Martyn about your bruise?"

"That's a different kind of question," Gran says, examining her fingernails, her right hand massaging her left. "Mrs. Martyn doesn't want to know that Harold knocked me down. People don't really want to know that kind of thing," Gran continues, her voice low, almost a whisper. "They ask out of concern and interest, but they don't want the truth. They want you to tell them you are fine, and thanks for asking." Gran stops and looks at Rebecca with a thoughtful, kind look on her face.

"We think people want the truth, we think the truth is best, but it isn't really what any of us want. You'll come to figure that out when you're older. Life comes with all kinds of bumps and bruises. There's no way to really understand it, any of it. We smile and say *Fine, thank you* when someone asks us how we are. So don't you go telling stories."

Gran pats Rebecca's hand and closes her eyes like she's ready to take a nap, leaving Rebecca to think about what she has said.

* * *

After a couple of hours, the nurse comes out and asks Gran and Rebecca to follow her.

"You can come in and see him now. He's going to be fine. Broken collar bone, broken ribs, and a broken humerus," she says, putting her hand on her own upper arm. "We're going to keep him in overnight, what with the throwing up. He might have hit his head, though he says not."

The nurse looks over at Chuck on the stretcher. "He says he's game to stay, but he hasn't eaten our food yet," and she laughs, her white uniform crisp and pressed, her hat pinned securely in her hair.

Chuck looks almost glad he's staying. There's no cast on his arm.

"Why no cast?" Gran asks.

"Oh, we've taped his arm to keep his shoulder from moving and we can't cast his upper arm where the break is, but the sling will immobilize it while the bones heal. No ponies for six weeks."

"What about chores?" Gran asks.

"No lifting or moving that arm or shoulder."

"No school?" Chuck whispers.

"Oh, there'll be school, young man. Broken bones won't stop you from learning," Gran says.

Rebecca hasn't said a word, watching the conversation with a frown.

"The doctor will have to write down the instructions and sign it for Mr. Prescott," Rebecca says, looking at the nurse. Rebecca's shoulders are squared, her hands in fists.

The nurse looks at Gran and Gran looks away.

"No problem," the nurse says. "I'll get the doctor to do that before he discharges Charles tomorrow. Now let's get him up to the ward and into a real bed."

"You go with him, Rebecca, and I'll go down and see if I can find Penelope. Okay, Chuck?" Gran says.

Chuck nods and gives Rebecca a pained look.

The nurse rolls the stretcher down the hall and into the elevator, and Rebecca hangs on to the one of the bars of the stretcher. The nurse is humming and smiles at Rebecca like they're old friends.

"I don't like it in here," Rebecca whispers to Chuck.

Chuck tells her about the X-ray and the doctor and the hurting, and his voice is beginning to sound like he's had an adventure.

The nurse wheels Chuck up to the nursing station and hands his metal file to the nurse sitting behind the desk. Rebecca thinks the nurse looks familiar, but shakes her head, not wanting to remember her.

"You're all set, Charles, for a night's stay courtesy of the hospital," the nurse says, ruffling Chuck's hair and giving Rebecca another smile before she heads off down the hall humming.

The new nurse gets up and wheels Chuck into Room 204.

"You've got your very own room for the night," she says. She turns the crank on the stretcher to lower him down. "You'll need to get into a gown for the night. I know it's hardly what any boy wants to wear, but bigger men than you have put our fine garments on without too much complaint." She laughs.

The nurse turns to Rebecca. "You can wait in the hall for a few minutes while I get him undressed, and then I'll call you back in," she says.

Chuck's shirt is already missing. They had to cut it off him so as not to move his shoulder too much. Cut it right off, Chuck said in the elevator. Rebecca walks out into the hall and leans against the wall. She had been in the room across the hall. Room 207. She looks at her feet, feels panic crawling up her spine. The not-quite green or beige walls, the flecked painted concrete floors, the smell of death. If not the smell of death, then the smell of the total absence of life, sterility, too clean, and the clanging of metal, as if nothing in this place has any measure of quiet. She sees a nun at the end of the hall coming toward her, her black robe flowing out behind her, and Rebecca feels like turning to run, taking the stairs down two at a time, but instead counts in her head. The nun turns in to a room before she gets to Rebecca.

"You can come in now," the nurse says, sticking her head out the door. "We're all set in here."

Rebecca walks into the room. Chuck's bed is cranked up high and the sides are up like he's a baby, like he might try to escape. The top of the bed is raised so he's in a reclining position. He has tears on his face that he wipes away when Rebecca walks up beside him.

"You okay?"

"It hurts."

"It would. You had quite the crash."

"I don't ever want to go home. Not ever," Chuck says.

"I know. But you have to."

Twelve

JOANNE AND DONNA PLAY AT THE BOTTOM OF THE PLAYGROUND field, slightly in the ditch behind the wild rose bushes when a baseball game is going on and behind the backstop the rest of the time. Rebecca watches the two of them head down to the playground when the bell rings for recess. They go wherever the other kids aren't. Joanne and Donna have cooties, both of them; they came down with cooties in grade two, as if that were the amount of time it took the other kids to figure out who was weaker, who fit on the rung at the bottom of the ladder.

Joanne is an easy target with her watered-down blue eyes and albino-like hair that her mother keeps cropped halfway down Joanne's ear as if a bowl had been placed on top of Joanne's head to guide the scissors. Her hair is like silk, perfectly straight, and it almost rustles. Her voice is high-pitched and squeaky, like she's never sure what she wants to say, but once she gets started she can't stop. To make matters worse, Joanne is tall, taller than most of the boys in the school and taller than all the boys in her grade. She tries to blend in with bad posture, rounded shoulders and her head pushed forward, but she stands out like a sore thumb. Joanne has no athletic ability aside from being told to stand under the basketball hoop. *I'll pass the ball to you,* most of the kids claim, but Joanne seldom catches the ball. She stands with her arms folded in front of her while the ball bounces off her and she tries not to wince. She stands in the outfield during baseball and when someone hits the ball out there, she puts her hands over her face and never moves. Cooties will do that to you, will take any confidence or skill that you might have been nurturing and suck it all right out of you, completely.

When teams are being chosen and Rebecca gets to pick, she picks Joanne, first time, no hesitation.

"Joanne," Rebecca says firmly, like it is the only choice to make, the only decision that makes any sense. Joanne never gushes or thanks Rebecca. She moves to her place in line and tries to look like she belongs.

"Why don't you pick me first?" Chuck asks.

"I can't," Rebecca says and won't explain any more than that. Chuck quits asking.

Donna is a different kind of cootie victim. Donna's cooties are almost self-induced. Almost. Marty McKelvie saw Donna picking her nose during quiet time for the six- and seven-year-olds. He stood right up and shouted *Donna's got cooties.* Even though Mrs. Bell told him to sit down and be quiet, the whole cootie thing stuck. Donna tried to explain, something about an itchy nose, but no one gave her the benefit of the doubt. Nose picking is a tricky business and not meant to be done when the likes of Marty McKelvie are prowling about.

Donna is an only child of parents who give in to every request, every demand Donna makes, or so it seems. She has an inventory of dolls and books and clothes that is both impressive and disturbing. Other girls in the class go to her birthday parties more out of curiosity than anything else. Donna invites every girl in the school no matter what age, like she's hedging the odds. She even invites Rebecca year after year after year.

Rebecca is not allowed to go to birthday parties. It's an unspoken rule. She doesn't have to ask for permission; she knows what the answer will be. No good clothes, no money for a gift. She's heard the stories of these birthday parties: the sleeping bags in the living room, the candy and pop, the loot bags filled with hair ribbons and pretend lipstick and playing cards and tiny books and candy cigarettes. She's heard about staying up all night, the ghost stories, playing Twister and Hide-the-Button, the whole thing sounding like a whopping amount of fun.

There was a time when Rebecca imagined having her own birthday party, greeting everyone at the door and accepting the colourfully wrapped gifts with curly ribbon on top and shaking the parcels a bit to try to guess the contents before putting them on the gift table, a table set up especially for gifts and nothing else. Fancy that, a table just for gifts. The thought makes Rebecca shake her head even now. She imagined punch and party hats and Pin the Tail on the Donkey and nickels and dimes and one whole quarter wrapped in wax paper and baked right into the cake. She imagined streamers and balloons and the house so clean it shone. Maybe she will have such a birthday party next year. That's when Rebecca will have a party, next year.

* * *

Donna jumps out of the junior classroom like she's a kung fu fighter, right in front of Rebecca, and shoves an invitation in Rebecca's face.

"I can't come," Rebecca says, putting her hand up to block Donna's advance.

"But," Donna starts to plead, because she's a pleader. She pleads to be first in the line-up for the water fountain, pleads to go first in show-and-tell, pleads about anything and everything that might put someone ahead of her. "I have three new Barbies and you can try on my clothes."

"Tempting," Rebecca says. "But no."

"I'm going to be eleven and I want at least eleven friends to come."

Rebecca turns and walks away. Donna stomps her foot.

"I don't have cooties," she shouts in Rebecca's direction.

"I know," Rebecca shouts back. "There's no such thing."

"Then why won't you come to my party?"

Rebecca stops and walks back to Donna.

"You can help yourself, you know. Quit bragging. Quit telling everyone about all the stuff you have. Eleanor never has a lunch. If you're so rich and privileged, then bring enough food in your lunch to share with her without her knowing you've brought it for her. No one cares if you have eighteen dolls and forty-three pairs of shoes. No one should care. You should care that Eleanor is hungry and that she can't see the blackboard properly. And quit asking me to your parties. I'm never going to come."

"Chuck is coming. I'm allowed to invite boys this year."

Rebecca turns around with a huge sigh and rolls her eyes.

"You just don't get it," Rebecca says.

Rebecca continues down the hall toward the playground door when she hears the sound of the piano coming from inside the storage room. She has been listening at the door for weeks, every day waiting for the right moment. She looks behind her and then knocks on the door, opening it slowly when Mrs. Martyn asks her to come in.

"Rebecca," Mrs. Martyn says, her hands resting on the keys, and looks slightly surprised. Rebecca doesn't sing in her choirs and never competes at the Kiwanis Music Festival. When the other girls show up at school with best dresses and shiny shoes for the big day at the festival, with hair pulled back into tight ponytails, Rebecca stays at home. "Can I help you with something?"

Rebecca shuts the door behind her and starts to dig in her pocket. She pulls out a wad of money and places it on top of the piano, coins and all.

"Can I buy piano lessons with this? I mean, is it enough for a few lessons? I can play a little bit." Rebecca squares her body to face Mrs. Martyn.

Mrs. Martyn hasn't spoken yet, stares at the money and then back to Rebecca.

"There's eighteen dollars and fifty-three cents. If it's not enough, that's okay," Rebecca says, starting to gather up the money.

"Oh, it's certainly enough," Mrs. Martyn says. "I was trying to figure it out in my head. But yes, yes," she says nodding. "Why don't you sit and play something for me."

Rebecca hesitates, and Mrs. Martyn slides over on the piano bench and then pats the bench with her hand, the motion that says *come and sit here*. Rebecca sits down and rubs the sweat that's leaking from her palms on her pants.

"I only know one song very well," Rebecca says. "My mother plays it."

And then Rebecca starts. Her eyes close and her fingers move slowly over the keys, pressing them gently and carefully, not wanting to make too much sound. She plays, without stopping, the song that has taken her six years to get right, playing in the shed when she is sure she is alone, crawling in the window and lifting the tarp, trying to hear the sounds, the notes in her head that her mother played.

Rebecca stops and puts her hands back on her thighs. They sit in silence for two or three minutes, and Mrs. Martyn's eyes are shiny. Her hand has been at her neck as if she is holding her head on.

"Oh my, Rebecca," is all Mrs. Martyn can seem to get out, as if no other words are good enough. "You play beautifully. Your mother would be very proud." Mrs. Martyn's voice chokes.

Rebecca's eyes close again and she breathes in slowly, as if she has been waiting all these years to arrive at this very place. *So like her mother.*

They work out a plan. Mrs. Martyn takes only a five-dollar bill from the wad of Rebecca's money. Mrs. Martyn says they will do a lesson whenever she comes to the school, maybe every two weeks, and she'll talk to Mr. Pedorski about allowing Rebecca to use the piano at recess to practise.

"Five dollars will cover the rest of the year," Mrs. Martyn explains and finishes up with it being her privilege to work with Rebecca. Rebecca doesn't smile, doesn't jump up and down. She relaxes her shoulders and her hands unfold.

* * *

The lunch bell is ringing and Chuck finds Rebecca outside the washrooms.

"Where've you been?" he asks.

"Helping Mrs. Martyn."

"Doing what?"

"Planning to take over the world. How's your arm?"

"Not bad. Donna says she'll invite me to her party if I let her carry my books."

"A win-win," Rebecca says and guides Chuck through the classroom door ahead of her.

"I'm not going to any stupid girl's party," Chuck says.

"You know you want to," Rebecca says with a laugh.

Mr. Pedorski is already shouting orders. He starts with his grade fives, who can't be expected to sit still. He gets them busy, then moves on to grade six and so on. It's a bit like juggling, Rebecca thinks, keeping all the balls in the air. On Fridays the whole class does art together and on Monday mornings they do spelling followed by writing.

"Good penmanship is next to godliness," Mr. Pedorski says.

Rebecca thinks that might be an overstatement but doesn't really care one way or the other. Chuck doesn't have to take any notes and his writing is terrible even when his arm isn't in a sling. He does his spelling verbally at recess, when the other kids without an arm in a sling are outside playing.

"It's the price you pay for an injury," Mr. Pedorski explains, as if Chuck has a choice.

The whole class has a spelling bee once a month on Fridays. It's usually an all-of-a-sudden spelling bee, the kind Mr. Pedorski suggests when no one seems to be doing any work, when everyone's spending too much time looking out the windows like they might make a run for it.

Mr. Pedorski calls the words out for each student, up and down the row, everyone standing by his or her desk. If you get a word wrong, you sit down, which seems more like a reward than a punishment. Rebecca usually makes it to the very end, the last one standing. If that happens too often she makes a mistake on purpose.

"Since when don't you know how to spell *procrastination*," Chuck says.

Rebecca doesn't answer.

* * *

Rebecca likes the bus ride home. She likes looking out the window as the bus groans and creaks past the farms on the River Road. The Sallingers' old concrete-block house was empty for three or four years before the Sallingers moved in. Now the snakes have crawled up from the cellar claiming squatters' rights.

"Sallingers should move out," Gran says every single time Gran drives past Sallingers' with Rebecca in the car on their library trips. "They're not going to win that battle."

Mrs. Visser's house is built right on the edge of a ravine and looks like it's slowly sliding in, too tired to bother not to. The house has the appearance of being tilted, and Rebecca imagines the cutlery sliding off the dinner table. Mrs. Visser teaches girls to sew. Rebecca would like to learn to sew. Her mother's sewing machine is in the hall closet behind some old blankets and worn towels. Mrs. Klein had told her not to throw away any old towels or sheets because you never know when you might need them, and Mrs. Klein was right.

Sometimes Rebecca imagines the bus never stops, keeps driving and driving, right out of her life and into another one. The bus would drive to a different time zone, maybe a different reality or time travel, and no one would recognize her, would smile at her on the street with a half-smile, a pathetic smile with head tilted slightly and a how-are-you-doing-Rebecca question that doesn't want an answer, and no one would look away to avoid saying *I have no idea what to say to you.* Maybe this bus could fly, take her to a faraway land.

A bank manager moved into Roddick and is building a new home on the river. The house has only the garage facing the road, has strange small windows above the garage, and there doesn't seem to be any way to get into the house as far as Rebecca can see. The siding is going on, a dark, sinister brown with darker trim.

The bus stops at Marty's house to let him off across the road from the banker's new house. Marty shoves at least two kids before he jumps off the bus, to get his quota of bad behaviour in before the end of the day.

A big gate stands at the end of the lane that leads to the new house, a black iron gate that would require a secret password to get through. And there's a sign with the same dark brown wood: *Bellwether Belgians* with *Bernard Tupper* printed underneath. Rebecca is certain there is a Mrs. Tupper because she's seen her walking across the road to get the mail. Rebecca wonders why Mrs. Tupper's name isn't on the sign.

The Belgians graze in the front field by the road, gentle giants, their huge golden bodies with flaxen manes and tails. They are majestic beasts, powerful, more pull for the pound than any other draft horse breed. They are bred for steady-as-she-goes. The banker likes the look of them in his front yard, their deep pedigrees firming up his own, Gran claims.

Gran says no one trusts a banker in the first place and then building a big fancy house doesn't help. No one calls him Bernie, and he corrects people when they put the emphasis on the wrong part of his first name. Rebecca practises in her head to check the different sounds. BERnard sounds a lot more important than BerNARD.

"Pretentious," Gran said on the way to the library one Saturday, looking over the seat at Rebecca and Chuck while taking a cigarette out of her mouth. "Bet you can't spell that."

"T—H—A—T," Chuck said and then laughed really hard.

Gran ignored him and Rebecca nodded, giving him a *well done*.

"The house doesn't even have a front door," Gran said. "What kind of a house has no front door?"

Rebecca asked Gran why no one trusts a banker. "You'd have to be smart to be a banker and trusting smart people can't be all that risky."

"It's an envy thing," Gran said. "People can't help it. They don't want strangers moving in being better off. It reminds them of what they haven't got and they forget all about what they have. It's always been that way. It's one of those rules that no one talks about."

Rebecca had more questions for Gran that Saturday, such as was Rebecca's mother not accepted, not trusted, was she an outsider, but they arrived at the library, ending the conversation.

* * *

Rebecca leans her face on the bus window and wonders if people ever envy her father. They can't possibly envy him now, but maybe before, before things all went so terribly wrong. Gran says the neighbours called Rebecca's mother *exotic*. Gran also says Rebecca's father had *landed a rare bird*, as if he coaxed Rebecca's mother into a cage with a shiny mirror and a little swing with a bell on it, like the budgie that came to school for show-and-tell with some kid from the junior class. The bird's feathers were an iridescent green. Is he green or yellow or both? He tucked his beak into his chest, shy, and didn't sing, not locked up in that cage. "He wants to be free, to fly on the breeze and float on the clouds," Rebecca said, looking into the cage and admiring him.

"Until a hawk eats him," Marty said.

Rebecca thought of giving Marty a big shove into the garbage can, but that only encourages him. She does say every now and then, when she can't stand him anymore, "Want me to make you cry again, Marty?" That usually shuts him up.

The bus lurches forward again, and Chuck and Rebecca bang heads.

"Don't sit so close," Rebecca says, and Chuck slides even closer to Rebecca.

"Look at my chin," Chuck says, running his finger along his jaw line.

Rebecca squints and looks closely.

"What am I looking for?"

"My beard," Chuck says.

"That may be overstating it," Rebecca says.

"I think I'll be shaving soon. Certainly before I get to high school."

"You could probably use a butter knife," Rebecca says, but she smiles at Chuck. "Be careful what you wish for. I think shaving could become a drag."

"A man's gotta do what a man's gotta do," Chuck says. His fingers are moving back and forth under his nose.

"Can't you see it?"

"Absolutely," Rebecca says, standing. "It's my stop."

Rebecca's house isn't visible from the road, not anymore. The spruce trees are taller and planted so close together that they are more like a hedge, no telling where one tree starts and another one ends. The fence along the road is tired and broken. There's no shiny sign that boasts of any family living here. There were letters on the barn at one time. *R. Archer & Son.* But someone, her father mostly likely, though she hadn't seen him do it, threw a can of white paint on the barn and now it doesn't say anything at all. It is a big blob of white. Rebecca used to think it would have been worse if he had drawn a line through *Son* and written *Daughter* above it, like a consolation prize. The blob of paint that covers most of *Archer* and all of *Son* is the better option, she thinks. Maybe one day when she is feeling brave she will hang from a rope and paint *Rebecca Archer & Father* or maybe leave him out altogether. *Rebecca Archer, Farmer Extraordinaire.* It has a nice ring to it.

"See you tomorrow," Chuck says as Rebecca walks to the front of the bus.

She doesn't answer, but she does look back at him when she crosses the road and wiggles her fingers at his face pressed to the bus window with his tongue sticking out and his eyes crossed. She smiles at him. He wants a laugh from her, but she doesn't have one. Not today.

The lane to her house is about six hundred yards long. She tried counting her steps one time and got lost somewhere in the nine hundreds. She is only on step forty-six when she hears a feeble baby's cry from the ditch. She drops her lunch bag and books and starts digging through the tall grass. The sound stops and Rebecca stops, too, waiting to hear it again.

Wah, the sound comes again, like a baby but different.

She moves the grasses apart and finds a young crow tangled in plastic twine, his wings twisted and some of his feathers worn right off. He can barely lift his head and when he sees Rebecca he doesn't even bother to fuss and flap his wings; he lies still.

Rebecca runs the rest of the way home and grabs a cardboard box from the porch and dashes into the house for a towel and a pair of scissors. Her father is sitting at the kitchen table with the newspaper in front of him, his hands tucked between his legs like he's cold.

"Why the hurry?" he asks, his voice slow and slurred.

"There's a bird. Hurt. In the lane," Rebecca says and runs out, slamming the door behind her.

The bird hasn't moved and isn't making any noise at all now. Rebecca wraps the towel around him and lays him in the bottom of the box. The bird's eye is on her, but he doesn't look afraid. He looks exhausted and starving and almost dead.

"Shhh," Rebecca says. "There, there."

She covers the box with the towel and walks carefully the rest of the way home. She brings the box into the porch and sets it down. She walks into the pantry off the kitchen and grabs a can of beans, while her father watches her with a confused look on his face.

"You brought it in the house? We can't have a bird in the house," he says, shaking his head.

"Yes, we can. I'm going to take care of him and make him better," Rebecca says, opening the can of beans.

"Since when do birds eat beans?"

"Since now."

"A crow," Rebecca's father says. "I don't know. No, I don't think this is a good idea," shaking his head again with greater fury and starting to get out of his chair.

"No, this is a good idea. And you're going to help me feed him when I'm at school," Rebecca says, pointing at him with a forceful plunge of her arm. "I take care of your cows and I've taken care of you and you're going to take care of my crow. Now start thinking of a good name for him while I try to get him to eat something. He'll need water."

Rebecca's father looks stunned, like he's been slapped across the side of the head. He opens and closes his mouth a few times.

"There's an eye dropper in the medicine cabinet. I can't remember what it was for. You can use that."

"I had pink eye. I was five."

Her father shakes his head, his eyebrows moving up and down on his forehead like they work independently. "Right, right," he says nodding.

"Yah, you remember," Rebecca says, not even bothering to look at him.

Thirteen

CHUCK LOOKS DOWN THE ROW OF DAIRY COWS IN THE BARN. THE cows stand with their heads trapped in steel stanchions, like prisoners in the town square, the constant clanging an annoying discord. Some are small Jerseys with fine legs and sweet faces, looking more like deer than cows and their milk creamy beyond creamy. Others are Brown Swiss with greyish-brown faces and large fuzzy ears, whose calves are heavy-legged and always chubby, an unspoken invitation for cuddling. The odd black-and-white Holstein comes in and out of the milk line when Harold gets the culls from the large dairy farm on the road to Kenora, a farm with no time for poor performance. These cows kick too much, are prone to mastitis, or are old and don't produce enough milk, so Harold takes them and their problems become his.

The cows swat their tails continuously from side to side, trying fruitlessly to chase away the buzzing, biting flies. The cows are uncomfortable, their udders full and heavy, and they dance in their stalls, throwing their heads up and down and shifting their weight from right to left, bawling their complaints, as if anyone might care.

Chuck hates milking cows, hates the early mornings, the unrelenting pattern of it, the endless list of chores that never shrinks, always grows, stretching out before him like miles and miles of chain, hates the tails that whack him in the face, stinging his eyes, tearing at his skin, hates the manure that leaks from the cows like a ruptured sewage line, the loose sloppy waste that splats into the gutter and sprays back up, landing in Chuck's hair and ears, the smell soaking in through his pores to take up permanent residence.

Chuck moves slower now, his arm and collarbone barely healed. Harold never let him miss a single day of chores. Gran protested, but no one was listening. Penelope told Chuck to use his right arm. She has obviously never milked cows; using one arm isn't an option. He had to suck it up, he told Rebecca.

"I can come and help," Rebecca offered, but she knew when Chuck shook his head, they both knew, she wasn't allowed on the farm.

"Like he'd do anything," Rebecca said.

"He might."

* * *

"Quit daydreaming and get on with it," Harold says, his usual impatient snarl hacking through Chuck's thoughts.

Chuck imagines saluting the man he calls Dad, referring to him as Harold only in his head, like they are acquaintances, having collided with some regularity on the street, nodding in passing, being familiar only with what's on the surface, the cover. Harold has never asked a single question of Chuck, not what's your favourite colour or what do you dream about or what place on earth would you most like to visit. Harold never asks Chuck what he wants to be when he grows up because that's not a question that will ever be posed; that question came with an answer, is a fact, a fact delivered at the same time Chuck's five-pound, slightly premature body was expelled from his mother, a fact that is no more negotiable than Chuck's blood type or gender. *He will be a farmer* was a certainty or Harold would never have entertained the madness of another child, another mouth to feed, and this runt of the litter had better goddamned well measure up.

Chuck wonders when Harold stopped imagining him in any positive light. Was it when he didn't grow quickly that first year? Was it because he didn't walk until he was fourteen months old, a story that has been shared as a joke, ridiculing Chuck? Was it when Chuck picked up a fork with his left and wouldn't use his right, no matter how many times his parents moved utensils from his left to his right, slapping his left hand?

"Stupid kid is left-handed," Harold said, his voice shocked and confused.

Or was it Chuck's blond curls that twist around his head, giving him the appearance of a cherub, while Harold's hair was poker straight and a mousy grey-brown, as was Penelope's.

"Where the hell did the blond curls come from?" Harold asked.

Did Harold ever love Chuck, even for one brief second?

Every word from Harold's mouth is an imperative, a command. *Stand up straight, hand me that fork, someone get this kid's hair cut,* each directive louder than the previous, Chuck wanting to cover his ears to block out the sound. Chuck used to imagine fishing at the river, Harold showing him how to put the minnow on the hook, impaling the leader line through the minnow's mouth, a small sacrifice for the joy of catching a fish, a sturgeon maybe.

"They put up a hell of a fight," Blake Patterson, an older boy from a few farms down, said once when Chuck came upon him while on one of his exploring hikes along the river. Chuck looks for unusual rocks and Indian arrowheads, filling his pockets with the treasure that Harold calls a useless waste of time. Blake was straining to land what he thought was a big northern pike.

"Grab the net," Blake shouted, breathless, leaning back and letting the pull on the end of his fishing rod support him.

Chuck had no idea what to do but waded out into the river, the water flowing right over the tops of his boots, and held the net below the surface of the water.

"Scoop him up," Blake yelled.

Chuck was a little afraid, never having fished before.

"Got him," Chuck said, lifting the net out of the water. The long-snouted fish wasn't done fighting and his continuous flopping startled Chuck; he dropped the net. Blake dropped his rod and grabbed the net from the water.

"This is no northern," Blake shouted. "This is a musky. My first musky. God, they're ugly," Blake said, lifting the net as high as he could. "Muskellunge. It means *ugly pike* in Ojibwa. Go figure. Talk about never being anything more than your name," and Blake laughed. "Where's your rod?"

"I don't have one," Chuck confessed.

"How can you grow up on the river and not have a fishing rod? It's practically the law."

Blake pushed his hands into big gloves, pulled a pair of needle-nose pliers out of his hip pocket, and, holding his knee against the fish, pulled the hook out of its mouth.

"Have to let this guy go. There aren't enough of them around to kill him. But hey, thanks for helping me land him. If I need a witness, I'll call you."

* * *

Chuck squats at the pail of warm water and iodine, the pail between the gutters where the cows stand tail to tail, a narrow walkway between them, wide enough to avoid being kicked. Cows never kick straight back; their legs go sideways in a lightning arc. Only horses can kick straight back. Chuck is painfully all too familiar.

The pail is behind the cow Chuck has to milk. He wiggles his fingers in the water and the water stains his fingers yellow-brown. A well-worn rag hangs off the pail. Chuck grabs the next tail and secures it with twine to the far back leg of the cow and then places the small three-legged stool beside the udder, repositioning the stool in the straw so it sits level, or nearly level. He eases himself down on the stool and carefully washes each teat, scrubbing off the dried manure and mud. The cow swings her head around as if to check him out. She looks like she is considering kicking him into the gutter, but most of the time she doesn't. Third cow from the end, Nadya, would just as soon kick you as look at you. She has a mean streak. No stool beside her udder. It's a balancing act to get the milk out while dodging her lightning-quick feet. Cows' forward kick gets him every time if he's not paying attention. Chuck is usually quick enough, but he's had his shins hammered a few times, making him cry it hurts so much. He's always careful around Nadya.

"You'll be a pot roast, you ugly brute," Harold says, pushing her tail straight up and over her back to pinch a nerve so she can't kick as easily. Harold's lips are pulled back and his teeth are jammed together.

"Hurry up and get her milked," Harold shouts, his face red from the strain. Chuck's hands move like magic, the milk streaming into the pail.

"There," Chuck says, jumping up from squatting and throwing his hands back like he's tied a calf at the rodeo. His foot catches the edge of the pail and sends the milk splashing in all directions.

"Oh, for the love of god," Harold wheezes out, dropping the cow's tail and whacking Chuck across the back of the head.

Just once Chuck would like to see Harold demonstrate one ounce of patience, would like to witness one act of kindness from Harold without an obligation or a complaint or an explanation. Just once he'd like to hear, *Well done, my boy.*

Your father had a hard time growing up, Chuck's mother said, like she was explaining why he doesn't like Brussels sprouts, her voice flat and unemotional, a monotone account of what she might consider his pet peeves. Chuck thinks about asking Harold.

"What happened?" Chuck might ask, and Harold would tell him, unload the burden of the horrors of his childhood, and then Harold would change, would become kind and patient, and they'd go fishing.

"Let that cow out," Harold shouts, pointing to Nadya. "Pay attention."

All the cows have names. Each year has a specific letter of the alphabet. So all the calves born that year have the same letter starting their name. Gran names the calves with Chuck's help. But Harold never uses their names, calling them any number of ugly things. *You bitch* is a common reference. *You goddamn stupid cow* is another. Never Lacey or Queenie or Maxine. They must have gone through the alphabet at least once because Gert is younger than Toots. Toots has been around forever, her long, spongy teats almost impossible to milk, her back no longer straight and flat, and her eyes look tired like she's earned a rest in the pasture, to wander and pull up grass where she so chooses, but she'll die in this stall, will most likely collapse where she stands, and Harold will tie a chain around her back legs and drag her out with the tractor and never once feel grateful for Toots' patience and tolerance and how she let Chuck's little hands learn to milk.

Gran knows the best names when she looks into the face of a newborn calf. She puts her hand under the calf's chin and then asks her what name she likes. Gran waits a second or two and then stands up, wiping her palms back and forth against each other. "Milady," Gran said, right after she named Melody the day before and Muffin the day before that.

The bull calves have no names. Harold kills them at birth, slits their throats as soon as their mothers have licked them off, and then drags the bodies to the bush for the wolves to eat.

"They're good for nothing," Harold claims.

Chuck doesn't want to think about it. He knows he has graduated from feeding calves to feeding cows to washing udders to milking cows, like packing a suitcase, and in time killing bull calves will be added. That's when he'll make a run for it, he tells himself.

Squeeze and strip, squeeze and strip, Chuck thinks, watching his hands work the teats. His hand cramps sometimes, but mostly it is an alternating rhythm, releasing one hand while squeezing the other. *Squeeze and strip,* he has heard those instructions about five hundred times too many. *Squeeze and strip, squeeze and strip,* while his father watches over him, ready to berate his small hands and weak wrists.

The cows milk better for Chuck than they do for Harold. They appreciate Chuck's gentle slowness, his taking time to let them know he is there and his deliberate movement that annoys the hell out of Harold. Their milk lets down immediately, a long full stream into the bright stainless steel pail, and the sound of the milk hitting the bottom of the pail is musical, a comforting sound, while bubbles gather on the milk's surface, creamy and thick.

Chuck finishes with Lacey. She stands perfectly still, her eyes closed, her mouth full of hay, like she has slipped into a deep trance while Chuck milks her.

"Okay," Chuck says, standing up from the stool and stretching out his legs. Lacey resumes eating, opens her eyes, and shifts her weight from one hind leg to the other. Chuck runs his hand down her back as he carries the half-full pail and dumps the milk into one of the four five-gallon milk cans that sit on a small wagon at one end of the barn.

When all the milking is done, Chuck pulls the wagon down the gentle slope to the milk house that stands in the shade of a large maple and a white spruce, trees that seem to be wrestling for the space, for top honour. The milk house fits completely into the trees' shadow no matter the time of day. Chuck is big enough only now at twelve, almost thirteen, to pour the milk into the cream separator on which is fitted a fine mesh filter. Chuck turns the separator by hand and as the contraption spins round and round, the lighter milk is skimmed off and pours out through a hose into a larger pail. The skimmed milk is fed to the hogs that are digging and fattening up in the pen furthest from the house.

The remaining cream is poured into three-gallon steel cream cans and set down in the corner of the milk house in a reservoir filled with cold water flowing in from the creek and flooding around the cans, almost completely submerging the cream cans before the water flows out the other end of the reservoir, keeping the cans cool and the cream fresh.

The cream is poured into one-quart jars as needed when neighbours come to buy cream. They can only come on Wednesday afternoons and Saturday mornings when Penelope is home from her job in the laundry at the Roddick Hospital. What cream doesn't sell or they can't use themselves goes to the pigs. The skim milk and leftover cream is mixed in with baked goods from the grocery store in town and vegetables scraps and turned into a disgusting mess of slop, and the pigs gobble it up, making happy rooting noises, their little stubs of tails wiggling back and forth.

* * *

"Don't be thinking you and that little witch down the road are taking your ponies out today," Harold says. "We're taking horns off."

Not horns, Chuck wants to wail, wants to throw his body down on the straw. *Not horns.* Cleaning out the chicken coop by hand, cutting tails off the piglets, or pulling their teeth. Anything but horns.

Chuck and Rebecca have plans to swim their ponies in the river. Rebecca will know when Chuck doesn't show up that Harold changed the plans without notice. Rebecca will toss hay down from the mow instead, or crush grain. She'll fill up the time with her own never-ending list of chores.

They take their ponies to the river sometimes, on hot days or days when they can sneak away undetected. Rebecca is afraid of the water, Chuck can feel it, but she never lets on. She faces the water and her face gets dark and angry. The colder the water, the angrier she looks. Daisy isn't keen on swimming but Prince leaps in like a crazy fool, and the strong current nearly sweeps Chuck away.

Rebecca shouts from the shore. "Do not let go of his reins," and Chuck holds on tight, more from fear of Rebecca than fear of the current.

Chuck tries not to whine to Rebecca, but sometimes he can't help it. She braces her back as if she's ready to carry him. He wonders if she ever cries, ever has had enough. Shouldn't he be the stronger one? Isn't it supposed to be that way? Maybe Harold is right about him; maybe he is a weakling.

After lunch Harold takes twenty minutes to sleep in the big chair by the fire. His head rolls on to his shoulder and he snores a deep resonating rumble that almost shakes the china in the cabinet in the dining room, the little bits of china Gran saves for special occasions, occasions that never happen. There's never a dinner with candles and cloth napkins or more than one fork sitting left of the plate or water glasses. None of that happens; every meal is the same: everyone collapsing at the table, grabbing a plate and cutlery, and not bothering with grace or waiting on anyone, stuffing his meal down his throat as if it could be the last meal on earth.

"Let's go," Harold shouts waking and leaping from his chair all in the same moment. "Chuck!" he hollers, tipping his mouth toward the ceiling.

Harold is in the shed gathering his tools, the big device looking like something out of a torture chamber, with long handles that scare the bejesus out of Chuck. The mere sight of the gougers, like a portable guillotine, makes Chuck's stomach pitch and turn.

"Get the calves locked in the corral," Harold shouts from the shed. "Grab this bag of lime."

Chuck wants to shout right back, *Which is it, Harold? Which job is first, because I know darn well if I do one, you'll shout about the other.* Chuck grabs the paper grocery bag about a third full with white dust, lime, to pack on the wound when the horn comes off, to stop the bleeding and prevent infection

"I told you to get those calves locked in," Harold says. "They'll figure out what we're up to and head to the front pasture. Hurry the hell up."

Chuck slides the locking board in place on the large swinging corral gate, closing the only exit from the corral. The heifer calves are milling around with wide suspicious eyes, their heads heavy with juvenile horns. They're over a year old, will take their place in the milk line when they've delivered their first calf at about two and a half years of age, replacements for the older cows that are ungraciously shipped for slaughter. In with the new, out with the old. The aggressive heifers use their horns against each other, but most of them carry their horns around like awkward crowns. Their horned heads won't fit in the stanchions in the barn, so the horns have to come off before they are turned out with the bull. Chuck asked his dad when he was little what would a dairy cow do in the wild; wouldn't she have her horns? What goddamn dairy cow lives in the wild, Harold answered, shaking his head as if Chuck were the stupidest kid on earth.

A couple of the heifers stop to wrestle, pressing their foreheads together to settle an earlier dispute, pushing into each other with every ounce of their bodies. Harold chases the first calf up the chute.

"Slam the head gate, slam the head gate," Harold yells, his voice panicked and crazed. "Stand bloody well back or she'll never put her head through. Back up."

Harold's voice bounces off the barn and slams with full force into the back of Chuck's head. The calf looks for an escape route but finds the space in the locking head gate too tempting, thinking once her head is in the squeeze chute, the rest of her body will follow to freedom.

"Slam it. Jesus, slam it," Harold yells again. Chuck hits the pin with his foot, and the heifer is trapped. "Gotcha, you bastard. I'll be glad when you're bigger," Harold says to Chuck.

I'll be glad when I'm gone, Chuck murmurs under his breath, not quite loud enough to be heard.

The calf digs her feet in and pulls, straining to free her head, her hind end falling under her. Harold slips the rope halter around the calf's ears and pulls it tight over her nose, winching her head down so she can't move more than a fraction of an inch. Harold pulls the gougers out of the pail of iodine and shakes off the excess iodine. Chuck shivers.

"Get your hand full of lime. Get ready," Harold shouts. "When the horn comes off, get in there and pack the lime on the wound as thick as you can. Keep packing it on until the bleeding is just about stopped. Don't mind the blood. It'll squirt you in the eye. No goddamned crying this time."

Chuck nods, not looking convinced, feeling his stomach heave. Harold slips the gougers over the horn and brings the handles together using all his weight. There is a horrible crunching sound; the calf opens her mouth, and her tongue hangs out while she bawls with the most horrific voice, snot pouring from her huge nostrils. The calf would have collapsed to her knees but her head is tied up tight.

Blood starts pumping in three or four streams aimed mostly at Chuck while he grabs a handful of lime and starts swiping at the calf, blood squirting into his eyes and nose, into his mouth had he not kept his lips pressed tightly together. He wants to shield his face with his right arm, but he doesn't dare. He can hear the *no-son-of-mine* chant in his head and wonders for a brief second what it would be like to be one of his older sisters, who never had to do any of this madness.

One morning to sleep in, that's all Chuck wants. To roll over when the sun finds his face. To reshape the pillow with a few punches and then slide back to sleep, over the edge into that place where colour and air don't exist, into early-morning dreams that are abstract and harmless, usually Chuck flying without a plane, using his arms and dipping and diving over hydro lines and telephone wires and around trees, flying beside Canada geese on their way somewhere, practising their precision maneuvers, Chuck tipping his hat to the goose in charge, never wanting to settle back down on earth. *Don't wake me, please,* Chuck begs to the gods of slumber.

Chuck can't remember ever having slept in past six, can't remember a single morning without chores. Not when he broke his arm or when he had chicken pox and a fever. Gran tried to block the door, but there was no negotiation; Chuck had to feed calves.

"It won't kill him," Harold said, shoving Gran out of the way while Penelope stood at the kitchen sink before leaving for work, having her usual breakfast: instant Maxwell House coffee and a cigarette. Penelope didn't react, didn't defend, didn't protest, leaned on her elbows on the kitchen counter and used her front tooth to get something out from under her thumbnail. Gran picked herself off the floor and asked Penelope if she had misplaced her mother instincts.

"Practise what you preach," Penelope said with the familiar sound of indifference.

Chuck went to the barn crying, but trying not to. He went to the barn every morning before school, before breakfast, before Christmas, before everything, pulling himself from bed like his blankets were thick tar clinging to his Superman pajamas, hanging on to his arms and legs, pulling at his ears and hair.

Geraldine and Frances got to sleep in, slept in past lunch before they moved to town. Harold pounded on their locked bedroom door until the screws in the hinges loosened, but the girls didn't let on they heard, even though no one could have slept through the din. They weren't afraid of Harold, and their blatant foolhardiness seemed like courage to Chuck. He couldn't imagine defying Harold with such ease, ignoring Harold's threats, not having to wait for someone to intervene and aim some good common sense at Harold's rage. The girls looked at Harold, their eyebrows up as if he'd startled them, and then returned to what they were doing, without even a hint of concern. All Chuck's defiance was under his breath, cowardly at best.

"Safety in numbers," Gran said, as if Chuck should have canvassed the neighbourhood for a brother. Any brother would have worked, but better someone older to take the brunt of Harold's fist, someone who would have grown taller and stronger than Harold and then could push Harold down and stand over him, threatening, daring, while Chuck rolled over in bed and went back to sleep.

* * *

I don't want to be a farmer, Chuck considers yelling at the top of his lungs, but instead he keeps packing on the lime until the bleeding is barely getting through, little streams of red spray that pump like someone is turning them on and off, on and off. Eleven more horns to go.

Lissie

Fourteen

ELISABETH OPENS HER EYES EVERY MORNING AND LOOKS UP. SHE can't help smiling at the puffy clouds she painted on her ceiling when she was nine, an attempt to make the room feel more like her room, like she belonged there, or the room belonged to her. She painted white swirls, thick marshmallow clouds, all over the ceiling, painted with brushes of every size while lying on a board between two stepladders, like Michelangelo.

Extraordinary, Charlotte said when Elisabeth finished the masterpiece. It's Charlotte's house: Charlotte Smythe, the woman playing the role of Elisabeth's mother, a tallish, thin, fair-haired white person. A woman with a name that can't easily be shortened. She's not a Char or a Lottie. She's Charlotte, and Charlotte is in charge.

Elisabeth wanted to shorten her own name to Beth, thought it would be a happier name, friendlier. She wrote *Beth* on her pages at school when she was six; fewer letters to figure out how to get the circles and sticks in the right places, fewer letters to write on her jacket and her lunch box and all things she must not share or misplace. Charlotte put an end to that. *Elisabeth is a proper name,* Charlotte said, drawing a straight line with a ruler through *Beth.*

Charlotte complained to the principal when a report card came home with a z in Elisabeth.

"Is it too much to ask your staff to spell a child's name correctly?"

The principal nodded, looking apologetic. "It's not a common spelling," the principal said.

"Precisely," Charlotte said, her voice never raised or lowered, but an even, soft monotone that left no room for discussion.

"And it's Smythe," Charlotte said, exaggerating the long vowel and the soft *th*. *Not Smith.* Charlotte instructed absolutely everyone involved with Elisabeth's education long before the first day of grade one. *Smythe,* Elisabeth rehearsed, over and over, to make sure she got it right, too

* * *

This morning Elisabeth watches the clouds on her ceiling from beneath the plump overstuffed comforter and thinks if she were to raise her arms and concentrate she might levitate and float up among the white wisps and swirls, airborne in a make-believe world. The stars would come into view as she floated, her arms outstretched, tumbling around in the constellations. Cassiopeia, Ursa Major, Orion's belt. Elisabeth regularly creeps through her bedroom window at night and stretches out on the garage roof. From there she can see the stars, keeping a list of those she is looking for and checking them off when she finds them. She also brings her sketch pad and records the stars on her paper, drawing her own constellations, giving them names and stories, a deep history with a happy ending. This star belongs to that star and together they belong to this group of stars, and so on and so on. Elisabeth isn't giving in to the tales that come attached to the constellations such as Andromeda, the daughter of Cassiopeia. Cassiopeia chained Andromeda to a rock so a sea monster could eat her and stop Andromeda's beauty from challenging Cassiopeia's beauty, Cassiopeia's extreme vanity causing such cruelty, thinking herself more beautiful than any other. Elisabeth changes those stories. In Elisabeth's story Cassiopeia let

Andromeda take the position of the brightest constellation in the northern sky, let her light shine brighter than her mother's.

Elisabeth likes the idea of floating around on her ceiling where no one will notice her when they come into her room looking for her. They will search under the bed and in the closet, they will tear back the bed linens exposing the bare mattress, they will pull the dresser away from the wall and look far into the back of the closet, but they will never think of looking up and she can hide there, suspended, watching a life that doesn't really include her anyway. She's not sure who *they* will be. No one has been in her room besides her mother and Mr. Domanski, but it could happen; some stranger might come looking, come asking for a child that fit her description.

Mr. Domanski from next door painted the walls and ceiling a muted blue while Charlotte watched from the doorway, a silent guard should any of the blue paint take flight and land on Charlotte's precious white walls.

Mr. Domanski is that kind of neighbour, helpful, never intrusive, eager to lend a hand, but never lurking and never using first names. He is very formal in a friendly way. *Good morning, Miss Smythe* and *How are you today, Miss Smythe*, with his eyes sparkling and his meaty cheeks rounding out his face when he smiles. He is always smiling and eager, as if today is the first day of something wonderful, as if he's always celebrating, but with a smile: no fanfare or loud outbursts from Mr. Domanski. Mr. Domanski is retired and has nothing but time on his hands, he says, so is willing to help Charlotte do almost anything. Except the roof. He won't get on the roof. Ladders make him nervous, and he shakes his head as if there's no explaining some things. *If you really need me to I suppose I could*, but then he winces.

"White would be much nicer," Charlotte said, showing Elisabeth five chips of paint that were all white: frost line white, snow white, cloud nine white, Oxford white, moon light. They all looked the same to Elisabeth: white. It was the only time Elisabeth held her ground.

"I need blue," Elisabeth said, wanting a bold and vibrant blue, cerulean or cyan.

"Blue is so cold," Charlotte said and shivered in a mocking way, but finally settled on azure: soft, quiet, without much voice at all. At least it has some colour, Elisabeth tells herself, but it is only a hint away from white, a whisper.

Charlotte's entire house is white. White walls, white furniture, white frames, white lamps, white towels. Elisabeth used an orange crayon to colour on the wall on the inside of the front hall closet. She coloured behind the edge of the big abstract painting that hangs over the couch, behind the clawfoot tub when she could fit under the edge of it and reach her tiny arm up on the wall; there she drew two round orange circles with stick legs and arms and very upright hair. Despite the walls being painted a fresh white every two or three years, the orange remains, like a signature: Elisabeth was here.

Charlotte's home is small but proper in the quiet part of town, a section that Roddick has cordoned off: no riff-raff allowed, no rule-breakers, no one who makes a fuss or publicly complains on any matter, no complaining about the frequency of the snowplow or how noisy garbage pick-up is or whether Mrs. Langille's garbage cans were left on their sides rather than upright, no complaints about the weather or taxes or the size of the melons at the Shop-Easy. Not a word of it.

Almost every driveway has two cars, has lovely manicured lawns that seem to say *nothing in our lives is out of order.* The residents belong to groups that require an invitation, a secret cloistered society that braces against change and the immigration of new ideas.

Charlotte's house blends in, and the differences are subtle, hidden under the invisible cloak of silence that Charlotte wears like a shroud. There are no grandparents, no aunts or uncles, no flock of cousins, no doors banging as children run in and out, no bikes abandoned in the driveway, no shoes scattered at the back door, no water-filled balloons launched like grenades. It seems that Charlotte fell from the sky, settling down like dust or snow, without making a sound, and no one can remember when she wasn't here and in her arms she held a baby with darker than dark eyes and skin a colour that has no name: not exactly red or brown and most definitely not white. Neighbours are too polite to inquire, too afraid to break Charlotte's silence in case they hear something that won't fit into their homogenous recipe for living.

"Aren't you lovely," Mrs. Campbell said at the drugstore, in the aisle where the greeting cards were stacked. Mrs. Campbell puckered her face and put her hands out around Elisabeth's head without touching Elisabeth, as if something about the child might be contagious. Mrs. Campbell looked at the insulin in Charlotte's hand, the tiny vials. "They are inclined to be diabetics," Mrs. Campbell said, as if she was confirming the one big secret of the universe.

"They?" Charlotte asked.

"Indians," Mrs. Campbell whispered, looking over her shoulder and shielding her mouth with her hand.

"Elisabeth isn't a diabetic," Charlotte said with no change in the tone of her voice.

"No?" Mrs. Campbell said, looking confused and wishing she hadn't said anything at all, even if she was wanting to be nice, to make conversation.

"No. Elisabeth has diabetes. There's a big difference," and then Charlotte guided Elisabeth ahead of her. "Always nice to see you, Joan," she said, but her voice didn't sound grateful, didn't sound one bit glad.

"What's the difference between diabetes and diabetic?" Elisabeth asked.

"Everything. Never mind about that," Charlotte said.

That was the end of the discussion. Did Elisabeth come with diabetes? she wondered. Was she born with it? Is that why someone gave her away, because she was too imperfect, too flawed from the get-go to be bothered with?

"You've done a generous thing, Charlotte," the ladies whispered at church with their eyes-half-closed smiles. "Opening your home to one of them."

Charlotte said nothing. She pulled Elisabeth into another seat, but children recognize when they don't fit. They can tell by the way others breathe in and out, by the shadows in their eyes, by the half looks, nothing full on. Children know. And they find each other, they find other children who know. Eventually.

* * *

Elisabeth's teeth are white and straight like Charlotte's, as though they shared the same braces, the same mould to make them look like they belong to each other. Elisabeth's hair is dark and coarse and twists into a French braid that Charlotte can do with her long thin fingers, supple like the rest of her. Elisabeth is small and compact. Charlotte's hair is blonde, a faded yellow. Elisabeth used to put her fingers in it when she was little, and it felt like feathers, soft and thin and limp.

Elisabeth smiles like Charlotte, when Elisabeth smiles. She smiles in a reflex to Charlotte's worried face. Charlotte looks closely at Elisabeth, like she's trying to recognize her, pick her out in a crowd, a look that says she has a secret she's trying to keep but keeping it is making her uneasy.

Charlotte's voice is mostly a purr, a soft rumble that has no sharp edges, no shouts or unexpected outbursts; everything is controlled. Elisabeth's voice doesn't sound anything like Charlotte's, but it still sounds foreign in her head, a sound she doesn't recognize as though its rhythm and cadence are adopted. Adopted. Like Elisabeth.

Elisabeth can't remember when Charlotte told her she was adopted. It was obvious. Elisabeth must have always known; her mother might have whispered it over and over with her lips pressed close to Elisabeth's ear. *I'm not really your mother,* she might have said. *My body never had to swell to hold your tiny folded body. I never had to endure the pain of getting you out. I am merely pretending to be your mother.* Those were the words Elisabeth heard in her head over and over and over.

Adopted may have been Elisabeth's first word. Not *dada* or some version of baby chatter, but *adopted.* The one word, waiting to find its way into a sentence. I am adopted. Someone gave me away, handed me over saying *I don't want this child. I don't want her. I want something else, something different. You take her.*

Elisabeth wonders if there is a sales room somewhere with a man sitting behind a desk in a suit with shiny trousers, the jacket on the back of the chair, with sweat circles under his arms, his sleeves rolled up. Does he thumb through a catalogue, scratching his head occasionally, as if trying to find a match gives him a headache?

Yes, well, we have a blond-haired, blue-eyed boy from good football-playing stock. Sure to be a handsome lad. Oh wait, wait, the man says, reading further, his finger guiding his eye. *He has colic and cries a great deal. No one wants that, especially someone like you, without a husband, I mean,* looking apologetic with a bit too much sympathy and his head tips to the side pretending he really cares when he doesn't. He keeps thumbing the catalogue pages, shaking his head intermittently and clicking his tongue on the back of his dentures.

Wait a minute. We might have a match here. A baby girl. Native blood, but she's lighter than most. Doesn't say why here. She'll be as silent as you. Won't ask a lot of questions.

Charlotte will sign some papers and rise from her chair and shake the man's hand. He will press a buzzer and a door will open and someone will carry an infant into the room. Charlotte is anxious, not sure at all, suddenly wondering why she thinks she can be a mother to anyone, her shoulders and fingers stiff, a cold sweat forming on her lower back, but she opens her arms and takes something wrapped up tight. That something is Elisabeth.

Next, the salesman shouts and Charlotte is ushered quickly from the room. *Good luck to you, Mrs. Smythe. You understand there are no returns, no exchanges. All adoptions are final.* Charlotte is escorted out. *Let me get the door,* with an arm firmly on Charlotte's back so she has no time to reconsider, to question the soundness of the decision to raise someone else's child, some stranger, some alien. Then the salesman slams his oversized red stamp down on the paper Charlotte has signed. *File Closed.*

Elisabeth can see the whole scene very clearly in her mind.

Charlotte brought Elisabeth home. *You may call me Mother,* she would have said. And then the husband put his arms out against the wall, bracing himself from the horror of this strange child, a child whose skin is different, whose voice has no sound yet but when it does won't match his own. So he packs his bags and slips away in the quiet of the night and leaves no note of explanation, no note of apology. He is gone and one suit jacket with a striped navy tie around the hanger hangs in the back of Charlotte's closet like a footprint left in the sand. He was here. But now he's not.

Charlotte keeps the white house in perfect order. There are no newspapers scattered, abandoned beside the empty coffee mug. No knife with remnants of jam and peanut butter sits in the sink. No fingerprints on the bathroom mirror. No socks under the sofa.

The piano stands in the corner of the drawing room; the room has a window on each side of the piano.

"No one draws in here," Elisabeth says with her crayons and sketch paper under her arm.

"It really means a room to withdraw to, a formal reception room, if you will," Charlotte says. "You may colour at your desk."

On the piano are photos, all with white frames of various sizes, photos where Elisabeth never looks at the camera, looks down and away instead. A small photo of Charlotte with a man is behind all the other photos, almost hidden, with Charlotte standing beneath his arm as one might stand with a stranger, someone she doesn't really know. Out front, larger than any of the other photos, is Elisabeth in a swing, suspended while Charlotte holds the chain, restraining, not letting Elisabeth fly. Who took this photo, Elisabeth wonders. Who put his hand up and said, *Say cheese?*

Elisabeth rolls over and buries her face in her pillow. The first day of high school is tomorrow. She shakes her head and holds her stomach as if it might leap right out of her body and run down the street away from her. She might as well fall down Alice's rabbit hole, her favourite book, except there's no solution, no sip of this or bite of that. If you don't know where you are, can't recognize any part of the landscape, then how on earth do you find your way home?

I don't want to go, I don't want to go, Elisabeth chants in her head, as if she can change the order of the universe. She tried it when she wanted to be taller, but it didn't work. Maybe this time it will. *I don't want to go to high school,* being more specific.

Maybe when Charlotte comes to her bedroom in the morning to wake her, Elisabeth can say something, can make some argument instead of her usual morning silence. Her clothes will be laid out like a carefully mapped plan. Elisabeth won't plead or beg, won't add a name like Mom or Mother or Mommy.

I won't be going to school. It would be ridiculous to walk into a classroom and pretend to be one of the students. Surely you understand.

Charlotte might acknowledge this fact with a nod and open the labelled dresser drawers that say *undergarments, slacks, socks, night clothes,* and so on, and place the clothes neatly back inside. But then she might turn to Elisabeth and say, *Now what?* And what will Elisabeth's answer be? Will she get a job at the variety store, will she clean rooms at the Midtown Motel?

It's not that she's afraid of school, afraid of having no friends. She's used to that, used to standing off to the edge of the play-ground, reading or sketching in her art book, sketching trees with-out leaves, picnic tables without baskets, vases without flowers. It's one thing to know on the inside that she doesn't belong, that she can't compare her chin or the position of her front teeth that protrude slightly as though she might have sucked her thumb. Charlotte would have put a stop to that, the disgusting habit of putting thumb or fingers or the end of pencils in one's mouth. Elisabeth can't compare the twist of her hair at her left temple or her uneven shoulders. She knows the colour of her skin and hair is so far removed from the white-blonde of her mother's hair and her blue eyes, but how does she explain this to strangers, have answers for teachers? *Whose child are you, who are your people?* To make Elisabeth's reason for being here perfectly clear, as if Elisabeth is obligated to explain.

Elisabeth wiggles deeper under her blankets, pulling the sheet over her head. She doesn't ask questions, not now. She might have when she was little, but the answers were vague and made Charlotte uneasy. Charlotte started every answer with, *Well, I don't really know.* Sometimes her voice trails off as if she has forgotten the question, but usually Charlotte pats Elisabeth's hand. *Use your napkin, dear,* she says, as if she knows Elisabeth is tempted to go wild and drag her face along her sleeve and Elisabeth doesn't really need an answer.

Maybe Elisabeth should rehearse the things she does know, compile them into a letter of introduction, a biography she can hand to anyone she meets who needs to know the facts. She will start at the beginning.

Elisabeth is a daughter, of sorts. She came without a name, naked, she imagines, wrapped in a tattered blanket and left at the front door of Mrs. Smythe's very white house. Mrs. Smythe called her Elisabeth, a name with some genetic distance from her own, a great-great-grandmother, a Red River Settler. Elisabeth is a stately name; Charlotte explains the connection as though the name itself will somehow hoist this child's genetics, connect them to Charlotte's by a sort of grafting.

Elisabeth Smythe. My name is Elisabeth Smythe. My name could be Hazel or Gail or Daphne, but I use Elisabeth because my mother says so.

Age fourteen. Born January 31, 1955. *Close enough.*

We'll celebrate your birthday on the day I brought you home, Charlotte says.

Brought me home from where? Elisabeth rehearses asking. She has a list of questions she keeps in a journal, wrapped in plastic and tucked under the rocks at the back of Charlotte's lawn, where the lawn falls away to a small narrow trench that keeps the lawn well drained. There are pages of questions and most of them sound the same.

Where did you find me? Who is my mother? What is her name? Will I bump into my mother on the street when I am twenty-three and will she know me? What does her voice sound like? Was she afraid to give me away? Was she relieved? Did she exhale as though released from an invisible prison? Is she right-handed? What is her blood type? Does she have diabetes? Does she look like E. Pauline Johnson? Does she talk in rhyme? Does she recite continuously the same lines from Pauline Johnson's poetry? *And up on the hills against the sky, / A fir tree rocking its lullaby, / Swings, swings, / Its emerald wings, / Swelling the song that my paddle sings.*

Elisabeth makes a new entry almost every week, digging up the book wrapped in plastic and then replacing it, moving it over several feet and back again the next time.

Elisabeth started recording questions when a magician came to the school to perform and chose Elisabeth to be his assistant.

"Tell the audience who you are," Malachi the Magician said. Elisabeth couldn't think of a single word to say.

"Your name," the magician said. "You know your name, don't you?"

"Elisabeth," she said. "With an *s*," she added quickly, in case anyone mistakes her for an Elizabeth.

"Let's give EliSSSSSSabeth a big hand," Malachi said, and everyone laughed. Everyone except Elisabeth.

She could have the list printed and bound with a leather cover to look like a legal document, something passed in the House of Commons.

Elisabeth Smythe. Five feet, one and a half inches. Eighty-six pounds.

235 Williams Avenue. The number 235 is easy to remember. Two plus three is five.

Size-five shoes.

Elisabeth Smythe. Plays the piano, but not very well. Sister Margaret will confirm if asked.

Elisabeth Smythe draws, loves to draw. Here is the proof, and Elisabeth will raise two of her favourite sketches: *Elm Tree by Moonlight* and *Frozen Swing*, marked Exhibit A and Exhibit B.

Elisabeth Smythe. Lost her front teeth when she fell down the patio steps. Had to bleed on the patio, not in the white house. She was going to lose her teeth anyway. They were already loose. *There, there. No harm done. No need to fuss.*

* * *

How do you go to high school when you have no idea of who you are? What if Elisabeth is so invisible that she is trampled in the halls and no one even notices her lifeless body as they step over her, around her, on her? Elisabeth accepts being invisible. It took her no more than four years of elementary school at Sixth Street Elementary to understand. Once she accepted that no one wanted to peel back the costume of her existence, she didn't have to muster any courage to get out of bed in the morning. There's a freedom that comes with being invisible, when you stop expecting more, when you know you are a secret too risky even to whisper about. Your head drops, your shoulders cave in slightly. You don't need to brace yourself; you don't need to lean into life, because everyone steps around you as if you were never here, leaving lots of space to slip through unnoticed.

High school is a whole new ball game. Standing in the light is far more terrifying than staying where you are. Elisabeth would beg if she thought it would have any effect on Charlotte. She could use the diabetes card, could fall down on the floor too weak to move, her eyesight compromised by low blood sugar, her muscles unwilling to do her bidding, her brain confounded, no speech to explain. But that would be crying wolf. Bad karma. Elisabeth has enough nights when she wakens from sleep, sweating profusely, her hands trembling, her body too weak to cry out. There is juice on her bedside table, but sometimes it is too late and she can feel herself sliding down a narrow tube into darkness, and when she wakes and finds her mother standing over her, wiping honey on her gums and tongue, Elisabeth cries.

You're all right now, Charlotte says. *Never mind the tears. Eat this*, and pushes three crackers thick with peanut butter at Elisabeth.

So no, she mustn't pretend her blood sugar has gone too low, because even the thought of pretending makes her wince. She lets her sugars run a little high, keeps a few candies hidden in the toes of her shoes just in case, so she won't have to bother anyone.

If only her mother would look at her, register her fear, give her a pep talk filled with encouraging euphemisms. But Elisabeth has practised her empty face for too long, has perfected it so no one, including Charlotte, has any clue of the longing and loneliness and fear that lie behind her dark-brown eyes that seem more black than brown, that used to hide behind her thick bangs until Charlotte insisted her bangs grow out and braided Elisabeth's thick black hair off her face.

There is no way out. She must go to high school, and most certainly she will die before day three or day four so it won't be long, won't be a drawn-out torture. She will die quickly, will hold her breath until she is quite blue, the blue she wanted in her bedroom, and then she will let it all out as she collapses on the floor in a heap and everyone will say, *Who is she that has died?* And no one will know the answer.

Fifteen

"YOU'RE UP," CHARLOTTE SAYS, COMING INTO ELISABETH'S ROOM after three brisk taps on the door. "You'll look your best today. Set the standard for yourself. Let your teachers know you mean to be the best student," all the words running together in a statement more than a request, with voice that says *get to it*.

Charlotte surveys Elisabeth's appearance, then runs her fingers along the labels on the dresser drawers, checking to be sure each drawer is pushed in tight, lines the hangers up in the closet, then turns to face Elisabeth.

"Your hair. I'll do it. Those blankets need to be tight," and then she turns to walk from the room. "Your breakfast is laid out," she says, stopping to put her fingers on the blue paint like it still isn't a good fit.

Elisabeth looks at her bed, the pillows fluffed, the sheet pulled back over the edge of the comforter, crisp white sheets that are washed every three days and pressed flat with the steam iron as though to sterilize them, wash every germ that has crawled from Elisabeth's body into the threads to hide there, to cling to the weave. Elisabeth sometimes considers tearing the sheets from her bed and dragging them through the garden and the back lawn, jumping on them and crushing them into the grass and then placing the sheets back on the bed, imagining Charlotte's horror.

Three quick taps again on Elisabeth's door and Charlotte's face appears.

"You're up."

Elisabeth looks at the floor and breathes deeply, wondering how many times this repetitive cycle will happen today. She sometimes bets with herself. It's getting to be a minimum of twice each morning, Charlotte coming in and going out and coming in again. *Don't make eye contact*, Elisabeth thinks.

"Your breakfast is ready. Your hair? It's important to set a good first impression. First impressions are important, you know. Your bed must be straight," and she pulls the comforter up tight and smoothes it with her hand. "Better. Your breakfast is ready."

Charlotte stops and frowns. She seems anxious and confused, hurried. "Breakfast is ready," and she shakes her head back and forth. "Your hair. I'll drive you to school, but just today. You should walk."

"No, thank you. I want to walk today."

"Yes, you should walk. I'm not driving you to school today. It's not far. You should walk."

Elisabeth sits at the dining room table, a crisp white napkin next to her plate. On her plate are a peeled and sliced orange, a piece of dry toast, a hard-boiled egg, and a glass of milk. Elisabeth eats alone while Charlotte reorganizes the cutlery drawer, lining the forks up and fitting the spoons one inside the other. Elisabeth has watched Charlotte enough to know the precise details of Charlotte's morning manoeuvres in the kitchen, turning the handles of all the mugs to face slightly right, checking the order of the spices on the rack over the stove. Elisabeth switched marjoram and mustard once to see what would happen, but it put Charlotte in such a state Elisabeth never did it again, though she often thought of it. Paprika and parsley. Turmeric and thyme.

Charlotte likes symmetry, but only to a point. A cluster of small baskets sits on top of the cabinets to the left of the sink, three baskets of varying sizes. They sit on their sides with nothing in them but potential space, their broad weave in a golden yellow, tinted slightly green, the only colour in the room.

Elisabeth's bag is sitting at the back door, leather with a long shoulder strap, her name engraved on a small brass plate on the inside of the flap, the bag an exact though smaller replica of Charlotte's lawyer bag that used to sit by the door ready, ready to go to the office, to write wills and powers of attorney and legal agreements, when Charlotte left the house. In Elisabeth's bag are freshly sharpened pencils, two erasers, a small binder with loose-leaf paper and dividers, the names of one subject on each divider, pencil crayons sharpened to exact points and tucked inside a small cloth bag with Elisabeth's name embroidered on it, a packet of tissues, and lunch money in a secret compartment that Charlotte rehearses with Elisabeth.

"Never remove the money in front of anyone and don't count it out. Decide what you'll have and get the coins out ahead of time. White milk, not chocolate. Soup or chili. No hot dogs. Disgusting things."

Elisabeth is obligated to practise her piano for thirty minutes before school. Every day. Monday to Friday, even in the summer. She starts with the scales. F major always gives her grief with the B flat and the change in fingering. Elisabeth winces when she makes a mistake, knowing Charlotte is listening from somewhere in the house, probably making an entry in a logbook. September 4. F major scale. Under the heading *Mistakes*.

Once when Charlotte was out in the yard, Elisabeth pounded the keys with her fists and Charlotte rushed in all breathless and flushed in the face.

"What on earth?" she said, her hands on her head as if her hair were going to burst into flames.

It was the only time she saw Charlotte lose her cool, come undone a little as if it were incomprehensible that such a racket could be coming from inside her house. Elisabeth had to practise an extra forty-five minutes that time to make up for the outburst, and fifteen of those minutes were spent on C major formula pattern scale with the right and left hand going in different directions, away and toward each other, requiring Elisabeth's total concentration.

When Elisabeth finishes, she tucks her books into the piano bench, the edges all neatly in line, tapped lightly to make sure the edges of the pages are perfectly straight. She calls up the stairs to Charlotte. "I'm on my way," trying to find the perfect balance between speaking normally and being heard and not venturing anywhere near shouting.

"Where are you going? Church? Today is Sunday?" Charlotte drops a stack of freshly ironed pillowcases, one hand smoothing her hair while the other smoothes the front of her sweater.

Church used to be an Easter thing with a fresh bonnet and white gloves and a crisp dress and sometimes a small lacy basket with flowers in it. Church used to be a Christmas thing, candles and carols and animated smiles as if being a Christian were a lot of fun. Church was Thanksgiving and holidays, but lately church is becoming a regular thing where Charlotte squeezes her fists and, with closed eyes and pursed lips, seems to be praying for something, or apologizing or saying something about regret. Elisabeth isn't sure which, but there is an urgency that grows as Charlotte's memory shrinks. Charlotte's usual poker face and gracious smile that never encourage conversation have been replaced by a bewildered face, a confused face. Women in church stare at Charlotte, not face on, but out of the corners of their eyes, glancing quickly to assess Charlotte's appearance. Reverend McFayden holds Charlotte's hand a little longer at the doorway after the service, and Charlotte leaves her hand in his as though it is her one resting place, as though she is silently confessing all the things that worry her in that simple holding of her hand.

* * *

Elisabeth waits, doesn't respond, giving Charlotte time to retrace her steps in memory, which seems to be taking longer and longer. It grows harder for Elisabeth not to jump in and remind Charlotte that she already said something twelve times, like a film loop that never stops. Elisabeth is tempted to finish Charlotte's sentences, to find the words that seem out of Charlotte's reach, but Elisabeth doesn't dare.

"School. You're going to school," Charlotte says, picking up the pillowcases. "It's not Sunday," she says, disappearing into the bathroom and shutting the door firmly.

Elisabeth imagines Charlotte standing in front of the mirror berating her image for being so flawed, for aging, for any number of things, but mostly for not being perfect. Elisabeth shakes her head and is on her way to school, her stomach flipping and flopping, her hands shaking. She feels like she might vomit right on the sidewalk, throw up her well-chewed orange and toast and leave it there as evidence that she is afraid.

She wishes Charlotte would rush out of the house this minute and tell her she doesn't have to go, that education can be found in many places besides the halls and classrooms of institutions, that the best education of all is life itself and why don't the two of them go on an adventure and see what they might discover, visiting historic museums and ancient ruins and finding the secrets of failed societies. Instead, Elisabeth examines her shiny brown penny loafers and yellow knee-high socks and avoids every single crack in the sidewalk all the way to school. She is wearing a blue tartan kilt and a bright yellow sweater, short sleeves with a band that climbs up her neck, her black hair pulled back tight and smooth and locked into a French braid, the ends of her hair tucked inside and behind the braid. Her fingernails are neatly manicured.

It's an eight-block walk to Roddick Central High School, a name that implies there might be another school at the edge of town, less central, but there's not. All the outlying farm communities feed their students into this high school, a sea of eleven hundred strange faces, most of whom will meet for the first time, will not have already worked out a pecking order while in elementary school, and the inevitable wrestling for top-dog position will ensue and Elisabeth won't have the shrubs at the side of Sixth Street Elementary playground in which to disappear.

Elisabeth breathes deeply and her pace slows. What would be the harm in dropping her bag and making a run for it, hitchhiking out of town? She has seen young people standing at the side of the road with their thumbs out, holding a sign that says *Kenora* or *Dryden*. She remembers one sign that said *Anywhere but here.*

"Never pick up a hitchhiker," Charlotte warned Elisabeth on one of their drives out of town.

Elisabeth considered reminding Charlotte that she doesn't drive, is only eight, but instead Elisabeth added the statement to the long list of things she should never do: never blow your nose in public; never leave home without money in your shoe, *mad money* Charlotte calls it; never wear the same underwear more than one day and sometimes less; never hang your private laundry, *underthings* Charlotte whispers, on the clothesline unless surrounded on either side by sheets or towels; never walk with your toes pointing in, an obvious sign of stupidity that has nothing to do with badly formed knees; never ever burp, not even in the privacy of your own room.

Elisabeth sits at the bottom of the lawn from time to time, rehearsing the many sounds she can make with a burp. *Deep* is her best belching word and has some definite resonance to it. Mr. Domanski heard her, once or twice, but never let on, observing the neighbourhood code of conduct. He smiles at Elisabeth, as if it is perfectly normal for someone to be sitting at the bottom of the lawn burping.

Elisabeth likes Mr. Domanski, asked him once if he would be her friend. *Absolutely,* he said, eagerly, as if he could use a friend, too.

* * *

Elisabeth recites in her head as she walks to school, the directions to her locker and homeroom. Up the cement steps to the main door, the big glass door that requires two hands to open, with a leaning back and pulling. Then down the stairs alongside the huge mural of the Roddick Central High Bears, a huge black bear with mouth open and gruesome teeth. Turn left instead of going into the gym. The gym is very large, with a divider that splits the space into two gymnasiums, so two games of volleyball can happen at once. A big stage is at one end with heavy purple drapes edged in gold, drapes that are faded and dust filled. Elisabeth had come many times with her mother to the final concert of the music festival and watched children climb the steps to perform for thunderous applause. Some played the piano; others sang; there were choirs and the high school concert band with no other competition, the one band for over a hundred miles east or west. Some played flutes and there were string quartets.

"You will do that one day," Charlotte said, leaning in close to Elisabeth's ear, but her voice was forceful and made Elisabeth jump. Elisabeth almost laughed. *Who are you kidding?* she wanted to say, but decided Charlotte's illusions didn't really hurt anyone. Elisabeth was fairly certain her musical skill was modest at best, judging from Sister Margaret's constant tongue-clicking and dramatic exhaling and a suggestion every now and then that Elisabeth take up needlework instead of playing the piano to keep her hands busy.

"Tempo, tempo," Sister Margaret says, drumming her small pointer stick on the edge of the piano. Elisabeth wonders if the nun ever thinks of beating Elisabeth with the stick and then would have to recite a few Hail Marys to keep her from going to hell. *Oh never mind,* Sister Margaret usually finishes with, or *What's the point* or *Lord have Mercy:* any number of indicators that she is not in awe of Elisabeth's raw talent.

Elisabeth keeps walking. Head down, don't make eye contact. Follow the hall until it opens on to a stairwell. Climb one flight and go right, through the carpeted hallways where the business classes are, as though this area is already noisy enough with the click-clack-ing of the typewriters, so let's keep the sounds of shoes to a dull muffled thud. Then through a set of doors that are kept closed in the event of fire, so that only those students on one side of the door will be consumed by fire, luck of the draw. First classroom on the right. 214. Mr. Quesnel.

All future grade nines were given the facts before coming to high school: pilot project this year, homerooms diluted with representa-tion from every grade; no pure grade nines to hide from the seniors, no safety in numbers; twenty-eight students in each homeroom, maximum of eight grade nines; a surplus this year, a bumper crop of potential juvenile delinquents. Charlotte added that last part.

Elisabeth is at the doorway of Room 214. Early. Too early. Looks like a ridiculous keener. She hesitates, wanting to check her schedule one more time to be certain she has the right room though she recited it and wrote the number down twenty-four times. Only four students are sitting in desks, scattered randomly, a safe distance between them to avoid contagions, to appear invisible, inconspicuous, part of a covert operation, looking in their books as if something is written there, all grade nines undoubtedly: who else would be early?

"Come on in," Mr. Quesnel says, his voice cheerful, planned cheerfulness, deliberate cheerfulness. He's the French teacher. He doesn't sound French. He doesn't look French. Elisabeth isn't exactly sure how a French teacher should look. A beret on his head and a baguette under his arm would do the trick, and Elisabeth smiles, on the inside.

"I'd guess your name," Mr. Quesnel says, "but I have thirty-two names on my list. I'm guessing you're not Joseph Pope or Colin Holmes," and he examines his papers.

Elisabeth laughs, a little, like a burp, a tiny eruption. For a second she imagines making up a name and a whole secret identity; she could be an exchange student from South America. *No speak English*, she could say.

"Elisabeth. Elisabeth Smythe. Grade nine," Elisabeth says.

"Here you are," and he makes an exaggerated checkmark on his class list. "Take a seat. You've got your pick," and he swings his arm in a grand gesture over the classroom to wave her in.

Elisabeth stands frozen, surveying the room, looking for an emergency exit.

"Sit here," says a girl in the far row by the windows, third desk from the front, and she taps the back of the chair in front of her. Her hair is a myriad of brown and gold, pulled back in a very loose long braid. Her clothes are baggy and sloppy, earthy looking, comfortable. She sticks out her hand.

"Rebecca. I'm Rebecca, your new best friend."

"Elisabeth."

"I know. We were in the same group on Grade Eight Day." Rebecca puts a look of mock indignation on her face. "You don't remember me? How can you not remember me? I was the Silent Wonder."

"No, sorry."

"Well, never mind, but sit here, Elisabeth. Elisabeth," Rebecca says again. "Seems a bit too formal. Liz. Beth."

"There's an *s* in Elisabeth."

"Then Lissie. Yes. That's even better. Lissie. We'll exaggerate the *s* sound. Lissie. Perfect."

"My mother will be thrilled."

"She'll get over it, Lissie. Now show me your schedule so we can figure out what classes we have together."

Elisabeth digs in her bag and looks for a minute at Rebecca, looks at her with a half smile on her face.

"What is it?" Rebecca asks.

"I was so scared this morning. I thought I'd throw up on the walk to school."

"So was I. So was everybody, if they are honest."

"Thank you," Elisabeth says. "Thank you, Rebecca." Elisabeth hesitates for a moment. "Does anyone call you Becky?"

Rebecca shakes her head. "We have a cow named Becky. She's not all that pleasant. No one uses a nickname for me. Not anymore."

"Me either," Elisabeth says.

"You'll meet Chuck at lunch. We all have the same lunch. Lissie, Chuck, and Rebecca. The Great Disenfranchised," Rebecca says.

"What does that mean?"

"I have no idea, but it sounds good," and Rebecca laughs again.

The two girls put their schedules together and discover they have most classes together except Elisabeth has art and Rebecca has physical education. Everything else is the same.

"Chuck has English and math with us, and geography. But I think that's it. He's doing some shop classes to keep his father quiet."

Mr. Quesnel calls the class to order as the last of the students wander in, the older ones trying to look peeved, bored. Mr. Quesnel tells everyone how the homeroom thing works: come in for attendance and questions and problems and start-your-day-off-on-the-right-foot sort of thing. A few stragglers, lost grade nine kids, come in after the bell buzzes, a deafening noise that makes a person feel like she's been electrocuted.

"Losers," some of the seniors mutter, sitting in their desks, the boys sprawled, legs in the aisles, boredom on their faces, trying to feel superior and look like it.

"Stand for the national anthem," Mr. Quesnel is saying. "And sing along."

Joseph Pope looks like he's been in high school for fifteen years; he has a full beard, he seems about twelve feet tall, and his lumberjack-sized body doesn't even fit in a desk. He refuses to stand for the anthem and Mr. Quesnel looks like he chooses not to battle it out with Joseph and lose, not on the first day of school.

Rebecca takes Mr. Quesnel at his word and sings "O Canada" at the top of her lungs. Rebecca's voice is crystal-clear and Elisabeth can't help humming along a little. Elisabeth gets the giggles halfway through, and Rebecca gives her a poke in the side.

"Pre-emptive strike," Rebecca says when she sits down, whispering to the back of Lissie's head. "Let them all think I'm crazy and then they leave me alone. Works like a charm."

"Something to say, Miss Archer?" Mr. Quesnel says.

"*Je ne parle pas anglais, Monsieur Quesnel.*"

"We'll see about that," Mr. Quesnel says, a smile on his face.

Mr. Quesnel is one of those teachers, one who goes beyond, who cares. Rebecca recognized that at their first meeting on Grade Eight Day.

"Don't be afraid of high school," Mr. Quesnel said. "Jump right in. Be part of your high school community." And he meant it, no platitudes. It was Mr. Quesnel who made Rebecca dare to imagine.

A voice crackles out over the loudspeaker, introduces himself as Mr. Binder, the principal. He couldn't have chosen a worse name if he tried. His voice sounds more like Mr. You'll-Get-The-Strap-If-You-Misbehave.

"Let's remember our dress code, girls, and no romance in the halls; keep your hands to yourself and no going to your locker between classes." He announces that Freshie Day is on Friday and that seniors are to keep their abuse to a minimum. No permanent markers. No duct tape. No locking grade nine bodies inside lockers. No damaging personal property. Joseph huffs loudly.

Elisabeth wants to take notes, barely resists, wanting desperately to get the rules right.

Rebecca raises her hand after Mr. Binder has finished his list of threats and welcome.

"Yes, Rebecca," Mr. Quesnel says, his head tipped to the side.

"Wouldn't it be better to start the first day of school off with the kinds of things you should do to get it right, rather than a long list of what you shouldn't do that will get you an all-expense-paid trip to study hall with the very friendly Mrs. Albert?"

"Examples?"

"Oh, I don't know. How about use your sunniest disposition. Skip in the halls rather than trudge. Join every club you can. Make sure you have breakfast before you come to school. Treat your teachers with respect. I threw that in for you."

"Point taken, Rebecca. I'll pass your thoughts along to Mr. Binder."

"Oh, and about that. He probably should change his name. Mr. Binder is inviting ridicule."

"Take your seat, Rebecca," says Mr. Quesnel, turning to face the blackboard, his shoulders wiggling slightly.

"Just saying," Rebecca says.

The buzzer for first class sounds and everyone rises automatically from their desks.

"Greet the day," Mr. Quesnel shouts over the din of shuffling desks and dragging feet. "See you tomorrow, Rebecca," he says, a smile on his face.

Once they are in the hall, Elisabeth leans over to Rebecca. "I thought you said you were silent."

"Oh, I was, I was. I'm taking a new approach to life. I'm tired of being silent. This will be more interesting. Besides, it shocks the hell out of people. It's like I just arrived on the planet and no one noticed me before. You should try it."

"Are you allowed to swear?" Elisabeth asks, a nervous sound to her voice.

"You mean *shit* and *damn* and that sort of thing?"

Elisabeth nods.

"No, not really. But who makes those kinds of rules for us? I am responsible for my own behaviour, for my own language. I am a separate entity," she says as if she's reciting a pledge of allegiance.

"Do you speak French?" Elisabeth asks.

"No. I rehearsed that one line to dazzle Mr. Quesnel when I found out I had him for homeroom." Rebecca laughs. "Another one of my pre-emptive strikes. Mr. Quesnel will keep us safe, Lissie."

They keep walking and Elisabeth feels strange, a bit giddy inside, like she has gas and might burp or worse. She holds her stomach.

"Rebecca," she says.

"What?"

"Can I call you Becca?"

Rebecca looks startled. Nicknames. The sound of being inside a family, of being tied to one another with an invisible cord that stretches and retracts at will. Rebecca watches families: families in cars, families at the park, families on the street, families that laugh, families that argue, brothers and sisters who push one another, who tease, who want to be first, want to be the favourite. *Is it me, Mommy? Am I the best? Do you love me the most?* Rebecca stares and sometimes her mouth drops open, caught in a trance, trying to time travel to a place where she had a family.

"I don't think so," Rebecca says, and a pained look creeps on to her face.

"We have math class. Room 319. I'm not very good in math," Elisabeth says.

"I am. You'll be fine."

Sixteen

REBECCA TAKES HOLD OF CHUCK'S HAND AND LISSIE'S HAND AND smiles at them both.

"Charles Prescott," Rebecca says. "We can round out our membership to three. Break the stalemate. This is Elisabeth Smythe. Lissie. She's one of us." Rebecca bows with exaggerated flair while Chuck stares as though a knife is jammed in his spine.

Elisabeth is tempted to throw her arms around Rebecca, but contains her enthusiasm. *Outbursts are a sign of weakness.* Elisabeth has heard that enough times that she can't possibly forget the sound of Charlotte's warning.

Chuck sits on his hands and doesn't say much. Rebecca nudges him a few times, squeezes his hand, offers him some of her lunch.

Elisabeth thinks Chuck looks like someone who is growing too fast, his feet too large for his body, clumsy and awkward. His hands are enormous, yet he is barely as tall as Rebecca, who has about two inches on Elisabeth. Chuck has pimples on his forehead that he combs his hair down over. His body is caved in slightly as though he is protecting himself, and he jumps at loud noises and seems easily startled. He doesn't look straight at Elisabeth, but talks in her general direction, tossing words out in the room for her to catch. He smells funny some days and his clothes look dirty, almost threadbare in some places. He picks at his fingernails, *a disgusting habit,* Charlotte calls it. *Don't you ever let me catch you chewing or picking at your fingernails.*

"Chuck and I have been friends since the first day of school," Rebecca says, a matter-of-fact sound to her voice. "We live down the road from each other. We're on the same party line. I'm older so I get to be in charge," and Rebecca laughs while Chuck nods.

"She does," Chuck says. "She is very bossy."

"He had a Mighty Mouse lunch box and I couldn't resist," Rebecca says. "Who can resist Mighty Mouse? Go on. Sing the Mighty Mouse song for Elisabeth."

"No thanks," Chuck says.

"Come on. It'll seal the deal. You know you want to."

Chuck grins at Rebecca like he can't help himself.

"Here I come to save the day," Chuck belts out, his arms raised over his head, and then he folds back up, looking left and right.

"See," Rebecca says. "Who can resist that?"

Lissie smiles, sees how the two of them fit together, sees how it must feel to collapse into the comfortable chair of friendship, a chair that holds you up in all the right places and lets you slouch where you need to, pure comfort and familiarity. Rebecca really *is* in charge.

"I was always in trouble at school," Chuck says.

"Not always, but often," Rebecca says. "He wasn't always in control of his legs, which used to take him out of his desk a little too often. I created a diversion so that our teacher wouldn't notice, and it worked most of the time. I'd ask some stupid question that required a lengthy answer, and Chuck would try hard to stop fidgeting. Boys should be allowed to learn while running on a treadmill or on roller skates."

"What is a treadmill?" Elisabeth asks.

"It's a running surface on a conveyor belt," Rebecca says.

"Oh right," Elisabeth says, not exactly sure.

Rebecca looks like she needs to protect Chuck, like she's running interference, her eyes keeping watch in case someone might try to hurt him. Elisabeth imagines Rebecca throwing her arms out in front of Chuck when they walk by the pack of boys that sit on the bottom of the steps that lead up to the cafeteria. *Faggot,* one of them burps at Chuck, with a laugh as if the word itself is hilarious, and Rebecca takes a step closer to the boys, almost daring them to say anything more. They don't, but Elisabeth can't be sure that Rebecca won't pound them out if they challenge her.

"You make it worse," Chuck whispers to Rebecca.

"No, I don't," she says defiantly. "I let them know they can't mess with us."

"No, you let them know they can't mess with *you*," Chuck says.

"Same thing."

The boys are always on the steps, gathered like packing dogs, coming up with nicknames for one another. Snout is one of the bigger boys whose hair hasn't seen a comb since kindergarten. He lumbers when he walks, a rehearsed walk, forced, trying to look uninterested and unruly. *Slob* would be a better name. Mutton carries thick paperbacks around in his back pocket and looks a bit like an alien from outer space trying to figure out his surroundings. Perpetually mystified. Slippy never seems to go to class and spends a lot of time on the steps with his elbows on his knees.

Dogs get courage from one another when they pack, courage to take down a deer. On their own they are lap dogs.

"Boys are much the same," Rebecca explained. "Gran told me that."

* * *

Elisabeth tries very hard not to follow Rebecca around school like a lost pup, even though she wants to sneak under Rebecca's arm, rest there, breathe deeply, find shelter. Elisabeth has never had a friend, has never crawled inside a fort and whispered about daydreams and nightmares, never invited someone from her class to a sleepover, to build a blanket tent in the drawing room using the large couch cushions as the frame. Never planned to run away with a friend and live in the forest in a secret underground fort that would have rivaled Peter Pan's Neverland. Never played house with a friend, tucking dolls into beds and comforting their cries with a *there, there*, patting their backs to return them to sleep. Never took turns with a friend to be the doctor and the patient in their make-believe hospital, never put on plays and pageants in the backyard, charging admission to neighbours and relatives.

On her own Elisabeth imagined a friendship, created Little Lisa, who lives in Elisabeth's closet, has lived there since Elisabeth was four. Little Lisa who never changes, never ages, who knows all Elisabeth's secrets, understand Elisabeth's tears when she can't hold them back any longer, knows when Charlotte is coming and hides. It is Little Lisa who negotiates with monsters hiding under the bed, Little Lisa who promises that Elisabeth will be tidier and quieter and ask less of Charlotte and will practise the piano harder if the monsters will leave, and they always do, but obligating Elisabeth to be not just a good girl, a better girl, but the best girl.

What will Rebecca think if she finds out about Little Lisa? Rebecca might laugh, might be outraged at Elisabeth's weak madness, might whisper to Chuck about this ridiculous girl who is so pathetic she can't even conjure up a real friend, needs to rely on her imagination not to be alone. Chuck and Rebecca have been friends since they were little, friends before they were fully formed people and they figured it out together, friends that fit like nesting dolls, friends at an age when trust is automatic. It might be too late for Elisabeth to join the team, but this could be her last chance to see the inside of friendship, to see what she's been missing, to see the world from the inside, standing next to someone who has no obligation to stand there with her but chooses to just the same.

* * *

Rebecca walks through the halls of the high school with a shield in front of her that repels those who think they might get too close or try to conquer her. It isn't confidence, it isn't rage, yet there is a smouldering, a readiness, and Elisabeth can't help watching Rebecca. It looks a little like *I don't give a damn,* but that could be a façade to throw predators off.

In math class, Rebecca sits beside Elisabeth, between Elisabeth and Chuck in the front row at the long mathematics table. The noisy, restless boys, the ones who can't control their laughing or their chatting or their sniffing and snorting, their voices awkward and cracking, sit behind. Rebecca never turns to face her, but when Elisabeth's shoulders stiffen or she drops her pen, Rebecca's hand shoots up.

"Wait a minute! Wait a minute!" Rebecca says, before Mr. Reinson even looks her way. "Back up a step. You're going too fast."

Mr. Reinson frowns, but he stops and faces the class and retraces his steps and starts again. Rebecca never says a word to Elisabeth or Chuck about it, goes back to work, her radar waiting. She does a lot of pointing to the blackboard and demanding that Mr. Reinson repeat himself.

"That doesn't make sense," Rebecca says at least four times in every math class.

Mr. Reinson's shoulders move up and down in frustration and on more than one occasion he invites Rebecca to teach the class. Rebecca says a firm no, but tells him *Do it right*. He threatens to have her excused, to explain herself to Mr. Binder. Rebecca gives him her most determined stare, and Mr. Reinson returns to his scrawl on the blackboard.

* * *

The three of them find a spot to eat lunch in the sunshine, out on the tennis courts, their backs against the school. Chuck and Rebecca's lunches are thin, a flat sandwich and a store-bought cookie. Just one.

"Aren't you eating today, Lissie?" Rebecca asks.

"I'm not hungry," Elisabeth says, feeling the coins in her hand. "My stomach really hurts, and my back. I feel like I've been kicked."

"You can bring a tray out here from the cafeteria."

"There's a sign on the cafeteria door that says no."

"I'll bring it out for you," Rebecca says. When Lissie doesn't respond, Rebecca shrugs and leans back and closes her eyes.

"God, I hate pimples," Rebecca says suddenly with her fingers on her chin. "I think God gives us pimples so we don't think too highly of ourselves, to keep us from feeling too perfect. For our own good, of course."

"Do you believe in God?" Elisabeth asks.

"Absolutely not," Rebecca says. "But I have to blame someone for this shit on my face." Then she laughs and Chuck laughs, too, a safe sound.

"My mother and I go to church, every Sunday. Every single Sunday," Elisabeth says, fatigue in her voice.

"Gran and I go sometimes, when Gran feels like it. She says she'd better keep in good standing with God seeing as she is getting so old and would hate like hell to go to hell. She thinks that's funny," Chuck says.

"That is funny," Lissie says.

"I used to go to church," Rebecca says.

Elisabeth waits as if there should be more to that sentence but Rebecca doesn't say anything more.

"You're lucky you don't have pimples, Lissie," Chuck says. The *Lissie* doesn't roll off his tongue yet, sounds like it needs a bit more rehearsing.

Elisabeth doesn't have any pimples, not a single mark on her face, but she feels anything but perfect. Charlotte warned her that puberty would fix that, would take that lovely pure face and mess it up, so better to be prepared. Now washing her face eight or nine times a day has been added to her list of chores.

"Do you have brothers and sisters?" Elisabeth asks, hesitating, trying to start asking the questions from her notebook that she hides at the bottom of the lawn.

Neither of them answer immediately. Chuck looks at Rebecca and then speaks slowly. "Two older sisters, grown up."

Rebecca closes her eyes and straightens her back. "Nope. Just a father. Just Robert Archer and me."

Then Elisabeth remembers, remembers Charlotte telling her about Robert Archer's car going through the ice, that families have tragedies and everything changes, your plans, how you view the world, all of it is fragile and happiness is an illusive idea, a bit like trying to catch a single snowflake on your finger. *But who puts their family in that kind of risk,* Charlotte said. Charlotte paced and wrung her hands and rattled on about life being short and didn't families have an obligation to follow the rules and play it safe, didn't they owe it to one another at the very least. That is when Elisabeth quit asking questions of Charlotte and made lists instead. Now she has done this terrible thing: asking questions.

The bell goes and Elisabeth jumps to her feet.

"I have art," she says. "See you later," and she almost runs into the school and up the stairs. She darts into the third-floor washroom where two girls are standing by the open window with cigarettes in their hands. They are startled and are ready to toss the evidence out the window, but then realize it is only Elisabeth. They relax and hold their cigarettes in a confident I-dare-you way. Elisabeth drops her head and hurries into a stall, suddenly no longer needing to pee.

"Jigaboo," one of them says, the corner of her lip lifted, threatening, chewing hard on her gum.

The rules say no gum at school, Elisabeth wants to say, but then imagines they might beat her up for speaking to them. She recognizes the cold stance of the girls, as if they are bracing against her, to keep her out, a reflex action. *Self-defense is an affliction of the stupid,* Charlotte said, but Elisabeth has no idea what that means, which is true of a lot of the wisdom that Charlotte is compelled to heap on Elisabeth.

Elisabeth squats on the toilet, wishing there was noise in the bathroom like a loud fan or a band playing. She cringes when her urine streams into the toilet, squeezing her muscles as though that might make her peeing silent, and then she notices her underwear stained with a dark streak of blood. She sucks in her breath sharply, thinking for a moment she might be dying, and then remembers *the talk* in grade seven, the class where the boys were taken to the gymnasium to talk about voices changing and hair growing in strange places and wet dreams, and the girls were told about this precious change that makes them a woman, *a very proud moment it will be.* Mrs. Pennymeades didn't tell the girls this, that Elisabeth's abdomen would squeeze itself like a vice and bend her double and the pain would radiate and circle round and round like an invisible python trying to wring every drop of blood from her body, out through her *lady parts,* or *vagina,* the technical word that sounds like a secret tunnel that leads somewhere strange, some foreign land that grows inside her body without her knowing it.

Lissie looks inside her bag and finds a packet of tissue and wads the whole thing up and fits the tissue inside her underwear. *Proud moment,* she thinks, suddenly wanting to slap Mrs. Pennymeades for lying. Her thighs are throbbing, her hips, every joint is complaining about Elisabeth becoming a woman. *Don't do it, don't do it,* her body is saying. *No good can come of this,* she mutters and pulls up her underwear and wiggles her skirt down over her hips.

"Wagon burner," the other girl says while Elisabeth washes her hands. She knows from the tone of the girl's voice that saying these things is another version of *fuck off.* Elisabeth has only heard the word *fuck* one time, with its ugly violent tone, the mere sound of it making her wince, a word she intrinsically knows does not belong in Charlotte's white world. She said it a couple of times into the mirror. *Fuck. Fuck.* Drawing out the *f* and chopping off the *k.* It is too ugly a word to use. So she says *shit* instead. That is easier. Do-able. *Piss* and *damn* round out her repertoire.

Elisabeth slips into the art room as the very odd, very red-headed Mrs. Ozark is about to shut the door.

"Cutting it close, Miss Smythe," she says, but pronounces it *Smith,* and Elisabeth cringes, almost looking over her shoulder for her mother to make the necessary correction.

Elisabeth loves art class, but struggles to follow directions. She wants to draw what she wants to draw. She wants to listen to the voice in her head that tells her how her hand should move. She blocks out Mrs. Ozark's instructions without realizing it and then must try for the rest of the class to figure out what she should be doing, feeling flustered and panicked. Mrs. Ozark's breathy voice, which sounds like she's an Olympic whisperer, makes the whole thing worse. But it's the only class where Elisabeth doesn't feel exposed and afraid of rules. It's the class where she gets lost from herself and from everyone else.

* * *

Rebecca will figure out that Elisabeth isn't worthy. Rebecca will look at her the way those girls in the third-floor bathroom looked at her. Elisabeth violated her own rules. She broke the silence by asking a question. She should adopt Rebecca's tactic of pre-emptive strikes. She'll avoid Rebecca and Chuck altogether and carry on as she is used to doing and then won't have to feel excluded or judged. She won't have to explain herself or share the secrets of who she is, because she has no answers, has no bloody idea where she came from, and what if they ask, what if Rebecca follows suit and asks a question of Elisabeth, wants to know her story. She can't start making things up now. She starts to sweat and her abdomen cramps again and she thinks she might vomit.

In English class Elisabeth sits in the row closest to the door, lets Rebecca find the perfect desk next to the window, doesn't look up when she feels Rebecca's stare, takes notes on everything Mr. Hawk is saying about Chaucer and Chaucer's language that might as well be Greek, writing every word she can scribble down on paper while he drones on about his passion for literature and its free ticket to anywhere in the world and beyond. She wonders how on earth Chaucer can take her anywhere, except the deep caverns of hell. She keeps her eyes on her textbook and on her watch.

Mr. Hawk is short, shorter than most of the boys in the class. He wears a plaid sweater-vest buttoned up tight over a dark-brown shirt despite the unpredictable heat of October, so his face is flushed and sweat gathers in tiny beads along his forehead and large wet circles form under his arms. When he leans over to read Elisabeth's work, some of the beads drop on the desk and she closes her eyes and feels squeamish and his hot stale breath makes her turn her face away. His hair is thick and seems to grow straight up, like grass. He looks uneasy, so he talks loud and then louder to hide his doubt.

The buzzer sounds. English is the last class of the day and students are moaning about staying awake, yawning and complaining, and Mr. Hawk ignores it all but looks like he is smouldering, ready to blow. Elisabeth jumps from her desk and runs all the way home, not even bothering to retrieve her jacket from her locker. She runs the whole eight blocks, her bag pressed against her chest.

She hurries through the back door despite the rules about quiet entries and into her bedroom, shutting the door behind her. Her body streams down the door into a pool of despair on the floor. Elisabeth knew high school would be too much, knew in her very cells that she can't fight back against the river that is flowing in her, trying to drown her. She braces for Charlotte's knock and insistence about noise, but no knock comes.

Finally, Elisabeth pulls herself up off the floor and opens the door and listens, waits, but the house is completely silent save the refrigerator's hum. Elisabeth's eyebrows start a scrum. This is so unlike Charlotte, not being here to interrogate her, though she calls it interest, concern. Not here assessing the damage to Elisabeth's clothes and hair, not here making a list of homework and obligations.

She goes quietly into the bathroom and locks the door behind her. She searches in the back of the bathroom closet, behind the towels and extra rolls of toilet paper and extra shampoo and toothpaste and bars of soap and everything they might need to see them through the apocalypse. She finds a plain shoebox with a label that says *sanitary napkins* and inside is all the necessary equipment for this horrible departure from childhood.

Elisabeth wanders through the house and finally into the garage where she finds Charlotte stacking old magazines on a shelf beside her car.

"I don't know where these magazines came from," Charlotte is saying. "Did you put them here?" she asks, and her voice has an accusing sound to it, with a look somewhere between annoyance and panic.

The magazines are *McCall's* that Charlotte saved for Elisabeth to cut out the *Betsy* paper doll with each month's new set of clothes.

Charlotte brought the magazines out to the garage only last weekend. I might need these, she said at the time.

"These magazines have been cut up," Charlotte says. "Who would do such a thing?" and she continues stacking and saying the names of the months aloud.

"What comes after March? January, February, March, March, March. We'll need to get a lock on the door."

Elisabeth steps in. "I'll get this," she says, taking the magazines from Charlotte and ignoring Charlotte's look of surprise. "You cut the paper dolls out for me. That's why they're cut up." Elisabeth flips through the magazines and lifts them up to the shelf. "They'll be safe here."

"Well, thank you, Elisabeth," Charlotte says, but with a frown.

"I have homework," Elisabeth says and turns to go.

"Yes, yes," Charlotte says wiping her hands down the front of her and patting the back of her hair to make sure her head hasn't fallen off. "Someone will call you for dinner. Piano. One hour."

Elisabeth doesn't bother to say she practised this morning, like she did yesterday morning and the morning before and the morning before that.

Seventeen

REBECCA AND CHUCK TRUDGE OUT OF THE SCHOOL AND WAIT BY their designated bus stop. Bus 239. It's an arbitrary number, but Chuck used to think more than two hundred buses lined up at the school and how would he ever find bus 239.

"They're all yellow," Chuck complained, getting all worked up.

Rebecca told him matter-of-factly there were eight buses. Eight, and she didn't chuckle or smirk. Chuck asked *Why not number the buses one through eight then? Why all the confusion to make a guy worry?* Rebecca considered reminding Chuck he worried about everything, but she reconsidered and shrugged instead.

They lean against each other, not having much to say, until the girl with two crutches arrives at the bus-waiting place. Ruth leans into her walking sticks as if she is permanently folded at the waist and every muscle in her body works independently without any cohesion or co-operation. Students walk around her, give her a wide berth and their indifference. They don't ridicule her or kick her crutch out from under her arm, but neither do they see her. She is a ghost, and Rebecca sees that Ruth doesn't look at anyone, no pleading eyes, no waiting for a smile or a nod.

"Hey, Ruth. Give me your bag," Rebecca says, the same greeting every day, and Ruth seems to snap back to the present. She wiggles out of her pack and Rebecca takes it from Ruth's shoulder.

Ruth is in grade twelve and rides the bus only to the edge of town, where her mother waits at the side of the road for her every day. Ruth never complains, her hip stuck out to one side, her shoes with thick heavy soles, and her back noticeably humped. Ruth has sparkling blue eyes and deep dimples in her puffy, pudgy face.

"Thanks, Rebecca," she says, breathing out heavily and easing into her front-row seat once she has manoeuvred the bus steps. No one else takes that seat. Not ever. Rebecca places the bag on the seat beside Ruth.

"I like your sweater," Rebecca says, and Ruth smiles. Every day Rebecca likes something. Rebecca likes Ruth's hair clip with the pretend sapphire, Ruth's birthstone, her woven vest with an Aztec design of reds and oranges, her new watch strap with a hint of lime green in the fake leather, Ruth's white teeth and her new razor-sharp haircut. Rebecca asks Ruth what she is reading if they have to wait for the bus. She asks Ruth her favourite programs on television and sometimes it's *My Favorite Martian* or *Mr. Ed* or *That Girl*. Usually, it's *That Girl*.

Rebecca asks Ruth what her plans will be next year when she is done school. Ruth wants to live in a city, a really big city like Winnipeg with concert halls and transit buses that pick you up and let you out where you want to go.

"You drop coins in the fare box beside the driver and then he tears off a transfer that lets you on any bus without paying again to get you where you want to go," Ruth says as if it is almost fantastical. There are art galleries and big department stores with elevators in them and someone to press the buttons and say which floor the doors are opening on. *Fifth Floor, Housewares,* and there are two more floors above that, plus the basement. The stores have stairs that move and climb all on their own; shoppers stand on these moving stairs and go to the next floor. Ruth could be a switchboard operator or take shorthand, and she types very fast. She could live right downtown and watch people out her window and peek in the baby carriages that line the front of Eaton's and the Hudson's Bay Company on Portage Avenue with babies tucked under blankets sound asleep while their mothers shop. And she could play the flute in the city orchestra. Rebecca listens without comment, her eyes never leaving Ruth's, and wonders whether Ruth will ever leave home or will keep going to grade twelve year after year after year and forget all about her plans.

Ruth's flute case protrudes from her pack. Rebecca asks her to play on the bus and Ruth sometimes plays if there is time. "Beethoven is my favourite," Ruth says. "Not as cluttered as Mozart or as busy as Bach, and not nearly so mournful as Chopin."

"Calms the savages," Rebecca says.

Rebecca and Chuck collapse in the sixth seat on the right side of the bus, the seat they claim as their own, their usual spot, not the front and not the back where the thugs sit, the boys who think bad manners make them cool and the girls who are impressed by those who cross the line of bad behaviour, girls who look weak and gullible to Rebecca, girls without their own opinions, who don't know their favourite colour or how to wear their hair unless they think the boys like it, girls who flock to these rule-breakers like seagulls to french fries. Rebecca has considered slapping some sense into them, but they're too far gone. They'll grow up to be the next generation's Penelope: angry and disappointed and wanting to blame.

Rebecca and Chuck are silent until the bus gets moving, its motor coughing into action, the rumble and roar giving them an element of privacy, blocking out any eavesdropping. The bus driver looks in his mirror to make sure everyone is behaving and sitting down, like he's doing his last check, threatens with his eyes, and puts the bus in gear.

"What's with Lissie?" Chuck asks. "She's been avoiding us."

"She's insecure," Rebecca says. "It'll pass."

"I don't like her," Chuck says.

"Of course you do. She's like us. Battled and bruised. Move over and make room for her."

"I liked things the way they were."

"They haven't changed. Not that much. Nothing stays the same forever."

Chuck shrugs, his usual acceptance move, and nods with his head while shrugging, a little nod, like it hurts to give in.

"I'm going to invite her to meet Otis," Rebecca says.

"In your house?" Chuck asks as if Rebecca is saying she is going to run naked through the streets.

"Yes, in my house."

"Robert isn't going to like that," Chuck says.

"He has a doctor's appointment next week. He has to go to Winnipeg to see a specialist about his feet. He'll be gone for a few days. Taking the bus."

"Wow. He hasn't left the house for more than a few hours for years."

Rebecca nods. "I know. I live there."

"Sorry," Chuck says.

"Why don't the three of us have supper together? I'll cook."

Chuck squeezes his eyes shut and winces with mock anxiety and then grabs his stomach. Rebecca ignores him.

"We could make one of those packaged pizzas. Robert hates the smell so I can't ever have one when he is home. Something about garlic. He thinks he smells garlic in everything. Would Gran pick us up after school? The three of us."

"I'll ask."

Rebecca rises from her seat as the bus lurches to a stop at her laneway. One of the boys from the back makes some comment about Rebecca's appearance, and she turns to face him with eyebrows raised.

"Really," she says, and the boy looks away. "Talk to Gran," Rebecca says to Chuck as she heads for the door of the bus and begins the hike down her lane. She waves over her shoulder, knowing Chuck's face will be pressed to the window waiting for her arm to shoot up and her fingers to wiggle in his direction as the bus pulls away.

Rebecca steps around puddles and grass growing up in the middle of the laneway, a laneway where the sucker trees are closing in, trying to reclaim the space as their own in an attempt to make it look like no one lives here, and it's working. The water in the ditch used to flow freely, with a few bulrushes that kept the water clear and fresh and the frogs visible. Rebecca used to wade into the water up to her knees, waiting patiently for a frog to come to the surface, resting his nose on the edge of the water, his eyes blinking, his legs stretched out behind him. Rebecca ate the honeysuckles that grew at the edges of the ditch, but now the grasses and scrub trees have taken over.

Rebecca stops in the lane and looks at the house, its shingles lifting in many places, some of them torn right off by fierce winds. The window screens never even made it out of the shed this past summer. The whole place looks decrepit and abandoned. Her step gets slower. At night, when she's in her bedroom and looking out, she can imagine that her home is solid and in good repair without broken door hinges and with windows that open and siding that is freshly painted, a cheerful yellow with white trim and red geraniums in window boxes, yellow tulips in early spring and green ivy crawling around on a trellis that leans against the house.

Lissie will faint when she sees this dump, Rebecca mutters.

She whistles when she is close to the house, and Otis appears in an elm tree along the lane and shrieks at her, his mouth open as he leans into his voice, his black feathers glistening.

"Clever bird," Rebecca says, dropping her bag on the lawn and flopping down beside it. She saved a bit of bread from her sandwich and has it in her pocket. Otis lands and hops onto her legs, tipping his head back and forth and pecking at her pocket.

"You looking for this?" Rebecca says, pulling her hand out of her pocket. Otis snatches the bread and flutters up to a branch on the small globe cedar that sags under his weight and dumps him back on to the grass.

"You're getting fat, Otis," Rebecca says. "Going to have to cut back on the sweets."

Otis hops back onto her legs and picks at her shoelace, pulling on one end and untying the bow. He pecks at her pocket until he figures out there are no more pieces of bread and flies off to berate her from the telephone wire.

Otis is never very far away when Rebecca is outside. He flies from tree to tree when she walks to the barn, sits on the fence while she throws hay in the manger for the cows, sits on the yard light beside the water trough while Rebecca scoops out the debris the cows have deposited there, sits on the bale of straw while she shakes it out for bedding.

Otis was scrawny and weak for several weeks after Rebecca found him. She fed him beans and bits of canned dog food, and he was happy to stay in his box while his feathers grew back. She came from school one day and found Otis sitting on Robert's lap staring into his face.

"Your bird can go outside now," Robert said. "He's been flying around the house."

"He can't go outside until he has a name," Rebecca said.

"Otis," Robert said, putting the bird back in the box. "Get him out of here."

"Otis. Good name," Rebecca said, and she imagined Robert sitting in his chair day after day running names through his head. Jack. Too close to Jake. Norbert. Not easy enough. Clive. More suited to a frog. Fluffy. Too cat-like. Otis. That's the one.

Rebecca used to imagine having a dog, a puppy that would tuck into a box at the end of her bed and when he whimpered, missing his mother and littermates, Rebecca scooped him up and tucked him under the covers with her, his face snuggled into her warm neck and his cold wet nose against her cheek. When he was big enough he waited for her at the end of the lane, though not too close to the road, and when the bus screeched and spluttered and burped her out at the edge of the road, her dog rose from his waiting place and wagged his tail and bounced around until she squatted to embrace him and then he licked her face. She made lists of perfect dog names: Henry, Clarence, Admiral, Buckley. Claude. Claude is a perfect name for a dog. But Rebecca never had a dog.

"A farm without a dog is not a farm," Rebecca proclaimed to her father when she was young enough to still try.

Rebecca tried to befriend several wild cats that moved into the barn. She found their litters of kittens once or twice, digging through the hay to watch their uncoordinated bodies trying to crawl, amazed at how tiny they were. Even though she never touched them, the mother cat seemed to know Rebecca had been watching and moved her kittens. Rebecca found dead kittens, three of them, their bodies entwined like a nest, shriveled and stiff. Rebecca buried them at the edge of the garden, dug a deep hole and placed them inside an old tea towel, wrapping them to keep them warm before she placed the soil back on top of them and then piled rocks to mark the spot. She didn't cry and she didn't look for kittens again. She put food and water out for the mother cats and the food always disappeared.

She even imagined a goldfish in a big bowl swimming laps and stopping to kiss the glass when she pushed her face up close. She asked Robert a couple of times, left drawings out in full view of a child with every kind of pet. His only comment was *We can barely feed ourselves.*

Her mother said she could get a dog when she was eight, when she was old enough to be responsible for it, to care for it, to keep it clean and teach it good manners, and to be prepared because pets don't outlive their owners; pets teach you about the cycle of life. But her mother had been wrong about that; pets don't die first. Rebecca had been responsible for too many years already, leaving notes and reminders for Robert and the endless list of chores that needed to be done: vaccinations and fence repairs and barn doors that had blown off, left notes when the water pump had lost its prime and when the mice chewed through the electrical line to the heated water bowl in the barn and the water froze solid. She left notes when the belt came off the grain crusher and when the spark plug was clogged on the lawnmower, but none of it seemed to get done. Robert hadn't earned a dog, but Rebecca had. She had Daisy. Daisy has been a good pet despite aging much too quickly.

Rebecca lies back on the grass, looks up at the clouds, and tries to suspend her thoughts, to stop her brain in its tracks so she can breathe and not think. The energy that is required to keep up the pretense of being happy and content is almost too much some days, many days, most days. Some days she wants it to stop, for it to be all over, for the empty fizzing in her stomach to stop and her shoulders to collapse instead of hanging on to the ends of her ears.

Otis lands beside her head and pecks at the elastic at the end of her braid, trying to pull it free. Rebecca jumps to her feet and runs toward the house, waving her arms and Otis is airborne right behind her. She slams the back door and drops her bag by the closet. Robert raises his chin off his chest, his hair sticking up in all directions, several days of growth on his face. Rebecca stops and looks at him.

"Did you even wash your face today?" she says.

Robert makes a fist with his right hand and pumps his fist as if he's lifting weight with his right arm.

"There's feed in the back of the truck. I got feed today," Robert says.

"You got it yesterday," Rebecca says.

"I can't remember," Robert says, his palm on his forehead. "Don't bother me with details. Drive the truck to the barn and unload it. I'll make supper," his voice getting louder with each word.

A large can of Heinz tomato soup is sitting on the kitchen counter. *I'd hardly call that supper,* Rebecca wants to say. They have soup and canned ham and canned vegetables and canned fruit and canned Klik, meat that Rebecca can't even identify. She made a meat loaf for him, followed the recipe in a magazine she got from the library. She served it up with a tablecloth and white paper napkins that she got from the dispenser outside the ice-cream truck parked in front of the park. Robert smelled the meat loaf, poked at it with his fork as if it might still be alive, and then shoved the plate away.

"I don't like garlic. I don't eat garlic. Is that garlic?" He looked at her bewildered and confused.

Rebecca got up from her chair, took his plate, and threw the whole thing in the garbage, plate and all. Then she sat down and ate her supper. She was eleven.

* * *

Rebecca grabs Robert's keys from the table and pulls her barn jacket on in one graceful movement. The jacket's zipper is barely holding the jacket together, the cuffs frayed and full of holes, but it fits her like an old friend. She bought it big, *big enough to last,* she told the woman at the church rummage sale. I don't want to buy another one before I'm done farming, and the woman had chuckled like she was humouring Rebecca, a sound that annoyed Rebecca.

The truck starts first try, and Rebecca slams it into reverse and lets the clutch out quickly. She considers driving the truck through the side of the house, driving right through the porch. Then Robert would have to fix the back-door hinge, and she almost laughs. She feels the familiar rage climb up her back and a scream waiting to burst out of her mouth.

She turns the truck around to drive to the barn but then pushes the clutch in and lets the truck idle for a few minutes. Rebecca looks at Otis perched on the shed roof. He tips his head back and forth as if he's trying to figure out Rebecca's next move. She runs her finger along the groove in the steering wheel, almost worn flat. She looks at the wad of keys hanging from the key ring that used to say something like Ford or John Deere but has long since been worn smooth. Keys, keys, and more keys. One key has a bit of red paint on it. It is an unusual shape, different from the others. She pushes the gas pedal a few times, revving the engine, and then lets the clutch out and heads down the lane.

Rebecca steers around the puddles in the lane and drives with one set of wheels crushing the grass growing up in the middle. She rolls down the window that will go only part way and turns up the radio. Johnny Cash is singing about a boy named Sue and Rebecca turns it up even louder.

It takes about ten minutes to get to Roddick. Her earlier rage and indignation are beginning to wane. She takes the back streets around behind the feed mill and comes into town from the east. Her left leg is beginning to ache from pushing on the clutch. She plans to be taller in her next life, to have longer legs. She stalls the truck twice at one corner where the grade of the road rises. The car behind her honks, and she considers getting out and yelling at the driver.

She turns on to Williams Avenue. She remembers number 235 on all of Lissie's books and inside her shoes and jackets. 235 Williams Avenue. She pulls up next to the perfect lawn and the very white house. She turns off the ignition and pulls out the keys and closes her hand around them. She closes her eyes and breathes in and out as though she is in a trance. Her shoulders rise and fall and before doubt or hesitation can settle in she throws open the truck door and strides to the front door and knocks firmly three times. She waits two or three seconds and then knocks firmly three times again.

The door opens only part way, and a tall, lean pale-blonde woman stands looking at Rebecca, something near horror on her face.

"Hi, Mrs. Smythe," Rebecca says, dragging out the Smythe moderately. "Is Lissie home?"

"Lizzie. Who is Lizzie? There's no Lizzie here." She attempts to shut the door, but Rebecca leans in closer.

"I mean Elisabeth. We call her Lissie, your daughter. Is she here?" Rebecca asks.

Charlotte starts to close the door when Lissie's face appears at her shoulder.

"Rebecca," Lissie says, startled, but with a smile growing on her face. No one has ever knocked on her door inquiring for her. She'd heard talk of the other kids at school. *I'll call on you later* were the words they used and it sounded like belonging to a secret organization. *I'll call on you.*

"Can you come out and play?" Rebecca says, laughing.

"How did you get here?" Lissie asks.

"You don't want to know. Wanna go for a walk?"

"Yes, I do. Wait here and I'll get my jacket."

"Sorry for my appearance, Mrs. Smythe, but I was on my way to the barn when I decided to drop by and see Lissie," and she smiles at Charlotte.

"Her name is Elisabeth. E-lis-a-beth," and Charlotte enunciates each syllable. "Elisabeth, you can't go out now. It's almost supper and you haven't done your piano or homework."

"It'll keep. I'll only be gone for a half hour or so," and she pushes past Charlotte as she zips up her jacket.

Charlotte looks bewildered and stands with the door open as Rebecca and Lissie walk down the sidewalk.

"Don't look at her," Rebecca whispers. "She can't see us if we don't look." And she laughs again.

"Did you drive here?" Lissie asks, leaning into Rebecca's ear.

"I did," Rebecca says, pressing her teeth together and pulling her lips back. "Yikes. I may have lost my mind."

"I didn't know you could drive," Lissie says. "You're not old enough to drive."

"I know," Rebecca says. "I feel a bit crazy. Alive and crazy."

"Charlotte is probably still standing at the front door about to have a stroke or ready to pass out from shock. I've never not done exactly as I've been told for, well, forever."

"Feels good, doesn't it? Kings of our castles. Masters of our domain."

Lissie laughs, loudly, a fresh sound that even she has never heard come out of her mouth before.

"Where do you want to walk to?" Lissie asks.

"Do you have any money? I need to copy some keys and I don't have a red cent."

"Yes," Lissie says, digging in her pocket. "I always have money. Mad money. What are the keys for?"

"Long story," Rebecca says, and she shoves her arm through Lissie's and they walk like they're in a three-legged race. "Where've you been, Lissie?"

Eighteen

"WHERE DID YOU GO?" ROBERT SAYS, HIS VOICE BARELY AUDIBLE when Rebecca drops the truck keys from shoulder height onto the kitchen table. He doesn't look at her, doesn't lean out of his chair into view.

"For a drive," she says, a nonchalant sound to her voice, but with an edge that says *I dare you to ask more*.

Rebecca looks at the stack of newspapers at Robert's feet and the three coffee mugs on the small table in front of him and at the bits of wood and ash built up around the woodstove, at the stain at the bottom right corner of the window where the outside is trying to get. The state of disrepair is shocking.

"The clutch is slipping on the truck," Rebecca says. "And when was the oil last changed, at the turn of the century? The tires are balder than bald." She wants to keep going when he puts his wrists up against his ears.

"It's rusting badly on the driver's side, almost right through the front fender. And the back door of the house is going to blow off one of these days and you'll find it in the plum trees." And with each statement she leans in closer and closer to her father.

Robert starts to rock back and forth, his eyes closed and his lips pressed together.

"Are you listening to me?" she says, pushing a chair into the table with her heel with more force than she intended.

Robert keeps rocking.

"This place is going to fall down on top of you one day," Rebecca says, standing in front of him now and pointing to the ceiling. "And maybe I won't be around to pull you out."

Robert holds his breath for a few seconds and then slowly exhales with each word.

"I pulled you out. I pulled you out," Robert says, nodding as if trying to convince himself, to confirm he had done something, more than should ever have been asked of him, his voice quieter with each declaration, like he is chanting, the *pulling out* part his mantra.

"Well, maybe you shouldn't have," Rebecca says, and Robert presses his eyes closed even tighter. She waits for a moment and then in a very quiet but firm voice goes on. "Maybe you didn't. Maybe my mother pushed me out." She stands and lets that sink in before she moves and grabs her bowl of soup off the table and flings it into the sink. The bowl bounces around, spraying soup in every direction, but doesn't even have the decency to break.

She slams her bedroom door and pulls her dresser in front of it. The gesture is almost laughable, because who exactly is going to try to get into her room, but she needs the feeling of locking the world out. Then she collapses on her bed. She doesn't feel like crying or breaking something or jumping out the window. She doesn't feel much of anything aside from fatigue and emptiness. Maybe if she ran a razor blade across her arm in small incisions she might perceive the sting and feel alive again for even those few seconds. Maybe she should join Robert and quit bathing and quit changing her clothes and start sitting in a chair opposite him, her school-books on her lap but never opened. Maybe she should keep her left hand in her pocket and never comb her hair and quit talking in full sentences. She'd grunt and groan when she answered the phone or went to the store.

Rebecca rolls over on to her side and pulls her knees up to her chest, trying to figure out her next move, trying not to feel the burden of guilt for striking out at her father. When did she quit trying to reach him, to take care of him? When did that all collapse? Did he quit trying right after he dragged her out of the water? She doesn't remember any of that now, not a single moment after the cold water froze her brain, made it stop storing details until she woke up in the hospital.

Does she hate her father? She shakes her head. She doesn't feel anything for him aside from moderate repulsion. She is obligated to live with this stranger who bears no resemblance to any member of her family. He has days when he gets up out of his chair. When he throws feed at the cows or plows the field, but then leaves it year after year without a crop. The hay sometimes makes it to the barn, and some summers the second cut sits and rots in the field and he runs out of feed for his cows so he has to ship them to market. Sometimes he gathers eggs and throws corn at the hens. But he never fixes fences, never picks up the mountain of twine that Rebecca has to drag into a pile in the spring and burn with the dead bodies that didn't make it through the winter.

She feels the familiar throb in her mouth, for over a week now, and sticks her finger in along her gum line to the top back molar on the left. The gum is swollen and spongy and when she pushes on it the pain is more severe. It smarts right up into her cheekbone, and she almost cries out. At least she can feel that, so she must still be living.

"Now what do I do?" she says out loud, holding a hand mirror in front of her face and exposing her teeth. She can't see back in her mouth far enough even when she pulls her lip out to the side. Something evil has crawled into her mouth and died, she thinks. She hasn't been to the dentist in years, hasn't had her teeth looked at since she was, well, since anyone was looking after her. She brushes her teeth faithfully, but she is losing the battle with this tooth. She imagines putting pliers in her mouth and yanking the decayed tooth right out.

Rebecca lies back on her pillow, her tongue fidgeting with the swelling on her gum, and before she has time to reconsider, she jumps off the bed and drags the dresser out of the way and throws open her bedroom door. She hurries down the stairs and digs in the pile of papers on top of the radio on the kitchen cupboard, looking for the telephone book. She flips the pages to H and holds her finger on Hewitt Dental Office while she dials the phone.

"Hello," Rebecca says, swallowing hard. "This is Rebecca Archer. I need an appointment to have a tooth looked at."

She wraps the telephone cord around her wrist. "No, I haven't been in since I was little, but I'm having trouble with a tooth." She waits a bit and twirls the cord some more. "Yes, that's right. Rebecca Archer. Next Thursday will work fine. I'll come straight from school. Thank you," she says, placing the receiver in its cradle.

"Who's going to pay for that?" Robert says without looking at her.

"You are," Rebecca says. "You are," and she jabs at the air in front of him before she takes the stairs two at a time back to her room, pulling her dresser over again, and then screams with all her force at her closed door. She exhales heavily. "That felt good."

What if she packed her clothes and ran away? She has no money. Are there shelters for homeless people? What if she went to England to find her grandparents? Maybe Lissie would lend her money, but Rebecca doubts Lissie carries around that much mad money in her secret hiding place.

Rebecca's hand closes in her pocket around the keys she copied. Who is she kidding? She can't go anywhere. She slides the keys under her mattress and collapses on the bed. She needs a job, she thinks, tearing a piece of paper from her binder. She smoothes the paper flat on top of her closed binder, smoothes it a few times while the ideas wiggle in her head. She could work at the library, putting books away, but lots of people volunteer for that. She could ask Mr. Lyons about restacking groceries on his store shelves, but the two helpers he has have been with him for a hundred years. The hardware store. That's it, she thinks firming her grip on her pen. Mr. Law already knows she means business when she speaks.

* * *

Dear Mr. Law, she writes, after she puts the date at the top of the page.

How are you? I am fine. She leans back and examines the letter from a distance and then crumples the page and tosses it at her garbage can and tears a new page from her binder.

Dear Mr. Law, she begins again.

Do you remember my mother? Grace Archer. Do you remember her bringing me to your store when I was little? Her walk was more of a glide, a soft, even step that floated, as if she might have been a fairy in disguise or maybe a ballerina. Do you remember how she rested her chin in her hand when she was thinking, when she was trying to decide which light bulb she needed or what kind of clothespins? She put her chin like that when she was thinking about the hard stuff, too, the real thinking, the thinking about disappointment and shame and hurt. She sneezed with everything closed up tight and her nose pushed into the crook of her arm. It was more of an implosion, and her teeth, her perfect white teeth. Do you remember her teeth? She had such a smile. I wish I had her smile, I wish I looked like her when I smiled. She used to smile at you as if she was a little bit shy but she trusted you. I could feel it even though I was little. Her hands were always soft and her nails always clean, but I never saw her fussing with them. Her feet were lovely, too. You probably never saw her feet. She didn't go barefoot when she went to town, but she did at home. She used to stand in her garden and wiggle her toes in the dirt. She told me the earth could heal a body if we let it. I'm not sure what she meant. She washed her feet at the well after, pumping water over them and rubbing the mud off with her hands. She didn't have dry rough heels or corns on her toes. She never wore jewelry and she didn't have a watch but she always knew the time. Did you know that? I think she had a special gift that measured the passing of time on the inside of her so she didn't need to wear a watch. Do you remember the sound of her voice, soft spoken, a bit whisper-like? She had a firm voice, but not very often. I worry I'll forget her voice, won't be able to hear its sound in my head. I don't want to forget. Not ever. Remember how she used to thank you when she bought anything and then she tapped the counter with her flat hand, gently, as if it was her signal to say goodbye. Thank you,

Mr. Law, and she tapped her hand as a signing off and smiled at you. You always smiled back. I think every inch of my mother was lovely, especially on the inside. She was kind and patient and I don't recall her ever being mad at me. Maybe that's how memory works when someone dies; the person left behind never remembers being disappointed, because that would burst the bubble, wouldn't it.

She bought a magnifying glass from your store once. She used it to pull a sliver out of my finger. I had to hold the magnifying glass because she needed two hands. She told me it wouldn't hurt if I was perfectly still and trusted her. I did and it didn't hurt. Not really. She kept talking with her quiet voice, the voice that had no hurry in it. She loved me, Mr. Law. I knew it. I knew it every second of my life and I knew it when she pushed me out of the window of the car even though she sounded angry and wanted me to leave her. She told me she would never leave me. Every night when she tucked me into bed, she promised she would never leave me.

My father used to be kind. I think he used to be kind. He used to fix things and he was strong and could lift me up over his head. He shrinks inside his jacket now as if it belonged to someone else and never fit him. I can't remember much else besides what my father is now. It's too hard. And it's too hard to remember Jake so I have erased him as best I can as if he never really existed because he didn't get a chance to be a person or a real brother and I wouldn't have been a good sister anyway. I really hope that's not the reason that Jake and my mother had to die. I wanted to blame somebody, wanted to blame someone in the very cells of my body, wanted to blame Jake, to make it his fault, but when I tried it always came back to me and how it must have been my fault. If I could have a job, Mr. Law, I could change my life and get away from remembering that it was my fault my mother had to break her promise.

I'm going to make a list of all the things I know about that will help me to work in your hardware store. I can fix a fence and know what kind of tools are required and I can change the belt on the grain crusher and know to let the tension off first and I can fix the cord on the skill saw if someone happens to run the cord through the blade because that can happen and I know to strip the wires down and use black electric tape to unite the two separated ends on each wire, white with white and black to black, and wrap the whole thing again in electrical tape and then it works like new. I know that a Phillips screw is much easier to turn than a Robertson and both are better than a slot and a hammer gets rounded after a while, after pounding nails for a long time, and doesn't hit squarely anymore and should be replaced, and to cut drywall the blade on the utility knife must be very sharp and once you cut through one side using a straight edge, then it snaps easily and it isn't hard at all and anyone can do it. And I will be polite and not make a face when someone can't pay the whole bill and I will never answer the phone sounding tired or annoyed no matter how stupid the question is.

Please, Mr. Law, give me a job. You won't be sorry. I'll soon be fifteen. Let me change my life.

Then she tears the eight pages of the letter in half and then tears them again and again until she can't tear them any smaller.

Nineteen

DR. HARBINGER'S OFFICE IS IN A LARGE HOUSE THAT HE RAISED his family in, a house that saw two sets of twins wear the wood on the stairs bare and the paint on the stairway walls permanently stained. It was Roddick folklore that Dr. Harbinger and his wife had given up on having a family after more than a decade of faithful effort without results. Then they looked at each other across the dinner table with a sense of resignation, and at breakfast they shared a friendly nod of acknowledgement before Dr. Harbinger collapsed into his newspaper and Mrs. Harbinger sipped her tea and ran her pointer finger along her upper lip and stared at the knobs on her kitchen cabinet doors, wondering if they should be freshened up. They were lulled into a place of acceptance. Then, without notice and in the span of eleven short months, they had four babies, which nearly consumed Mrs. Harbinger's sanity and undoubtedly halted their intimate relations. There may have been some accusations flung at Dr. Harbinger from time to time, when the volume of babies crying reached glass-shattering decibels. *You did this,* she may have hissed from between clenched teeth and Dr. Harbinger would have had no recourse but to shrug. Sex had been his idea; Mrs. Harbinger only went along with it because it was easier than not.

The wide front staircase that mounted an assault to the front door of the Harbinger home was flanked on either side by gardens, gardens chock full of pansies and petunias and primroses and all flowers pink. The steps and railing used to gleam a brilliant white, but since the twins grew up and moved on and Mrs. Harbinger died there is hardly a fleck of white paint remaining.

The home's expansive living room became a waiting area when Dr. Rafferty and a host of doctors in the summer joined the medical team to manage the influx of patients who seemed to have all their injuries and illnesses from May to October. The old house had undoubtedly been grand at one time, with its high ceilings and wide wood trim. The dark wood appeared less sinister with the light shining in the huge front windows. Smells of cinnamon buns and savoury stews and a myriad of other culinary masterpieces used to waft through the house, arousing patients' appetites.

Rumour had it the twins carried out their most creative mischief when the waiting area was full. There was talk of a toboggan crashing down the wide steep staircase leading down from the second floor, of indoor garden-hose water fights of all things, and parades complete with the clang and crash from pots and pans. When they were older the four girls enjoyed working on their tans in the front yard or on the roof of the summer kitchen with the tiniest of bathing suits that had never seen the water. They lathered on a baby oil–iodine concoction and turned their transistor radios up loud. Dr. Harbinger ignored them, pretended they weren't even there, shaking his head as if their very existence was a total mystery to him. Mrs. Harbinger fussed, waved her tea towel at them as she would have had they been a swarm of black flies intent on getting into her kitchen.

Mrs. Harbinger died from cancer, proof that doctors don't know everything, can't even keep those they love alive and safe from disease. Apparently, Mrs. Harbinger had never uttered a word about the mass she felt in her lower left abdomen, and Dr. Harbinger's hands no longer wandered there. By the time the ovarian malignant growth came out of hiding there was no battle to be waged.

Mrs. Harbinger merely died in a whisper, closed her eyes, and slid away leaving Dr. Harbinger alone, ashamed, and even more eccentric than before.

* * *

"What are we doing here?" Charlotte asks, stopping and leaning into her heels as Elisabeth tries to direct Charlotte up the sidewalk to Dr. Harbinger's front door.

"Dr. Harbinger wants to see us," Elisabeth whispers, trying to use her most assuring voice.

"About what?"

"Let's go in and see."

Charlotte relents, but tightens her grip on the purse she is clutching to her abdomen as though at any moment some lowly criminal will dash around the corner and snatch it from her. She is armed and ready.

"These steps used to be white," Charlotte says, pulling on the rail for support. "Really white. And the trim," she says, pointing to the peak of the roof. "It was a lovely home."

They sit in two chairs in front of the window. Mrs. Zielinski, who laughs like she has the hiccups, each eruption louder than the one before followed by an emphatic sigh, shifts down one seat so Charlotte and Elisabeth can sit together.

"Thank you," Elisabeth says with a smile, but Mrs. Zielinski has already returned to her magazine.

Jennifer Thompson is standing with her baby swaddled in her arms, Jennifer moving her upper body back and forth and bouncing gently in her hips to keep the baby sedated. Everyone who comes in has to swoon over the baby, making clucking sounds and talking with their lips puckered in a language that makes no sense.

"I don't care for babies," Charlotte says, her eyes half closed and her head shaking firmly. Elisabeth looks uncomfortable, her shoulders pulled up, worrying about being asked to leave. Surely there are rules for this sort of thing. Appear interested and polite. *Is that so hard?* Elisabeth wants to snarl.

"Everyone fawns over babies, goo-ing and drooling like idiots," Charlotte says. "I don't like them."

Wasn't I a baby once? Elisabeth wants to ask. *Did you like me?* But she doesn't. Tries to pretend Charlotte hasn't said a word.

"Would you like a magazine?" Elisabeth asks, holding up a stack of *Life*, *McCall's*, and *Family Circle*. "Read one," Elisabeth says, adding a hint of firmness to her voice.

"No," Charlotte says, not even bothering to sound polite.

Dr. Harbinger's nurse Freda calls Charlotte's name, and Charlotte leaps to her feet like she's won something.

"First prize," Charlotte hollers, and Elisabeth wonders where on earth this stranger has come from, this woman who wears Charlotte's clothes and walks with Charlotte's floating gait yet sounds nothing like Charlotte. Who is this woman who has taken possession of Charlotte's language and replaced it, turning Charlotte into someone else, into this confusing stranger?

Charlotte and Elisabeth stand for a minute looking uneasy as Dr. Harbinger points toward two chairs in front of his desk. He shuts his office door behind him, and his face begins to turn red.

"Sit, sit," he says with an urgent arm gesture as if he's got somewhere to be very soon. Elisabeth eases into one of the chairs, but Charlotte remains standing, looking bewildered. Elisabeth pats the chair next to her.

"Sit with me," Elisabeth says.

Charlotte shakes her head and her knuckles begin to turn white as she squeezes the back of the chair.

"Oh, for the love of god, sit down, Charlotte," Dr. Harbinger says, shoving his glasses to the top of his head. He begins mopping his chin with his broad flat hand. He has yet to raise his eyes to either of them.

Elisabeth wonders why Dr. Harbinger addresses Charlotte and Elisabeth with their first names and yet they are obligated to call him Dr. Harbinger, and she wonders if she will ever become someone that people will keep a respectful distance from by virtue of what she has accomplished or studied. *Oh, yes, Dr. Smythe. She's very important. Knows the alphabet off by heart. Went to medical school. Can count by nines and that's no easy feat. Can hop on one foot.* Elisabeth chuckles and Charlotte flinches.

Going to medical school is the only criterion Elisabeth can think of. That and maybe becoming a minister. She's never heard anyone call Reverend McFayden by his first name. No one enters the church and waves up to the altar and shouts, *Morning, Harvey.*

"Your front steps need painting. They should be white. Like they used to be," Charlotte says and gives in, sitting slowly as if she imagines someone pulling the chair away at the last second. Dr. Harbinger ignores the paint complaint.

"I've been around a while," Dr. Harbinger says as if that somehow accredits him to be all knowing.

His degree is framed and hangs on the wall behind his head, but is slightly askew. Elisabeth is certain Charlotte knows to the eighth of an inch how far off level the frame is. Elisabeth is tempted to reach up and straighten it. *Can't have anything not perfect, can we, Charlotte,* Elisabeth imagines saying, and she almost giggles despite the very serious conversation she knows is coming.

Dr. Harbinger contacted Elisabeth directly, came right to the school and had the office call her down. She feared for a minute she might be getting expelled when the crackle came over the loud speaker in English Class.

"Mr. Tucker, please send Elisabeth Smythe to the office," the office secretary said, barely able to hide her lack of interest.

Elisabeth nearly jumped out of her skin when she heard her name. She thought being called down was reserved for those students caught skipping or smoking. Elisabeth hadn't so much as walked in the out door, hadn't broken a single rule in her life, but what if there was a mix-up in identity, someone who looked like Elisabeth had shoplifted or tried to light the school on fire. She gave Rebecca a quick glance before she got out of her desk. Rebecca was sitting up very straight, a fierce look on her face, her eyebrows at a steep angle.

"Righty-oh," Mr. Tucker said, as if he was sending Elisabeth down for a tea party.

Had Elisabeth forgotten she had a dentist appointment? She ran her tongue over her teeth to see if she could tell if a cleaning was overdue. Has someone died? Someone would have to be Charlotte, because she is the beginning, middle, and end of Elisabeth's family. Two people don't exactly create a family. A family should have more players, a lineup of characters with their votes for favourite meal, his turn to take out the garbage, her being grounded for bad behaviour and making the others seem better. Two isn't enough to be a family, not a real family.

Elisabeth put her feet down quietly, one foot ahead of the other in silent deliberate haste. Dr. Harbinger was waiting in the hall by the office; his hands were stuffed deep in his pockets and he was pacing. Elisabeth knows Dr. Harbinger. He saw her when she had her tonsils out at nine and strep throat before that. He had looked in her ears and under her tongue in case some disease was hiding there. He gave her a tetanus shot before she started school. He told her not to cry while he flicked an air bubble out of the syringe and held the menacing needle up in front of her. He peeked in her underwear at the last minute, making her squirm with embarrassment, like he was checking to see if she had the correct girl parts or wasn't hiding another copy of herself in there. He had given her all the rules that went with having diabetes: the when to eat, the what to eat, the how much to eat and how much insulin went along with each step and how to convince herself the needles don't hurt.

Diabetes didn't have a beginning that Elisabeth can recall; it had always been there, like the birthmark on her left arm where it folds in the middle, a small red swirl that she used to pick at to see if it would disappear. She had to pretend she cared about having diabetes, about what she ate, pretend that she was paying attention to the clammy feeling at the back of her neck or the dizziness in her head and the blurred vision when she needed sugar. She had to notice the irritation and belligerence that boiled up inside her and the dry mouth and the insistent bladder when her blood sugar was too high. Some days she didn't care at all and wanted to put her hand up and say *No more needles,* to shout it at Charlotte, who insisted she fill the syringe and stand over Elisabeth to be sure she followed through.

I'll do it, Elisabeth said to Charlotte when Elisabeth was eight. Charlotte was stunned as Elisabeth lifted her shirt and squeezed her skin on her abdomen and slid the needle under the skin and pushed the insulin into her body and didn't cry though she wanted to. She didn't even wince. Dr. Harbinger didn't know about any of that, but he still came to the school to find her, to tell her what to do.

"Elisabeth," Dr. Harbinger said, putting his arm on her back and directing her into a corner. "I had them call you down. I need to talk to you about your mother. Mr. Binder said we could use his office. She's all right, your mother," as if in an afterthought he decided to put Elisabeth at ease. He nearly shoved her though the door. *I'm a busy, busy man,* his hurried urgent tone said.

Elisabeth hadn't asked if her mother was okay, still slightly numb from the walk from English, wondering what she might have done wrong, not certain she wouldn't be charged with some offence punishable by death.

Dr. Harbinger collapsed in a chair as if all the air had gone out of him and immediately began cleaning his glasses to buy himself time. He yanked his white wrinkled shirt out at the waist and massaged the lenses back and forth inside the shirt and stuck his long legs out in front of him.

"Mr. Domanski was in to see me the other day. He claims he woke up one morning to find your mother digging through his deep-freeze. She said she was looking for her brother's papers. I didn't know she had a brother. Did you?"

Elisabeth stared at him.

"Has there been a lot of behaviour like this? Confusion? A bit of paranoia? Panic?"

Elisabeth nodded, wondering if she was to blame, the stress of raising a child that didn't belong to Charlotte. Was he saying it was her fault? What did he want her to do?

"I need you to bring your mother in to see me so I can run some tests. I've called her several times, but she won't come. She won't even listen. Hangs up the phone," he says, clicking his tongue against his teeth in frustration.

Elisabeth nods slowly, like she's been asked to play a part in a covert operation where national security is at risk and she has no choice but to comply. *Your mission, should you choose to accept it.*

"Nine o'clock next Tuesday. I've booked an hour's time for her. Then we'll meet again the next Tuesday at the same time to discuss the results and plan a strategy. I'm fairly certain I know what we're dealing with," Dr. Harbinger said, exhaling dramatically and pulling his feet back under him, and Elisabeth didn't ask. She wasn't sure she was allowed to ask a question. He had the power.

* * *

"I am an expert on dementia," Dr. Harbinger is saying, snapping Elisabeth's attention back to the present.

Elisabeth doesn't see any certificates on the wall that boast of his acute intellect on the *conundrum of muddle,* as he calls it. Charlotte's left hand is pressed over her mouth, the right squeezed into a fist on her lap. She isn't looking at either Elisabeth or Dr. Harbinger. Her eyes open and close deliberately.

Dr. Harbinger's violin is resting against the wall, out of its case, ready if he suddenly has the urge to play. Dr. Harbinger is inclined to do that. Sometimes between patients and sometimes while a patient is in the room. He has been known to play to settle an unwilling child, or so rumour has it. Most residents of Roddick who have been a patient of Dr. Harbinger have heard the lovely whine leaking out from around his office door, the gentle high-pitched melody that makes everyone pause and listen, and most crying cease. People stop mid-stride or mid-sentence and hush themselves as Dr. Harbinger drags the bow across the strings of his violin, his eyes closed and his upper body weaving back and forth, as though every cell of his body is playing along.

Dr. Harbinger plays in a band. Alan Watt plays the saxophone. Alan is a quiet, white-haired lawyer, tall and willowy, who stands and sways like a limbless tree when he plays, a look of the sublime on his face, as if all the intricacies of the law that cause people to battle each other in court are forgotten while the music from his saxophone drifts up and envelops him, as if the saxophone allows him to forget about the intrusions that life flings at him. Shirley Sutherland plays the piano, her knees bouncing and her whole body joining in with her head thrown back in laughter and her very red lips stretched into a huge smile. She wears red high heels, the right kicked off so her foot can work the sustaining pedal. Herman Gray plays the bass and the hair he combs over comes loose when he really gets into the music, but he doesn't seem to care. Dr. Harbinger plays his violin like a rock star, his mouth open in a huge long oval and his bow almost animated, dipping and diving. They don't have any record deals in their future, but they do have a *shitload of fun,* Dr. Harbinger can be counted on to say.

"We've done the tests," Dr. Harbinger says, flicking Charlotte's file with his pointer finger, pushing the file away from him and toward Elisabeth, as if the file might be holding something contagious that would cause him to break out in hives and suddenly forget his name.

"It's all in there," he says.

Charlotte squirms as if she's trying to moult her skin. Elisabeth remembers finding the car keys in the crisper drawer of the refrigerator or the same small load of white clothes washed and dried continuously without ever getting soiled, the reminder notes left everywhere, the shorter and shorter sentences and the concentration that has Charlotte's lips moving slightly as if she is chanting *I can remember, I can remember.* Charlotte doesn't seem to be getting any worse. She still has moments, long stretches where she appears perfectly normal, her memory well and accounted for, her voice returning to its hushed but severe state. She tends to get confused when she is nervous or anxious, though when Elisabeth was little she could hardly remember an incident when Charlotte wasn't exactly sure of every step she took and every word that left her mouth. Perhaps Charlotte has used up her quota of controlling life, as if she is only allowed a certain amount and choosing to worry about labelling drawers and lining up coffee mugs has consumed the amount of control she was given, consumed it more quickly than those who don't care how their beds are made or whether their lawns are edged perfectly.

"Charlotte can't count backwards by threes or fours or repeat a list of five words." Dr. Harbinger says.

"Why would I want to?" Charlotte says, her usual quiet, deliberate voice replaced with an almost-shout, a bite to it. "There's no sense in that."

Dr. Harbinger crosses his arms in front of him. "This disease can't be conclusively tested for," he is saying. "There's no blood test, no urine test, no X-ray that clearly indicates the disease, but rather a pattern of behaviour and forgetfulness." He cleans his glasses again.

"The early onset of this disease has a genetic component, the experts speculate, which is, of course, no concern to you, Elisabeth. I wish I knew more of your mother's history, but she has been quite tight-lipped on that subject. Haven't you, Charlotte," Dr. Harbinger says, raising his voice as if Charlotte's hearing has been affected by the dementia too. "I knew nothing of a brother that she may or may not have, no medical history of her parents whatsoever, or of any family members."

Charlotte turns her whole body to face Elisabeth and leans in close. "You are," Charlotte says, but closes her eyes and doesn't finish the sentence.

"What's that?" Elisabeth says, but Charlotte turns her face away.

"In simple terms, Elisabeth," Dr. Harbinger says, "your mother has dementia. It's called Alzheimer's. I'm sorry. Charlotte, do you know what this means?"

Charlotte jumps out of her chair and slams her purse down on Dr. Harbinger's desk.

"You talk as if I am not in the room, as if I've left the building and the two of you can conspire about decisions that are mine alone," Charlotte says. She picks up her purse and pulls her jacket in tight around her, fumbling with the zipper and then not bothering.

"I am not her mother," Charlotte says, shaking her head and leaning forward like she is sharing a secret, her lips pulled up into a snarl.

"I think Elisabeth is aware of that," Dr. Harbinger says, clearing his throat and perhaps considering a lecture on ethics and politeness.

"But," Charlotte says, positioning her upper body over Dr. Harbinger's desk even further so her face is inches away from his, her finger raised and pointing directly at him, "I know who is."

Twenty

THE THREE FRIENDS ARE SPRAWLED OUT UNDER THE HUGE MAPLE tree on the south side of the school, under the guise of doing homework on possibly one of the last warm days of autumn. No one is admitting it, but the silent wish is for each day to crawl by. Teachers are asking about post-high school plans; university and college applications have to be filled out. There is a buzz that comes with being in the final year of high school, an almost paralyzing buzz as if, with no notice, these students who are slightly more than children must be able to imagine their lives after graduation. There is bravado and boldness, from some, but it is all a façade.

Roddick isn't an affluent community; it is isolated, set apart from the big city, and not everyone has a choice about his or her future. Some, if not most, have little notion that anything else exists beyond Roddick's reach. Many of the students can't wait to be free, can't wait to run from the school on the last day of classes, and want nothing more than a job, a paycheque so they can slip into the realm of adulthood, to follow in the same path as their parents and never look back.

Rebecca doesn't answer any questions when Mr. Currie calls her down for her guidance appointment. She is vague about her plans. "I've got it all worked out, but thanks, Mr. Currie," Rebecca says, holding up her hand to halt his interest. And he sighs an I-tried sigh and checks her name off his list of graduates.

The future never seemed real or possible or inevitable to Rebecca, but now it is knocking on her door. She can't even begin to entertain the thought of leaving Robert. He will decay in his chair, sit there day after day not eating, and there would be no one to poke him, no one to put a mirror up to his mouth and say, *Just checking, Robert. Just checking.* The cows will starve; the barn roof will fall in on Daisy, who doesn't move much these days. The grass will grow and cover the house, the trees leaning in to create the final camouflage, and no one will remember he even lives there. And no one will remember her mother.

She imagines Robert holding a family meeting with his financial papers in front of him, a gavel to call the proceedings to order, glasses perched on the end of his nose.

"What do you see yourself doing in the future, Rebecca? Tell me a bit about yourself, your dreams and ambitions. Math? Sciences? Chef? That was a spectacular meat loaf you made not so long ago. I may not have adequately demonstrated my appreciation. We'll get to that, but first things first." He leans back in his chair, stretching his arms over his head with his wrists settling behind his ears, and his legs reach out in front of him. "Go ahead. I'm all ears."

The thought is too absurd, so Rebecca tries hard not to think about the future, doesn't let it in, shows indifference to dreams and plans.

Chuck isn't sure he's had much of a choice about anything, ever, as if his feet slipped into concrete shoes the moment he was born and all he can do is shuffle them back and forth to imagine he is moving when he's not moving at all.

"I'm going to be a pilot," Chuck says.

"So you've said," Lissie says.

Chuck winces. He knows he drones on about the Norseman. He can't help himself.

"Rebecca never complains," Chuck mutters under his breath.

"Would there be any point?" Rebecca says.

Chuck works on the dock at Rainy Lake Airways in the summer, has worked there since he was fifteen. He rides his bike to work no matter the weather. Some days, when the wind is intent on holding him back, Chuck leans into his handlebars, trying to make his position as aerodynamic as possible, but fifteen miles each way is almost too much some mornings. A transport truck's wind stream knocked Chuck right off the road once and he lay in a heap in the ditch for a minute or two trying not to cry, trying not to blame Harold, trying to refill his lungs, a three-ring circus of emotions.

Harold grudgingly gave Chuck permission to work after a whole lot of quiet asking. It took Chuck weeks to find the courage to ask. He considered not even asking, and going ahead with his work plans in secret, but decided that wouldn't end well. So he laid the groundwork, starting with wanting to be more of a man, like Harold. He nearly choked on those words. He had no intention of being like Harold with Harold's squared-off fingernails like rusty chisels, pushing his slick, faded-brown hair back from his forehead, leaving lines along his scalp where the hair oil seemed to pool, with his black-brown eyes and heavy eyebrows that moved toward each other as if they were duelling, the never-smiling face with a temper that sizzled below the surface like sausages frying on the stove, snapping and spitting.

Chuck talked about the importance of earning a good day's wage and never uttered a word about airplanes, and Gran kept perfectly quiet on the subject. Any hint of a dream in the conversation would have met a veto from Harold. Harold would have vetoed Chuck if it had been possible. *We didn't need this kid,* Chuck heard Harold rant to Penelope on more than one occasion.

When Harold did finally concede to Chuck's job, though, it felt more like Harold's success than Chuck's: it came with all sorts of conditions. No one was going to drive him, and Harold forbade Gran from interfering, pointing at her in a menacing manner. Gran sometimes broke the rules and met Chuck on the highway at the end of his workday. She put Chuck's bike in the trunk and gave him a ride until they were a mile from home. She let Chuck and his bike out on the side of the road with instructions to give her enough time to get home and blend in. Sometimes she pulled into the overgrown orchard and sat in her car until Chuck had a chance to get home ahead of her.

"We'll pretend we're undercover agents," she said. "We work for Parry Mason."

Harold agreeing involved some fist waving and pounding on the table and some threats, complete with swearing and criticism and accusations, none of which was new to Chuck. Chuck has developed an almost impermeable armour where Harold is concerned. Plus, Chuck has to turn over half his wages to Harold to make up for the extra work Harold has to do. Chuck is a lazy son of a bitch, Harold says, so his efforts don't amount to a hill of beans, but still. Chuck has to feed calves in the morning before he leaves, which means a very early start, but he doesn't care. He gets to stand on the dock next to the Norseman and breathe in with awe and feel the magic of her, every single time he stands beneath her. He climbs around on her floats, using the struts like a jungle gym, and he even puts his face against her fuselage as if she were alive.

The bush pilots take pity on him as he drags the mountains of tourists' gear from the car park down to the dock, listening to the tourists chatter as though they had flown the aircraft themselves, the male boasting akin to pounding on their chests and roaring their Tarzan yell.

Chuck lifts coolers and sleeping bags and boxes of food and tackle and listens to warnings of *Don't damage those rods* and *Careful that doesn't go in the lake.* Most of the dudes, as the pilots call them, try to bring too much, and once the cart is on the weigh-scale the avid fishermen have to thin out their gear. No one ever leaves a case of beer behind.

The conservation officer is there with reminders of limits and rules about transporting fish, leaving a patch of skin on each fillet and freezing them flat, and being aware their catch will be examined upon their return. Don't take the rules lightly, warns the young woman in a uniform, handing them a brochure. Her uniform is pulled over a bathing suit. She ignores the innuendo and flirting from these lumpy, balding, middle-aged men. As soon as the aircraft is away from the dock, the uniform comes off and the conservation officer switches to tanning mode, and Chuck tries not to stare at the breasts leaking out of the bikini and the waist that is sleek and smooth above hips with a meaty behind that almost cries out to be touched. Thankfully, Chuck is more certain of his passion for the Norseman and distracts his attention away from the bronzing maiden, though he steals a couple of glimpses whenever he can, using his best rehearsed spy technique. He imagines putting his body on top of hers, their arms and legs blending together, while he stands on the dock flushed and sweating.

After Chuck pumps all the water from the floats while the Norseman stands ready at the dock, and wipes her windscreen and drags the heavy fuel hose away from the walkway, he starts slinging gear up to the pilot, who decides how best to stow the load to keep the Norseman properly balanced. While they wait for the fishermen to drain their potatoes and get last-minute instructions, Chuck climbs in and sits at her controls. He spouts Norseman facts to his captive audience: wingspan fifty-one feet, length thirty-two feet, three-bladed propeller nine feet long, cruise speed one hundred fifty miles per hour, range nine hundred thirty-two miles, ceiling as high as seventeen thousand feet. Chuck starts every sentence with *Did you know*, his voice breathless, and he doesn't care whether anyone is listening. Most of the tourists have no idea how special this Canadian-built Norseman is. They don't know that over nine hundred of them were manufactured starting in 1935 and ending in 1959 and that the RCAF used seventy-nine of them and that more than seven hundred were built for US Army purposes on floats, skis, and wheels. He throws that fact in for the American tourists who make up most on the list of the fly-in fishermen looking for an adventure in the mosquito- and black fly-infested northern wilderness. Some do more beer drinking than fishing and return to the dock after two weeks sunburned, bug bitten, a little less swaggering, their wallets a whole lot lighter.

Chuck pushes the Norseman away from the dock and watches with envy while the pilot with the thick black beard and straight white teeth fiddles with the controls. The engine of the Norseman turns over and the big prop in the centre of her face swings around in a belch of smoke and then catches, vanishing into a perfect circle. She taxies to the bottom of the bay where the pilot turns the great beast into the wind, adjusts her flaps, and pushes the throttle full forward. The Norseman groans as she leans back on her floats, then growls as she picks up speed and pulls the air with her propeller, and then roars as she lifts off the water, one float first, usually the left, the right following, and as she clears the trees she purrs and Chuck's arms involuntarily shoot above his head, and the bikini-clad conservation officer turns her face away from Chuck muttering something about *boys*, the sound of disdain in her voice.

* * *

"When?" Lissie asks, with a hint of judgement in her voice.

"Soon. Before I'm done growing up," Chuck says. His laugh sounds nervous and the voice is different in his head when Lissie is around, as though her presence still makes him uneasy.

"Oh, soon. I thought you meant you had a real plan," Lissie says, having long ago given up the compulsion to apologize for busting up Chuck and Rebecca's twosome.

"It's a real plan," Chuck says. "I'm going to fly a Norseman. Like the one at Rainy Lake Airways. BSB."

"What does BSB mean?" Lissie asks while Rebecca rolls away from them, seemingly intent on what she is reading, letting her arm collapse on the side of her head, covering her ear.

"It's her call letters. You can read it on the underside of her wings when she flies over," Chuck says. "She has massive wings and you can't help but know it's the Norseman when you hear her take off. If the wind is right, I can hear her from home."

"Why are airplanes and ships and storms and hurricanes considered female?" Rebecca asks, lying on her back now and trying to touch her toes to the grass above her head.

"Because men want to control them," Chuck says, trying to sound wise.

"What do you know about women?" Lissie asks.

Nothing, Chuck would like to say. *Bloody well nothing.*

"I've spent almost my entire life with Rebecca. What's not to know?"

Rebecca snorts.

"Oh, boys are such an open book," Lissie says.

"Food, a bowel movement, and sex. That's all they need, Gran says, and in that order. Except Gran says shit and I can't pull that off the way she can." Rebecca laughs, shaking her head remembering Gran's advice. "Good ole Gran. She swears like a pro."

"I don't think that's fair," Chuck says. "About boys." He drops his pen. "What do I know?"

The three of them are quiet for several minutes, reading and jotting down notes and trying not to feel awkward.

"What about you, Lissie?" Chuck asks with suspicion in his voice.

"Art school or art history. Charlotte says I can't make a living being an artistic dreamer," Lissie says. "You need credentials. You need letters after your name." Lissie does her best impression of Charlotte.

Rebecca rolls back over on her side, her back toward the other two. *A dreamer,* Rebecca thinks. How can dreaming survive in the madness of this reality? How can they dare to imagine dreaming?

"You can be anything you want with your marks, Rebecca," Mr. Currie said.

What about money? What about responsibility? What about life having his heavy boot on my throat? These are all the retorts Rebecca wants to fling at him, but what would the point be. Mr. Currie doesn't understand her lost childhood, the frustration and rage that grow in her like a mould, a fungus that is raw and sore, consuming her patience and tolerance, and even her memories are fading to make room for the angst and anger that she has to will away or count to keep under control and that control, on some days, feels very fragile.

* * *

"I want to have sex," Rebecca says, sitting up quickly and crossing her legs.

Chuck and Lissie look at each other, not sure they heard Rebecca accurately. Chuck frowns. Lissie raises her eyebrows.

"With whom?" Lissie asks.

"*Whom?* Really? Proper grammar at a time like this?" Chuck says, trying to distract the conversation.

"Don't look like I said I wanted to rob a bank," Rebecca says.

"I'm not sure I want to have this conversation," Chuck says.

"I'm curious. We were in the boys' change room last week for Phys Ed class," Rebecca says, ignoring Chuck and feeling thankful the future plans discussion is derailed. "The Beaver Brae Bronco girls were here from Kenora to play volleyball. They had the girls' change room. It says *Julie M is easy* on the change room wall. It got me thinking about sex." Rebecca runs a blade of grass along her upper lip. "It's only natural."

"Boys are stupid," Lissie says, a sound of conviction in her voice. "Sorry, Chuck, but why do boys write that stuff?"

"We're not all stupid. Everyone knows Julie Mitchell is easy."

"What makes a girl easy and a boy not?" Rebecca asks.

"I wanted to talk about airplanes and flying," Chuck says. He will never confess that he's been imagining Rebecca naked for a couple of years now. His mother caught him with his hands under the covers one night and told him he'd go blind if he pulled on that thing. The thought of being blind filled him with terror considering the number of times he had been pulling on it, so he backed off for a bit, but it was too tempting, hanging right there within perfect reach of his fingers, and it made him feel better to hold on to it. There had been a little boy at the beach one summer day, a toddler with his diaper on, and he trotted around with one hand in his diaper. Chuck heard the mother say something about a boy and his penis, and she pulled his hand out of his diaper and slapped the toddler's hand and made him cry. *It's embarrassing,* the mother said to her friend.

Rebecca started smelling good at about age thirteen. Chuck asked her what the smell was.

"Deodorant," she said, like he had three heads. "Give it a shot."

He hadn't said more than that.

He imagined putting his face below Rebecca's ear and letting his tongue run along the smooth skin on her neck. The image made him sweaty and his heart pounded and he felt a tightening in his underwear that made him squirm, so he quit imagining those kinds of things when she was around and instead remembered Harold kicking him in the rear end and the toe of Harold's boot tearing the flesh around his anus. Chuck had fallen to the ground sucking in his breath with gasps, his lips pursed. That memory settled down any urges.

It isn't just Rebecca. He looks at Janet Anderson in math class, her sweater stretched tight over her very generous bosom, *jugs*, the boys call them, and Janet has no problem flinging them about and colliding them into boys whenever she has the chance. Rebecca says breasts are power, the bigger the breasts, the more power, but Rebecca keeps her breasts harnessed and hidden beneath sloppy sweatshirts and loose tops. She isn't one to flaunt, which makes Chuck work harder to imagine something heaving on Rebecca's chest, straining to be set free. Chuck imagines a bodice ripping open like the one on the cover of Gran's books.

Then there is Lori Hickerson, whose skirts are so short there is hardly any leg not visible, and the idea of her underwear being almost in full view—almost—makes his eyes water and his breathing quicken. He listens to the boys and their bragging, one trying to keep ahead of the other. Most of it made up. Things about undoing bras and pulling skirts up and underwear down, and the stories all flood back in Chuck's mind when he is trying to sleep, and one thing leads to another and then some more pulling on that thing.

* * *

"You have to admit, it is a bit confusing. Girl feels curious and wants to check out a boy's body parts and she's easy. Boy feels curious and tries to check out a girl's body parts and he is somehow knight-worthy," Rebecca says. "Doesn't make a lot of sense."

"Charlotte would lock me away in the tower if she knew I was thinking about having sex. I'd get several hours of lectures on teen pregnancy," Lissie says.

Chuck and Rebecca exchange a look; they both know that Charlotte isn't giving any lectures these days.

"I don't think my parents know what sex is," Chuck says, laughing.

"Oh, they know all right. They know," Rebecca says, and Chuck moans and covers his ears with his hands and hums loudly.

"Still," Rebecca says. "I've been thinking about it."

"You wouldn't," Lissie says, moving in closer.

"Probably not," Rebecca says. "Brian Fischer has asked me out more times than I can count. I danced with him at Homecoming and he did some heavy-duty hip pushing against me. I thought it was a little more than obvious. He'd probably be willing."

"Willing is an understatement," Chuck mutters under his breath.

"What?"

"Nothing."

"Richard Hare would probably have sex with a fence post, so if I was desperate, I suppose. But where and how? So many things to consider. Robert never leaves the house so I can't exactly do it there."

"No, thank you, Jesus," Lissie says.

"I'd hate to die not knowing," Rebecca says.

"Do you have plans to die?" Lissie asks.

"You never know. You never know."

"Can we talk about airplanes now?" Chuck says, a bit of a whine to his voice.

Rebecca shrugs and Lissie picks up her papers and begins writing again.

"Fire away," Rebecca says. "I'm all ears."

"Well, you've spoiled it now," Chuck says, wiping away the sweat from his forehead.

Twenty-One

REBECCA KEEPS THE KEYS SHE COPIED WITH LISSIE'S MONEY hidden between her mattress and box spring, hidden with the other treasures: her mother's picture, a newspaper clipping about Rebecca's mother playing the piano, one of Jake's baby socks, and Rebecca's first toothbrush.

Up and down, not back and forth, her mother said, looking over Rebecca's shoulder in the mirror. That's it, her mother said with her smile revealing perfect white teeth, her hand letting go of Rebecca's wrist, while Rebecca stood on a wooden crate at the bathroom sink, pretending she was tall, tall enough to see in the mirror.

The toothbrush is one of Rebecca's favourite memories of her mother, second only to the image of being held, wrapped tightly in a flannelette blanket, her mother tucked in the rocking chair, Rebecca's nose up against her mother's neck, her mother's humming vibrating through the blanket to Rebecca's skin, a gentle buzz while she rocked. Rebecca isn't sure she remembers or imagines it, but has added the details of her mother wearing a long white nightgown with smocking at the chest and a row of fine cotton lace crocheted at the edge around her neck and a white ribbon at the end of her braid. The humming is hushed, *Hush thee my baby to rest,* and it is late spring, the sun reluctant to set, arguing with the moon over whose turn it is, the frogs singing in support of the moon, sending the sun to set, with its pinks and oranges clinging to the horizon as a last farewell, all the details needed to make the image real, something to hold on to, and the rocker is moving gently forward and back, forward and back, the floor creaking beneath it, almost silently, one breath above silent, forward and back with each beat of Rebecca's heart, forward and back.

Rebecca used to wrap a blanket tight around her, pulled it around her body, under her arms and then over, like she was a human jellyroll. She sat on the edge of the bed, her eyes closed, and she leaned forward and back and sometimes side to side, imagining her mother whispering about how perfect Rebecca is, and Rebecca tried to smell apples and lavender. But she can't be sure now if there ever were apples or lavender. *There, there,* her mother whispered. *There, there.*

Rebecca looks at the collection of treasures. She puts the yellow toothbrush with its tiny bristles, the bristles bent and discoloured now, against her teeth. *Up and down. Up and down.* She pulls her lips up in a snarl to examine her teeth in the mirror. She remembers losing her first front tooth, wiggling it back and forth, then pressing her thumbnail under it and closing her eyes really tight while she popped it out. The sound of the tissue tearing away from the tooth made her stomach feel squeamish, but when she found the shiny new quarter from the Tooth Fairy under her pillow the next morning in recognition of her bravery, she was willing to pull the whole lot of her teeth out. That was the only quarter the Tooth Fairy ever left. Rebecca put a collection of teeth under her pillow in an envelope for almost a year. Nothing. The Tooth Fairy forgot all about Rebecca, didn't want Rebecca's faulty teeth. Her adult teeth grew in straight, or straight enough.

Rebecca puts her two fingers in Jake's sock, red and blue stripes, boy colours. Where's the other sock? Where are the shoes and the learning to tie laces? Her father duct-taped Rebecca's laces when she couldn't tie them tight on her own. She was learning how to tie when her mother left her, when her mother chose Jake instead of her; she hadn't quite mastered lace-tying, not exactly sure where the loops went and which one to do the final pull on, not able to look up at her mother for reminding. When her laces came undone, Robert slapped a piece of duct tape over the top of her shoe to keep the laces from trailing on the ground. So Rebecca practised on her own to get it right. She didn't like the tape or the sound of Robert's tongue clicking on the roof of his mouth or him tearing the tape with his teeth. That's so long ago now. Why does she bother with such memories, why isn't her mind used for creating new ones, striking out on her own, slamming shut the book of her broken childhood? Why are her memories frozen on one or two years, as if nothing else happened worth remembering, worth storing for later?

The newspaper clipping is a story about Rebecca's mother playing the piano for a performance at the JA Mathieu Auditorium the summer Rebecca's mother was seventeen. The clipping is taped to thick paper, the tape yellowed and brittle now. Rebecca keeps it inside a folded-over piece of cardboard so the delicate paper won't tear. She imagines her mother sitting at the piano, a long black gown and white gloves to her elbows. No one can play the piano with gloves on, but still. Rebecca's mother stands on the stage, smiling down at the audience, closing her eyes slowly in thankfulness to them for coming. She tips her head slightly, humbled by their encouragement, but once she sits at the piano she is transported to some other dimension where her music is the language and the very air she breathes. Her fingers fly over the keys and her eyes close as if her fingers need no guidance, know all on their own which direction to go, which keys to press, when merely to brush the keys and when to put her whole weight behind it, almost standing up and leaning over the piano. And when she finishes she breathes deeply for a few seconds, waiting for re-entry before she stands and bows.

How could someone so talented, so beautiful, so poised and perfect marry someone like Robert, who no longer bathes? Has Robert long ago forgotten Grace's beauty and perfection, forgotten to honour Grace's memory?

The keys: which one is which, of the three she copied from Robert's collection that he clung to as if they opened the vault of the world's wealth and secrets? One key opens the shed door, one opens the trunk, and she's not sure what the third key is for. Why hasn't she used them? She traces the edge of the key with her finger. She holds them up, a string connecting them all, and they sound like a wind chime, a delicate tinkling.

Does she really want to know what's in the trunk, what her father has hidden away from her? What if it's something sinister or rotten? What if it's something she doesn't want to see or know? She can't change her mind once she opens it and looks. It will be too late and then she will have to add regret to her list of lonely longing, add it to the emptiness that runs from the top of her head to the soles of her feet.

She puts Jake's sock up to her cheek and rubs it back and forth. She can't remember him wearing this sock, can't remember it hanging off his foot as he staggered around the house with his arms over his head, celebrating being alive, celebrating walking without holding on, celebrating freedom, as if he could measure his own growth. *Look at me,* he would say if he could talk.

Can she remember him? Really remember him, the tiny bits of detail, the creases in his wrist, which fingers close first on hers, which teeth came in first, the sound of his new voice, his first voice, before it became real, when his voice was more a promise than a sound? Can she remember him at all? Or has he become fiction? Some character she invented with a cherub face and blond curls and blue eyes that sparkle like a cliché. Maybe he is actually pale and thin and his skin greyish, his eyes cloudy and dark. She thinks she remembers his thick feet, pudgy and fat, and how she thought she might bite his toes off because they were so cute and it made her grit her teeth. She mostly remembers disliking him, wishing him away when he climbed on her mother's lap, and envying him when Robert hoisted him high over his head so Jake could put his baby hands on the ceiling while he giggled. She had been a bad sister, not really a sister at all, hadn't shared her toys or taught him how to dunk his cookie in milk. When her mother asked Rebecca to watch him while she ran to the garden or the clothesline, Rebecca became a human shield to prevent Jake from touching anything, and he collapsed on the floor wailing in protest and she rubbed her hands together with success. She had thought his tiresome antics to blame, but maybe she should never be trusted with children, must not be a teacher or a Brownie leader or a babysitter. She wished Jake away.

If Jake had lived, would Robert be different? If her mother had lived but not Jake, would Robert have blamed Rebecca's mother instead of blaming Rebecca? If Rebecca had also drowned, would Robert have started over, created a new family, and forgotten his loss? Would he have found another wife who would place her hand on Robert's shoulder when he needed steadying, set a steaming cup of coffee in front of him in the morning while they exchanged knowing glances, a look that said *I'm sorry* for yesterday's argument, a smile that promised something, a stare that counted on him to do the right thing?

Rebecca curls up in a ball and pulls a pillow over her head and clutches the keys and sock and toothbrush to her chest. She thinks about yesterday's conversation about leaving high school and the end of this façade of living, the end of having somewhere to go every morning Monday to Friday, the end of writing things on paper that no one will read again or remember, the end of math equations and logarithms that will never help her solve the riddle of why to keep breathing. She has no money to imagine something away from Roddick and Robert, and who will carry on his pretense of being a farmer if she leaves? Who will listen to his silence and decipher when he needs supper or clean underwear or a wide berth?

The dream of building bridges is the stuff of juvenile foolhardiness. Her marks are good but not great. She looks at bursaries and scholarships, few of which she has any chance of securing, and none without Robert's co-operation. Where would she go if there were no limit, no restraints on the choices she could make? Would she travel a world she has no knowledge of? Would she hunker down in some commune and become an ingredient in a recipe for better living with no single purpose or identity? She reads about such places, where rules are arrived at collectively and every undertaking is for the greater good. She has no ability to blend in. She never played basketball or volleyball where she learned to be a team. Despite Chuck and Lissie, everything in her life has been about being alone.

Does she dream of climbing mountains or running marathons? Does she awaken at night seized by a plan, an urge to fly the nest? She doesn't have any dreams at all, not anymore. She may have had some once, but even that notion is too long ago, something imagined.

She isn't serious about wanting to have sex, the proclamation she made to Chuck and Lissie. She wanted the conversation about the future to stop, because she couldn't breathe, couldn't bear to listen to Chuck and Lissie actually making plans, thinking they can make plans, imagining something will change in their lives. Sex was more an announcement to feel alive, to shock her system with a made-up confession. She doubts she will ever open herself up like that and let someone in, let someone's skin touch her skin.

She wonders what it would be like to be that intimate, that naked, that exposed with someone. How much trust does someone have to have to do such a thing, to strip down to nothing and stand, willing to be judged, and not to run and hide. Would it be easy to pull another person right to you, let your legs wrap around him, and try to eliminate anything separating you, letting your instincts driven by hormones guide you? Surely that is impossible to do.

She knows boys well enough to know that there's not one to be trusted. Except Chuck. She doesn't mean to group him in with the boys who stare and sweat over breasts and bare legs, who have a weapon in their pants that they'd like to brandish as if they were fencing, with thrusts and parries and fancy footwork. Boys want to close their eyes and drive this thing into something that will stop the ache, and nature has predisposed them to do such things, to reproduce. Gran warned Rebecca about that when she went to high school. Watch out for teenage boys, Gran said. They've got one thing on their minds, just the one thing.

Rebecca read about sex, went to the library and looked in the tiny drawers under the subject headings. She flipped to *sex*, but kept her thumb under *sewing* in case anyone looked over her shoulder. There were a number of titles. One was marked *See reference desk*. She imagined a book with such vivid details and photographs it must be kept under lock and key, behind the reference desk. The book probably required a signed waiver that if opening the book caused fainting and striking the head, the library would not be held accountable.

Rebecca scribbled a few titles and corresponding numbers on a tiny piece of paper taken from the stack of papers on top of the filing boxes. She wandered through the library trying to look inconspicuous, tried to look like she knew exactly what she was doing, though she was pretty sure a light was flashing over her head to let everyone know she was looking for books about sex.

She found *A Teenager's Guide to Life and Love* written by Dr. Spock and *The Basic Writing of Sigmund Freud*. She shoved the list in her pocket and left the library, not bothering to smile at the new librarian with the bright-orange hair that hung in perfect waves to her shoulders. She didn't look up at Mr. Mayhew, who came to read the paper at the library every weekday. *Yesterday's news is easier to swallow,* he said every single time Rebecca made eye contact with him, and she had to agree.

After five trips to the library and unfruitful searches through the shelves, Rebecca decided the books were hidden in various places, not grouped together in one reference section so the library couldn't be accused of encouraging behaviour of a sexual nature. She's pretty sure that's how it would be referred to, considering the taboo quality all adults seem to attribute to sex or anything close to it.

She and Chuck and Lissie call it wrestling. They walked to the river late one night, when Rebecca did another of her truck-stealing joyrides. They parked about a half mile away and crept around like cat burglars. They peered into the back seat of a couple of cars where they saw bodies engaged in what looked very much like wrestling, hurried wrestling, as if they were being timed. Chuck and Lissie nearly split a gut, but Rebecca found the whole thing confusing and it made her uneasy.

Eventually, Rebecca came right out and flatly asked the librarian for a book that explained such things, saying she was doing a project on it. She had no one else to ask, so she asked the librarian Mrs. Greer, who winced and frowned and took a deep breath and then walked ahead of Rebecca to the science section and pulled a book or two from the shelf marked *Psychology and Human Sexuality*. She walked from section to section, pulling books off the shelf and finally handed Rebecca a book entitled *Sex Education*.

"This was published in the UK," Mrs. Greer said. "It's worth a read for the sheer madness of it," and she piled a few books up on Rebecca's arms.

Rebecca found a private cubicle and spread her notebook out and began to read. She opened first the sex education book, published in 1962, and began to read it randomly. She couldn't help but laugh. The instructions were quite clear; the man is in charge. A woman shouldn't put face cream on in front of her husband, though she should clearly put face cream on, so it becomes a covert operation: wait until he is asleep to slip into the bathroom and apply beauty-improving cream. And obey, a woman must obey her husband. A man's satisfaction is much more important than a woman's, but still a woman should give a slight moan to signify her pleasure and silence to demonstrate her reluctance. A man must have written this, Rebecca thinks and sets the book at the far end of the desk, opening another, *Was Jesus Married?*

She remembers the talk given to twelve-year-olds. The boys and girls were separated, the boys sent to the gym with Mr. Pedorski and the girls kept in a small cluster in the classroom so they would feel safe and secure. The girls were told about the secret place inside their bodies and the boys were told what to call their appendages and protrusions and all things scientific.

"Not one word about how it works or how we are supposed to feel about this equipment that seems to have a mind of its own," Chuck whispered. "It's embarrassing." Rebecca said she didn't bother listening.

Rebecca watched animals enough while growing up to appreciate this instinct to mate. She doesn't want to mate, to reproduce, though she has imagined caring for a baby, holding her close and whispering about safety and forever and all those things that children should hear. She can hear the infant's kitten voice, her hair soft and down-like, her fat fingers closed around one of Rebecca's own fingers. Rebecca promises she will keep her imaginary baby safe from the world, safe from disappointment and hunger, safe from nightmares and grief, safe from Robert.

Twenty-Two

THE HIGH SCHOOL ORCHESTRA IS FRONT AND CENTRE, CHAIRS pulled in an arc around a wooden platform upon which Mr. Cranston stands, king of the castle, glasses down at the end of his nose, his suit shiny and smooth where he sits, his tie narrow and ragged, too ragged for a man of such power. Dispersed like a dusting of sugar are graduating band members wearing golden gowns and mortar boards, obligating those non-graduating band members to strain their necks around and over to see Mr. Cranston wield his conductor's baton in a threatening manner. Graduates run around like ants, looking excited, a pretend version of dignity, on the verge of laughter or tears, both at the ready. The flutes and clarinets and saxophones and trumpets are blowing an E, all trying to find the same pitch, concert pitch. The sound isn't melodic or harmonic, it sounds like an argument, and Mr. Cranston frowns and points to various students to tighten their mouthpiece, a look that says *Shape up and do it now.*

"Fix that embouchure," Mr. Cranston says in a snarl, smacking his lips together to demonstrate the correct position of the lips and then smiles immediately, a fake smile, but a smile just the same, as if he knows he must contain his frustration for this one event, assure the parents their precious progeny are in good hands.

Mr. Cranston is well known for his outbursts, his temper and his slamming of doors in the music room, his shouts of *Is there not a musical bone in any of your bodies?* at the top of his lungs while standing on his desk chair. One student, a boy who made attending high school a life's calling by taking two years to finish each grade, dared to challenge Mr. Cranston. *We only have one body; go back to grammar school.* Mr. Cranston stopped shouting. His face became ashen and his hair, what was left of it, nearly burst into flames. He pointed to the door like the Grim Reaper in a Dickens novel. It was almost legendary. Messing with Mr. Cranston is never a good idea. *Crazy Cranston.*

Rebecca wanted to play in the band. Mr. Cranston demands participation in the band, and those students who don't participate have an entire grade point deducted for apathy. A whole grade point, and then added some singling out in class and threw in a bit of humiliation for good measure.

Rebecca plays the clarinet, B-flat clarinet, in music class. To be in the band meant Monday-evening practices and early-morning practices before school on Thursdays, neither of which could be accommodated by Robert's hectic schedule of sleeping in his chair and reading the newspaper, both in equal parts. Rebecca considered tearing the *Winnipeg Tribune* from his lap and beating him with it.

"This is about life outside," she wanted to scream, hammering him with the newspaper. "There is life in here. I am life," and she might have pounded her chest or put his hand on her face, his good hand. Instead, she snatched the newspaper off his lap and tore it into pieces before crumpling the whole mess and throwing it in the wood stove. He didn't react, didn't move a hair.

So she doesn't ask for rides to band or volleyball or track or the dentist or the bank or anywhere. She tried to find someone to carpool with, but that implied returning the favour and unless she planned on stealing the truck every other week, the plan wouldn't hold up. She even tried to coerce Chuck to take up an instrument, but he wasn't having any of that. Gran would have driven her had Rebecca asked, but she couldn't bring herself to ask, to need something from someone, something she can't pay for.

The band holds a concert twice a year, a fundraiser for new instruments and repairs and band jackets and music. Rebecca feels a disturbing envy when the music starts, when the sound moves about on the inside of her, like it has climbed in her ear and she can feel the music in her fingers and toes and in the pit of her stomach and in her chest where the bass seems to come through and the pounding of the tympani drum that echoes in her very core. Music is in your genes, Rebecca's mother said. It's fixed there, without choice, so you must never waste it. It is meant to be shared, to be put to use.

* * *

Parents are finding seats in the large auditorium, chairs dragging along the floor, people calling out to one another, mothers anxious, fathers awkward, younger siblings confused and forgotten.

"Two seats over here," one student usher calls out, waving his arm above those seated like he is landing an airplane.

Several groups rush over, like chickens to falling corn, to grab up the seats. Those in the front row look like they've been camped there for days, jackets on the backs of chairs, the grandmother left to chase off intruders.

"No, no," she repeats several times. "These are saved."

"All of them?" hopeful guests ask in disbelief, thinking of shoving her off to the side, but slink away in disappointment instead, wishing they had come earlier, wishing they had a grandmother to use as a placeholder.

Graduating students flow in and out the side doors of the gymnasium while teachers try to corral them, like they are herding kittens, telling them to be quiet, to wait in the hall, to calm down, but the energy can't be contained. Principal Binder walks on to the stage and taps the microphone several times and the sound system squeaks and squawks, painfully loud, and guests gradually stop their conversations about lake levels and tourist lineups at the Bridge and hay yields and begin to quiet, barely able to resist making one more comment, one more hello.

"I would ask all graduating students," Mr. Binder says, pointing and shaking his head to those in the band wearing gold, "to gather in the hall to my right, for those of you who have not already done so as you were instructed to do upon arrival." Mr. Binder is shaking his head, trying not to look annoyed but undoubtedly thinking none of these graduates can follow directions and how on earth are they going to survive in the real world. "Let's get this show on the road," he says, smiling down from his position of superiority, wondering how he has made it through one more year in this god-forsaken land of snow and mosquitoes, extremes of both, mentally calculating the number of days until his retirement.

It takes Miss Banks to raise her voice as loud as she can to ensure the graduates are all lined up in reverse alphabetical order. She calls out each name and the students are mostly co-operative. Those not graduating, whose marks didn't quite make the grade, have had their names stroked out on the master list, a perfectly straight line drawn with a ruler and red pen.

Rebecca and Chuck and Lissie don't stand together, their surnames scattered through the alphabet: Archer, Prescott, Smythe. The three of them came together; Gran drove them calling herself the graduation chauffeur. She had a single rose for each of them, a white rose, even one for Chuck.

"Men don't get flowers," Chuck protests, holding the rose up to his nose and closing his eyes as he breathes in.

"Charlotte would approve," Lissie says, and Gran smiles.

"Pretty smart for an old bird," Chuck says, giving Gran a little shove from the back seat, and Rebecca pinches him. "That's what she calls herself. She knows she's old," Chuck says with a whining defense.

"It's rude," Rebecca says.

* * *

Rebecca is wearing one of Lissie's skirts, a long one in browns and golds that gathers at the waist. She wears a soft gauzy white blouse that Gran gave her, loose fitting and softly hanging from her shoulders. Her long hair is pulled back in a loose ponytail secured with a white ribbon at the base of her neck. Lissie is wearing all white, a white tailored suit. *For Charlotte*, Lissie says with a smile, her dark hair pulled back in a tight bun, her darker-than-dark eyes wearing a hint of soft purple eye shadow. Chuck's pants are almost too short, but Gran squeezed every inch she could out of the hem. His white shirt is clean and crisp, ironed to perfection, and he is sporting a tie, a man's tie, not a clip-on, a real grown-up tie with black and grey stripes. His hair is smoothed back, his curls modestly contained and his puberty pimples gone. Chuck looks manly, suddenly taller than Rebecca. She hadn't really noticed this before.

Robert isn't coming. Rebecca didn't show him the announcement, never mentioned she is getting the physics and mathematics awards. Charlotte is in care at the Roddick Nursing Home for the weekend, where she can be watched and contained. She doesn't like going there, puts up a huge fuss, as if she is a cat being stuffed in a bag, suddenly all arms and legs grabbing hold of anything, with a whole lot of screaming.

"Elisabeth," Charlotte cries at the top of her lungs. "Call my brother."

"You don't have a brother," Lissie says, or she nods and agrees to call him. "I will, I will. Don't worry," but nothing calms Charlotte. She is afraid and angry and confused and every emotion in between.

Lissie has a woman who comes to stay with Charlotte while Lissie is at school. Some days Lydia can hardly make it through the day of trying to keep Charlotte indoors, using locked deadbolts on both the front and back doors. And other days, Charlotte is peaceful and content, folding laundry and looking through boxes of papers. She doesn't say much except to ask Lydia when she might be leaving, as if Lydia is the one thing between Charlotte and freedom.

Chuck's parents are coming.

"Gran shamed them into it," Chuck says. "Harold will have to wear proper shoes, but I wouldn't be surprised if he shows up in his barn boots and drags manure all through the front entrance."

Gran takes a long drag on her cigarette while Rebecca and Lissie wince. Chuck isn't getting any awards, no recognition for best wood-worker or least-likely-to-electrocute-himself-in-shop-class. Lissie is winning the art award.

"Hands down, Roddick High's finest artist," Rebecca shouts as though she is the town crier, and Lissie giggles.

Rebecca hasn't told her friends she is playing the piano and singing after the valedictorian's address. Mr. Quesnel asked her to do it, said he knew it would mean a lot to everyone, but Rebecca isn't exactly sure who *everyone* is. She confided in Gran, told her how scared she is, how she isn't sure she can do it, but Gran shook that off like nonsense.

Gran put her hand on her chest. "You just do it," Gran said, very firmly. And then nodded as if there were no room for doubt and backing out now.

Rebecca practised at school during her spares and lunch break. Mr. Cranston told her she was doing a fine job and asked why exactly she wasn't in band and then shook his head like he understood the madness of her existence. Mr. Cranston gave her an A in music despite her absence from band.

"The Long and Winding Road," the Beatles' version of it. Mr. Quesnel said it was short and perfect for her voice, but said she could sing "O Canada" if she preferred, at which they both laughed, remembering her grade-nine debut singing the national anthem at the top of her lungs.

Rebecca considers drinking a bit of whisky to take the edge off, but is afraid she will slur her words or maybe worse, maybe fall off the piano stool. She might have tried a doobie, but she has no idea how to smoke a joint so she decides to tough it out. Saying the word *doobie* makes her feel like a fraud, but she is thinking of adding smok-ing to her list of things to do that scare the hell out of her. Learning to swim is on the list—also sex and eating sushi, which she read is raw fish and the notion of such food makes her gag, but she can be worldly if she tries. At the very top of her list is cut ties with father.

She isn't sure she can ever strike that out as having been done, but still, it's good to have on the list.

She checks the program and sees it shows merely *Musical Number*, so if she makes a run for it the orchestra can fill in with another round of "Pomp and Circumstance."

The hall lights flash on and off and Miss Banks puts her finger to her lips and everyone is quiet, or doing their best version of quiet, and she smiles, suddenly humbled by their youth and their enthusiasm and their innocence, and nods at them.

"Well done," she whispers. "Well done."

Travis Enge appears in full Scottish gear, his kilt and tunic and feather bonnet. Travis plays in the Legion band and everyone in town knows Travis, the man in charge of maintenance for all the schools in the district. If you have a problem, any problem, you call Travis; he's that kind of a guy, a rescue guy. Travis stands at the back of the auditorium and plays three blasting notes and then begins to march in place as the graduates form a line behind him and then begin the slow procession up the main aisle to the seating next to the stage, while Travis plays some Scottish marching song that everyone knows without knowing.

The audience is on its feet, snapping photos and waving to children, privately thanking some higher order for getting the kids this far without disaster. It all feels a bit like a magic show to Rebecca, a sleight of hand, smoke and mirrors. What is she graduating from and where is she headed? She marches along with the rest of her class, most of them thankful that thirteen years of study are behind them. Rebecca and Lissie have no one to wave to; no one has pressed her finger to Rebecca's name in the program with a huge sigh of relief, making certain she hasn't been overlooked. No one is ready to beam when Lissie gathers up the art award, looking left and right to take credit for Lissie's genetically wired talent. Gran catches Rebecca's eye and points at her and nods, and they both know what she is saying.

Rebecca doesn't hear the introduction from Mr. Binder or the singing of "O Canada," though she does stand and sing. She is staring at *Musical Number* in the program and wondering how she could possibly have agreed to this. What was she thinking? What business does she have thinking she can fill her mother's shoes, that her limited talent will honour her mother? *So like her mother.* Rebecca chants her grandmother's words in her head. *So like her mother.*

* * *

The academic awards are handed out. She crosses the stage and sticks her hand in the direction of the school board trustee and mumbles something that resembles *Thanks.* She doesn't cheer when Lissie's name is called for the art award, doesn't even clap. She is frozen in her chair, hardly able to breathe.

No wonder her father never leaves the house, hardly leaves his chair, Rebecca thinks. She isn't much different from him, but their chairs are different sizes: his fills a room and her chair spills out the door and into school. She thinks she might throw up.

The valedictorian walks to the podium while the audience claps its welcome. He opens a book to read from while everyone quiets down. He is class president, an every-guy's-guy sort of guy. He plays football and track, has good marks and good teeth and the right kind of haircut, not too long or too short. He works at the grocery store restocking shelves and carries out groceries when someone needs help. What is he going to tell his graduating class? That life is easy, simple, and straightforward, that there are no surprises or bumps, that the graduates get precisely what they deserve, what they have earned? He could have given a recipe for carrot cake for all Rebecca knows because she refuses to listen and can feel anger begin to bubble and boil inside her, and she wants to smash something, wants to tear down this building, this school that has held her prisoner for five years, a school that allowed her to hide and be invisible and not matter, a school that demanded she blend in as one of the collective.

She hears Mr. Binder call her name, twice maybe, before Brian Allison shoves her with his knee. She shakes her head and stands, catches Chuck's eye, and takes note of his confused face as if she has been part of some hilarious prank behind the scenes.

Rebecca walks to the centre of the stage, the piano on her left and the podium on her right. Her whole body feels wooden and hollow. She can hear whispers behind her and sees Mr. Binder's hand extending in her direction. Instead of going to the piano she walks to the podium and nods at Mr. Binder as she brushes past him to stand in front of the microphone. She switches the microphone on and it squeaks. She doesn't say anything for what seems like several minutes but is probably more like seconds. People are adjusting themselves in their seats and clearing their throats.

"I dedicate this to my mother," Rebecca says, and her voice comes out loud and strong and surprises her, as if someone else has spoken for her. She turns and walks to the piano and moves in between the piano stool and the keys, gathers up Lissie's skirt, and slowly sits down. She leaves her hands on her thighs and breathes deeply once or twice and adjusts the microphone pointing into her face. Three flats, she says in her head. Just three flats. E flat major. Nothing too hard. Simple. No really high notes. She can sing it if she can swallow the fountain of saliva that is bubbling up inside her mouth.

She makes a fist with each hand over the keys and slowly opens her fingers and lowers them to the piano keys. She is transported to the shed, to her mother's piano hidden under the dirty tarp, the mice making nests inside its working parts, and she plays, plays and sings for her mother. She doesn't hesitate, doesn't miss a note or a beat, doesn't feel another person in the room, doesn't notice the temperature or the amount of light or the sounds of people breathing. They have all vanished and in this moment she is the only person on earth.

The music rises up from the piano, from her throat, floating weightless on the air, and Rebecca feels the sound leave the room, leave the school, leave this earthly plane. *Mommy,* she whispers when her fingers rise from the keys.

She opens her eyes and rises to stand beside the piano, as her mother had in the photo, and bends at the waist with a gentle bow. She can't tell if anyone has applauded or is deathly silent because she looks up at the audience and sees her father limping out the door at the back of the auditorium.

Twenty-Three

"WHAT DO WE DO NOW?" CHUCK ASKS OVER A COKE FLOAT AT THE Husky House, their go-to place. Not many other kids come out to the Husky House on the west end of town: too obscure, too far from downtown. There are no tables here loaded with Coke and fries and smoking teenagers. No gangs making plans to climb the water tower and spray paint an obscenity or two. No dares to streak naked through town or lift Mr. Angelini's Volkswagen Beetle and place it sideways in his garage. Besides, that's already been done.

Lissie and Rebecca shrug their shoulders and look at each other, sucking hard on the thick ice cream saturated with Coke, the ice cream fizzing and melting and flopping inside the glass. Chuck lifts his feet off the floor and spins the chrome stool around as if he is on a midway ride, but his legs are too long now and they collide with Rebecca's and Lissie's knees so they both make him stop. Chuck looks disappointed and Rebecca wonders why boys take so long to grow up.

Chuck is almost six feet, yet he has the maturity of an eight-year-old, still cries on occasion when Harold puts a good beating on him. Chuck shows up at Rebecca's door with tears and a bleeding nose and a cracked fat lip. One time Harold pulled a whole handful of hair out of Chuck's head, leaving a noticeable and bleeding bald spot. Chuck really cried that time, snot pouring from his nose, his shoulders convulsing, and Rebecca, barely able to contain her rage, had to force herself into silence. She led Chuck out to the yard to sit under the cedar that used to be a small round ball and now is tall and thick and awkward, like Chuck. She wiped his nose on her sleeve and wondered how on earth a kid claims back his life.

* * *

Robert rises from his chair and stares out the front window at the two of them, Rebecca's arm around Chuck's shoulders. Rebecca can see Robert with her peripheral vision as he surveys them, the way he might a pending thunderstorm or a fire threatening the house, and then he pulls the drapes closed with his right arm, his left hand in his pocket.

Rebecca picks up a stone at her feet and hurls the stone at the window—*a twindow,* Robert called it when he and Rebecca's mother put the window in, *with two whole sheets of glass with air in between,* as if the window had been flown in from the Taj Mahal. The stone bounces off the window frame and hits the small pane of glass on the side of the main window and cracks the glass all the way across the pane. The curtains remain closed.

"What are you doing?" Chuck says, his crying paused.

"I'm pissed. I feel like breaking something. In fact, I'm going to cut down this cedar bush. Look at it," Rebecca says, pointing to it with both arms. "It's hideous. An eyesore. This whole place is an eyesore." She grabs the axe from the woodpile beside the shed and practically runs back to the lawn and the cedar. She starts pounding the trunk with the axe, bits of bark and wood flying in all directions, and Chuck jumps out of the way.

The tree eventually topples over and Rebecca keeps smashing it with the axe and Chuck looks at her biceps and shoulders flexing and rippling with every swing of the axe and strokes his own muscles, a look of defeat on his face.

"There," she says. "That's better. Let's go see the beavers."

Chuck falls into stride with her. "You scare me sometimes," he says.

"I scare myself."

* * *

Rebecca looks longingly at the big table in the corner of the Husky House, the round one with a single seat that wraps around the large chrome table, the red vinyl on the seats split in a few places, the seat worn and collapsed where people sit, naturally spaced. The table is for families, families with a mother and father and several kids. No one else can sit there, families only. Rebecca imagines a whole scene where she and Jake slide into the back, her mother and father the end posts, the protectors, and nothing can get at her and Jake. They flip through the songs in the jukebox menu at their table and Rebecca gets to choose happy songs: Chubby Checker singing "The Twist," and she and Jake stand on the seat and wiggle in their shoes while Robert and Grace laugh. And they never worry or care about the reaction of other customers, be it envy or annoyance. Rebecca might choose "Locomotion" and dance with her arms over her head and Jake laughs until he hiccups and then her mother says, *Shhhh*, but her eyes are still laughing, wishing the moment would never end. It is a perfect supper outing, and Rebecca orders a hot beef sandwich, open-faced. Her father begs her to try something different because she always orders a hot beef sandwich, but her mother smiles, knowing that you can't risk getting something you don't like so why spoil a good thing; that's what makes it a favourite. They come to the Husky House every Saturday night and maybe on Wednesdays. As Rebecca gets older the conversation shifts from childish topics to planning Rebecca's future. They discuss which university she might attend and what she will study. Jake interrupts because he is approaching puberty and his hormones are making him obnoxious and smelly. Rebecca's mother says, *Now Jake. It's not your turn, dear. This is Becca's time to be the centre of attention.* And Jake hangs his head in submission, plotting his next outburst. *Don't leave me,* he finally says, whispering in Rebecca's ear, and then he blushes.

And Rebecca feels the familiar ache in her stomach that brings her back to reality.

* * *

"Lydia can't manage my mother," Lissie says. "Not anymore. She has given me a month's notice but would like to quit earlier if she finds another job." Lissie sighs. "Dr. Harbinger says it's time." Lissie picks at the edge of the menu, then flattens it again with her fingers, presses the edge smooth, and looks at Rebecca, a pleading helpless look on Lissie's face. "I hate the idea of the nursing home. It's a horrible place that smells like urine and death."

Lissie knows Charlotte is no longer in charge of her own life, has gone from fierce to pathetic, certain to confused.

"Bloody disease," Rebecca mutters. *Old-timers*, people call it, but Charlotte isn't old.

Lydia talks too loud, disturbs Charlotte's peace. "I've asked Lydia to use a softer voice," Lissie says. "Or at least I tried to."

Rebecca knew what to do when she was visiting. Lydia was shouting at Charlotte about drinking her tea.

"Good grief," Rebecca said, her voice raised and speaking directly into Lydia's face. "She can't remember. She's not deaf."

Lydia looked annoyed like she might have a comeback, but Rebecca stared at her, eyebrows up, hands open, leaning in toward Lydia. No one can argue with right.

* * *

"Charlotte keeps talking about papers and her brother and is obsessed with looking through boxes," Lissie says.

Lissie explained about finding Charlotte crying in her room, behind her bed, a box of papers spread out on the floor.

I can't remember, I can't remember, Charlotte kept saying over and over, looking up at Lissie like a helpless child.

"What could I say?" Lissie says to Rebecca, her voice cracking and her eyes filling. "*There, there* doesn't do a lot of good."

"What did you do?" Rebecca asks.

"I tried asking her what was bothering her, but she covered her head and began to rock and hum and said *no, no, no* until I thought I'd go mad," Lissie says.

Maybe Charlotte wants to have a brother, makes one up so she isn't alone at the end of her life, stuck with an adopted child. Those were Lissie's words. Maybe Charlotte wants to pretend she has someone of her own flesh and blood who can donate blood, his blood, to drive the disease out of her body, if it were that easy. And maybe he lives in an imaginary place. Lissie wonders if Charlotte has been adopted, has no one to turn to, no real family, no one with matching genes and blood type. Maybe she feels totally and utterly alone.

* * *

"Charlotte might like it there," Rebecca says to Lissie.

"It has beige walls. Charlotte will spontaneously combust," Lissie says.

"We could paint her room white," Rebecca says.

"I suppose. What if she has to share a room? Charlotte can't share a room. Charlotte is no good at sharing."

"I'm sure they have single rooms."

"How will you pay for it?" Chuck asks.

"Charlotte has lots of money and she put my name on all of it before she lost her memory, or so Mr. Tinkess from CIBC says."

"I play piano at the Roddick Home once a month," Rebecca says, offhandedly. "It's a nice place."

"For who?" Chuck says.

"What?" Rebecca says, lifting her lips from the straw.

"Who do you play for?"

"For *whom* does she play, you mean?" Lissie says.

Chuck groans and rolls his eyes. "I think I graduated high school so no need to correct me any longer. Okay?" He nods his chin at Lissie and she laughs at him.

"The inmates," Rebecca says. "Some of them dance when I play the old tunes. They really enjoy it."

Rebecca thinks of Flo and Shirley, who lock fingers, bounce a couple of times in place to get their rhythm, and then shuffle and glide around the room. They grit their teeth and concentrate while they swirl and twirl and laugh only when the song has finished. The nurses clap and cheer. Some of the residents sit in their wheelchairs and drool, but she notices one woman, who looks more dead than alive, tapping her fingers on the arm of her wheelchair and her head moving back and forth in time to the music, especially when Rebecca plays "On the Sunny Side of the Street." Some part of the woman is still alive, and Rebecca finds that comforting. Maybe some part of Rebecca's father is alive, even if he pretends he is dead. Another woman puts her hands under her chin like she has a big surprise, a happy one, and she can hardly contain herself. And another holds a doll wrapped in a blanket. She rocks the doll back and forth, tenderly putting her lips against the plastic face, her eyes closed, murmuring something in the plastic ear, the mothering instinct in her by way of gender genetics, not choice. There are only a couple of men.

"Where are all the men?" Rebecca asks the nurses.

"Men don't last very long once they get in here."

Rebecca nods.

* * *

"How much money?" Chuck asks.

"Chuck," Rebecca says, a snap to her voice, like she's warning a child of bad behaviour.

"It's okay," Lissie says, patting Rebecca's arm. "I have no idea. But enough. Mr. Tinkess says so."

"How do you like that? One of us is rich," Chuck says, shaking his head and lifting his shoulders in disbelief. "Who'da thunk it?"

"I wouldn't say *rich*," Lissie says. "I think I'll have to be careful with the money."

"How long have you been playing at the Home?" Chuck asks.

"Years," Rebecca says.

"Years? Why on earth wouldn't you have told me that? I thought you told me everything," Chuck says, and he looks wounded.

"It didn't seem newsworthy."

Everyone is quiet trying to digest the thought of one of them having money, and Chuck draws the last of the ice cream from his glass through his straw and makes a loud slurping sound, but neither Rebecca or Lissie reacts. They stare straight ahead at the coffee cups and the pie cupboard and at Joanne in her mustard-coloured waitress dress with the tear under her arm and the apron stretched tight over her belly. Joanne has worked at the Husky House forever. Her *career,* Joanne calls it. The idea of slinging coffee and pie and deluxe hamburgers for an entire lifetime makes Rebecca smile.

"Maybe we should make a plan," Chuck says. "Write it out. We'll work at our jobs for the summer and save all our money and then head out to travel the world."

Rebecca wonders how it is possible that Chuck still has dreams, can imagine a better life for himself, despite Harold trying to beat it out of him, despite Penelope's indifference. What world exactly were they going to travel, some make-believe world with pyramids and castles, with deserts and oceans? It is all make-believe. There is an invisible dome that fits down over Roddick and if you dare to leave you will perish, you will forfeit your memories, your past wiped clean and all that was will never have been.

Lissie works at the drugstore, the Clinic Pharmacy, smiling at customers when she feels like it, getting a discount on her insulin and shampoo. When she's not steering customers in the direction of bandages and aspirin and hair dye, she's wiping dust from the shelves and moving the old stock from the back to the front, a constant migration of products. There are certain things that no one asks for; the customers wander the store trying to look invisible, like they know what they're doing. It's usually when husbands come in to pick something up for their wives. *Personal hygiene.* That's what the pharmacist calls it, as if the description requires a secret code and no one should really know about menstruation, nor talk about it, as if they might whisper *Third aisle, bottom shelf, behind the facial tissue, wear this disguise.* Rebecca bought a huge box of Kotex when she had shed the embarrassment of being a woman. She dropped the lifetime-supply-sized box on the counter with an almost defiant air. "This should see me through to the next century," she announced while the clerk merely smiled and Lissie busied herself in the tooth-paste aisle.

Craig Kelly came into the drugstore one day and went right to Lissie and asked for condoms. Lissie blushed and pointed to *Family Planning*. Craig winked at her and she blushed some more. "I'll be needing the big box," Craig said. "The really big box."

"Oh, good for you. The directions are on the box," Lissie said, in the best bored voice she could conjure.

Craig taunted Lissie most of the way through high school, stopped at her locker and leaned against the wall, smiling at Lissie as if he were the handsomest guy on earth, as if not one cell in his body were made of anything but confident conceit. Craig asked Lissie to the prom and before she could stutter a response, he said, *Just kidding*. And she laughed, as though she was part of the joke rather than the butt of it, but inside she felt a little piece of her soul die, felt it take its final breath and sigh in defeat. Craig is dating Julie and they made out in the corner of the gymnasium by the stage every opportunity they could until Mr. Binder suspended them for an *indecent display of lack of self-control*. Lissie wonders about kissing like that, faces pressed together, practically swallowing each other, and when exactly the breathing happens. She feels a strange envy when she watches them, Craig's hands all over Julie's body. The thought makes Lissie shiver a little.

Craig asked Rebecca to dance at the fall semi-formal in their final year of school, and Rebecca looked at him for a second or two, a look of total disgust on her face, and then told him to fuck off. Chuck and Lissie burst out laughing while Craig was speechless. Rebecca turned and resumed her conversation with Chuck and Lissie as if nothing had happened, and Craig crept away muttering under his breath.

Chuck still works at Rainy Lake Airways, for the summer and into the fall while the weather holds, before the ice threatens.

He doesn't ride his bike to work but uses Gran's car, though he has to turn over his paycheques to Harold every two weeks. Harold had to hire two Mennonite boys, eleven and twelve, to help with haying and chores.

"They are stronger than you and half your size," Harold said to Chuck.

Chuck merely nodded. *Don't wake the demon* is Chuck's motto. He still has to feed calves in the morning, slop the pigs, and throw corn at the chickens. The farm is falling into a greater state of disrepair, Harold unable to keep up. Harold's cursing increases in proportion to the farm's decline, as well as his bouts of violence: breaking things, throwing plates against the wall, and dumping the cutlery drawer all seem to release his pent-up rage.

Chuck convinces his boss to write a cheque for half his pay and give Chuck the rest in cash, and he hides the cash in a tin box in the haymow between two floor boards. He never flashes money around to make Harold suspicious. He gets tips occasionally from tourists and uses that for spending and gas money. How far can he get away from Harold on his savings? Not far enough.

Chuck's job at Rainy Lake Airways is winding down for the season. He can help turn some wrenches and buck rivets over the winter while the Beech 18 is in rebuild and the Grumman Goose has some major repairs performed on it, but those will be irregular hours followed by irregular pay. He has to save for flying lessons. He has saved twenty-eight hundred and seventy-six dollars. When he got to a thousand he thought he was the richest kid in the whole country. He saves only the full dollars and spends the change on gum and root beer. He climbs into the barn's haymow once a week and digs the tin out from between the boards and counts the money, slowly, hoping it has reproduced miraculously, doubling, then tripling. But it's always the same: no more, no less.

Chuck started writing down a plan. Where he will go to take flying lessons and how much money he will require to live in his own apartment and how he will figure out such things when he has no one to ask who might know. Mr. Currie in Guidance gave him a brochure on flight training from Confederation College, but the cost scares Chuck.

"There is financial aid available," Mr. Currie said. "Get your parents to fill out these forms."

Chuck didn't answer, felt the air drain quickly and completely out of his lungs.

He hasn't told Rebecca about writing the plan, the list of questions, the scribbled answers. He can't imagine leaving her behind, leaving her doing Robert's chores and making Robert's meals and living Robert's life, can't imagine leaving Rebecca frozen, stuck in her glacier-like life. He isn't sure he can.

A gap has formed between the two of them. Rebecca doesn't mother Chuck, doesn't boss him around and make him try harder, the way she used to. She still listens to him whine and complain, but she no longer holds her hands on her hips, her eyes open wide, her eyebrows considering leaping off her forehead. *What are we going to do about that?* she used to say but doesn't anymore. She listens. *We.* That was the best part. *We.* She and Lissie seem tighter now, and Chuck feels slightly pushed to the side. It's not a good feeling.

* * *

Rebecca works for Mr. Law at the hardware store. He lets her have *flexible hours*, he calls it, when she has to deliver a calf or take horns off with the vet or fix fences. She knows her tools and her way around fixing things. She is friendly but keeps to herself. He tries to slip a few extra dollars on her paycheque.

"You made a mistake on my pay," Rebecca says and asks him to write her a new cheque.

"Don't worry about it," Mr. Law says, but Rebecca holds her ground, refuses to leave until he writes a corrected cheque.

Rebecca knows the right gate latch to keep the Henderson kids in the yard and the right filter for Mr. Albertini's furnace and the best washer for Mrs. Klein's kitchen sink faucet. She keeps her head down and works hard and pays her father's account as soon as it comes due. She doesn't break the rules or challenge them, but Mr. Law sees something boiling beneath her skin. She is all business, doesn't hang around with the other summer staff discussing pranks or plans, doesn't show up late on Saturday mornings with a hangover from the night before. She looks used up, old, certainly older than she should look. Her shoes are scuffed and worn. Her jeans are threadbare. Norma, Mr. Law's wife, brings some new clothes to Rebecca from time to time, scuffs them up beforehand to make the clothes look used and then puts them in a Shop Easy grocery bag, making certain all the tags have been removed. Mr. Law hands the bag to Rebecca in an off-handed manner.

"Mrs. Law thought you might use these. She's cleaning up the girls' room and getting rid of stuff." That's the only way he can get Rebecca to accept help. She says thank you without fanfare or emotion. He wants to change things for her, alter this empty road she is on, take out the bumps and even the dips. Life wears people out, Mr. Law thinks. At ten or fifty or eighty, but eventually life wears people out. He resigns himself that Rebecca got worn out ahead of schedule.

Twenty-Four

CHARLOTTE IS SMILING AT LISSIE. NOT A REAL SMILE, NOT A SMILE that starts in the eyes and then pulls the whole face into service. It's a smile that only slightly lifts the corners of Charlotte's mouth, and not evenly, as if one side of Charlotte's mouth can't be bothered to participate. It's a smile that Lissie recognizes, that makes her nervous, fearing Charlotte is planning an escape, an assault of some sort, like she might tip the kitchen table over and launch water balloons from behind it, aimed at Lissie, to keep her back.

Charlotte is sitting on her white couch in her white clothes, a white turtleneck no matter the weather, but an orange or deep-blue pin on her left chest, as if that one shock of colour is all she needs to feel alive, to direct all eyes to that spot and away from the details of her, inviting the focus on this work of art with its bold colour so strangers or neighbours aren't looking in her eyes for signs of life and honesty, or examining her jaw set too firmly and wondering why.

Charlotte looks small and helpless, shrinking away, the look of bewilderment a constant now, or mostly constant. The notes left around the house no longer make sense to Charlotte, no longer guide her through the day like a seeing-eye dog.

Lissie finds the notes, gathers them up, and puts them in a box. The most recent one she removes from Charlotte's hands. *Do something before it's too late,* the note says.

"Am I late?" Charlotte asks, looking at the note. "I don't want to be late. I must not be late."

Lissie clucks to Charlotte like a mother hen. "You're on time. Lots of time," Lissie says. Charlotte relaxes.

Charlotte's hair that was always perfectly smooth, its edges crisp and sharp like the hairdresser had taken concentrated effort to get each hair the exact same length, is now crumpled and flat at the back as if Charlotte has become two-dimensional and all the sides of her that she can't see in the mirror no longer exist. Her teeth have yellowed. She can no longer sit still for the dentist, can't contain her anxiety long enough to get her teeth cleaned. All the energy it takes to keep up the pretense of her existence has consumed her stores; none is left. Her lips no longer sport her signature bronzing, her fingernails no longer painted the polished pearl she couldn't be without.

Lissie swallows hard, walks over to sit next to Charlotte on the sofa, and takes her hand.

"We're going for a car ride this morning, Charlotte."

"Why do you call me that?"

"It's your name. You are Charlotte and I am Lissie."

"You are not Lissie. You are Elisabeth."

"I know, but it's nice to have a nickname."

"Nicknames are for dogs."

"Nicknames are friendly and they mean you belong to someone."

"Why don't you call me *Mother?* I've been your mother for a long time, longer than anyone else was your mother. Longer than *she* was your mother."

Lissie takes a deliberate breath. "Did you know my mother?" Lissie asks, keeping her voice quiet, with no change, no urgent sound, barely breathing and her heart is pounding, like she might be going to receive the secret code to the Royal Vault, pounding like her heart might burst through her skin and bound around on the floor, colliding with the furniture and the walls.

"No," Charlotte says, a sad sort of resigned sound to her voice. "I never met her. Jonathan didn't." Charlotte stops in the middle of her comment and takes a deep breath and stares right into Lissie's face. "Shhhh," she says, pulling her finger to her lips. "I can't trust you. You'll tell Elisabeth." She lays her head back against the couch and closes her eyes, pulling a small blanket up to her chin. *You can't see me. I'm not here.*

Lissie waits, afraid to make a sound. Jonathan? Who is Jonathan? Is this all manner of fiction, some movie Charlotte may have watched?

Charlotte's breathing gets deeper and deeper until Lissie thinks she has fallen asleep. Charlotte takes three long breaths followed by a pause, as if she is willing herself to leave her body, to take flight. Lissie watches her, Charlotte's hollowed cheeks and her eyebrows filled in now, not the slim sleek line they used to be.

"My mother was Irish. MacLaren was her family name," Charlotte says without opening her eyes.

A family name, Lissie thinks. Something a person takes along with her, no matter where she goes, that's like a road back to where she started. A family name. Lissie's chest hurts. She doesn't know the details of Charlotte, doesn't know where she was born or where she went to school or what that life looked like.

"Elisabeth looks like her, the same chin, the same high cheek bones. My mother was beautiful. I never looked like her. Not a bit."

Lissie feels a pounding in her head like her brain might explode and blow bits all over Charlotte's white house. Someone will come in and gather up all the pieces but will have no idea how the pieces fit together. Charlotte doesn't move her head or her hands, as if she is completely paralyzed and speaking is all she can do, giving out these bits and pieces that she can no longer contain.

"My mother said I must always tell the truth. Everything will turn out right if you tell the truth." Charlotte's head is shaking, back and forth like she is trying to deflect pain or toss some thought out of her head. Her lips continue to move, slightly, but no sound comes out. "I don't think that's true," she finally says.

More silence. Lissie lets go of Charlotte's hand, feels the urge to grab Charlotte's shoulders and shake the truth out of her, shake the cobwebs and darkness, the sludge and pretending. Which words are madness and which are some link to the past? There's no deciphering key, no way to crack the code. The years of rehearsed silence have brought them both to this place, with no road map, no trail of crumbs to guide them back. Lissie is afraid, really afraid, that whatever truth resides in Charlotte's memory is at the edge, ready to slip away and be forever lost.

Lissie leaves the open-ended comments alone and wonders how she is going to get Charlotte into the car. There must be another Elisabeth, Lissie thinks. She can't begin to entertain the possibilities of Charlotte's rambling words. Today is moving day, but no need to rush, no need to put Charlotte on high alert. Slow and steady, Lissie has learned, works best.

Lissie moved Charlotte's things a bit at a time to Charlotte's new room at the Roddick Nursing Home. Lissie told Rebecca they should rename the place the Last Stop Café. An entire life is lived working toward something, moving forward, to arrive here, at this horrible place. This is the sum of a life. The searching, the building, the creating.

"To get here," Lissie says, and the thought makes her feel sick.

Lissie painted Charlotte's room cloud white, Charlotte's favourite. She bought new bedding for the tiny single bed that looks more like a child's bed. She bought new pillows and a white comforter with a single blue band across the lower half. It is queen-sized, though, and Lissie had to fold the comforter in half to make it fit. All the twin-sized comforters had child prints: Batman, Spider-Man, Flintstones, Jetsons, Josie and the Pussycats. Not exactly Charlotte's style.

A woman stood in the doorway while Lissie painted, the woman wringing her hands and looking unsettled.

"Who said you could?" the woman said, pointing an accusing finger at Lissie until a nurse came and took hold of the woman's shoulders and turned her around.

"Come and help me tidy the magazines," the nurse said, and the woman smiled.

* * *

"Fuck," Charlotte shouts, sitting upright as if she's been stung, and Lissie nearly falls off the ottoman.

Charlotte never used to swear, not a single *shit* or *damn*, and she would rather have choked to death than say *fuck*.

Swearing is the lowest form of communication. People swear who have nothing intelligent to say. Those were Charlotte's words, a warning aimed at Lissie before she went to school, when Lissie tried out a *shit* for size when she stubbed her toe. The word flew out of Lissie's mouth and she was as surprised as Charlotte. Charlotte was outraged and a good yank on Lissie's right arm got that message through, along with a dash of cayenne pepper on Lissie's tongue.

"There'll be none of that," Charlotte said, and the tone of her voice left no room for negotiation.

The last few years have changed Charlotte's position on the matter of swearing. If Charlotte can't find a word that fits, *fuck* seems to do the trick. She even said *cocksucker* in the grocery store. Charlotte wanted a box of Alpha-Bits. *No sugared cereals* had been a mantra Lissie was obligated to live by. Lissie had the urge to wag her finger at Charlotte's face and repeat the rule. *Rule Number Five Hundred and Forty-Three, Charlotte. NO SUGARED CEREALS*, stressing each syllable. So tempting.

"Cocksucker," Charlotte said, standing on her toes and straining to reach the box of cereal. Mrs. Garner from the church office stepped back, her eyes wide like she'd been slapped, a full-frontal assault, and Lissie only barely resisted a knee-slapping guffaw: the cliché of it was too perfect. Charlotte turned and smiled at Mrs. Garner and stuck out her hand like they'd never met and then moved on down the aisle at super-human speed.

Grocery shopping with Charlotte gave Lissie no end of tales to share with Rebecca and Chuck. It wasn't funny, wasn't the least bit funny when you really thought about it, but laughing seemed the only way to get through it. Charlotte felt the need to buy several jugs of bleach and started loading them into the cart if Lissie wasn't paying attention.

"You can never have too much bleach," Charlotte said, and as Lissie unloaded them, Charlotte reloaded.

It was that way with all manner of strange things: panty hose, charcoal briquettes, tomato soup. They didn't own a barbeque and they never ate canned tomato soup. So Lissie quit taking Charlotte to the store, to any store. It was too confusing, and people asked questions of Charlotte to make conversation, to be kind, but Charlotte couldn't find the answers, couldn't put a sentence together quickly, and swearing often resulted. Then it was awkward for everyone.

Charlotte loves doing laundry, is content to fold towels and pillowcases and handkerchiefs. Lissie set Charlotte up with the iron in the kitchen. While Lissie worked on her homework at the kitchen table, Charlotte ironed. Making everything smooth and creaseless calmed Charlotte, and she spent hours at the sink trying to get a single stain out, as if that were her one quest: keep life stain free.

* * *

"I'm going to take you for a car ride and we can have lunch out," Lissie says, trying to use her most convincing voice, her it's-an-ordinary-kind-of-day voice.

Charlotte nods and gets to her feet.

"Now," she says. *Now*: a sound that is halfway between a question and resignation.

They take a drive along the river, upstream from the paper mill, the old log booms still in the river, the current obvious and visible, bits of wood and twigs being swept along, like they have somewhere to go and need to get there in a hurry. Charlotte's decline is like the river, picking up speed as it reaches the dam, tearing away at any resistance in its path. There's no hanging on to the banks or the log booms; there is no point in that because the determined current will get her and drag Charlotte under no matter what. There's no going upstream. Not now.

They have lunch at the A&W, the run-down orange and brown hamburger shack on the edge of town. Charlotte loves the root beer, now, not before, in the baby mug, easy to hold and sip from. Lissie leans across Charlotte and locks the passenger door. It has become the pattern.

Lissie watches the waitress stroll from the kitchen toward the car, more of a saunter, in no particular hurry, a pencil behind her ear and under her cap, the cap pinned off centre to give her a foreign appearance. The coin bank is tied to her waist, ready to make change in a hurry. She looks bored and is chewing gum, her lip pulled into a snarl.

"You can turn your headlights out now," she says. "What can I get you?" flipping open her order book and pulling the pencil from her ear while looking over to the next car as if it is much more interesting.

What can you get me? Lissie thinks. Where would she start if she could have anything? Would she ask for the answers to the questions in her journal, buried in the back yard, the long list of *I wonders? You can get me a cat. I've always wanted a pet. You can get me a career as an artist. You can get me an identity, a history, a family tree that doesn't start with me, that isn't a single-stemmed mutant with all its branches hacked off, that doesn't look like a log, a piece of driftwood found on the shore with no identifying features. You can get me someone who has my chin and the same bridge of my nose and someone who laughs the same because of genetics.*

"Two whistle dogs," Lissie says, and adds *please,* quickly so the waitress won't think Lissie forgot. "With fries and three baby root beers. That's three."

And Lissie smiles, the smile that is meant to say *I'm okay, don't give me a second thought, my life is perfect. Bring me the food and don't take too long, because the silence in here makes me want to run for my life.*

"Shit," says Charlotte. "I left the iron plugged in."

Lissie looks at her watch every few minutes, her stomach starting to ache as if a python has taken up residence inside her body.

She squeezes her eyes shut. Snakes. Scary things. Silent. She touched one once and was surprised by its warmth, as if its scales and legless body were merely camouflage to keep people away when really snakes were gentle creatures, left to slither around, lower than low. She checks her watch again.

Two p.m. sharp. She is set to pull up in front of the Last Stop Café at two p.m. where two attendants will be waiting to help her get her mother in, to take Charlotte and lock her up and throw away the key, where nothing will be hers and all the rules of privacy and no sharing will mean nothing. Charlotte will be living in a commune of madness and if she has a lucid moment in the night and wakes to find her white house gone, her life gone, she may scream and then scream some more, but no one will know her and her screaming won't unlock the door.

"Time to go," Charlotte says. "I want to go home."

Lissie nods and turns on her headlights. The car hop comes and retrieves the tray, the garbage piled up on top, napkins and papers, hiding the fact that only two baby root beer glasses are on the tray. The third is in Lissie's purse.

As soon as Lissie pulls up at the front door of the nursing home, Charlotte rolls herself into a ball in her seat.

"No, no, no," she cries, looking at Lissie for help. "No, no, no."

"It's okay, Charlotte," Lissie says, putting her hand on Charlotte's back. "Shhhh," she says.

The attendants take Charlotte's arm and she begins to wrestle, all arms and legs, her slightly weakened body restored in this moment, as if she might lift a car off a baby or stop a locomotive on the tracks. Dr. Harbinger appears behind the clump of wrestling bodies while Lissie stands frozen, helpless, her hands tucked into her chest. Charlotte lets out a wail that must be heard most of the way through town, a wail that may have let out every hurt she has ever experienced, every disappointment, every slight, every heartbreak; it is all there in that single but prolonged wail.

"Charlotte," Dr. Harbinger says, looking over his glasses and mopping his head with his handkerchief, his go-to action. She pictures him standing over an opened body in the operating room, sweat dripping from his forehead and him pulling a sterile handkerchief from his pocket and mopping up the sweat. "Pull yourself together," he says. "This is quite a display."

Lissie thinks Charlotte has every right to make a ruckus, to make up for all the years of controlled emotions, for the years of precise comments, for no surprises, for never letting her guard down. *Scream away, Charlotte,* Lissie wants to say. *Scream away.*

Twenty-Five

REBECCA AND CHUCK AND LISSIE HAVE PLANS TONIGHT, A celebration, a celebration of survival. Lissie brought the sloe gin and Chuck brought the cola and Rebecca stole her father's truck. It isn't exactly stealing anymore, not now that she can drive legally, but she doesn't ask and somehow stealing the truck makes her feel more alive than just taking the truck. She revs the engine and slams the truck door as loudly as she can, daring Robert to run out and try to stop her. But he never does.

They drive to the river on the other side of town where the willows are scattered along the shore, their long weeping tendrils forming a natural tent, a hideout. They have lawn chairs and cigarettes and were going to bring a bit of weed but have no idea where to find any or whom to ask.

"You have to have connections for that sort of thing," Rebecca explains.

Chuck and Lissie laugh.

"What does that even mean?" Lissie asks.

"Well, my little innocents," Rebecca says, her hands on her hips, "our circle of friends consists of you and you and me," pointing emphatically at one then the other. "Are either of you dope dealers? Are you packing? I didn't think so. We need to broaden our base of friends if we are going to partake in contraband."

Chuck shrugs. "I'm going to try it," he says moving his chair into position. "Before I die."

They set their chairs up in a semi-circle of sorts and each fills a glass; it is a collaborative effort. Lissie pours the sloe gin, measuring the alcohol in a jigger she found in a kitchen drawer.

"This isn't exactly how I imagined this playing out," Rebecca says.

"We need to be precise," Lissie says.

"The apple doesn't fall far from the tree," Rebecca says, and Lissie nearly drops the bottle.

"Oh, my god. You're right. I'm Charlotte. I've taken over for Charlotte. God help me."

"Keep pouring," Rebecca says.

Chuck handles the ice and Rebecca tops the glass off with cola.

"Cheers," Rebecca says, raising her plastic Texaco glass. The other two follow suit.

"To us," they say in unison.

"I brought a notepad," Lissie says, digging in her bag. "To write down all the things we're celebrating."

"This is kinda losing the feeling of rebellion. A jigger. Notepad. If we were knocking off a gas station we'd stop to clean the washroom and wash the windows," Rebecca says.

"Come on. Don't spoil my fun. Who wants to go first?" Lissie says.

"I will," Chuck says. "Here's to surviving thirteen years of mandatory education."

"Hear, hear," Lissie says and takes a swallow. "This tastes like cherry coke," she says.

"Not too bad, not too bad," Chuck says.

Rebecca stands staring at them as if she can't quite see straight and Lissie and Chuck have gone out of focus, and then she drains her glass in one gulp. She winces and opens her mouth as if her throat is on fire.

"Let's break this down, then, into high school's best and worst memories," Rebecca says. "We did have some of the strangest teachers God ever put breath in."

"Mr. Doroshenko," Chuck says, slapping his knee. "Best and worst. He took his shoes and socks off in economics and cleaned between his toes."

Lissie and Rebecca groan together.

"Gotta love that accent," Rebecca says. "Remember when the whole class tried to sound like him when we spoke up in class and he didn't even notice?"

"What a guy," Chuck says. "I will never forget John Maynard Keynes and fiscal and monetary policies or the Combines Investigation Act."

"That's because we wrote the same test forty-five times," Lissie says with mock indignation.

"Don't exaggerate," Chuck says.

"Okay, forty times."

"That's better."

"He used to stand on his desk and do his impersonation of Brock's Monument," Rebecca says. "You have to admire that kind of courage."

"Courage? How is that courage?" Lissie asks.

"He didn't worry about being judged or following some sort of teacher's rule book or socially accepted norms. He left it all out there in the classroom. I think that's cool," Rebecca says.

"He killed me," Chuck says.

They remember Mrs. Benkowski, who didn't dye her hair quite often enough, and Mr. Legg, who didn't know a mint would be a good thing before he started leaning over desks and giving math advice, and Mr. Arnason, who spent more time looking down girls' tops than checking their work.

"Oh, he thought he was so subtle, but we all knew what he was up to. I kept a book under my chin so he couldn't see anything. But Ellen Frankiewicz knew what he was up to and I think that's why she got an A. Gave him a good view," Lissie says. "He was icky."

"Icky? He was an asshole. Someone should have punched his lights out," Chuck says.

Rebecca can't help smiling at Chuck's outrage. *He's growing,* she thinks, and hopes he keeps growing right out of Harold's reach, hopes Chuck flies out of that nightmare and into a life of his own.

"What are you smiling about?" Chuck asks.

"Nothing. Just remembering."

They remember Mrs. Kerr in the cafeteria; she always had a smile as she poked hot dog wieners with a fork and filled plates with the day's special, a smile that said *You belong here, I see you.* Even the kids who didn't have a friend in the world got that smile and they raised their faces for that moment.

"Everyone remembers Mrs. Kerr," Rebecca says. "She was the best thing about high school. Mrs. Kerr and Thursday's Tuna Surprise."

"To Mrs. Kerr and Tuna Surprise," Chuck says, and they drain another glass.

"To Mr. Quesnel," Rebecca says quietly.

"Why are we toasting him?" Chuck asks.

"For making French tolerable," Lissie says.

"For seeing us," says Rebecca, her hand on her chest. "And for caring if we are okay."

"To the end of French," Chuck shouts. "Cheers."

They all laugh as if they have been out of school for years and are digging through their memory trunk for the best bits, never mentioning not belonging or staying on the sidelines. They don't talk about dances and stealing kisses when no one is looking. They don't talk about homecoming parades with floats, or football games where Jamie Domanski ran for a touchdown, his arms stretched over his head like he really won something, his excitement contagious and pure, the rest of the school cheering and jumping up and down and blowing noisemakers as if this might very well be the best day ever, as if Jamie carries the ball for each of them, as if his winning makes them all winners.

They don't talk about track and field meets or volleyball tournaments or school plays. They don't talk about parties or dates or going to the Royal Theatre and sitting on the worn velvet seats and holding hands. They know nothing of the reality of being a carefree teenager whose only responsibility might be to brush her teeth or take out the garbage.

"I think that's it for growth for me," Lissie says. "Here's to being five foot two and holding since I was twelve."

"Hear, hear," Rebecca says, her words slurring slightly now.

"I guess this is it for me, too," Chuck says. "I did pushups and hung from the barn rafters, but this is it," he says, putting his hand flat on the top of his head.

"That was only going to lengthen your arms, Gorilla Man," Rebecca says.

"Do you suppose we've outgrown pimples?" Chuck says, running his hand over his chin. "I shaved today," like he has been nominated for a Nobel peace prize. "That's three times this week."

"What a man," Rebecca says. "Here's to manhood," and Rebecca punches the air with a left and right hook.

"Yah, shaving. That's all men have to worry about. We get stuck with periods," Lissie says.

"Don't, don't," Chuck says, putting his hands over his ears and humming. "La, la, la."

"You can celebrate getting Charlotte moved," Rebecca says. "That's a big thing."

"That wasn't a celebration," Lissie says. "More of a sad exhale."

"Yes, but you survived it. That's the celebration," Rebecca says.

Lissie goes over every single morning to have breakfast with Charlotte and every night after work to read to her and brush her hair. They kept Charlotte sedated at first to prevent her injury as she tried to open windows and claw her way through doors. She is calmer now, more resigned.

Rebecca and Chuck go with Lissie to see Charlotte, once every week or so. Lissie brushes Charlotte's hair and the bristles on Charlotte's scalp relax her, or so Lissie likes to think.

Rebecca closes her eyes and sighs, an understanding sound.

"You can celebrate knowing how to comfort Charlotte by brushing her hair. My mother brushed my hair to get me back to sleep when a monster came out from under the bed." Rebecca's head falls back on her chair and she runs her fingers gently across her own temples. "It's the feeling of love. I can feel it even now." A tear rolls down her cheek but she doesn't bother with it, and Chuck and Lissie wait.

Chuck runs his fingers through his own hair and shrugs. "No one ever brushed my hair to calm the demons."

"Time to light up," Rebecca says. "Where are those smokes?"

Lissie digs in her bag. "Here. In here somewhere," she says. "I bought Du Maurier because I like the red package with the flip-up lid. Look, it's like the cigarettes are on bleachers, all tiered like that," she says, opening the pack in front of them.

"Who brought matches?" Rebecca asks.

"I did, I did," Chuck says, using his mock juvenile voice and holding up a lighter that he snitched from the top drawer of Gran's bedside table. He flips the lighter's lid open with its metallic sound and runs his thumb along the starter and a flame appears like magic. He holds the flame at the end of each girl's cigarette and tells her how to suck in. The flame climbs up inside the cigarette. He leans back in his chair and blows the smoke straight up above him.

"You look like a pro," Rebecca says.

"Nineteen years of watching Penelope," Chuck says. "My head hurts and I feel dizzy."

"Me, too," Lissie says and leans to the side of her chair and vomits with no warning whatsoever.

"Eat crackers, Lissie. Alcohol and diabetes don't mix. Eat some cheese, too," Rebecca says.

Rebecca only pretends to smoke, pulls the smoke into her mouth and holds it there and then lets it all go in one poof that doesn't look like smoking at all, not the required long stream of steady smoke. The whole thing is a bit disappointing.

"Maybe it's more about how you hold the cigarette that makes everyone feel so damn cool," Rebecca says, holding her hand out to the side with a drawn, bored look on her face as if she has been smoking for years, and then she laughs. "I don't think I've got what it takes."

Nobody states the obvious. They are nineteen doing what most of their school cohorts had done at fifteen or sixteen. Chuck saw a couple of ten-year-olds behind the arena lighting up like they knew what they were doing, and he remembers an inexplicable envy to break the rules and not fear the consequences. It looked like freedom to Chuck, freedom to choose, even to choose badly.

"Better late than never," Chuck says, but he wonders when he swallows another mouthful of sloe gin if it is really worth it. "Who's ready for another drink?"

"May as well be sick as the way I am," Rebecca says. "Who said that? Someone said that when I was little but I can't think of who."

Chuck pours another drink for each of them.

They listen, listen to each other breathing, Rebecca pulling on the willow's leaves and running them up and down against her cheek. The sun has set, painfully early, meaning August is gone, September is gone. It is officially fall and they won't be going back to school. The kids from their graduating class who had post-secondary education plans have gone, left town with big ideas. The streets seem emptier, as if the clatter of back-to-school activities has quieted or moved off altogether.

"Gran says most of them will be back," says Chuck.

Rebecca thinks about the ones who left, the ones who tried to break free, tried to imagine a fresh start, tried to imagine independence and freedom, but can't pull it off because in the end leaving is too hard for most people, their old ordinary life pulling them back.

"Hear the crickets?" Rebecca says. "It's their fall voices, their last hurrah before the frost."

"They're noisy," Chuck says. "There's one in my closet. I can't find it to smack it."

"They're ugly with things sticking out of them," Lissie says, shaking her head. "They crunch when you squish them." She makes a disgusted face.

"Remember the poem we learned in fourth grade? 'Some One' by Walter de la Mare?" Rebecca says, standing up from her chair with her arms at her sides, and recites the whole poem with exaggerated diction.

Lissie joins in at the end. *"Only the busy beetle / Tap-tapping in the wall, / Only from the forest / The screech owl's call, / Only the cricket whistling / While the dew drops fall, / So I know not who came knocking, / At all, at all, at all."*

"I remembered," Lissie says, clapping her hands, and then holds her stomach and sits down again.

"You have a good memory," Chuck says.

"I wish I didn't," Rebecca says. "I wish I could forget."

Chuck puts his hand over Rebecca's.

"Mr. de la Mare wrote that poem in the last century. The last century," Lissie says, her hands out to receive an explanation for something so incredible. "He lived to be eighty-three."

"I wonder how old we'll get," Chuck says.

"Maybe we should die young, before anything can spoil us, jade us, make us see life as it really is," Lissie says.

"Too late. We'd have to die at birth," Rebecca says.

More silence. More listening. More waiting. More drinking and more smoking.

"Robert said that," Rebecca says, slapping her thigh with her open hand. "It was Robert."

"Said what?" Chuck asks.

"May as well be sick as the way I am. When I was little. When my mother put some new dish she'd made in front of him. *May as well be sick as the way I am.* It was Robert. I knew someone said that."

"Good for you, I guess," Lissie says.

Chuck puts his pointer finger on his front tooth. "Seems impossible that Robert ever told a joke or said something funny," he says.

"No kidding," Rebecca says and tries to remember when Robert was anything else than what he is now, when he was carefree, when he laughed when he danced with her mother, when he looked at her mother as if he was really seeing her and seeing her so clearly that it almost hurt, but Rebecca came up with nothing.

"Remember when farting was your single most enjoyable achievement of the day?" Rebecca says to Chuck.

Lissie snorts.

"No, really. He was beyond proud. He is an excellent farter."

"What is it about boys and farting and burping and all things smelly?"

"There is no explaining some things," Chuck says, looking pleased.

Lissie burps and sighs.

"See. Burping is a good thing," Chuck says.

"Eat some more crackers and cheese, Lissie. Keep the carbs going in," Rebecca says.

"Guess what I found in Charlotte's box of secrets," Lissie says between bites.

Both Rebecca and Chuck turn their chairs to face her, their eyes a bit wider despite the alcohol haze.

"Aren't you going to guess?" Lissie says, as if it could have been a pearl necklace of untold value or a treasure map or the answers to life's confusions, but they don't guess.

"My birth certificate," Lissie says, her voice slightly slurred and her eyes only half open.

Rebecca's hand flies to her mouth.

"I know," Lissie says. "I have a birth certificate. Guess what my birth name was?"

Chuck and Rebecca don't move, afraid to make a sound.

"Aren't you even going to try?" Lissie whines. "You're spoiling my fun and I'm going to throw up again if you don't guess." She stomps her foot.

"Jane Doe," Chuck says. "Gertrude Crapinski."

"Not even close," Lissie says. "Elisabeth Smythe. I was born Elisabeth Smythe," and she holds up her pointer finger.

"What?" Chuck says. "Charlotte is your birth mother?"

"Not so fast," Lissie says, wagging her finger. "Not so fast. Nothing that simple. I was born Elisabeth Smythe to Jonathan Smythe and Loretta Windigo."

"Who the hell is Jonathan Smythe?" Chuck says.

"I think he might be Charlotte's brother. She has said his name several times in the last year," Lissie says.

"Whoa," Chuck says. "This is crazy talk."

"Loretta Windigo," Rebecca says quietly. "Your mother is Loretta Windigo. She sounds beautiful and artistic."

"Maybe Charlotte is in some sort of witness protection and changed her name," Chuck says.

"You have a mother," Rebecca says.

"Oh, it gets better," Lissie says, lifting the glass to her lips again and swallowing hard. "Jonathan Smythe and Loretta Windigo and infant child crashed into Great Slave Lake while aboard a De Havilland Beaver flying out of Fort Resolution. All lives lost. I have the newspaper clipping." She takes another swallow.

Chuck can hardly sit still and turns to Rebecca expecting some sort of reaction. "Are you hearing this?"

Rebecca nods, but looks dumbfounded, as if none of the information is getting in. "You have a mother."

"So the infant child was you, except you didn't die," Chuck asks.

"I don't think I was even on board," Lissie says. "I think Charlotte was looking after me. I found a letter from Jon and I'm guessing Jonathan was Jon and he was asking Charlotte to look after me while he and Loretta had a honeymoon."

"Holy crap," Chuck says. "You're a bastard."

"Chuck," Rebecca says, just short of shouting.

"I heard it in my head first and thought it was funny. It wasn't," he says.

"I know," Lissie says, raising her glass. "Here's to me, finding out I am not an orphan, except now I am officially an orphan, but a different kind of orphan."

"We're all orphans," Rebecca says.

"To Lissie," Chuck says.

"To us," Rebecca says, and they all drain their glasses.

"Where's Fort Resolution?" Chuck asks.

"It's in the Northwest Territories. I looked it up on the map. It's on Great Slave Lake," Lissie says.

Rebecca looks at her feet and picks at a loose piece of rubber on the sole of her running shoe, and her mind is racing and no words seem able to find their way together into a sentence. "Lots of secrets," she finally says.

They sit and drink and light more cigarettes and dig their shoes into the sand in front of their chairs and don't say another word.

Rebecca finally moves, squeezing Lissie's hand, and smiles at her. "Good stuff, Lissie," she says. "Good stuff."

Lissie smiles back. "It's a weird feeling," and her head wags from side to side like she might fall asleep. "I have to go home," Lissie says, trying to get out of her chair. "If I don't go now I might never be able to get up."

"You have to eat first. I have to know you're going to be okay," Rebecca says.

Lissie nods and eats four more crackers and a slab of cheese.

"I'll drive you," Chuck says. "If I drive slowly down Eighth Street I can probably get to your house without crashing." He burps out a small laugh. "But no guarantees."

Lissie is green and bent over at the hips. "Why do people do this?" she asks, heaving again.

"Maybe they work their way into it, do a bit of alcohol training," Rebecca says.

"Amateurs," Chuck says, feeling proud but not exactly sure what he is proud of, and he belches again.

Rebecca stands and hugs Lissie, holds her tight, and doesn't really want to let go. Lissie goes all loose in Rebecca's arms, putting her head on Rebecca's shoulder like a small child, and they stand all together while Chuck drapes his arms over both of them.

Twenty-Six

CHUCK DRIVES LISSIE HOME, HELPS HER GET HER KEY OUT TO open the door. Neither of them can get the key in the lock easily. Lissie gives up and hands the key to Chuck, who fumbles around for a minute or two.

"Got it," he says. "Score."

The door opens and they fall in. The house sounds strange, empty with echoes. Lissie looks at Chuck as if she knows what he is thinking.

"It's weird, isn't it? It's as if no one lives here anymore. It's hollow. And I can't remember what it used to sound like," Lissie says. "It's as if all Charlotte was to me was a part in a play and nothing was real and here is the empty stage, the actors gone."

Lissie waves Chuck off and collapses on her bed, her jacket and shoes still on.

"Charlotte wouldn't approve," Chuck says. "Rebecca says to put a glass of juice by your bed," he says, heading for the kitchen.

"Watchdog Rebecca," Lissie says. "Guard-dog Rebecca. Angel Rebecca. Guardian angel Rebecca. She has to keep us safe. Can't help herself. I'm going to get a dog."

Chuck sets the glass of juice on Lissie's nightstand.

"Lissie, eat something before you go to sleep. Rebecca will worry. She has worried enough, don't you think?"

Lissie groans. "Get me the jar of peanut better and a slice of bread. You could tell her I had a steak dinner and she would still worry. I like how she always pretends she's so controlled and so subtle, but we both know she is scared to death something will happen to us. You know that, right?"

"I don't know what I know," Chuck says, digging the peanut butter out of the jar and spreading it thick on the slice of bread.

"Go easy," Lissie says. "I'm not having a meal here."

"Do as you're told," Chuck says and laughs. "I think the sloe gin is wearing off. My head is clearing." He watches Lissie chew. "We didn't get much on our list of celebrations."

"We got enough. We made it. We're just about there."

"Are you okay here alone?" Chuck asks, looking around behind the door and in the closet, sweeping his arm under the clothes.

"I'm too tired to be afraid," Lissie says. "I pretend my ancestors are watching over me, the owl and the eagle."

"You've never mentioned those ancestors before," Chuck says. "Something new?"

"Something old. I am Cree or Ojibway or something in between. My skin might not be the right colour and my hair might not be straight enough, but my genes are, the part that you can't see."

"Wow."

"Yah, wow."

"I didn't know you thought about that stuff," Chuck says.

"You didn't ask."

"You didn't tell."

"She said, he said."

"I suppose. I'm sorry, Lissie. I never thought it mattered to you."

"Well, it does. I just didn't know how much until now. I'm falling asleep," and Lissie is gone, snoring almost immediately.

Chuck pulls the piece of bread from between her lips and wipes the peanut butter off her mouth onto his sleeve. "That's what friends are for," he says.

Chuck crawls back in behind the wheel of Robert's truck. He taps his palms on the steering wheel as if that might be the cue for the truck to start on its own. He shakes his head to clear away the dizziness and rolls the truck slowly down the street leaving the lights off. The streetlights are bright and he can't remember ever being in town at this hour. He has no idea what hour it is; he doesn't wear a watch.

He sneaks up behind Rebecca, her head back, her feet on Lissie's chair, which Rebecca has pulled over in front of her. Chuck considers scaring Rebecca, but she looks so peaceful, her eyes closed, the moonlight sneaking through the willows enough to illuminate Rebecca.

"I know you're there," Rebecca says. "You can't sneak up on me when you drive Robert's clunker."

"I guess not."

"Did you crash and burn?" Rebecca asks.

"Not that I noticed."

Rebecca drags her chair out from under the tree and into the moonlight and collapses in it again.

"You okay?" Chuck asks.

"Just dizzy. I'm never smoking another cigarette. You?"

"Same."

"Lissie okay?" Rebecca asks. "Did she —"

"Yes, I fed her peanut butter and bread and there is juice beside her bed like you told me. She didn't stay awake very long."

"Did you put the orange juice by her bed?"

"Yes, I said I did," Chuck says with a groan.

"We're pathetic," Rebecca says. "Whose idea was this?"

"I think it was yours."

"No way. I'm not taking the fall for this," Rebecca says.

"That's quite the shocking news about Lissie's birth certificate," Chuck says.

"Yes," Rebecca says, her voice quiet and hesitant. "Secrets."

"Her house is so empty."

Rebecca doesn't respond and drains her glass and then tosses it in the waste can that is chained to a post nearby.

"She said something interesting about Charlotte playing the role of her mother, but I can't remember the rest of what she said. It was deep, though."

"Deep?"

"Yah, and she talked about being Cree or Ojibway. Did she talk to you about that?"

"Sometimes. She was curious. She wanted a sense of community, of belonging. I think we all want that. Lissie is caught in the middle of being white and being native. One's a shadow of the other, but which one."

"I never thought about it," Chuck says.

"Men don't. I don't think men think about much," Rebecca says.

"That's not fair."

"Wanna swim?"

"Swim? Are you crazy? The river will be freezing."

"We can tough it out."

"You hate water," Chuck says, but he's thinking, *You're afraid of water*. It's the only thing he knows of that scares Rebecca. He has never seen Rebecca swim other than riding Daisy in the river.

Rebecca starts pulling her T-shirt over her head and unzipping her jeans.

"I'm going swimming," Rebecca says, the statement sounding more like a threat than an announcement.

"The current is strong here," Chuck says, but Rebecca is running toward the water.

"Shit," Chuck says, and follows her, peeling off his clothes as he goes.

Rebecca is in the water up to her waist, her arms tucked into her chest, trying not to scream from the cold. She is wearing her underwear and Chuck has never seen any girl in her underwear, not even his sisters; he isn't sure where to look. He wants to look directly at Rebecca's body, to see what she's been hiding behind loose clothes her entire life, what is really underneath her peasant tops and sweatshirts and baggy jeans. He wants to put his lips on her chest, on the meaty part that presses out of her bra, and smell the space in between her breasts that he is sure will give off some hypnotic aroma that will mystify him and send him floating off the ground. He is thankful the water around the lower half of his body is so bloody cold, protecting him from his natural intentions.

Rebecca lowers herself into the water, squealing and shivering. Chuck sits beside her.

"I don't know how to swim," she says.

"Neither do I," Chuck says. "Let me hold your hands and let your body go, let your feet stretch out in the water."

Rebecca holds Chuck's hands like she might never let go and lets her head lie back in the water.

"Kick your feet," he says.

Rebecca kicks her feet, urgently at first, trying to force her body to stay on the surface of the water, but then she relaxes, the cold numbing, and she wiggles her feet up and down, suspending her on the surface of the water for a moment, the moonlight landing on the white of her stomach.

"You're swimming," Chuck says.

"I am," Rebecca says, her voice a whisper. "I am swimming."

Chuck holds her head in his hands, and her arms spread out and her legs go limp.

"I'm tired, Chuck. I'm so tired."

Chuck nods in the dark and then bends down and puts his lips against Rebecca's, presses them there all soft and thick and heavy, his eyes closing automatically and he feels a tingling right down to the soles of his feet.

Rebecca turns her head and slips under the water, Chuck still holding her hands. She jumps up, pushing her hair back off her face.

"It's so cold," she screams, and the two of them run from the river.

Twenty-Seven

REBECCA SCREAMS AND KEEPS SCREAMING, ONE LONG WAIL THAT stretches out through the barn, up the spider-webbed, dust-filled stairwell to the dimly lit mow, out the windows where the broken glass barely hangs on to the frames, up through the roof where the loose tin has torn away leaving gaping holes for the rain to pour in. Wings flap and flee, birds taking to flight, alarmed mice scurry, and dust loosens. The wind stops to listen, not wanting to compete. The clouds pause in the sky, no longer making shapes and telling stories. The trees stay bent, the leaves shaken loose; the gate stops swinging, its rusty hinge suddenly seized. The wail starts to flatten, starts to lose its force, dropping in volume, the sound of defeat crawling in, defeat and fatigue and being used up and being alone.

Daisy is on her side, her head back and one back leg elevated off the ground, frozen in the death pose. Rebecca jumps over the manger rail and tries to lift Daisy's head, but her tongue is protruding, cold and blue. She is dead.

"Daisy," Rebecca cries, an explosion of grief in her guts.

Daisy is all that is left that connects Rebecca to her mother. Daisy, the pony Rebecca's mother chose, that she bought with her egg money and a bit of savings she had. The surprise, the yellow ribbon leading from Rebecca's bed to the barn, Daisy's snowy-white face looking at Rebecca, all trusting when Rebecca ran into the barn with her mother on her heels.

She's yours, Rebecca's mother had said.

Rebecca pulls Daisy's heavy head into her lap and tries to close Daisy's eyes, but they won't stay closed. Daisy's eyes are staring, but she can't see Rebecca, has left Rebecca alone in the miserable barn, in her miserable life. A sound of anguish heaves up from inside Rebecca.

"Don't leave me," Rebecca sobs. "Don't leave me. Please, Daisy. Please," and she buries her face in Daisy's mane.

The cows gather around Rebecca, their breath creating a fog in the cold March air. They are watching, moving closer in a circle of sorts, their noses outstretched, curious about this death, recognizing Daisy's strangeness. The cows drop their heads while Rebecca's sobbing finds its fatigued end, her breathing returning to normal from its ravaged hiccupping. The cows wait, shifting their weight from left to right. The birds come back to perch on the rafters overhead, the swallows and the starlings. The sun has climbed higher, its light dimmed by a layer of flat grey clouds, barely higher than the trees. The whole day declared dull now, empty. Rebecca slumps against Daisy, every ounce of her energy and courage consumed.

Rebecca imagines the last moments of her mother's life, the struggling, trying to claw her way through the glass. Did she gasp and choke? Did she try to hold her breath? Or did she know, know instantly when the ice cracked and gave way, that there was no point in struggling? Did she give in and relax after Rebecca was through the window and safe? Did Jake float up from his car bed, out from under the books and toys, once the car was full of water and did Rebecca's mother draw Jake into her arms and press her lips against his cheek and did Jake think he was back in the womb, his mother's heartbeat becoming his own?

Rebecca lay in the tub when she was small enough to fit, the tub filled as deep as she dared, and rolled her head back, under the water, her arms at her side, completely submerged, and became her mother: welcoming the end, ready, sure that Rebecca would be fine, forgetting Rebecca was six years old, not yet done with her mother's hand to guide her. Rebecca held her breath and then let it out, watching the bubbles find their way to the surface, and then she tried breathing in, letting her lungs fill, but she couldn't do it, didn't have the courage her mother must have had. Rebecca choked and coughed and gasped. It had to be that way, her mother certain and unafraid, or Rebecca would have gone mad, grief having won.

* * *

"What's happened here?" Robert says, standing over Rebecca.

Rebecca is lying in the manure and filth with her head on Daisy's cold neck, Daisy's tongue hanging from her mouth, no life to hold the tongue in place, Daisy's head in Rebecca's arms.

"Death," Rebecca says, without looking up at him. "Death has happened here."

Robert remains standing, off to the side, his left hand jammed in his pocket, his customary pose. His shoulders droop even lower, if that is possible. He makes a sudden gesture toward the cows and they scatter, and he puts his right hand out to Rebecca like he might help her up, but she turns away.

"Help," Rebecca says. "You're going to help me now. Now, Robert? Now? After all these years of nothing. Of no sign that you were still alive other than your breathing."

"I'm your father."

"Is that right? Is that what you call this?" she says, her arms gesturing around the dilapidated barn, her voice getting louder with each word.

"I'm your father. Don't call me Robert. It's disrespectful."

"Disrespectful. Well, well, well."

She pushes Daisy's head off her legs and lays it gently down on the manure pack. Rebecca pulls herself to standing. Robert puts his right hand out again

"It's too late. You don't get to help me now. You gave up on me," she says, pushing her flat hand forcefully against his chest.

Robert nearly falls over backwards, his body slamming into the wooden pen wall. "And I'm giving up on you. Fourteen years of hoping and waiting is long enough."

Rebecca moves toward Robert and then stops.

"Why did you even pull me out of the car if you had no intention of saving me? Why didn't you just leave me there?"

Robert stutters some sounds, shakes his head, stays in the same position.

"You are pathetic," she says and pushes past him. He doesn't turn to follow.

Rebecca backs the tractor into the pen, ties a chain around Daisy's neck, tears dripping off her chin. Robert hasn't moved, his right arm hanging limp at his side. Rebecca ties another chain around Daisy's back feet. Robert still doesn't move. Rebecca climbs into the tractor seat and lets the clutch out slowly, the tractor easing away from the dead pony, the chain tightening, and Daisy's body starts to move as the tractor pulls the pony from the pen. The dead stock truck will pick her body up, like a grim reaper touring the neighbourhood waiting for a farmer to call and announce another death.

Rebecca pulls Daisy's lifeless body behind the granary. She finds a canvas tarp in the back of the shed and covers Daisy, pulling the tarp tight and securing the edges with stones. She collapses on the edge of the tarp, willing her body to stop breathing, her heart to stop pounding in her chest.

She can't leave Daisy here, can't leave her rotting under the tarp, waiting for the dead stock truck driver to winch her decomposing body into the back of the truck. She can't do it. Instead, Rebecca builds a fire pit, a funeral pyre. She digs a hole in the field as deep as the feeble trip bucket on the tractor can dig, tearing off the soil one layer at a time until she has created a basin in which the last of Daisy's remains can be covered. Rebecca fills the tractor's bucket with stumps and logs and broken fence parts, with old shutters and window frames and doors that have blown from the barn, old rotting bales of hay. When the pile is of sufficient size, Rebecca returns to Daisy's body, removes the tarp, and secures the chain around Daisy's neck and legs. She raises the bucket and Daisy's body is lifted from the ground, swinging back and forth like a clock's pendulum, Daisy's mane and tail reaching for the ground, her head swaying, her eyes still open, her tongue protruding.

Rebecca lowers Daisy onto the funeral pyre and climbs on the pile of wood and debris, loosening the chain and pulling it free. All the while Rebecca sobs, not bothering to wipe at the tears and snot pouring down her face, impairing her vision. She trudges to the garbage barrel and retrieves a stack of newspapers, not even opened and read, and tears the paper, crumpling it into huge balls, and jams it into the oversized burn pile. She empties the contents of the lawnmower's small gas can onto the pile and lights a match, flicking it on the pile. It explodes into flames, knocking Rebecca down. She is tempted to jump into the flames with Daisy, tempted to find her own escape from this empty horror of her life.

Instead, she feeds the flames all day, dropping load after load after load on top of the fire, the fire that quickly consumed Daisy's thick, heavy tail. After hours of feeding the flames, most of Daisy has vanished, and Rebecca pushes dirt and stones over top of the hole in which the bits of Daisy's remains lie and covers them completely.

Rebecca hasn't eaten, hasn't paused, is covered in soot, her jacket singed, her hair shriveled in places from the heat and flying embers. It is done, and she staggers to the house having left the tractor in its place, carefully backed into the open-sided shed.

Rebecca showers, rinses her mouth with hot water, letting the heat pour over her, softening her muscles, the steam rising up around her. She is still crying, the tears washing off her face and down the drain, her shoulders convulsing. It is a foreign feeling to let the heartache out, and she can't stop, can't put the brakes on to get back to her composed self that seems too long ago now, as if the old Rebecca has slipped down a steep slope and the new Rebecca is holding on to the edge by clinging to a small branch. Is she strong enough to get up and over, to pull herself to safety? She keeps crying.

She dries her hair roughly with a heavy towel, nearly pulling the tangled mess from its roots, and then stares into the mirror.

She looks old and worn; her eyes are flat, dull. She wishes now she had punched Robert, knocked him down. Her compassion has been tainted. Left to ferment, her empathy turned to disgust. Maybe he'll stay in the barn, stand frozen in the deep manure, and never come out again.

Rebecca drags a brush through her hair, not bothering with untangling, and gathers the long, sopping-wet mass into an elastic. Water runs down her face and neck and soaks the edge of her T-shirt. She pushes a toothbrush back and forth across her teeth with such vigour that her gums bleed and she spits the red guck into the sink. She swipes at the light switch on her way out of the bathroom and slams the door. She marches up the stairs, stomping on each step, and throws her bedroom door open, the door slamming into the wall, the door handle stopping a fraction of an inch before embedding in the plaster, the shoe box filled with stray socks doing its job as a doorstop.

Rebecca looks at her neatly made bed, the comforter pulled tight, the sheet folded back smooth and white, the dandelion painting on the wall, the white ruffled curtains she remembers her mother sitting at the dining room table making, the sewing machine humming as it hammered out the stitches. She puts her fingers under the edge of the mattress and heaves the mattress off her bed.

Exposed are her treasures, like litter hiding under her mattress. She snaps up the string with the three keys and marches back down the stairs. Her eyes are wild and her jaw set like her teeth might snap off at any moment. The first key fits into the shed door lock, the lock giving way with a loud click. Much to her surprise, the trunk is light and slides easily out from under the workbench. The second key isn't the right fit so she tries the third key and here she stops, bracing herself like a weightlifter, closing her eyes and taking deep breaths to calm the frenzy.

The heavy lock drops to the floor and before she can reconsider Rebecca lifts the lid on the trunk, her eyes closed and her stomach bubbling and gurgling, her hands shaking like she has palsy.

She stands over the trunk, hands in front of her, fingers spread, as if the contents of the box may harbour some contagion that will grab hold of Rebecca, trick her into opening Pandora's Box.

The trunk is neatly stacked full with the photos from the top of the piano. Underneath some loose papers is a small square tin. Rebecca puts her fingernails under the edge of the tin's lid and pulls. The lid springs off and inside is a packet of thin blue tissue-like envelopes, all sealed and bound, each bearing the same writing, neatly tied up with a string. On the front, in a combination of printing and writing, is her name: Rebecca Archer. The return address says *H Claydon, White Gates, Leeds, England.* H Claydon; Rebecca's grandmother writing to her. She tries to read the date on the postmark, but the ink has smeared in the damp trunk. She counts the envelopes. Eleven. There are eleven letters. What is this? Why hide these letters? What could her grandmother possibly say that Robert didn't want Rebecca to hear, that he would rather she felt completely alone than risk? The letters weren't even opened, hadn't been disturbed in any way. What madness is this?

Under the frames, Rebecca sees one dirty white plush arm and as she lifts the frames out of the trunk her mother's teddy bear looks up at her, his half-marble eyes still in place, the red stitched mouth smiling at her. A sob bursts from Rebecca's throat and she pulls the bear into her arms. He smells of mould and dust. She traces around his eyes and the brown embroidered nose, some of the threads loose and broken. One of his legs is hanging on by only a few stitches and some of his stuffing is trying to escape. She folds her arms around him, squatting down on the cement floor, unable to process her find, the discovery of a thread, a connection that means she hasn't been alone all these years.

Rebecca finds an empty cardboard box and wipes the cobwebs and dust from it. She lifts the framed photos from the trunk and stacks them in the box along with the letters and teddy bear. Under the bear is an official-looking document that says Deed/Transfer of Land. A lengthy description of feet and minutes and seconds and easts and wests with wheretos and therefores and thences, all manner of strange words and the unfamiliar language is followed by her mother's name and Rebecca's name, owners of *said property*. She puts the document in the box with the frames and photos and bear and the tin.

She drops the trunk's lid and shoves the trunk under the work-bench with her foot without bothering with the lock. She lifts the box and heads to the house, leaving the shed unlocked.

"No more locks," she shouts toward the barn.

There is no sign of Robert. Rebecca is beyond caring, has moved into the fight zone, the taking-care-of-business zone. She kicks her shoes off at the back door, one shoe leaving a dark stain on the wall where it hit.

She takes the box to her bedroom, shuts the door behind her, and pulls her small dresser in front of the door.

"Keep out," she shouts at the door, stamps her feet, and screams one long blast.

She empties the frames from the box, placing them around her room, the frames balancing on the window ledge and the apple crate: pictures of her mother, of Jake, of her grandparents.

She pulls the knot in the string that holds the letters and care-fully opens the first, the blue onionskin paper thin and fragile. She starts to read, the fingers of her right hand covering her mouth as if to contain the surprise, the shock of a voice reaching out from the past, breaking through the impermeable dome that descended over her life, using up almost all the air and leaving her and Robert playing the same song, doing the same dance that neither of them put any heart into.

She reads slowly, about her mother, about her perfection, about loss and truth, about inheritance and hope and remembering, about pregnancy before marriage, about what ifs and if onlys. She takes in every word, every comma and period, each sentence being pulled inside her and warming the cold loneliness, thawing the emptiness and loss.

"Mommy," Rebecca whispers while reading the stories of Grace's youth, bringing Grace back into focus, into the present, about her amazing achievements as a pianist, playing with the London Philharmonic Orchestra. Rebecca pulls the teddy bear under her chin and holds him firmly there against her body, the last of her tears soaking into his soft plush face.

Twenty-Eight

REBECCA KNOCKS ON LISSIE'S FRONT DOOR, KNOCKS THREE TIMES, the sound she used to imagine on her own door, a friend standing on the back step, her face pressed against the glass, full of ideas for an adventure, ready to head for the swings to see who can pump the highest or spin the fastest on the merry-go-round, to discuss breaking rules and mischief, to complain about little brothers and chores and gossip about friends and voice independence and singular purpose, to plan the future for next Saturday, next year, when they are grown and what and who they will be.

Can Rebecca come out and play? Those magic words would make Rebecca's mother scoop Rebecca's face into her hands and kiss her nose, the action saying she recognizes Rebecca has grown up, can go out to play with her own friends, choose her own path, be real and authentic. *Have fun,* her mother would have whispered, her head tilted slightly to the side as if she can't believe Rebecca has grown up so quickly, is able to go on her own. Someone knocking on her door surely meant Rebecca belonged to something beyond herself, she was connected and the world outside her back door was there for her, included Rebecca on the roll call list.

Rebecca Archer.

Here! Rebecca acknowledges her presence by raising her arm, now welcome to join in, to take her place in the community.

But no one ever knocked. Just Chuck. That time when he got his bike and whenever Harold beat him.

* * *

Lissie opens the door, her hair loose and short around her face, the tight French braid gone. Lissie cut her hair the very same day she moved Charlotte into the nursing home, as if she became someone else, was taking charge of her existence. *No more French braids, thank you.*

"Rebecca," she says. "Where have you been? I've called you a dozen times."

Where have I been? Who knows, who can answer when she's lived her life frozen, frozen in grief, forgotten by the living, invisible, a living ghost, still trying to break free from the ice and cold water and sinking car, still looking behind to see if her mother is coming through the car window with Jake in her arms, still fighting with Robert not to pull her out, to let her stay with her mother?

"Horses will run back into a burning barn. Did you know that? They want to get back to the safety of their stalls, even when the barn is engulfed in flames," Rebecca says, shaking her head.

"What? What are you talking about? Was there a fire? Are you okay?" Lissie pulls Rebecca through the door, not bothering to ask about the suitcase at the end of Rebecca's arm. "How did you get here?"

"Horses will do that, even though it makes no sense," Rebecca says.

"What's happened?"

"I walked," the questions and answers out of synch.

"What?"

"Nothing. Absolutely nothing," Rebecca says, and her voice has an empty sound, as if she were speaking from several floors up, the words barely discernible. "Everything has changed."

Lissie leads Rebecca to the sofa and pushes her gently down and then sits beside Rebecca and puts her arms around her and pulls her in close, and they sit and say nothing, the suitcase still in Rebecca's hand. The tall grandfather clock in the hallway pounds out the minutes and blares the hour, but they don't move until Rebecca drifts off to sleep and her hand slips off the handle of her suitcase and the suitcase topples over with a hollow thud.

* * *

"What are you going to do?" Lissie asks quietly, not much more than a whisper.

"I'm going to Fort Resolution. We're going to Fort Resolution."

"Where?" Lissie shakes her head. "What are you talking about?"

"We're going to Fort Resolution."

"What on earth for?"

"To find your family."

Lissie lets out a blast of air and sits up straight with her hand on the back of the sofa to steady her.

"I'm not sure I understand you. We can't go to Fort Resolution."

"We're going," Rebecca says. "We're going all right."

"I don't know anyone there. I have Charlotte. And this house. And what about you? Robert? And bills and jobs? We can't go, we can't pack up and go this very minute."

Lissie stops talking, and Rebecca stands and walks to the kitchen table. She opens a notepad on the kitchen table, shoving Lissie's sketchpad and charcoals off to the side.

"There's a flight every Tuesday and Friday," Rebecca says.

"Rebecca, wait a minute. I need to catch my breath. Slowly, tell me slowly."

"You need to find your family. You have family. You have cousins and aunts and uncles and maybe even grandparents. They are out there and they don't know you. They think you are dead. You have to go, and I'm going with you."

Rebecca pauses to let the facts soak in to Lissie for a few seconds. She taps the pencil on her notepad.

"Mr. Law has given me time off work. I went right to his house and asked," Rebecca says, looking slightly mad. "I can't believe I did that."

"I don't know, Rebecca," Lissie says, wincing and squeezing her hands in and out of fists.

"Of course you can. We can," Rebecca says. "We've nothing to lose. We'll do it together."

The front door bursts open and Chuck is standing in the doorway, his legs slightly apart, his body braced like he's been shot and can barely stand. His curls are messed, standing on end like a mad scientist, and he has a bloodstain on his shirt, the knuckles on his left hand bloodied and scuffed.

"Rebecca," he says and starts to cry.

Rebecca jumps up from her chair and her arms are around him. "Tell me," she says, and Chuck seems to turn to jelly, shapeless and soft.

"He took it all, every dollar."

Lissie hands Chuck a tissue. Rebecca waits, letting Chuck get it out as he can.

"My secret stash. I've been saving for four years." Chuck blows his nose loudly and Lissie puts her hand out for the snotty tissue, but he shoves it in his pocket instead.

"He found the tin under the floor boards in the mow." He looks up at Rebecca, his curls holding on to his forehead and the tips of his ears, and the sadness is leaking out his eyes and nose, from every pore of his body. "He never goes up there." Chuck sobs again.

The disappointment fills out the space in the room, like a noxious gas that seeps into every corner and crack. Chuck stamps his foot hard and stands up straight.

"I punched him out," Chuck says, showing Rebecca and Lissie his bleeding knuckles, and he smiles, the kind of smile that is about surprise and discovery. "I think I maybe broke his nose," and he begins to look pleased with himself, like he's shared a secret. "I dropped him like a sack of shit."

Both girls start laughing, taking their cue from Chuck and he laughs even harder.

"He never saw it coming. My first pre-emptive strike. Remember, Rebecca?"

Rebecca nods and laughs.

"It felt great. Nineteen years of rage in one punch," he says. "And then I took my money back."

"You what?" Rebecca says, her eyes wide. "Tell me."

"After I punched him out I marched up to his room and in the top drawer of his dresser was all my money except some that he had already spent. But I took the rest and I waved it in his face before I left."

"Oh my god, Chuck. You're a superhero," Rebecca says while Lissie jumps up and down.

"I can't go back there. He'll kill me."

"You don't need to," Rebecca says.

"What are you two doing?" Chuck asks.

"We're going to Fort Resolution," Rebecca says, looking over at Lissie.

"We are going to Fort Resolution," Lissie repeats with exactly the same tone and sound.

"Not without me," Chuck says, slamming his fist into the arm of the chair. "Where exactly is Fort Resolution again?"

* * *

They are at the bus depot, each with a small suitcase, looking braver and more certain than they feel on the inside. Rebecca has her list, her map, her notepad. Lissie has the birth certificate and the newspaper clipping.

Mr. Balducci writes out their bus tickets and collects the money from Lissie.

"It's only right that I pay," Lissie says again, and both friends shrug sheepishly.

"How's that father of yours, Rebecca?" Mr. Balducci says without looking up from writing the tickets.

"He's dead," Rebecca says.

Mr. Balducci drops his pen and his eyes fly wide open. Chuck and Lissie gasp.

"What?" Mr. Balducci says. "I didn't hear."

"Oh, he's still sitting in his chair in the living room with the newspaper on his lap. He still looks alive. Still changes his clothes from time to time. He still opens a can of soup with the electric can opener I bought him. But he's dead, all right."

"What do you mean?"

"My father died the March I was six, sank to the bottom of the lake with my mother and my brother. He just hasn't quit breathing yet."

Mr. Balducci looks dumbfounded, at a loss for words, shaking his head with discomfort.

"I guess you wanted me to say *fine*," Rebecca says. "*Fine*. My father's *fine*, Mr. Balducci. Don't you worry. Is that our bus out front?" she says, stooping to pick up her suitcase.

Mr. Balducci nods, still looking stunned.

"I guess we're on our way," Rebecca says, opening the door to the bus-loading zone. "The days are getting longer and warmer," she says to Chuck and Lissie. "Spring is here. I heard a meadowlark this morning. Heard her clear as day."

"You and your meadowlarks," Chuck says, a teasing sound in his voice.

"Isn't it early?" Lissie asks as they climb the three big steps on to the bus.

"Early? I thought it might never come," Rebecca says.

"We'll have to take turns sitting together," Chuck says.

"No problem," Rebecca says. "You two take the first shift."

Acknowledgements

HOW DOES ONE THANK ALL THOSE WHO MADE THE PATH smoother, who kept the destination in sight for me? Without the kindness and encouragement from Lisa Moore, I doubt very much this book would be a reality. I am so very grateful. I thank Loraine Currie for our "dailies" over the last thirty-five years that kept me afloat during life's storms and for reading, and reading, and reading some more. I thank Hazel Lyder and her Downtown Bookstore, a place where I found friendship and a safe place to be and write. I thank Allison Kirk-Montgomery for being ready to save me whenever I needed saving. I thank Stephanie Sinclair, my agent, someone who cares if I am uncertain. I thank NeWest Press and Leslie Vermeer for gently guiding me closer to perfection. I thank my sister Sherry Moran and my brother Laurie Stewart for their love and for our shared childhood that contributed to this tale. I thank those "real" people who let their names and characters show up on the pages of this book. You know who you are and what you mean to me. I thank all those with whom I collided on this life's journey, who helped fill up my memory book with wonderful stories.

Most importantly, I thank my daughters Aimee, Samantha, Laurie, and Thea for their unlimited faith in me, for knowing I was a writer before I did, for their cheerleading and their beautiful souls. I am so fortunate.

And I thank my father, who left me much too early, before I was ready to let go his hand, left me wrestling with grief in what seemed like a losing battle. I have prevailed.

Wendi Stewart grew up on a farm in Northwestern Ontatio and now makes her home in Wolfville, Nova Scotia. She has been published in *The Antagonish Review*, *The Leaf*, the *Owen Sound Sun Times* and in *Every Second Thursday* (Glenmalure Publications). She currently has columns appearing in the *Fort Frances Times* and the *Chronicle Herald*. *Meadowlark* is her first novel.